THE FORGOTTEN TALE OF LARSA

First published in 2014 by Bluebird Publishing House

www.bluebird-publishing.com

© Seja Majeed 2014

Design © Anna Dittmann 2014

The Forgotten Tale of Larsa is a Registered Trademark.

The right of Seja Majeed to be identified as the author of this work has been asserted.

A catalogue record for this book is available from the British Library.

ISBN 978-0-9929055-0-7

Printed in the United States.

www.theforgottentaleoflarsa.com

THE FORGOTTEN TALE OF LARSA

SEJA MAJEED

BLUEBIRD PUBLISHING HOUSE

Dedicated to the memory of my uncles,
and to all the innocent lives lost in my beloved homeland, Iraq

PROLOGUE

My father once said that a man's freedom is worth more than the price of gold. Freedom cannot be bought, sold or given, he explained; it can only be respected as a birthright. I didn't understand what my father meant until this very moment; I was the princess from the Garden of the Gods who had become the slave of an emperor. As I sat on my enemy's horse, weeping openly, I remembered Marmicus. With each breath I took, I pictured his eyes, which were as deep as an ocean, and his lips, as shapely as the hills of the desert. I remembered the way he had looked into my eyes as we lay together for the last time. That night, I saw his happiness and sorrow painted across his face.

Although he had longed to shield me from the barbarity of war, it seemed that I had fallen victim to a far crueller fate. I had lost everything. Everything except my memories ...

1

SITTING SILENTLY UPON A LAVISH THRONE MADE FROM PURE GOLD was the Assyrian emperor, Jaquzan. He was no older than thirty-five, but he possessed an aura of great maturity, as if he had lived a life that had spanned an eternity. In his hands lay life and death, and beneath his feet an empire that stretched as far as the horizon. Jaquzan had the body of a man but the power of a god: kingdoms survived only by his permission and mortals lived only by his kindness.

'The Dark Warrior has arrived, sire,' said a guard, nervously, as he approached his master.

'Allow him forth.'

'Yes, sire.'

The Dark Warrior entered the chamber, his lips curling upwards in an arrogant smile.

'I have brought you what you wanted, sire. I made sure it was specially crafted to your liking.' Nafridos bowed before his cousin, and commanded his slaves to open a velvet sack he had brought as a gift.

Jaquzan's expressionless face suddenly flickered with a trace of uncharacteristic human emotion; a careful observer would have seen his pupils dilate like those of a wild creature finding its prey.

'Bring it to me.'

The slaves rushed to him, bowing like the soulless beings they were as they timidly offered him the sack. Jaquzan was an unpredictable creature of uncertain, and dangerous, moods; no one could ever tell what he was thinking, or anticipate his next move. Jaquzan slowly removed the white linen covering from the orb-like object he clasped in his hands. His cousin was right – the gift was one of a kind, truly something of a rarity. At last, he possessed the jewels of Persia and they were far more glorious then he had ever imagined.

'You have done well.'

'Only well?' said Nafridos, adopting a playful tone as he watched his cousin stare at the gift, his patience finally rewarded with the things he had desired for so long.

'I tried my best not to disfigure his face too much, but his squirming made it an impossible challenge. You should have seen him beg for his life – it would have made you laugh.'

The emperor sneered. At last, the centre of the world had finally fallen at his feet. In his hands was a powerful jewel that had once commanded the legions of the Eastern hemisphere. Jaquzan glared at the severed head of the young King of Persia. His skin was covered in dried blood and had turned tough like leather. The face of a wealthy man rotted in the same way as a poor man's. His black tongue hung off his thin lips like a dead animal's. Jaquzan showed no sympathy for the king, who had clearly been tortured before he was butchered and decapitated.

'What were his final words to you?'

'The same as every other king I have slaughtered for you. "Kill me, but spare my family from death."'

'Is that all?'

'No. He said, "I am Persia. I am the centre of the world. Today we both shall die free."'

The Dark Warrior grabbed a chalice and poured himself some red wine to celebrate, before settling down upon a sumptuously carved and decorated divan, luxuriating in the extravagance of the Assyrian palace. War was a wearying game, and the only pleasure Nafridos ever derived from playing it was at night, when his skin was bathed in cool water by his concubines. This was not to say he did not enjoy it: he revelled in the business of butchery; it was his one purpose in life, something at which he was very good. Over time, Nafridos had developed a reputation for ruthlessness. The people called him the Dark Warrior with good reason: whenever he left the battlefield, every inch of his body would drip with blood, such that his skin appeared black.

'When will your war against the world end?'

'When there is only one god on earth, found in me ...'

Nafridos laughed loudly.

'I see your harshness grows by the day.'

'It grows at the same rate as my tolerance,' replied the Assyrian emperor. A cruel smile cracked his sculpted face as he imagined the world falling at his feet.

'Then with the bones of your captives I shall build temples in devotion to you!' the Dark Warrior roared, as he lifted his chalice into the air to toast the Emperor of Assyria ...

2

Princess Larsa possessed a beauty that was rare and unearthly; it attracted the eyes of men and the envy of women. Her eyes were large and brown, and her skin white, and soft as silk.

Sunlight flooded through the open windows, warming her youthful skin. She could hear the birds singing beyond the palace balcony as they always did; they were the first to wake her, just before her servants came to her bedroom. A new morning had arrived, bringing with it a new duty, something for which Larsa felt unprepared. She dug her face into the pillow, wanting to hide away from the bright light, her arms stretching out as she tried to rid herself of the haziness of sleep, but her hand unexpectedly hit something: someone was sleeping beside her. Larsa woke up with a burst of happiness spilling through her: it was a joyous surprise.

'You're home! When did you arrive?'

'In the early hours of the morning. I didn't want to wake you. You looked so peaceful sleeping.'

'You should have woken me! Next time I'll command you to – it's the only way I can be certain you will.'

Marmicus laughed at her forceful, though touching, reprimand.

Of course, she was right: it was the only way he would accede to her request. He had been watching her sleeping, gazing at her beautiful oval face and waiting for the moment when her almond eyes would open to see him lying beside her. The more Marmicus looked at her, the more he realised how much he had missed her company. He brushed her fringe away from her eyes.

'Your eyes become more beautiful with each new morning.'

'Then stay here, and I shall never let them wander over other men.'

Marmicus laughed aloud. He loved the childish things she said sometimes. Only he had the pleasure of seeing her act like this; everyone else saw a façade of royalty.

'Are you trying to make me jealous, Larsa?'

'Is it working?'

'Yes.'

He leant in and kissed her tenderly, his lips softly brushing against hers. The tight feeling of war disappeared altogether. Larsa put her hand to his chest, feeling the intense beat of his heart against her palm as they kissed, but the thought of him leaving her again made her stop.

'What's the matter?'

He could tell she was worried about something: it was unlike her to draw away from him like that.

'Every time you leave, I feel that my heart sails away with you. I hate being alone here without you. I don't know what to do with myself when you're gone.'

'I'm here now – you don't need to worry about me.'

'I know you are, but you'll leave again, and I'll have to wait for you. I wonder how I'll cope without you. I may have inherited my father's throne, but I'm afraid I won't lead my people the way he wanted. I don't know anything about power or war. All I know is that

I love my people – that's all.'

'A woman who understands love is far wiser than a man who understands only war; our kingdom is blessed to have you as its ruler, and I'm blessed to have you as my wife.'

'But is that truly enough? I'm a queen by birthright, not by honour or wisdom. I've never seen war as you have, or lived the life of an ordinary woman; I don't know anything about hardship. All I've ever known are these walls, and the stories told by those inside them.'

'Men would trade their lives not to experience battle: you're blessed, not cursed, Larsa. You need to use this gift to your advantage – speak of peace as the friend it is, not as an enemy.'

She knew Marmicus was right. Even so, it failed to settle her nerves; the inauguration ceremony was fast approaching, and she didn't have any time to learn about the ways of the world. Larsa stared at the floor, feeling ashamed of her naivety; the only solace she could ever find was with him, and she was grateful that he had returned. She rarely left the palace. When she did, a huge crowd of people would always follow her, making it even more difficult for her to interact normally with anyone or live the life of an ordinary woman, something she so deeply desired.

Marmicus understood the position she was in, and knew it would take some time before she would fully settle into her new role.

'Look, the fact that you're even questioning yourself means you will be a good ruler. I've met kings who would rather die than question themselves.'

Larsa smiled. She wasn't quite sure if he was exaggerating or telling the truth.

'I have a meeting with the Counsel of Priests today. I'm certain they'll obstruct me because I'm a woman who knows little about the affairs of men. I need you to come with me.'

'You don't need me to come; just believe in yourself the way I believe in you.'

'I'll try,' she said with a half-smile. Marmicus could tell it was a forced one. Nothing he could say would convince her; she had to learn it for herself, and only time could do that. 'Why didn't you come home when my father fell ill? I waited for you every day, praying you'd come before he died.'

'I came as soon as I heard the news. You know I would have come if I had known.'

'I thought something had happened to you.'

'Nothing will happen to me, I promise.'

'You can't make a promise like that – it's like the sea promising never to touch the shore; it can't be kept. You'll never be safe until men learn to live in peace.'

'Should the earth be plagued by a thousand wars, I will always return to you, Larsa.'

'It's not about our love. I just don't want you to make a promise you can't keep.'

Marmicus clasped her hands, wanting to reassure her. He had not realised just how much his absence had affected her: she needed him more than ever, especially now that her father had died.

'Do you remember the sacred words of our kingdom?'

'Of course. "Allegiance lies in the heart of the sword."'

'Then you'll know that every sword held by every hand is always carried for the love of something. I carry mine to protect you and to make you happy. It's all I care about, Larsa. You're everything I need, and if ever you should feel uncertain of this, I want you to remember these words, just as I do. They'll strengthen you with courage in the face of whatever tomorrow may bring.'

'Allegiance lies in the heart of the sword,' the princess whispered again, this time with conviction. His warmth comforted her and alleviated the deep loneliness she felt inside. 'I still can't believe my father is dead; he was so strong, so healthy.'

'I know,' said the Gallant Warrior as he leant in, lovingly kissing her on her forehead. 'He will never be forgotten.'

3

There was nothing on earth quite like the Temple of Ishtar. So beautiful was this monument that even the gods had reason to wage war for possession of it. Like a living mountain, the colossal temple spiralled upwards, encircled by lofty pillars and overhung with lush, terraced gardens fed by gushing fountains. Even at night, the temple's glory could be seen: a gigantic torch lit up its top, its flame guiding lost travellers towards the sacred Garden of the Gods. So bright were the temple's flames that the mighty hearth appeared as a star in the vast desert sky, lighting the path for wanderers in search of the Garden of the Gods.

Hidden from view inside the structure were spacious passages and galleries that led worshippers to the main chamber belonging to the goddess Ishtar. Once they entered the great chamber they would bow before Ishtar's magnificent stone statue, which reached as high as the lofty ceiling. With her long almond eyes and voluptuous body, she seemed to peer into the eyes of each worshipper, as if looking deep into their soul at what they desperately desired. When all else had failed, only Ishtar had the power to answer their prayers. Today, the tranquillity of the magnificent temple was overtaken by the quarrelling of the Grand Priests who sat, restive and agitated, waiting for the princess to arrive.

'What an impertinent girl!' the Grand Priest of Ursar blasted furiously, his voice echoing. 'What an outrage! Does she have no knowledge of who we are? This is the reason women should never be permitted to rule – they have no awareness of time. They should remain figures of beauty, appreciated only by the eyes and never by the ears. It's what the gods had intended for them.'

He rose from his seat in frustration and paced up and down the chamber; his reflection sparkled across the long pool of water that marked its centre line.

'She has certainly shamed her father; he would have never kept us waiting like this.'

The temple echoed with the complaints of unhappy priests who had been waiting for some time, their faces contorted with outrage. It was unheard of to keep the Counsel waiting.

'Men quarrel like wolfhounds! Their rantings are devoid of all reason,' a strong voice declared, from behind the priests. The most powerful woman in all the land had heard their insults, and she was not impressed. Even so, the Grand Priest of Ursar remained where he was. He never could conceal his disgust from anyone; being polite was not worth the effort, even for royalty.

'How dare you keep this Counsel waiting? Your behaviour is nothing more than a symbol of your female impertinence!' he declared furiously. His opulent robes flickered beneath the fiery torches, while his beard shimmered like strings of silver.

'Calm yourself, oh scholar of the gods. I may be a woman, but I can be as ruthless as a man,' replied the princess. She walked on, followed by a long line of servants. One servant brought up a beautifully engraved wooden chair, positioning it in the same spot where her father had once sat before the Counsel of Priests. 'As for the rest of you, the real obscenity doesn't lie with me, but with this Counsel, for you all speak lovingly of the gods, yet you have chosen to quarrel among yourselves in their house. I doubt the gods would be pleased.'

'Forgive us, Your Highness, we are all friends and allies of your kingdom; none of us have come here to insult you,' said the young Priest of Xidrica. His voice was soft and humble, unlike that of his counterpart, who possessed the arrogance of a king.

'Then quarrel we shall not, oh noble one.'

'Thank you, Your Highness. You have indeed taken your beauty from your mother and your wisdom from your father.'

Even though the princess appreciated the gesture, the compliment failed to work its charm. She knew that the Counsel had not assembled simply to flatter her, or congratulate her for becoming their soon-to-be-inaugurated queen; they had come for a purpose, something that must be of great importance.

'Let us not pretend any longer. Like my father, I am wise in matters of the mind. We can all be certain that none of you have journeyed through the scorching desert simply to pay me a weightless compliment. So who is going to tell me the real reason you've decided to call upon me?'

Finding out would be harder than she had imagined. The Counsel fell silent. Nobody dared move in their seat; it was as if they all wanted to blend into the background. After all, no one wanted to have the responsibility of passing on bad news.

'Well?'

Again, no one answered: it was obvious that they all knew the answer, but they were too afraid to voice it. It occurred to Larsa that she preferred them when they were squabbling; at least then she knew what troubled them. She looked across the chamber, searching for someone brave enough to give her an answer, but everyone was acting so peculiarly – some even avoided making eye contact. Something was wrong; she could feel it. A rush of uncertainty came over her, and she tried hard to hide her nerves. If they knew she was nervous, they would use it against her.

'I am still waiting. Will no one speak? Just a moment ago you were all adamant that I hear your thoughts. What has changed?'

The Grand Priest of Ursar finally rose; the responsibility fell to him to tell her the disastrous news. He was, after all, the most powerful of them. Holding his long cane, which amplified his grandeur, the frail priest stared deeply into the princess's eyes and quietly uttered the words, 'War is coming …'

4

I forgot how beautiful the sun looks; somehow the prospect of war makes everything seem all the more glorious,' Larsa whispered to Marmicus. They were watching the evening sun dip lower into the horizon, settling over the fertile kingdom of the Garden of the Gods. The sky was painted with glorious shades of orange and pink that blended together like a painting, and the kingdom was calm; nothing could unsettle it, not even the rustling of the palm trees or the coming of war.

'I feel the gods are displeased with me. I must have wronged them somehow for them to curse my kingdom so soon.'

'Nothing can curse a man other than his own deeds. The gods have nothing to do with what's happening here – only the desires of selfish men can set fire to peaceful lands.'

'I know you don't believe in the gods, but I feel they're watching over us, even you.' She turned towards him, seeking reassurance.

Marmicus knew it was difficult to accept the prospect of war, but the first thing any ruler needed to do was to be strong in the face of the enemy. This wasn't the time for Larsa to doubt herself – there was too much at stake.

'Have I done something to provoke this war? Why has it come so soon, when I've barely ruled for a day?'

'You already know my answer.'

She walked away from the balcony, infuriated by his cold reply: Larsa needed his comfort, but his mind was worlds away. She sat upon the divan, wanting to collect herself. There was so much to think about, and she didn't know where to start. This was all new to her, although not for him. Marmicus approached her, feeling a slight guilt for his short response. Larsa pretended not to care, but her eyes betrayed her.

'The more you doubt yourself, the more power you give to your enemies. If you want to help your people then you have to be strong for them.'

'You always think of the people before you think of what I need or how this will affect us. Think of me, for a change,' said Larsa. She needed a husband who would comfort her, not a selfless warrior who comforted and thought of others. As much as it was noble, it was often irritating.

She made a sweeping gesture with her arm. 'None of this means anything to me if you're gone. I don't want you to fight in this war. I won't let you.'

She couldn't bear to have him fight again, not so close, not when the enemy was just beyond her borders. At least with distance there came some small degree of emotional remove. If he died, what would she do? She could barely cope without a mother and father; she knew she couldn't survive without him.

'You know our homeland means everything to me. I cannot neglect my duty just because you're frightened that I may die.'

'And yet it's easy for you to neglect me without question? Is it wrong for me to ask my husband to be by my side? You make me sound as if I'm acting selfishly when all I want from you is to be here with me! I've come to live half a life; I won't do it any more. I can't.'

Her face scrunched up with resentment; she would not be made to feel guilty for her suffering. He had sacrificed his own happiness for the sake of others – and he may be loved by the people – but it had come at the cost of her happiness.

'Why do you deny yourself the right to live your life?' she said. 'You're entitled to smile just as I'm entitled to love. After this war, there will be a thousand battles waged by others who will summon you to fight alongside them and, if the cause is noble, you'll accept their challenge and leave me here. I can't live my life on the thread of hope that you'll return to me unharmed. I want us to be a family – I want to be a mother one day and I want you to be alive to see our children grow. Is it selfish of me to ask you to live for us?'

'You want to be a mother?'

'Yes,' she replied, heatedly. 'I feel I'm ready now. I wasn't before.'

A huge grin appeared on Marmicus's face; one which he tried to hide – they were in the middle of an argument, after all.

'Why are you smiling? Don't you want to be a father some day?'

'Larsa, I have never been happier than I am at this moment.'

'Really?'

'Of course.'

The faint dimples in his cheek revealed themselves as he smiled brilliantly. 'There's no other woman in the world who I'd want to carry my child. I love you so much.'

A voice interrupted them.

'Forgive me, my lord, but shall I tell the Counsel that you will not be joining them?'

'No, let them know that I will be joining them shortly.'

'Yes, my lord,' replied the soldier.

'We will discuss this later. I must go now,' he whispered as he gently kissed her and strode out of the chamber, and towards the Temple of Ishtar.

5

It was not very often that the Counsel agreed on matters, but tonight they had hoped to make an exception. They were losing precious time while the enemy was gaining valuable strength.

'We've got no choice in the matter; we must attack, and protect the walls of this city,' declared the Grand Priest of Ursar.

He had had enough of listening to pathetic suggestions by the other priests; it was action that was needed, not idle deliberation.

'If we fight without the gods' blessings, we'll certainly lose this war. I say we should call upon the gods, and ask them to show us some signs of triumph before we rush into combat,' the young Priest of Xidrica said. His love for the gods was as evident as his nobility, but it was a quality deeply unappreciated by many of the Grand Priests; the only quality that seemed to unite them was the love of pocketing power for themselves.

'I think we should send Jaquzan gifts of gold. Maybe this generous act can tame the wild beast, even if it is only for a short while?' said another.

'You buffoon! Jaquzan doesn't value peace, and he doesn't need any more gifts. The entire world is falling at his feet, and he has everything any man can ever dream of. We have only one option, and it's to attack now. Besides, we are Grand Priests, not peasants. Let the people fight and let us marvel at their victory – their deaths will ensure our survival, which is just as it should be.'

'Enough!' roared Marmicus, who had at last broken his silence. No one understood combat more than he did. He lived it and breathed it every day; it was his gift and his curse.

'War without honour is not an option! If we attack, then we shall attack honourably. My men will not be drawn into a battle with cowards as their leaders and greed as their cause. Their sacrifice will not be any man's gain, and their names will not be tarnished by this Counsel's greed, or for the sake of clay gods who can't even answer their prayers. If any of you forget this, then you'll enter into battle alone, for I will not command my soldiers to follow you.'

'Marmicus, we'll lose this war if we do not act with haste; let us attack while the lion is still caged.'

'Where there is no faith, there can only be certainty of defeat.'

He turned his back on the Counsellors and paced towards the magnificent stone statue of Ishtar, which overshadowed them; it was the only way he could possibly remain civil. The Grand Priest had angered him greatly with his selfish remarks; it was as if the lives of his soldiers had no value at all: he was commanding men to enter into battle and selflessly die for him without so much as a nod of gratitude for their sacrifice. It made him feel sick to his stomach. If anyone else said anything along those lines, Marmicus knew he would snap and the consequences would be lethal.

'Perhaps you'll change your mind once you've heard the news?' said the Grand Priest of Ursar. He would not back down so easily, not when his position was on the line.

'What news? What are you talking about?' asked a Counsellor, and a murmur of curiosity went round the chamber. Could there really be news that would so drastically change the Gallant Warrior's mind?

'Yesterday I was sent word, from a reliable source, which has changed the balance of power in favour of our enemy. Persia has fallen into the hands of the Assyrians; now all that remains of it are the ashes carried by the winds. The greatest empire that has ever rivalled Babylonia has been defeated. If we are not careful, our kingdom will follow suit.'

His news was shocking – unbelievable: the kingdom of Persia had always seemed an all-powerful force, ruling over every land in the region. The Persian army was remorseless, with a military might which slammed down like the fist of a god on anything, or anyone, that got in its way. Its demise had proven the Counsellor's point: Jaquzan was not to be underestimated; he was only to be feared.

'So, you see, comrades,' said the Grand Priest of Ursar, 'this is why we must attack now. If we are not careful, we shall be trampled on by the Assyrians. What difference does it make if we fight for the people or if we fight for our own cause? The result will be the same: some shall live, while others shall die. Let the people fight, and let us remain watchful over our positions – no man here wants his scholarly throne ripped from beneath his feet for the sake of protecting another man's honour!' He looked at the Counsel, whose heads were nodding in unison as if being bullied into agreement. 'The time has come for us to embark upon war. Death is death and life is life – the only difference is that we deserve to live for longer.'

Marmicus turned, looking back at the Grand Priest. His face showed sheer disgust, while his fist instinctively tightened around the hilt of his sword.

'Have patience, Marmicus. His greed will be judged by the gods.'

The Priest of Xidrica could see the fury in Marmicus's eyes. His temper had eclipsed his reason: he was as a volcano, about to unleash hell on earth; nothing could hold him back.

'I have fought many battles. I have seen many die and some live, but in all the wars that I have fought in, the purpose has always been the same: it has been to protect this kingdom and all those who serve it. You stand here before me now in your opulent robes, feasting on the fruits of this kingdom without thanks, and speaking of war as though it is nothing more than a game for your amusement: as if the scars inflicted by our enemies will heal in time and the cries of men who fought courageously to protect this kingdom will be carried off by the winds, only to be forgotten. But you know nothing of war – for cowards have no place in the armies of the brave.'

The Grand Priest shrank back into his seat like a child scolded into submission. He had been humiliated in front of his fellow priests: it felt as though sand had been thrown into his eyes and smoke had been flung into his lungs. *One day, oh Gallant Warrior, you shall learn to bite your tongue, or you shall live to regret it …*

'Know this. Jaquzan may have an army of thousands, but he does not have the honour or the devotion of my men, who fight for the people and for the love of this kingdom. We shall not be defeated if our hearts are devoted. Men have waged wars for a thousand years and more, but none shall ever conquer like this. War will come and, when it does, our battle will never be forgotten.'

'Allegiance lies in the heart of the sword!' roared the Counsel in clamorous approbation. In one brief moment the Gallant Warrior had united the hearts of men – except that of one man, a serpent who secretly carried hatred within his heart, and was cunningly plotting to kill him. *Enjoy your moment of glory, oh Gallant One, but it will not last long, for soon you shall squirm because of the treachery that runs through my veins ...*

'What then do you propose we do, Marmicus?' asked the noble Priest of Xidrica. His eyes lit up with inspiration as he absorbed Marmicus's speech.

'I propose we do this ...'

6

'That's their plan, sire,' Nafridos said, feeling pleased with himself. The news sent by the Serpent was invaluable; it had revealed Marmicus's military tactics, giving the Assyrians the advantage when war came; it was indeed worth a thousand plates of gold.

'What makes you certain it's not a trap?' Jaquzan asked, swirling his chalice in a hypnotic rhythm.

'It's not a trap; he gave me his word.'

The Assyrian emperor gave a long stare, reacting only with a subtle twitch; his cousin had amused him with the stream of words that flowed so freely from his lips. Carelessness was a trait that Jaquzan despised above all things; he was the master of self-preservation, whose every emotion was crafted with a purpose. 'Don't let your stupidity and ignorance blind you, cousin – only a fool trusts someone who has already betrayed another. It's like saying that you trust the sea when it has already sunk your ship.'

He rose from his magnificent throne. It weighed five thousand minas and had been carved from solid stone; on either side of it were two Lamassu, the Assyrian winged bulls which were the symbols of his empire; their human heads and hoofed feet guarded him against adversity. Though he was not superstitious and did not believe in the spirits of the Lamassu, they had been passed down to him from his ancestors, and it was out of respect for them that he kept them as symbols of his kingdom.

He walked into the open, terraced gardens, taking his chalice of wine with him; the green lushness contrasted with his jet-black hair and glowing skin, which appeared tight, and smooth. He was a handsome man, no older than thirty-five, but his expressionless features made him appear older than his years, and somehow less than human.

'Do you want me to ignore their plan, and go ahead with the attack as if nothing has been said?'

'No, we will not ignore the plan, but we shall tread with caution, for we do not wish to be stung twice; that means you will pay close attention to every matter, and you will not confuse what you *think* to be true with what you *know* to be true, for even the oh-so-honourable Marmicus is certain to have an ounce of mischief.' He paused for a moment, staring at a garden spider that had weaved a delicate web over the stem of a white rose. He approached it, staring at it blankly; it quickly tried to conceal itself, hiding within the curls of the white rose petals. Jaquzan lifted his chalice and spilt red wine over it, watching carefully as the creature tried to save its webbed home from his callous hands.

'How unfortunate for the Gallant Warrior,' said the emperor. 'For soon his wound shall itch from a far deadlier bite.'

'What are you planning to do to him?'

Like his master, Nafridos had heard rumours of the Gallant Warrior who fought fearlessly for justice. He felt a connection with him, as if he was his living opposite, and for this he was bound by blood to kill him.

'Patience, dear cousin ... patience ...' Jaquzan whispered, as brutal thoughts of conquest entered his mind. 'Patience ... for even the spider needs time to weave its web before he catches his prey, and I shall indeed catch mine.'

7

Marmicus watched the princess play the Babylonian harp, singing along with it in her beautiful soft voice. Every time her fingertips flew across the strings of the instrument, it felt as though she was tugging at his heartstrings. He listened to her sing a verse from the story of Gilgamesh. How perfect she was; a combination of beauty, intelligence and, above all, kindness made her the angel she was. When his world seemed filled to the brim with chaos, Larsa had always brought him the peace he needed; he had been searching for it endlessly, finding it only when he met her. Larsa smiled, gazing at him with her large brown eyes, her long hair tumbling over her supple, exposed body. She cherished their moments of intimacy; how gentle and loving he was. Her skin still smelt of his passionate kisses, his embrace. She returned to the divan, lying beside him in the privacy of their chamber. Even with war so close, her world felt safe at moments like these.

'I know my father would have been proud of you today. Every word has been reported to me. You spoke with honour and courage before the Counsel; you made me, and our people, proud,' she whispered, resting beside her husband upon the bed. She traced his toned chest with her fingers, appreciating their time alone together.

'I just said the truth; nothing more and nothing less.'

'That may be, but men are often careless of truthful words … others have neglected them while you have always embraced them. That's why the people love you, and so do I.'

'Wars can't be won with words, Larsa; I wish they could, maybe then I could sleep at night without seeing the faces of every man I have killed.'

'There's no reason for you to feel guilty for what you do; you've always been the defender, never the attacker, on the battlefield. There's a difference.'

'The actions of a soldier reflect only the orders of his leaders; those men on the battlefields are not the attackers, they are just following orders. I know this because I was one of them – I can't blame them for the selfish acts of their kings. Before I served your father I did everything that was asked of me by my commanders. I never questioned anything when I should have, I killed men who need not have been killed, Larsa – those are the faces that haunt me, not the eyes of kings that have been killed, but theirs …'

Marmicus slowly untangled the princess's arms from around his muscular chest, and rose from the divan; every time he thought of his past life he felt impure. He could not bear Larsa to be near him when he remembered his old way of life – how different he was now.

'I can't imagine what you've seen,' she murmured. Sometimes she wished she could see the world through his eyes, even if it was just for one day; at least then she could comfort him properly.

'War is a savage affair. If men are not careful, it can strip them of their humanity and leave them soulless.'

'But I would be a better queen if I knew what my people saw, what war really means.'

'Why do you wish for something like that?' asked Marmicus sharply. Even though he loved her naivety, sometimes she would say things that were beyond childish. 'Never wish for something like that, Larsa. I don't want you to see war; it's something that can't easily be forgotten by the mind.'

'You can't protect me from what is coming, Marmicus; soon enough I shall see war, and when I do I'll be strong like my father.'

'No, Larsa, you won't.'

'What?'

'I don't want you to be here. I want you to leave this kingdom and head to one that can shield you from war. If our kingdom is conquered you'll be the first in danger, and I won't let that happen.'

'You speak as though we've already lost this war! We will win so long as we have you to defend us. I know it.'

'I am not immortal, Larsa. I'm one man, made of flesh, vulnerable to his weaknesses, just like any other. I can't lead the army if all I can think about is your safety. I have to be able to think with clarity, to focus on what's coming, and if you're here I'll put my men at danger. I need you to go.'

He could tell from her expression that she was offended by his reaction: her lips always parted slightly; it was a subtle sign that only someone who knew her intimately would recognise.

'How can you expect me to leave? This is my homeland and soon I shall become its queen; I will never walk away freely from my people or my duty. I'll stand and fight with our people, just as I promised my father I would.'

'I am not asking you to go – I'm telling you to. I've already made the arrangements. Tomorrow you'll leave, and journey towards the Kingdom of Aram, where it's safe. The decision has already been made.'

'I'm not a soldier for you to command; no order is above me, not even yours. I'm the heir to the throne and will soon be your queen!' declared Larsa. She could feel her hands shake nervously. This was the first time Marmicus had ever commanded her to do something against her will; it was unlike him to be so forceful.

'This isn't the time to be stubborn, Larsa. If we don't win this war, there'll be no kingdom to rule over or return to. If you love me, you'll do this for me.'

He had always regarded her resilience as an attractive quality, but not tonight – there was too much for him to think about and her stubborn attitude was not helping.

'Why do you choose to torment me with your absence? Isn't it enough that I have given you my heart and my body? What more can I offer you?' she uttered in desperation, unable to understand why he was talking to her like this. Where was the man she had fallen in love with, who wanted to spend every waking moment with her?

'I'm not pushing you away; I just want to protect you from all of this, that's all. All my life I've fought in battles, knowing only hardship and pain, and your love has been the one thing that has offered me the peace that I've always wished for. In your hands lies my freedom. Without you, I am a prisoner of war.'

Larsa embraced him, feeling the weight of his words hit her like a pile of rocks. What she was about to say would cause her more agony than she could ever have imagined, but this was not the time to be selfish; she would endure the pain for his sake alone.

'I love you too much to willingly hurt you. I'll leave our homeland only because I would never want to be the cause of your unhappiness or the author of your imprisonment,' she whispered. Her lips trembled as she spoke; it felt as though her heart had fallen at her feet. She realised in that moment that the fate of her kingdom now rested with him.

'I'll leave tomorrow but only on one condition – otherwise I won't go.'

'What is it?'

'I need you to promise me that nothing will happen to you,' she said, with tears in her eyes, which began to roll down her cheeks. 'Swear to me that our hearts will unite once again like the sea upon the shore and the moon against the sun. There can be no power on earth that can separate us from each other. I need you to swear this to me, and I'll go willingly into exile for you.'

'I promise you we'll return to each other the day this war ends. I give you my word,' replied Marmicus as he tenderly wiped away her tears. Though he had made this promise, he knew deep down there was no guarantee that he would survive; but he would rather lie and know that she was safe, than tell the whole truth and have her remain in danger. The truth was that this could be their last night together.

'Then before I leave there's something I need to tell you. It's troubled me since my father died, but it's more of a suspicion than anything else,' Larsa said, feeling the need to free her troubled heart.

'What is it?'

'Before my father died he called upon me to sit by his deathbed. He was so weak, Marmicus; every time he breathed I could hear him grow weaker. I watched him dying and, all the while, I didn't know what to say to comfort him. I alone was allowed into his chamber. If anyone else tried to enter, he would start screaming. It made no sense; even the Grand Priests weren't allowed to pray over him. I couldn't understand why he was behaving like that; you remember how much he loved the Counsel? He always called upon them whenever he was in need, but that night he didn't wish to see any of them. It was as if he was fearful of them – or of someone. I can still remember the look in his eyes every time the door creaked a little; there was terror within them and it frightened me.'

'Didn't he mention anyone's name?'

'He couldn't speak properly; he just screamed with pain. Anything he said was incomprehensible – even when I tried to talk to him, he would babble words I couldn't understand.'

The memory of her father dying in her arms was painful for her to recall. She was still grieving for him; they had grown extremely close since her mother had died giving birth to her young brother, who had followed his mother into the afterlife a few days later. Since then, her father had raised her, offering her all his love and attention.

'I want you to think back. He may have left you a message of some kind.'

'He didn't.'

'He must have. Tell me anything – a shred of a memory, even. It's of great importance, Larsa; a traitor may be sitting among us.'

'I'm telling you he didn't; nothing he said made any sense, it was just noise. By the end, he couldn't even whisper my name, or see me.'

Larsa abruptly removed her hand from his tightening grip, feeling angered by his lack of sympathy for what she was going through. She was not accustomed to death as he was: Marmicus lived by the sword while she had only lived a life of peace.

'Wait ...' she said. Her voice dipped in tone as her lips trembled with emotion, for what she would say would reveal more than treachery. 'The only thing I can tell you is this: when the Grand Priest of Ursar entered the chamber, my father squeezed my hand so tightly that even I became fearful ...'

8

As the Serpent sat among the Counsellors he felt sickened by their self-righteous sense of superiority. *Ignorant fools! Soon I'll slash your beards off and use them as fuel for my fire.* His eyes traced their pious forms with sheer disgust. All this time he had served their gods obediently; in so doing, he had gained the greatest respect from them. But he could no longer live a lie. Within himself he felt chained to serve a false god rather than his own desires, denying himself a throne that was worthy of his name. Every time he entered the temple, he felt repulsed by the sweet, sickly smell of honey that clung to the air like a stain on the robes of an emperor. *I was born to rule: no one shall stand in my way*, the Serpent thought as his mind filled with venomous ideas of how he would destroy the sacred Garden of the Gods ...

9

'What beautiful pleasures you've indulged us with, oh King Nelaaz!' a guest yelled.

The sound of wind instruments and heavy drums beating had made it difficult for King Nelaaz of Aram to hear his guests speak, although he cared little once the half-naked belly dancers entered the grand hall. Their exposed flesh made him drool with thick saliva: an uncontrollable reaction to their shapely figures. They shook their bodies, encircling the assembled guests.

'No need to thank me; my women are your women, so long as we do not share them at night!' he laughed. The King of Aram had handpicked each belly dancer himself; it was one of his favourite pastimes, along with eating and drinking.

The dancers twisted and turned like cobras, dancing to the tune played on wooden whistles and drums, and in their hands they held large swords which they then placed on their heads, balancing them as they danced. The combination of naked flesh and the risk of death was an enticing combination for any man: some were so excited by the sight that they gnawed at their lips, biting them in excitement. In a circular movement the belly dancers shook their hips and swirled their toned muscles in and out; some shook their breasts as they seduced and infuriated their audience.

'There are three things I love deeply in this world. Can any of you guess what they are?' King Nelaaz yelled. He wiped his ginger beard with his sleeve; it was soaked in wine and frothing saliva.

'I can't think what they might be,' replied Fallus, chewing a grape with little finesse. In fact, he could not be bothered to think at all at that moment; all his attention was focused on the large thighs of the women who gyrated before him.

'I love my wealth, my palaces, but above all, I love my women!'

King Nelaaz suddenly grabbed the closest dancing girl his chubby little hands could reach, forcing her to sit on his sweaty lap as he began to fondle her, showing no restraint at all. With his thin lips, hidden beneath his ginger beard, he smothered her neck, moistening it with kisses. It looked as if the belly dancer was actually enjoying his slimy touch – succumbing, perhaps, to the lure of wealth over intelligence.

'To all the gods! And their women – may they forever delight us with the pleasures of their lips, and the sweetness of their hips!'

'To the gods and their women!' cried the guests. They all raised their chalices and gulped down the wine like uncivilised animals, the sweet intoxicant quenching their thirst, making them roar happily at anything.

'Your Majesty ...'

A servant rushed in, trying his best to dodge the dancing women and the lethal swords which moved with them.

'What do you want? Go away.'

'A messenger has arrived from the Garden of the Gods, Your Majesty.'

'Let him call upon me tomorrow. I'm busy.' King Nelaaz chuckled as he squeezed the girl in his lap, pressing her bosom close to his chest, while she twirled his ginger beard in her fingers.

'Your Majesty, he says it is a matter of urgency, one which cannot be delayed.'

'There's nothing more urgent than satisfying a king's desire, is there? Now go away. Tell him to report back to me tomorrow, or perhaps the day after that – if I'm lucky.' He winked at the dancing girl, his gaze every bit as perverted as his touch.

Realising the situation, the servant whispered into the king's ear. Few words passed his lips, but they were enough to alarm the king, as he shot out of his seat. The dancing girl fell off his lap; shamelessly, she crawled onto another man's lap, and his eyes were quick to enjoy her curvaceous body, his hands to grab her tight.

Dabbing the beads of sweat from his forehead, King Nelaaz rushed out of the chamber as quickly as his short legs would carry him. *Why must the gods always curse me when I am in the company of a beautiful woman?*

'Well, bring him in! Hurry up, boy, be quick!' King Nelaaz demanded as he sat down, his fat bulging from either side, spoiling the elegance of his throne and reminding everyone present of his greed.

'Yes, my lord.'

As King Nelaaz waited impatiently for the messenger to enter his chamber, he felt nervous; he had warned his servants never to disturb him when he dined with guests, especially when he was being entertained by beautiful women, yet they had done so. It showed a measure of courage, but they had better have a good reason ...

'Your Majesty ...' said the messenger. He bowed respectfully before the king. It was quite clear that his presence was unwanted.

'Come on, young man, I don't have all day. Can't you see I have guests waiting for me? What's this urgent news you speak of? Hurry up; be quick.'

'Her Royal Highness Princess Larsa is travelling towards your kingdom this very moment.'

It was an unexpected delight. 'Ah, I see she's finally accepted my marriage proposal. Good for her. I knew she would come round to the idea. I've always said that a beautiful woman like her should have as many husbands as any man.'

King Nelaaz smiled while rubbing his belly in a child-like fashion. He had asked to marry the princess on numerous occasions, but her father had always rejected his proposals, knowing him to be an unsuitable spouse. The big-bellied king already had three wives of his own, and was old enough to be Larsa's father, but even so he remained ever hopeful that she would change her mind and fall in love with him. *Perhaps she has come to her senses now that her father is dead? What if she does wish to marry me? Yes, I am certain that she does.*

'Well, has the princess accepted my marriage proposal or not?' His eyes lighting up with excitement, he could not wait to hear the answer.

'No, my lord, the princess has not accepted such a proposition,' said the messenger. He watched the sweaty king sink into his throne like a goat sack deflating. The news was obviously disappointing for him; no false smile could hide his disappointment. *I'm sure the princess will change her mind when she arrives. I'll try my best to seduce her with my charms and fatten her up with my food ...*

'If the princess doesn't wish to marry me, what on earth causes her to come to my kingdom? It can't be for its beauty or my hospitality; my kingdom can't compare to her own.'

'She is seeking refuge, Your Majesty; the Garden of the Gods is readying itself for war.'

'War?'

'Yes, Your Majesty.'

'That's impossible. No one would dare declare war against you, not with Marmicus as the kingdom's protector – besides, all the kings of Babylon have signed a treaty of peace.'

'That's true, Your Majesty, but the enemy is not a Babylonian.'

'Then who's threatening you with war? Is it your own people? They can be ungrateful little pests.'

Realising the nature of the question, the messenger took time to reply; he wanted to compose himself properly before he did.

'Well, who's waging war against your kingdom?' the king repeated, impatiently. 'Hurry up, boy! I don't have all night – can't you hear my guests enjoying their time without me?'

'The declaration of war has come from the Assyrians, and the fall of Babylon shall follow if nothing is done to stop them.'

'What? Have you gone mad?' shrieked the king. 'You expect me to welcome the princess into my kingdom with open arms when you're on the brink of war with Jaquzan? Why, that's suicide!' He rose from his seat, panting and shaking his head vigorously; he could not believe he had wasted his energy listening to such a foolish proposition, especially when there was only one possible answer. Absolutely, indubitably, undeniably: never! 'What indignity is this? Your kingdom will crumble into sand and you seek for mine to be buried along with it! I can't allow that to happen! I'm a king, with a king's throne; if I allow the princess to enter my gates I'll become a peasant, and what man desires to wear rags on his back? No, tell the princess she isn't welcome here. Quickly, go – tell her at once to return to her kingdom, wherever she may be. I will not have her here! She's not dragging me down into her tomb.'

'I understand your fears, Your Majesty, but it was at the request of the Gallant Warrior that she enters your kingdom's gates.'

King Nelaaz paused abruptly, his lungs wheezing with fret and worry. The messenger's final words were chosen for a reason; the mere mention of the Gallant Warrior's name was enough to alert any king to his obligations.

'Marmicus ...' said King Nelaaz as he returned to sit on his throne. His happy mood had been shredded into pieces; even the image of servant women dancing or bathing in a pool of wine had little appeal for him. *Damn the gods for cursing me with bad timing, and damn them for giving me this wretched heart of loyalty!*

'If I show allegiance to your kingdom, then I fear mine shall be buried alongside yours. Even so, I can't refuse a call for help from a brave warrior like Marmicus. His Sword of Allegiance has kept my walls protected in difficult times, and without him my people would have overthrown me.' King Nelaaz could hear his guests laughing louder and louder, while he shifted uncomfortably in his chair. 'I know I shall live to regret this decision. Go forth quickly and tell your princess that my home is her home and that the Kingdom of Aram waits anxiously for her arrival. Quickly! Before I change my mind.'

10

Marmicus stood, absorbing every glimpse of her silhouette, until eventually he could see her no longer. The Royal Caravan which carried the princess into self-exile had blended into the distance as if sinking into the sweeping sands of time. Only peace could unite their hearts once more – nothing else on earth.

As Larsa held on tightly to the reins, she watched her kingdom slowly vanish, and each step taken by her camel drew her further towards an unwelcome destination. Granules of sand flew in the hot dry air, and she peered out from under her veil, the white silk fabric shielding her from the harsh winds. Everything that was beautiful about her kingdom was now disappearing into nothingness. She could see only sand, which ran on for miles, bearing no signs of life apart from rare trails made by lizards and lonely wanderers, all of whom searched for a better life. Her journey had just started, yet she felt ill-prepared. The further her Royal Caravan travelled, the more intense her feeling of loneliness became; she was not accustomed to seeing an empty horizon. This was the first time she had left the Garden of the Gods, and the sun had barely moved before she missed it greatly. It was a magical land that resembled no other, always a feast for the eyes – heavenly gardens blooming with wild flowers and fruit trees, nourished by mighty rivers. *Oh, Marmicus, my love, I beg you to restore peace to our homeland so that our hearts can unite once more ...*

11

As the sun laid its head to rest beneath the earth's belly, Larsa stared out into the abyss. The desert was cloaked in darkness, with only the cold light of the moon shining upon its sands. Her servants and guardsmen had set up camp. She wished they would invite her to sit with them, but being of royal blood meant she was too noble for their company. She stared deeply into the fire, watching its flames dance to the breath of the chill wind, her beauty illuminated by the gentle glow that warmed her face. *Oh, my beloved Marmicus, now at last I have entered your world and felt your pain.*

'You needn't fear, Your Highness, the Kingdom of Aram doesn't lie too far from here. We should be there soon; perhaps in two more days,' said the Royal Commander who sat with her. He had been directly appointed by Marmicus to protect her from the nomads who travelled the desert searching for vulnerable wanderers to steal from.

'Yes, but my kingdom lies far from here, that's what grieves me. Marmicus was right – the life of a soldier is an unenviable one.'

'I understand.' He smiled as he peeled an orange then graciously offered it to her. Larsa thanked him for the offer, but she couldn't bring herself to eat.

'There's no greater torture on earth,' he said, 'than absence from one's homeland – always wandering, searching for something you can't find. I've felt this many times; every soldier has.'

'How do they cope with it?' Larsa was holding onto the golden pendant of Ishtar. Its eight-pointed star had astronomical significance, mirroring the heavens above them. Its soft metallic sheen stood out against the roughness of the wasteland like the spines on a cactus. She had hoped to find some comfort in its presence, but all it did was remind her of the homeland she had left behind.

'Every man has a purpose in life. Remembering that purpose always gives a soldier strength in times like this; even when the world is against you, there is always a reason to stand up and keep fighting.'

'What's your reason to keep fighting?'

'Mine is just a simple dream.'

'There's beauty in simplicity. What is it?'

He offered her a slice of orange, which Larsa took this time, not wishing to appear ungrateful.

'I want to care for my wife, to make love to her each night, and watch our infant grow taller than me. They are all that matters in my life; I'd sacrifice everything for them. They're the reason I keep fighting – to know that they're safe and happy.'

'That's a noble dream, one many would envy. Do you have a son or a daughter?'

'A son, only three months,' he smiled. His voice was full of unrestrained fatherly love; he had just parted from his newborn and already missed his cries so much.

'May the gods grant you a long life so you can watch your son grow tall and your wife grow old.'

'I'd rather watch my child grow tall and my wife remain young,' laughed the commander. A smile broke across the princess's face; she understood the importance of a father in a child's life. Whenever her father, King Alous, had journeyed away, he would always return home with a gift representing the land he had visited, and he would sit for hours with her, talking about what he had learnt, and why he had brought her back that special gift. Such intellect and wisdom as she possessed came from him. *Oh, Father, if it weren't for you I would have become as lonely as this moon and as empty as this land …*

'Will you not tell me what you live for?' the soldier asked.

'My dream is no different from yours. I live to love another.'

Her heart felt heavy for Marmicus; war had made the desert his second home, as well as his battleground. The world demanded so much from him; she only realised that now, not knowing the extent of his invisible wounds. This journey had offered her a small glimpse into his reality, and now she regretted arguing with him about petty things. If only she could go back and be the understanding wife he needed. *A life by the sword is cold as its touch …*

'The Gallant Warrior loves you dearly, Your Highness,' said the soldier, sensitive to the princess's meaning. 'Some say that it's because of his love for you that our kingdom has survived these troubled times. He fights to protect you – every soldier who has served alongside him understands this well.'

'You're mistaken; Marmicus fights to protect the people – they're all that matter to him. If anything should ever befall me, he'll remain loyal to the people and will never cast aside his duty.'

She gazed at the soldier who sat opposite her; his words were touching, but she knew the depths of her husband's love for his homeland: nothing in all the world would change it.

'Only a woman as modest as this moon would think that. Your people know his love for you, and I believe one day you will learn it too.'

He rose from the golden sand, stretching his hand out towards her. 'Come now, you must rest. We have a long journey ahead of us tomorrow and you too need sleep, just like anyone else in your kingdom.'

12

Days had passed since Larsa departed for the Kingdom of Aram, seeking refuge from the war. However, Marmicus had not yet received news of her safe arrival. It left him feeling anxious. He had instructed her to send word as soon as her feet touched Aram's soil; it was unlike her to forget such an important request. Unable to think clearly, he headed towards the mighty Temple of Ishtar, looking for solace in a place where few would expect to find him. Marmicus had never believed in the gods or their power; to him, they were nothing more than clay statues shaped by the hands of power-hungry men. Tonight, however, for some strange reason he felt drawn to them.

Marmicus stood in front of the gigantic statue of Ishtar; her finely carved eyes looked down at him, as if mocking him in his time of weakness. He could not understand why anybody would believe in her mythical powers: all he saw was stone, no godly power or divine right that made her superior. Marmicus envied those who believed in her powers. Their faith gave them hope. If ever they faced a problem, they would turn to her, believing that she would offer them justice, either in this world or the next. Their faith made the world more beautiful, for wherever there was a wrong committed against the soul, it would be undone by the justice offered by Ishtar.

'Strike me so I can believe in you!' he roared. His voice echoed through the empty chamber. He secretly wanted to believe in her power, but no amount of anger could rouse the goddess of fertility to strike him down; she remained as she was, motionless and unmoved by his desperate plea for guidance.

'Even if Ishtar struck you with a thousand bolts of lightning, you'd still find ways not to believe in her power. Isn't that right, Marmicus?'

There was only one woman in the kingdom who knew him well enough to say that. Marmicus turned, feeling somewhat embarrassed that his childhood friend had seen him behave as he had. It was unlike him.

'I see you've not lost your wit, Sulaf.'

'Nor my beauty, or do you suggest that I've lost that?' Sulaf chuckled. She paused for a moment, gazing at the man who had captivated her heart since childhood; he was the source of all her desires, as well as being the object of her affliction over the years. She walked towards him, cheekily smiling at him as if taunting him with all his childhood secrets. 'I remember when your father used to drag you here by the arm; even then you'd always find ways to escape Ishtar, and I'd be punished for not telling them where you had hidden! Do you remember those days?'

'Always,' smiled Marmicus, happy to see her.

'So what brings the mighty Gallant Warrior to the Temple of Ishtar, when you've denied her powers for so long?'

'Exactly the same reason as you. I need guidance in a time of uncertainty ...'

'Guidance?' asked Sulaf. Her eyebrows drew together in confusion. She knew Marmicus, yet she had never imagined he could say such a thing. 'If I remember correctly, you said the gods are just tablets of stone which should only be used to protect the walls of a kingdom, never the hearts of men?'

'You remember my words better than I do.'

'That's because I've had time to ponder over them. It's been a long time, hasn't it?'

'It has.' Marmicus paused, and they stared at each other, feeling glad. 'Since you bring up the past, didn't you say that you'd never marry, and yet you have?'

'Time can change a person and make them do things that they would have never imagined doing when they were very young. I see time is starting to do that to you.'

She strode past Marmicus and placed her small offering on the colossal stone plinth. Painful memories of her marriage flooded into her mind: her husband had been a brutal man with no understanding of her dreams. Although her skin glowed with the beautiful stain of the sun, it had once been bruised and bloodied by her husband's fists. 'My marriage is my greatest regret in life; I should have remained true to my word and not married at all. It seems that the gods have a way of cursing those who do not stay true to their word.'

'Forgive me. I didn't know my words would cause you any distress.'

'There's no need to apologise for the behaviour of another; sometimes we must endure hardships so that we may know our strengths. Besides, my son and I are now safe from his fists. I'm sure you know, my husband died soon after my son was born. I will never forget that day; I wept with relief, not sorrow.'

Marmicus nodded uncomfortably, unsure how to react; all he knew was that he felt happy to see her again after all these years. Sulaf had not changed much; she had grown into a middle-aged woman, but her features remained the same. She still wore the same mischievous smile, her skin appeared more tanned, and her hair remained thick and black – a few grey strands, but hardly visible. One obvious change was the look in her eyes; they had somehow lost their sparkle, as if they had grown tired of the world.

'You have not changed at all,' said Marmicus.

'We all change, whether we like to admit it or not. No one can withstand time, not even those who are most fearful of it,' Sulaf said with a rush of emotions spilling through her.

He was drawing her in again. If she was not careful, all her past feelings for him would be reawakened, and this was not what she needed, not now, not when she had finally overcome the anguish that her unrequited love had caused her. 'The people say that we are at the brink of war. I didn't believe them until I saw you standing here. Your presence is enough to warn any doubter that war is coming.'

'The people always have a way of knowing everything.'

'So the rumours are true?'

'The people will know when the time is right; now is not the time.'

Sulaf sat down on the steps of the statue of Ishtar; she needed a moment to compose herself. Her hands were shaking, so she pressed them flat against the cold stone, trying to conceal her alarm. The news was shocking, incomprehensible: in a matter of months the Garden of the Gods may no longer exist; instead it might resemble the wastes of hell. Every land that had been invaded by the Assyrian army had been flattened and destroyed. What could make her homeland the exception? The idea frightened her deeply.

'Today I watched two children playing in the same fields where we used to play; they were playing the game of kings and warriors, as we once did. One child pretended to be an emperor, but the other child pretended to be someone else entirely. He pretended to be you, and with one swing of his Sword of Allegiance the emperor was defeated.' She stared into Marmicus's eyes. He was a man respected by many but intimately known to only a few. 'I know you well, Marmicus, but in all the years that I've known you, I have never seen you look defeated.'

She pushed herself away from the pillar and walked towards him. Although she was not as gloriously beautiful as the princess, she possessed a confidence that made her attractive in other ways. 'I want you to remember one thing, if nothing else – there is more to this land than the princess or the palaces you have surrounded yourself with since your return. Don't let your love cloud your senses, for you may find that even the purest love can turn to poison. I have tasted love's poison, I've drunk from its chalice – I know it all too well. If the heart is not careful, it can weaken the soul, and this kingdom can't afford to have a weak warrior as its defender. Remember that.'

Sulaf had loved him ever since they had played together in the green fields. There had been a time when they had been inseparable, but their friendship changed when he met the princess. Each day Sulaf watched him slip away from her, falling further in love with someone else; like the trickling sand of an hourglass, the prospect of them ever being together ebbed and died, until eventually he had no more affection to offer her.

'You've got no reason to fear; I won't let anyone destroy our homeland. But thank you for your words.'

'There's no need to thank me; you'll always have my friendship and my guidance whenever you should need it.'

And you will always have my love whenever you choose to embrace it, Sulaf thought as she walked away from the secret object of her desires.

13

For a brief moment Larsa thought she had returned to her homeland. The Royal Marquee that sheltered her body from the intense heat of the sun was filled with luxury that seemed misplaced in the desert. All that she really needed was water, and fire, and yet her marquee had been filled with beautifully decorated chairs, rugs, and even a table. The smell of incense permeating the stale air comforted her, strangely, as she slept. If it had not been for the sound of camels groaning and shifting outside, she would not have known where she was. She rose from the cushioned bed and moved towards the makeshift door, which flapped in the dry wind like the sails of a ship. While she had slept peacefully among her lavish cushions, her servants had only sheepskins and the sand for comfort. It made her feel guilty. *I must undo my wrong*, she thought, watching one servant struggle to lift a heavy sack filled with wheat onto a camel's back.

'Wait!'

'What's the matter, Your Highness? Is there something wrong?'

The servant was alarmed to see the princess standing in the sun when there was cool shade for her inside the tent.

'Let me help you.'

'I can manage, Your Highness; it would be an insult to your name.'

'The only insult would be if you should refuse my help when I have offered it,' she said softly.

To her servant she appeared altogether too delicate to undertake such a tiring chore.

'He can lift it, Your Highness,' said another subject.

'I know he can, but I want to help.' Larsa's voice grew stronger as her passion rose; she would not take no for an answer. 'I want to be of some help. Please – it will mean more than you know.'

'As you wish, Your Highness,' replied the servant, making space for her hands to grip the leather sack. Only a gracious ruler would offer to use their own hands to ease the burden of their people. The princess reached out her hands to grip the goatskin sack. All this time she had felt like a stranger, lost in a swirl of sand, not knowing how to behave or what to say to her servants. But she felt compelled to find her place; there was no sense in feeling homesick. She helped her servants lift up the heavy sacks and tie them on the camels' backs. Deep down she had feared the desert, for her rule did not extend there. Now her fear seemed petty, for the desert had become a place of liberation – it gave her the freedom to act just as an ordinary woman would. In the desert, there was no one to judge her behaviour. She wiped the sweat that ran from her forehead with her sleeve, and a refreshing breeze swept past, cooling her body. For a moment she looked out into the distance, trying to enjoy the sight of the rippling sands that stretched out in front of her, and she noticed a strange movement on the horizon – it was hard to make out what it was exactly. The blinding light made her vision turn blotchy, and coloured specks danced before her eyes.

'What's that over there?' she asked.

'I don't see anything.'

'Look again – over there.' She pointed into the distance. A faint shadow dipped across a hill, running down as if chased by a thick cloud of some sort, but the sky was a brilliant blue – no clouds could have created such an illusion. Larsa stepped forward. Whatever it was, it had intrigued her. The object appeared to be getting bigger, and was heading in their direction. The servants stopped what they were doing, huddling together, trying to make out what it was.

'It looks like people. They must be merchants; this route is filled with them,' said one.

'No, they can't be merchants – merchants travel only by camel, and those are men riding horses,' said a second servant. He could make out the shape of horses galloping; the image flickered in the heat like a mirage, becoming sharper with every second. The dark specks contrasted vividly with the bright orange sands of the desert.

'It looks like a small army, but not large enough to seize a kingdom, had there been one near here,' added another servant.

'Alert the guards immediately!' declared Larsa. 'There may be too few to seize a kingdom, but there are enough to seize this camp. They're coming for us – I can feel it.'

Nothing can prepare a person of conscience for watching another die. Even if they don't know the other person, or what kind of life they may have led, somehow they will still find themselves screaming, begging their killers to spare them. But those who have unjustly killed once will find themselves repeating the same sin, for murder is an obsessive habit. Larsa could do nothing but watch the annihilation of her soldiers; vastly outnumbered, they had advanced on their enemy and been killed before her eyes like goats by grey wolves. Innocent men, who had sung and laughed the night before, were trampled by horses as they lay on the ground in agony. Their screams had slowly turned into faint whispers; those left alive were bleeding to death. No compassion or relief was offered by their attackers.

The commander who had so lovingly spoken of his wife and newborn child was the first to die; he fell off his horse when it reared and plunged, and as he stood up, a swiping blow hit him from behind. At first Larsa thought the blade had missed him; the commander stood motionless for a second or two, staring vacantly into the clear blue sky as if he were in some kind of trance; then he fell sideways. But this was not enough for his murderer; the Assyrian galloped back, wanting to finish him off once and for all, and desecrate his body The soldier hacked at his body; his blood splattered everywhere as the blade flashed up and down. Every time the knife was plunged into his body, Larsa thought of the commander's wife and infant, and all the things they had dreamt of doing as a family. Today all their dreams had been spat on and set alight. Finally, the commander's body lay on the ground, unmoving; the hooves of the soldiers' horses trampled on him, crushing his face and those of the others, until eventually all were unrecognisable. Ambitions and dreams built by good men had been reduced to rubble, and bodies lay scattered on the ground like desert rocks, ready for the vultures to feed on.

Nothing that was said or done now could make any difference to their fate. The princess – along with her servants – was at the mercy of her attackers. None of her soldiers had had any chance of survival: they were hopelessly outnumbered from the beginning, and all they could do was try their best to fulfil their duty and protect the princess from danger.

Larsa covered her ears, trying desperately to block out the gargling screams of her soldiers; she could hear them calling out the names of the gods, but where were they? Why had the gods not stopped this from happening? Others shrieked the names of their loved ones, wanting to remember their faces before they died.

Larsa shook her head like a crazed woman. The Babylonian poets had lied to her – there was no beauty in death, nothing glorious to be held or attained, just as Marmicus had explained. Everything the poets had described in their recitations was an extravagant lie. This was the real face of war: sheer brutality spawned by uncivilised actions, and for a short moment she stared into its eyes, seeing what inhumanity lay within it. The vultures circling above, and the grotesque smell of blood which drifted on the winds, brought to Larsa a deep and terrible chill. It was a smell Larsa had never come across before, and breathing it in made her feel nauseous and unclean, as if the sins of her enemy were being painted onto her skin.

Even if Larsa survived the bloody combat, the prospect of being violated was real. To be touched by someone else, once, twice or countless times – the thought disgusted and appalled her. She would rather kill herself. She looked at her servants, who were thinking the same thing: rape was imminent for her, and death was inevitable for them. Her stomach, full from the night before, began to heave. Overcome, she fell to the ground, her head becoming light and her vision foggy.

A servant rushed to comfort her, but the princess pushed her away.

'Leave me!' she shouted, willing herself to be strong as she tried to stand up.

'You don't need to witness this, Your Highness; the sight of death isn't meant for a ruler of peace.'

He pointed towards the Royal Marquee, reminding her that she could shield her eyes from the gruesomeness around her. Larsa nodded, and began to walk towards the flapping tent, until something inside her made her stop in her tracks. She remembered her father's words: *Remember, my dear child, that a ruler's heart must always be as strong as the walls of his kingdom. So build your heart into a fortress and never surrender to a moment's weakness. No force on earth can destroy you unless you willingly surrender to it …*

'No … I can't,' she said, turning back to face her fate. Her servants had shown bravery, when she had shown nothing but fear. 'Only a coward would turn their head from the sight of bravery, and I'd never wish to be that person. If ever there was a time to be a real leader, it's now, in this moment.'

The enemy had gathered some distance away, and now she could hear the thunder of hooves behind her. They were coming for her; only a few minutes separated them.

'Gather together, quickly!' she said. 'If this is my last hour, then let me depart this world with a clear conscience.'

Her servants rushed to her. They had served her since she was born; now they would watch her become a woman.

'I will not lie to you; I am afraid. I've never seen war, and I know nothing of it, but what I do know is that I love my people and my kingdom. Never would I wish to disgrace them, so I'm left with a choice. I can either walk into that tent, and let my fear take hold of me and control me as it did a moment ago, or I can stand firm and look into my enemy's eyes with the same courage as my soldiers. I know we are outnumbered, and I know we are defenceless, but – make no mistake – we are not helpless. Those men died for us – they left behind their dreams so that we can live our own. I will not disgrace them, and I know you won't either. So let the beasts come, and when they do, let them see our strength – we will never surrender to them. No sword they possess can strip us of our humanity or make us heartless like them. Whatever is destined to become of us is by the will of the gods, but what we do right now, in this final hour, is by our will alone.'

Larsa gripped the pendant of Ishtar. Whatever happened, she would not abandon it, not when she needed her courage the most …

The Assyrian soldiers arrived in a cloud of sand thrown up by their galloping horses; hundreds of faces encircled the Royal Caravan, which stood like a single tree in an empty desert. Nothing could separate the soldiers now from their prize. They sniffed the air like wild dogs as they gathered around the camp, making a human wall to prevent anyone from trying to escape. Their iron jaws and slate teeth screamed madness and sexual hunger; it was clear that these men had lost their humanity a long time ago.

The Dark Warrior jumped off his black stallion and walked towards the princess. He had not expected her to be as beautiful as she was, and her porcelain white skin was evidence that she had lived a privileged life. Nafridos wiped away the blood on his cheek, as if wanting to make himself presentable. Larsa may not have known about war, but she could tell straight away that he was a man who enjoyed killing: his broad athletic shoulders and unusual iron sword, with its jewelled pommel, defined him as someone who earned a living from it.

He stopped in front of Larsa and glared. A face like hers was meant to be admired; it brought only tension within the bodies of men, for desire has a way of making men feel things that only a woman can satisfy.

'One rarely finds a jewel among the debris.'

'My beauty isn't yours to admire. If you want to kill me then do it quickly; save me from your flattery.'

'I see you're in a rush to die? Don't worry, it'll come soon enough,' Nafridos sneered, as he gently slid his blade against her cheek, running it down the length of her face. There was the pungent stench of death on the weapon, like iron mixed with salt water; it made her feel sick. 'Shush, don't fear me, princess, I'm not your enemy – not for now.'

'You're a liar as well as a butcher.'

Nafridos laughed brutishly, and so did his men, who watched him play with his victim like a toy; they all knew she would afford him much amusement. Her resistance would only entertain him.

'I'm much more than that, princess – I'm madness in all its glory,' he whispered softly into her ear, his warm breath tingling the surface of her skin. 'Do you see these hands? They're going to set fire to your people and, after I'm done with them, I'll go on to behead your husband.'

'Threats can easily be made, but destiny is never one to be tried.'

'We have a poet!' shouted Nafridos to his comrades. They were cheering him on, urging him to taunt the princess. 'I can taste your courage, princess, but if I were you I wouldn't say such foolish things to a man who holds a butcher's knife in his hand, unless you want your beauty to turn into something less comely.' He sniffed her hair; its scent was alluring, but it was out of place on a battlefield.

'Go ahead, kill me, I won't stop you.'

'And why would I want to waste such beauty? No, I've got better ideas.'

Nafridos began to slide his blade along her chest, cutting through the soft fabric of her garment; it was the only thing separating him from her skin. Her bravery was truly remarkable. As he cut through her dress she barely moved, giving only the slightest whimper. Nafridos had never seen such bravery. All the queens and princesses he had violated screamed loudly, but Larsa barely trembled. If only she knew that her resilience was only fuelling his desire! It was like a spark that ignited an unquenchable fire within him; nothing would stop him from doing to her what he pleased. 'Now hush and be silent, or be silenced by me.'

The Dark Warrior turned his attention to the remaining servants. Killing men was a pleasure for him; something for which he had a talent. Only a couple of minutes had passed since he had butchered the Royal Guardsmen, offering them no mercy, and now his hunger for death had returned.

'Kill the men first,' he said to his men. 'You have my permission to have your amusement with the women. Once your bodies are satisfied, kill them all. Leave no man or woman alive. Everyone must die.' He turned to the servants. 'Today you shall all greet death, and when you do, be sure to tell the gods that the time has come for them to surrender to a new power.'

'What about the princess?'

'Her fate is in the hands of our emperor; she belongs to him for now. These are your orders and this is their destiny. Kill them.'

'No! Don't!' Larsa screamed. 'Let them go, don't harm them!'

The women were dragged by their hair. They tried to fight off the soldiers, but could not stop them from ripping their clothes and pinning them down. Chilling cries followed as the men were slaughtered, knives swiped across their necks in the manner of ritual execution.

'Where are your hearts? Have you no compassion?'

'Hearts?' Nafridos said, walking back to the princess. It was as if he could taste the sweetness of her innocence against his lips. 'They're buried beneath the earth, where your body shall soon lie. Now say your farewells, princess, before you find they can no longer hear you.'

14

King Nelaaz of Aram was a man stifled by bad luck and he knew it. No matter how much energy or wealth he poured into his kingdom, hoping to gain favour with his people, they would always turn rebellious, branding his ideas as laughable and calling for a republic. The short-legged king's round physique, his spotty and sweaty complexion, had led him to being nicknamed the Clown King of Aram; a name which – if uttered in his presence – carried an immediate sentence of death. In a last attempt to try to save his throne from the hands of disloyal men, King Nelaaz of Aram had asked Marmicus to intervene; it was his last hope of saving his slipping power from those who wanted to disembowel him. Fortunately, Marmicus had agreed to step in, buying some time for the sweaty little king to make the necessary reforms to please his people, and momentarily halting the civil war that was on the verge of erupting. King Nelaaz understood that he owed to Marmicus not only his throne, but his life. Had it not been for his pledge of support, he would have been overthrown and fed to the lions. Despite all this, King Nelaaz was not one to mull over things too long, and his lavish parties always cheered him up when protests erupted on the cobbled streets of his territory – and today was no exception.

'I can't imagine why your people have any reason to despise you; I've never seen such gracious hospitality in all my life,' said a guest. He savoured the rich smell of roasted pig served with vegetables and wild fruits. Food was laid out along the length of the table, catering for the endless number of guests who celebrated for no reason at all. As in all parties thrown by the chubby king, they enjoyed the company of the women who sat on their laps, joyously feeding them as if they were babies.

'Whenever I'm in the presence of food, I make it a rule never to speak about politics. I'd rather save myself from the indigestion,' said King Nelaaz. His little nostrils sucked up the rich aroma of succulent meat; his stomach had been rumbling since his guests had arrived, and finally he could relieve the pangs of hunger.

'Every meal must be blessed with a toast! We're waiting for yours, oh beloved king,' laughed a guest, a concubine sitting on his lap, pouring wine into his mouth.

'Of course, only if I must.'

'Yes, you must!' they cheered.

King Nelaaz staggered to his feet, his knees cracking under the pressure of his weight. He raised his chalice of barley beer into the air, wanting to toast his friends and allies – many of whom he did not know, but trusted. 'My father, rest his soul, gave me a good piece of advice. He said that a man's body is a temple where his food goes to worship, so eat well and you'll certainly please the gods. And, if not, at least you have a reason for your woman to stroke your belly at night! To the gods and all their women – may they be pleased with us all!'

Laughter erupted, each man toasting his fellows and digging into his food with unmannerly gusto.

At last I can eat, thought King Nelaaz with a sense of relief as he grabbed the meat, drawing it close to his thin lips, the grease running through his ginger beard. *Ah, sweet paradise, I have patiently been waiting for you …*

Suddenly the chamber doors slammed open, to everyone's alarm, and a group of men entered, holding swords as if prepared for war.

'By the grace of Ishtar, what's going on? Who gave you permission to barge in here like this?' shrieked King Nelaaz. He wiped the oil from his mouth, having barely sunk his teeth into the meat. At first he had thought a rebellion had reached his palace, but the news was far worse.

'We've been sent here by order of the Gallant Warrior.'

Sibius barged through, pushing men out of his way as he approached the king. He handed over a clay tablet bearing the seal of their leader, which was more than enough evidence to authorise his entrance – and even if it was not, no man would dare defy such a symbol or disgrace it in front of him.

'In that case, join us! Come and sit down, all of you, I expect you're all hungry from your long journey. Send in more wine and more women; our guests from the Garden of the Gods are worthy of a thousand slaughters and more.'

There was no better time for the princess to join them, thought the king. An image of her getting drunk and falling onto his lap entered his mind. She was a delightful creature; no doubt she would be even more delightful if she were wearing nothing.

'Well, what are you waiting for? Aren't you going to feast with us? There are plenty of women to go round; there's no need to share.'

'We're not here to celebrate with you; we've come to seek news of the safe arrival of the princess. These are the Gallant Warrior's orders, and we will not defy them even at your insistence.'

'Arrival ... what arrival? The princess hasn't arrived in my kingdom.'

'Are you certain of this?' Sibius was in no mood to be trifled with, especially by an idiotic fat king whose face appeared to be as swollen as his feet.

'Of course I'm certain. I've been waiting for her since I got word that she was coming. Tell me, when do you expect she'll arrive? Will it be today, or tomorrow perhaps?'

'So, all this while, you've neither heard from her nor sent word back to our kingdom warning us of her absence?'

'Well ...' said the king, realising he was in dangerous waters, 'I've been extremely busy ...'

Sibius glanced at the king; the look on his sweaty face said everything. The sheer idiocy of his behaviour was beyond comprehension. How could any rational man have failed to act, especially when they were on the verge of war?

'Do you understand the gravity of what you've done? Your behaviour has jeopardised everything.'

He turned to leave. The guests' silence revealed the seriousness of the king's offence. King Nelaaz wished he had not invited them; at this moment he wanted only to curl up in bed alone, a rare occurrence in itself.

'Wait!' he called, trying to stop Sibius from leaving. 'Perhaps the Royal Caravan is lost. I'm told that on cloudy nights such as these it's difficult to find my kingdom. I'll send my men to search for them in the desert. Yes, I'm sure they are lost.'

'Then let's hope, for your sake, that the princess is still alive, because if she isn't, rebellion will be the least of your worries,' replied Sibius, marching off with clenched fists and fearful heart, anxious to deliver news immediately to his friend, Marmicus.

King Nelaaz had sent a search party to find the princess in the desert, dead or alive. His soldiers had been combing the desert for days, their heads pounding with heat exhaustion as they trekked beneath the sun for hours on end. The king's idea was folly from the start. They all knew it would be impossible to find the princess: the featureless desert stretched for miles and she could have been anywhere; it was like searching for a ring in a sand dune. What made matters worse was that none of them knew what the princess looked like, so every time they found travellers they stopped them, rushing to look into their tents. If they found a beautiful woman, they immediately suspected it to be her, dragging her away with them, only to be told by their commander that it was not the princess.

'My lord, the men are growing weak, and are in need of some rest. We must give them time to recover from the sun's daggers,' said a lieutenant, mounted like all the officers. He trotted beside his men, watching them battle to carry on. The combination of rough sand and leather sandals digging into their skin made the journey an excruciating one.

'No, we have to go on, we must keep searching. I don't care if your skin turns to chalk and your mouths burn with thirst; none of you will leave this desert until we've found the princess. Do you understand? Now keep searching.'

Like many of his fellows, the commander had grown tired of rectifying problems caused by his king. If it were not for the pledge given by Marmicus, King Nelaaz would have certainly found his head mounted on a spear by now. Of course, if they did not find the princess, Marmicus would happily do the job for them.

'We've found something,' declared a foot soldier, pointing into the distance. 'Over there …'

A massacre had taken place at this spot in the vast reaches of the desert. The foot soldiers tried to dodge the scattered bodies that lay everywhere, all of them covering their noses as they tried not to breathe in the stench of rotting carcasses. They were seasoned soldiers, accustomed to the gruesome aftermath of battle, but none of them had ever seen such foul mutilation as this. Whoever had killed these people had wanted to leave a message behind for their enemies – butchering them was not enough.

'May the gods have mercy on them,' said the lieutenant. He was staring upwards. Thrust into the ground were long metal spikes, and the severed heads of the Royal Guardsmen were mounted on them, their eyes deliberately left open, while their hair blew eerily in the wind like reeds. Flies infested the area; they were laying eggs in their open mouths and nostrils. 'Assyrian bastards! Was killing these men not enough for them?'

'Forget your pity. Our orders are to find the princess, and we won't leave this place until we've found her, dead or alive,' the commander replied.

Soldiers began to use their weapons to turn over the bodies, careful not to tread on severed arms and legs. The stench was awful. Vultures circled above, waiting for them to leave.

'How are we supposed to know which one's the princess? It's impossible to tell by looking at these corpses.'

'Search for her beauty.'

'No beauty of this world can survive such brutality,' said one soldier.

'Over here! I think I've found something!' yelled another soldier, picking something off the ground.

The commander leapt off his horse and covered his nose with his sleeve.

'Give it to me,' he demanded, snatching the object. 'Where'd you find this?'

'It was over there, lying beside her body.'

The golden pendant had been delicately inscribed with encrypted words, giving the jewellery meaning.

'What does it say?' asked the soldier as he looked on. The golden object shimmered in the commander's rough hands.

'It says "Allegiance lies in the heart of the sword",' he replied. His finger softly traced the engraved words.

'What does that mean?'

'It means the princess is dead,' replied the commander as he peered at the headless body of the young woman. Her head was nowhere to be seen in the carnage; they must have taken it with them. He knelt down and looked at the remains of her decomposing body. The young woman had obviously tried to fight off her attackers – her fingers were broken, clearly showing a struggle.

'She was raped, then killed,' said the lieutenant, brushing the flies away from his face. He hovered over her, trying to gain as much information as possible; he knew the last moments of her life must have been cruel. He examined her partially naked body; her dress had been ripped and her legs exposed. It was enough evidence to show she had been ravaged, no doubt a number of times.

'We've found what we were searching for. Bury her body. Make sure you leave no trace of her misfortune for anyone to see. We can't afford to anger the Gallant Warrior with such barbaric truths.'

'What about the rest of the bodies?'

'Leave them for the animals.'

The soldiers began to dig a large ditch, attempting to conceal the truth. If only they had known that the headless body they had found was not the princess, but a slave woman …

'By the glory of the gods, what am I going to do? What if they don't find the princess? What if she's dead?' shouted King Nelaaz.

'You must keep calm. No good can come from speculating,' replied his advisor.

'Speculating? Why, there's nothing to speculate about. If they don't find the princess, one way or another I'm dead. What man wants the Gallant Warrior as his enemy? I certainly don't, not after all he's done for me!' blasted the king, heatedly. His bulging belly heaved up and down with his short breaths; for once in his life he was unable to set aside his troubles in favour of food or a naked woman. The sweetness of ripened apples had finally turned sour in his stomach, leaving him choking on foul bitterness. 'By the gods, I've been cursed! I can feel it within the pit of my stomach; those hungry peasants in my kingdom have cursed me with their wretched prayers, I just know it. I can hear them cursing me in my sleep.'

‚We've found her!'

‚Well, where is she? By the gods, I demand to see her now.'

‚I wouldn't advise it, unless you wish to see a corpse,' replied the commander. He had returned from the desert as quickly as he could.

‚Don't speak to me in riddles, boy, I have neither the energy nor the patience to unravel their meaning. Now, tell me where the princess is. You said you found her – where is she?'

The commander jumped straight to the point, breaking the news without any niceties at all.

‚She's dead. Most likely raped before the Assyrians killed her.'

King Nelaaz looked at him dazedly; it was a strange reaction, as if the news had gone over his head.

‚Dead? That's impossible! No one would dare kill the sacred daughter of the Garden of the Gods!' He could not bring himself to accept such news; nor could any of his advisors. Larsa was unlike any other royal soul; she was considered a deity with the purest blood, sent from the gods themselves in all their glory. Every royal from the Garden of the Gods was seen as a descendant of Ishtar herself.

‚I don't believe you.'

‚I knew you wouldn't, so I brought you this,' said the commander. He took out a golden pendant from his pocket; its soft metallic sheen was partly obscured by the dried blood splattered over it, hiding its beauty.

‚What's this?'

‚It's proof,' he said, handing it over to the king, who looked at it for a few seconds, then passed it along to his advisors. Only they could guarantee its authenticity.

'It's the royal pendant of Ishtar,' said one advisor.

'Indeed. Look at the back – see what's written across it.'

The advisor turned it over. Engraved on the shiny metal were the sacred words of the kingdom.

'"Allegiance lies in the heart of the sword",' read the advisor aloud.

'I found it lying beside the body of a headless woman. I have no doubt in my mind that it was the princess.'

'A headless woman?' said King Nelaaz, sinking into his chair. The news was getting more disastrous by the minute. He put his hands over his head, not wanting to hear more. This was it; the end of his mortal journey. It was only be a matter of time before he would be thrown to the lions, just as the people had wanted. The spectacle would be a celebration for them.

'By the grace of the gods, what am I going to do? When the Gallant Warrior hears of this he'll crush me with his fist.'

'Does the Gallant Warrior know of this misfortune yet?' the advisor asked pointedly. His long nose twitched. He had a cunning ploy, one that – if implemented properly – might save them all from the fall from power.

'I haven't sent any news yet. I'm waiting for His Majesty's instructions.'

'Good. I've got an idea. It's rather far-fetched but I think it may just work,' said the advisor. All his plans had worked well in the past, and there was no reason why this one would not work too.

'I'm listening. What is it?'

'We can't change the fact that the princess is dead – but, then again, we can't afford to send a pile of bones to Marmicus. It would simply reveal this kingdom's negligence. So if we can't bring her back to life, then let us at least pretend we tried our best to protect her from the Assyrians. We can say that our soldiers got there and fought to protect her, and that many of our men died alongside her, but it was too late – they had already killed her. That way, we can't be blamed for her unfortunate death, but at the same time we can preserve our valuable allegiance with Marmicus.'

He was right: the idea was far-fetched. But it did have potential.

'We don't have her body, unless you're suggesting we go back and dig it up,' said the commander. He had trained himself to always think a step ahead; it was important for military personnel to assess the strengths and weaknesses of any suggestions.

'We can always find a woman who looks like her. The king has plenty of women at his disposal; it's only a matter of choosing which one,' said another advisor. It would mean killing an innocent woman just to facilitate their deceit. The commander looked at the king, who said nothing; the idea was cunning, however deceitful. Nevertheless, it might be their only option. The choice was entirely the king's.

'What if Marmicus sees the body and realises it's not her?' said King Nelaaz. He was beginning to feel uncomfortable with the suggestion.

'He won't. Not if the body lies beneath an inch of gold. We'll make sure she's ready to be buried; no one will see the body below all that gold. It'll distract the eyes,' said the advisor.

'By the gods, I forbid it. It's plain wrong! I can't lie to Marmicus, not like this anyway, especially when he's saved me from my own people and given me his allegiance.' For once in his life the king wanted to do something right; but in times of war it was never wise to develop a conscience.

'This is our only option, unless you wish to greet Marmicus with a pile of tattered flesh and dried bones,' insisted the commander, becoming convinced of the plan's viability.

'Don't be silly, you fool! Of course I don't, but I don't want to deceive him like this. I'm not giving you permission to do this. I won't do it.'

'If you don't agree to this, Your Majesty, you'll have no throne to sit on, and no palace to shield you from your own people who, in case you have forgotten, are out to kill you,' said the advisor, leaning towards him almost devilishly, desperately wanting to convince him to accept the idea. There was nothing to lose from trying it. 'If it helps your conscience, then think of this act as a sign of friendship offered to a man who has just lost his wife. If Marmicus knew the true extent of his loss, he'd have no strength to shield anyone from harm, including his own people. We must try to cushion the blow. It's in his interests – after all, sometimes we must commit a small wrong for the greater good.'

'Perhaps you're right,' said King Nelaaz. 'Death is death. We can't resurrect the princess, or undo the curse which has befallen her kingdom. She's now just a pile of bones, while I'm still a king made of flesh and in need of some comfort. I suppose all we can do is let the Gallant Warrior mourn her death in the most appropriate fashion.' He was trying his best to convince himself of the idea; rationalising their plan was already starting to make him feel much more at ease with it. 'Very well, go ahead and kill one of my whore women, and make sure she looks like the princess. You can have all the gold you need to conceal her body. If we're going to do this, we must do it right. By the gods, let's just hope it's enough to put everything right; if it isn't, then I'll not only lose my throne and my gold, but my favourite whore, no doubt. I can't think which is worse.'

'It's a shame that such beauty has to be wasted; you should have brought her to me – I would have given her a memorable last night,' said King Nelaaz, looking over the lifeless body of a young woman. Her smooth white skin, long dark hair, wide eyes and heart-shaped lips bore sufficient similarity to the features of the princess; it was the reason why she had been singled out and killed. 'Who was she?'

'A temple maid.'

'Any man would be committed to the gods after seeing her there,' said the king, biting his lip. Whenever he saw a pretty face, he couldn't stop himself from imagining what it would be like to be sleep with the woman; it was a disgusting habit.

King Nelaaz loomed over her. He had not noticed any sign of violence on her body, but quite frankly he didn't wish to know the details. The only thing that was important to him was whether Marmicus would believe it was the princess. He walked around the slab several times, watching the undertakers carry out their preparations; the powerful fragrance of frankincense irritated his nostrils. Her skin glowed brightly; it had been moisturised with a concoction of essential oils. They poured strong perfume over her, mixed with saffron leaves and fresh pollen. Using a soft brush, they gently painted the perfumed dye onto her face, spreading it evenly along her neck and down her shoulders – only the wealthy could afford such a thing. Eventually her body looked as if it had been covered in gold leaf, the scent of death had been clouded with perfume, and her skin appeared refreshed as if life still ran through her veins.

The longer King Nelaaz watched, the more he realised just how expensive this lie was becoming. The servants pulled a garment over her head, drawing it across her shoulders and down the length of her body; its encrusted jewels sparkled brilliantly as the light hit them. The dress had been stitched with gold thread. The vibrant colours contrasted with the simplicity of the white material.

'What's the world coming to? Who could ever have imagined that a temple maid would be given the burial of a queen?' he said, watching the undertakers trying to lift her up. Her muscles had not yet hardened; she had been killed just an hour or two before, giving them enough time to conduct their ritual without difficulty.

'They've arrived, Your Majesty.'

King Nelaaz nodded, acknowledging the servant's words. A rush of nervous energy filled him. He wished he could have a drink to settle his nerves, but there was no time for that. Every ounce of gold spent on this deception would be wasted if Sibius didn't believe their elaborate story. Of course, if he did not, they still had the option to get rid of him and bury all traces of the enterprise.

King Nelaaz watched the undertakers add the final touches: they lifted a solid gold funerary mask from the table and placed it over the dead girl's face, concealing her features. It fitted perfectly over her eyes, nose and lips. They lifted her head gently and tied an elaborate necklace around her neck, its golden leaves and white pearls cascading all the way down to her chest.

'This had better work,' said King Nelaaz. For some reason his feelings of guilt had disappeared completely when he realised how much had been spent on the plan.

'He's here!' said a servant, rushing in.

'Don't let him see her until they've finished. We don't need another body on our hands.'

The king walked out of the chamber, preparing himself to break the news to Sibius. *Only the gods can make this plan work*, he thought.

15

'You're good with children. I'm surprised you've waited so long for your own,' said Sulaf.

Marmicus laughed aloud. The boy was trying his best to attack him, but he easily dodged his strikes, despite giving him ample opportunity to beat him. He could tell Zechariah was getting exasperated; now the time had come to give a real lesson in the art of swordsmanship. Marmicus flexed his wrist; the movement was quick, but gentle enough not to harm the little boy. The weapon flew out of the boy's hands, landing on the grass at his feet.

'You should never treat your sword as just your weapon, Zechariah; you must think of it as a friend, worthy of respect.' Marmicus handed it back to him. The optimism and determination in the boy's eyes reminded him of his own eagerness to learn when he had been that age.

'But it's a sword, Uncle Marmicus, not a person!'

'You're wrong; it's much more than a sword – it's the one thing you have to protect yourself when you're facing your enemy. You need to know your weapon better then you know yourself. If you don't, you'll die.' He stopped for a minute, wanting to explain exactly what he meant. 'Look, if you strike your sword too hard against your enemy's blade, the blade may tremble, and you'll fail to strike a clean blow when you need it the most. But if you strike it too softly, then the blade can bend and you'll be left open to attack. That's why a warrior needs to learn how to control the rhythm of his weapon; he needs to know everything about it. Only then can he protect himself and maintain perfect balance. Once you've done this, the power of your weapon can truly be unleashed and people will honour you because of it. Now I want you to try again but, this time, embrace your sword as if you were about to embrace your destiny.'

The little boy concentrated hard on his weapon – the heft, the way the light shone off the metal and how his fingers closed around the grip. He tried to absorb every little detail.

'Are you ready to embrace your destiny?'

'Yes.'

The boy flung himself forward, attacking with greater control and self-belief. His thin arm scythed through the air as he swiped his blade, determined to triumph; Zechariah had improved his swordsmanship in a matter of seconds. His weapon clashed against Marmicus's own, with more skill and rhythm than before. Sulaf watched, feeling proud, and in awe of Marmicus's way with her child. She could tell he was ready to be a father, and she wished that she could be a father to her own son. Marmicus tried to prolong the battle as long as possible so he could boost the little boy's confidence. Finally, he angled his weapon perfectly, as he always did on the battlefield whenever he wanted to end a fight. True to his style, it resulted in a clean win. 'You've learnt to let your passion ignite your strength. You'll make a good commander one day.'

He gently handed back his weapon to the young boy. Marmicus could see himself in the boy's eyes, which were filled with a longing to protect and serve, just as his had been when he was young. Teaching the boy strengthened his desire to become a father, and he could not wait for the war to be over so he could realise his dream.

'Do you think I can become as great you, Uncle Marmicus?'

'Every man is the master of his destiny, Zechariah. You will become only what you strive to be in life. Remember this always.'

'Come on, Zechariah, it's time for you to say your prayers to the gods,' said Sulaf. The affection between man and boy was too much for her to bear; she had always dreamt of a future with Marmicus, but her reality was too different and all too lonely.

'Please, Mama, can I stay for a while longer with Uncle Marmicus?'

'No, Zechariah, the sun has set and it's late. Besides, prayers to the gods should never be delayed, you know that.'

'I don't see why I have to pray to the gods. You always say our prayers are never answered by them,' Zechariah said. His head hung in disappointment. He wanted to spend more time with his inspiration; he knew he would be the envy of all his friends once they found out.

'If only you could teach him to be more passionate about the gods.'

'I'm the worst person to teach your son passion for the gods! Besides, passion can't be taught, it can only be felt.' Marmicus laughed. He winked at the boy as if to support his rebellion against the gods.

'Don't encourage him,' Sulaf said. She reached for Zechariah's sword, taking it out of his hands and tapping him lightly on the back. The truth was that she wanted to be left alone with Marmicus; spending time with him was all she had ever desired. They both watched him walk away and enter the modest mud-brick house.

'I thought you had forgotten this place; it's been years since I've seen you stand here.' She wrapped her shawl tightly around her shoulders. Now that the sun was setting, the valley became a cold place.

'I'll never forget where I grew up. This is where I belong.'

'What are you searching for?'

She looked at Marmicus curiously; she knew everything about him, and knew when he was being evasive. The truth was, he was lonely without the princess and he had come seeking companionship.

'Why are you looking at me like that? Can't a man remind himself of the beauty he once knew and the memories he once shared?'

'Every man is entitled to his memories, but why do you look to the past when your future is more glorious?'

'Without Larsa, I have no future; I only have a duty that must be fulfilled.'

'No, Marmicus, your future lies with the glory of your sword, or have you forgotten that?' said Sulaf angrily. She could no longer restrain the bitterness she felt towards Larsa. It was because of her that she had been denied the sweetness of love, and now it seemed she would deny Marmicus his rightful destiny. 'I hate it when you speak of her as if she is the centre of the world. She isn't.'

'What do you want from me, Sulaf?'

'I want you to seize the glory you were born for.'

'Those who have never witnessed the barbarity of war would claim glory can be found upon the battlefield, but there is no glory in death. I've looked into the eyes of men and I've seen their fear time and time again. Glory is just a word used by kings to force men into battle when they're too cowardly to fight themselves. No man wants to die for glory, not when he has everything to live for.'

'Then what are you fighting for?' she asked. 'What is it that keeps that sword in your hand? Is it love? If it is, then our kingdom is already doomed because soldiers will not fight for that, they will not bleed for it and they will not die for it. They fight only for glory, and for the honour of their names. They need a leader who understands this, not a warrior who follows only his heart.'

'My men never fight for glory; they fight for a meaning far greater than that. This kingdom owes itself to the passion of its warriors, who die to protect their families and friends. Nothing else matters to them but their survival. This is what unites wise men and divides selfish rulers.'

'The only passion in war is to conquer and to kill, but you refuse to see this – instead you're blinded by a child's love. What does the princess know about the sacrifices you've made to get where you are? She's never suffered the way we have. She knows nothing of the ways of our world.'

'Don't disrespect the princess! I allow you to disrespect me, but never the princess.'

'There's nothing disrespectful in revealing her youthfulness compared to yours,' said Sulaf as she shrugged off the Gallant Warrior's threat. She knew Marmicus all too well; he would never harm her, no matter how far she pushed him. It was something she took for granted, indeed exploited. She walked towards him, staring deeply into his eyes as she stood in front of him. The man she knew was lost somewhere beneath that false façade he wore … he just needed to be awoken, stirred with the emotions he had once felt for her. She pressed her hand against his cheek, sliding it gently across his jaw, her eyes lost within his. 'Are you willing to sacrifice everything for the sake of one woman's love, to die for her and to bleed for her? Is this what you truly want to be remembered for?'

'No,' replied Marmicus. 'I'll sacrifice everything I have only for Larsa …'

'Then you have chosen to sacrifice us all with you,' she said, disappointed with his words. For a brief moment Sulaf had thought his reason had returned.

'I am not the man I once was, Sulaf, can't you see that?'

'No matter how hard you try, you will never be able to escape what you were born for,' replied Sulaf. 'War is your throne and death is your crown; it comes hand in hand with who you are and it can never be pushed away, no matter how much you choose to deny it. Every warrior dies for glory, only to live on in legend. This is who you are, Marmicus, this is what you were born for. Deny it, and you deny your very existence on earth.'

Her voice oozed with seductive power; still, no amount of seduction from a woman's lips could ever tempt Marmicus to look elsewhere.

'I swore to protect this kingdom and I'll do that. Whatever my reasons, they are my own. I've already given you my word; now it's up to you to believe it.'

He walked towards his stallion. Man and beast shared a unique and unwavering friendship. He mounted, wrapping the leather reins around his hand.

'How can I not concern myself with your affairs when my future and this kingdom's future lie in your hands?' Sulaf asked. She watched Marmicus, not knowing if this would be the last time she would see him.

'Your future lies beyond this kingdom now. Take your son and head towards one that can protect you. War is something that cannot easily be forgotten, especially by a child.'

Marmicus turned his horse and galloped away.

16

'Where is all your courage now?'

Nafridos watched the princess being pulled behind his horse. Her wrists were tied together with dry rope, which was beginning to slice through her skin. Every time the horse jerked, she gave a scream as it cut into her. The burning friction was too much for hands that had never experienced anything but indulgence. The Assyrian soldiers looked on, saying nothing; her ordeal would not stop until she reached the Assyrian kingdom. Their commander always played with his victims as if they were toys, and killed them only when he had grown tired of them. It was just a matter of time before Nafridos lost interest in her.

'Try to smile, princess; looking sad is never appealing to any man.' He laughed, jerking the rope hard; he wanted to hear her scream again, but louder; it excited him. This unexpected wrench hurt more than all the others Larsa had endured, and she yelped, crying and screaming at once.

'Why are you doing this to me? What have I done to you?' she sobbed. Her head ached with dehydration as hot tears rolled down her face.

'I'll cut the rope if you smile for me. Now, smile, let me see the beauty behind all that misery. Go on, smile!'

Larsa could not bring herself to do it: even if it meant that the excruciating pain would go away, she just could not do it. How could she even pretend to satisfy her enemy when he had butchered all her soldiers and servants? It would be a treachery to them.

'I'm waiting ...' he whispered softly, as if he wanted to reveal a more gentle side of himself to her.

'I'd rather die than gratify your cruel and perverted urges,' declared Larsa, spitting on the ground, ready to endure her punishment.

'Then die you shall!' said Nafridos as he took hold of the dry rope again, and breathed in. 'Be strong, princess, for I assure you that this will hurt more than you can imagine ...'

17

Marmicus rode back to the palace, Sulaf's words fresh in his mind. He now wished he hadn't left so abruptly – it could be the last time they would ever see each other. What if something happened to one of them? Would this be the last memory they shared of each other? Their friendship had been strained ever since Marmicus had met the princess. Sulaf could never warm to her. It was as if she felt threatened by her existence. Whatever her reasons, Marmicus knew he had to do something about it; he couldn't leave things the way they were. He thought about what Sulaf had said, wondering how he could have acted so selfishly. All he wanted was the life of an ordinary man. Deep down he knew that Sulaf was right: someone like him could never be entitled to such a life. The world expected so much of him, and neglecting his duty would mean neglecting his people. It dawned on him that he had overreacted. It wasn't like him to take things so personally. All he could think about was the princess and why she hadn't sent news of her safe arrival. Was this her way of punishing him for asking her to leave the kingdom? If it was, then it was childish and selfish of her. Maybe Sulaf was right; there was a twelve-year age difference between them. She was only twenty, while Marmicus was thirty-two.

The gates of the palace opened for him, and Marmicus galloped through, passing the lush gardens. Waiting by the palace entrance was one of his servants.

'My lord, where have you been? I've been searching everywhere for you.'

'Has the day come when I fight for freedom but have none to call my own?' he smiled.

'Forgive me, my lord, it's just that Sibius has returned. He wants to speak with you urgently; he says he has news about the princess.'

'Where is he?'

'He's in your chamber. He's been waiting there for some time.'

Marmicus jumped off his horse, rushing to see his friend. He hoped Sibius had brought good news. He had need of it ...

18

'I've never been happier to see you! How was your trip?' asked Marmicus as he embraced his friend. Sibius tried to smile, but it was hard to conjure up a convincing one. He appeared tired and gaunt; he hadn't slept for days.

'Sit down,' said Sibius, wanting to make sure Marmicus was well prepared for what he was about to hear. They were like brothers: they had met when they served as foot soldiers in the army, and every time they were reunited it felt like the ending of a war which they had somehow survived.

'Well? How's Larsa? Is she well?'

'Sit down and I'll tell you everything,' he replied, pulling out a chair for him. His face was sombre. Marmicus felt a cold sweat break out on his face. He quickly sat down, saying nothing. 'What's the matter?'

Sibius hesitated. How could he break the news gently to him? Was there even a way to do that?

'She's angry with me, isn't she? Has she said something to you?'

'I wish it was that,' said Sibius, trying to stop him; he didn't want him to get ahead of himself.

Marmicus tapped his fingers on the table, waiting for Sibius to say something, but he didn't. He felt nervous just looking at him; Sibius had a strange look on his face; the princess must have said something which put him in an awkward position.

'Come on, aren't you going to tell me what's going on?'

Sibius covered his mouth, trying to stop himself from blurting out the news. He walked away quietly, steeling himself. There was no way to avoid the answer: he would have to tell his friend that his wife was dead, knowing full well that it would destroy him.

'It's about the princess … something has happened,' said Sibius, trying to force out the words. Marmicus stopped tapping his fingers – he hadn't expected that response.

'What are you talking about? What's happened?'

Sibius said nothing. He froze, not wanting to say more.

'Is she hurt? Tell me!'

Marmicus stood up.

'Why aren't you saying anything?'

The long pause sparked rage within him. Sibius was deflecting every question he asked. Unable to contain himself, Marmicus rushed to him, pinning his friend against the wall, blood rushing through his veins.

'Tell me what you know, or I swear I'll kill you!'

'She—' said Sibius. 'I'm sorry …'

'How? Where is she?'

Sibius didn't reply. Marmicus punched the wall, his hand just missing his friend's face as he threatened him in hope of a quick answer.

'I'll ask you one more time. Where is she?'

'She's dead, Marmicus. They all are. The Assyrians—'

Marmicus released his grip and stepped back, stumbling as the truth hit him. This couldn't be happening. How did this happen? The princess was supposed to be safe; she was protected by guards. Marmicus shook his head in denial, his body and mind rejecting his friend's words.

'You're lying. She can't be.'

'I'm not. I swear.'

Marmicus leaned in to Sibius; the pit of his stomach felt heavy.

'Who told you that? Who said it?'

'I saw her body myself; she's dead. I'm so sorry.'

Marmicus covered his face with his hands and turned away. He couldn't breathe. His chest hurt. Larsa couldn't be dead; she just couldn't. 'Not like this! Not like this!' he shrieked, unable to control the rush of emotions that came over him. Feelings of guilt overtook him. It was all his fault that this had happened! He shouldn't have pushed her away: if only he had listened to her, she would still be alive. He pressed his hands flat onto the table as he leant over it. He needed something to hold on to; his head was spinning. Suddenly a manic urge took hold of him. He flung the table on its side, unable to contain his agony. Sibius tried to stop him, pulling him back, grabbing him by the shoulders, but Marmicus fought him off and sunk to his knees. Anger unlike anything he had felt before erupted inside him. Sulaf was right: love could turn into poison. He had discovered this in a matter of seconds. Marmicus fell to his knees. Nothing could stop the crushing pain he felt in his heart; the one thing he loved most in the world had been savagely stolen from him. How could this have happened to him? He had sent her away in order to protect her, to prevent any harm coming to her, but now she was gone, hunted down and killed by the Assyrians.

'I know this is hard for you,' said Sibius, crouching beside him on the floor. 'If you want to honour her, think of your revenge for now, it is the only way to survive this …'

He took the pendant of Ishtar from his pocket, handing it over to Marmicus. He had cleaned off the splattered blood that had tarnished its golden shine. Marmicus didn't say anything; he just stared blankly at the pendant, drawing in shallow, choking breaths. Right now, he didn't want to know how she had been killed or what her last words were or, even worse, if she had been violated first. He could barely take in the knowledge that she was gone.

'I'll leave you alone. Try to get some rest,' said Sibius, feeling his agony. He got up, leaving him to grieve alone.

Marmicus held the pendant in his hands, kissing it, smelling it. The princess had always worn it around her neck. Her scent was still on it.

'My beautiful Larsa, what did they do to you?'

19

'Where are you, Marmicus? Why haven't you come for me? I need you,' Larsa whispered to herself. The beauty of her oval face was marred by small cuts and grazes. Every time her captors pulled the rope she was unable to stop herself from falling. Her porcelain-like skin had been battered by the sharp edges of stones on the desert floor. Larsa couldn't understand why Marmicus hadn't come for her – news of her disappearance must have been sent back to him by now. Even if it hadn't, Marmicus must have sensed something was wrong, because she hadn't sent him word of her well-being or safe arrival. Deep down, she knew he would never abandon her, but a niggling doubt ate away at her confidence. What if for some reason he had chosen to forget her altogether?

'Welcome to the land of Assyria,' said Nafridos as he stopped before the gates of the kingdom with his prisoner. He looked down at her from upon his horse, and the bones in his neck clicked as he twisted his head, wanting to see her reaction as she passed through the mammoth gates; it was as if she were a helpless lamb walking in the midst of hungry lions. Larsa knew he was staring at her, she could feel his eyes on her, but she looked away, not wanting to give him the satisfaction of her acknowledgement. Despite everything she was going through, she still tried to present a façade of bravery – it was the only freedom she had left.

Larsa could hear the voices of slaves, pulling ropes to release the gates and let her captors in. She shuddered; it dawned on her that soon she would meet Jaquzan, the man who commanded such ruthless warriors. Larsa tried to cast the thought aside, looking instead at the two gigantic Assyrian winged bulls that stood on either side of the gates. They were tall as trees, made from solid stone, their eyes staring fiercely into the distance to terrorise any enemy that dared come their way. They couldn't be missed; the statues imposed themselves on the flat land with their huge human heads, long bull-like bodies, and clawed feet – but even the statues looked miniscule in comparison to the towering walls of the kingdom. The Assyrian walls soared high into the sky, as though to stop even the birds from flying above them. They had been designed to prevent any enemy climbing over them to enter the city, and their existence reminded the princess of a definitive truth: that these were the gates of an ungodly prison designed to enslave people.

The mighty gates finally opened. Waiting on the other side were thousands of people lining the streets, some laughing and clapping, others standing silently as they were forced to witness her humiliating entrance. No one would have imagined that a princess walked in their midst; her clothes were tattered and ripped, her knees scarred and bloody, and her lips crusty from her aching thirst. Larsa felt that until this moment she had been living her own lie; that what she knew of mankind was all wrong. Questions kept running through her mind: what had she done to deserve this? How could any woman put up with such depravity, with being beaten until her resistance was eventually broken? Any dignity she had once possessed now trailed behind her, lost somewhere with the fragments of her inner self. Larsa wished she had died along with her servants; somehow the thought of death seemed more merciful than this …

ॐ

Glory greeted her captors, who had finally returned home with their much-heralded prize, and for this they were treated like kings. Rose petals were thrown into the air, softly drifting with the winds as they fell gently onto the heads and shoulders of her captors. Larsa felt sickened: how could murderers be celebrated like this? They were greeted like heroes instead of what they truly were – brutal and sadistic killers. Larsa wished she could cover her ears; lambskin drums were beating loudly in the background, their draining, dull tone beating in pace with her heart as she walked among the thousands of spectators. Lining the long road which led to the emperor's palace were beautiful black slave women; they were standing in front of the crowds, pouring rose water upon the ground to wash the blood and dirt from the feet of oncoming soldiers. Unknown to the princess, many of these women had once been queens who ruled the different tribes of Abyssinia; they too had been taken from their lands and turned into slaves, for each of them the happiness of their past lives was now like a thorn beneath their skin. Larsa gazed at them; she could see sympathy in their eyes for what she was going through, but in the eyes of those around them, none at all.

'Help me, please. Stop this!' she cried. Tears rolled down her cheeks, leaving streaks in the dirt on her face. No one responded to her pleas; they simply stood there, some cheering, others watching soullessly, showing no emotion as she was dragged away. Unable to take in the humiliation, Larsa shut her eyes, wanting to block out all the faces that glared at her, but she didn't even have that luxury.

'Open your eyes. I want you to remember the day a queen became a slave,' said Nafridos, but Larsa ignored his words, her naked feet bleeding as she stumbled on, her head hanging in exhaustion. It was the humiliation that was the most agonising sentence; she couldn't bear to be watched and judged by people who saw her crippled in this way.

Nafridos turned to one of his soldiers. No one would disobey him, especially not in front of his people. The Assyrian soldier knew exactly what he had to do.

'He said "open your eyes" – do it now!' the soldier yelled, holding a leather whip above his head. Larsa ignored him as she shut her eyes more tightly; at this moment she found beauty in blindness. The soldier looked to Nafridos, waiting for the command to act; a small nod was all that was needed.

'Do it,' he said.

The soldier marched ahead, falling in a pace or two behind the princess. He swung the leather whip above his head, his wrist moving quickly and his massive biceps glistening in the sun. The people looked on as he threw his arm forward, the lash following in a long and deadly arc before landing on Larsa's back with a resounding crack which drew a gasp from the crowd. A scream of agony rushed from her lungs.

'Why are you doing this to me? Why? Where's your humanity?' she wept, unable to hide the pain. The whip scalded her back like boiling water; a deep gash immediately appeared, and Larsa could feel the rush of blood flowing from between her shoulder blades. 'Please … I beg you … stop this.'

Suddenly, the roaring crowd fell silent, as if coerced into submission. The pounding of the leather drums also halted, and everything that had once vibrated with energy surrendered to stillness. Larsa looked up. The sunlight burned her eyes but it didn't matter; she needed to see his face, she needed to know what her enemy looked like.

'Jaquzan …'

Larsa knew it was him: standing before her on the highest point of the Assyrian tower was the man who now owned her soul. He was looking over his subjects, watching her from where he stood, waiting for her to come to him. The crowd knelt, bowing down like slaves before their master, their foreheads touching the ground as they surrendered to Jaquzan's ultimate supremacy. Everyone prostrated themselves, except for Larsa, but there is always foolishness in bravery …

❧

Pure hearts attract stained hands, for wherever there is good on earth, evil finds joy in destroying it. The unavoidable hour had come for Larsa to meet her enemy. Every minute that had passed since her capture had been leading up to this definitive moment when she would finally glare into Jaquzan's eyes and recognise what evil lay beneath the surface of his skin. The final stretch had arrived. Larsa walked through the long corridor leading to his throne room, its high walls colourfully painted with visions of war that glorified violent death. Each carved image revealed that oppression, tyranny and conquest had prevailed above hope, honour and freedom. Larsa turned her face away, unable to absorb the grotesque depictions of war; they seemed to carry on forever, lining the corridor. If Marmicus lost this war, another portrayal of Assyrian victory would surely be added to the long list of battle scenes depicted on these walls. The idea frightened her immensely. She imagined her worst nightmare, Marmicus's lifeless body lying on some nameless battlefield, butchered and headless like the others surrounding her now. Larsa quickly banished the thought from her mind. *I can cope with anything except that …*

Exhaustion and dehydration gripped her, sucking every ounce of strength that remained inside her. Her body felt heavy; she could no longer carry herself or drag her feet further. Knowing that Marmicus was safe was the only comfort she had; it gave her the will to survive the pitiless situation in which she found herself. Larsa imagined Marmicus's face, remembering the way he had lovingly looked into her eyes and kissed her neck during their last intimate moments together. His memory added warmth to a body that had succumbed to a world filled with cold. Since her capture, one question kept running through her mind: why had she not been killed? There must be a reason for her survival. Larsa knew her enemy could have killed her at any time, but Jaquzan had specifically ordered that she remain alive. Whatever his reason, it couldn't be any worse than what she had already endured. Her body and mind were prepared for anything – or so she thought …

There are few men in the world who are able to command others without having to say a single word. Jaquzan was one such man. Even in silence he possessed the ability to influence others; in fact, very little ever escaped his lips. After all, words are used to impress people, but a powerful man has no one to impress. The princess recognised the depths of Jaquzan's power almost immediately, and she saw the fear he wrought in her captors; brute men, so confident in the desert, were now hushed in the throne room, wanting desperately to disappear into the background. Even the cruel smile on Nafridos's face had vanished; he too had surrendered to his master's power, as if Jaquzan were able to control his mind without saying or doing anything.

Larsa was pushed to the ground in front of the emperor; her knees scraped on the floor as she was forced to prostrate herself. Now that her captors had completed their assignment, they were curious to find out what exactly was going to be done with her. After all, very few of royal blood had ever escaped the throne room alive, and those who had were thrown to the lions. Larsa lifted her head, wanting to see Jaquzan's face; maybe he wasn't as sadistic or cruel as his cousin? A person's humanity can always be seen in their eyes, but the princess would have to wait to look into them, as all she could see was a faint silhouette of a man sitting upon an exalted throne which spiralled upwards as if it were some sort of dark cloud hanging from the sky. The throne was unfit for any mere mortal to sit upon; it seemed possessed of an immortal presence, as if it were some kind of mythical creature, only capable of being tamed by absolute power. Its mere existence proved that humility had no place in Jaquzan's destructive world.

'Untie her hands,' the emperor said faintly, almost in a whisper. No one could tell if the gesture was done out of mercy, or if it was the beginning of another sinister sequence of events.

'With pleasure,' replied his cousin. Nafridos pulled her up, twisting her left arm as he did. Her skin was hot and feverish – touching it gave him an extraordinary feeling. Using his cherished dagger he cut through the blood-stained rope which bound her wrists together. A faint whimper left her lips, secretly pleasing him. Her wrists were swollen and bloody; the coarse rope had blistered them. As soon as the rope was undone, a rush of blood swept back to her fingers, which tingled with pain.

'Bring her into the light – let me see her face!' said Jaquzan.

Nafridos nudged her forward using the hilt of his dagger; the pommel dug into her back, hurting her.

'What do you want from me? Why am I here?'

'Be thankful, princess. Many have stood where you are now, begging for their lives as you now beg, perhaps, for death.'

'I'm not afraid to die for my freedom,' she declared, looking upwards, her head following the long, towering tiers of the throne that overshadowed them all. The guards looked at her with astonishment. No one had ever addressed the Assyrian emperor with such courage or stupidity before. Her strength appeared to seep through the pores of her skin. It only proved what Jaquzan was already thinking; that behind her beautiful face was a naive mind.

'Then you choose to die for nothing, for freedom is what freedom has always been – enslavement to an ideal,' replied Jaquzan without hesitation. He moved into the light. As he did, he revealed his face to her: his features were perfectly symmetrical, almost unnaturally so, as if every detail of his face had been skilfully shaped by a sculptor's hands.

'You're wrong. Freedom is to live without fear, to speak when forced to be silent, and to move when threatened by others. I will never give it up, and nor will Marmicus. He's going to come for me; he's going to set me free and, when he does, he's going to destroy you.

You'll beg for your life just as you've made others beg for theirs.'

'Let him come! When he does, I will crush him and scatter his ashes over your dreams. Now, bow in the presence of greatness.'

'Never!'

Jaquzan smiled. It was a rare reaction, and seemed unnatural, given what she had just said to him. The more Larsa spoke, the more Jaquzan learnt of her weaknesses without her even realising it. He was analysing her face, dissecting everything about her. She could not know that he possessed the ability to read people's characters by their reactions and behaviour.

'When will mankind learn that bravery is nothing more than unrefined arrogance, something which can be easily crushed by the hands? Now, watch as I begin to crush yours ... I can tell from your eyes that your greatest weakness is your humanity. I shall show you what inhumanity lies before your feet. Open the doors and bring forth my slave.'

Larsa turned, watching the doors open behind her; a woman was dragged in, her mouth frothing with saliva like a rabid dog. Whoever she was, it was clear that she had lost her mind a long time ago. She bit at her captors' hands, scowling, kicking and blabbering at them as they dragged her in; nothing she said made any sense. The slaves dumped her in the centre of the throne room. For a moment she sat there dazedly, rocking back and forth, humming as if to a baby. Larsa listened to her singing. Her voice was melancholy, while oddly soothing, but her calm persona completely vanished the moment the emperor moved in his seat; somehow, that small, subtle movement triggered something inside her, as though awakening her into madness. She began to shriek, her lungs bursting out with a relentless screech akin to a thousand screams. Larsa pressed her hands against her ears, desperately trying to block out her cries.

The slaves rushed back to her, pushing her flat against the stone floor, stretching out both her arms and struggling to throw a rope noose over her head. Larsa watched as the woman tried to fight them off, her hands crazily clawing at them, until eventually she gave in.

'Do you know who this woman once was?' asked the emperor, watching the princess from his colossal throne. Larsa shook her head; even if she tried to guess the answer she felt it would somehow lead to a trap.

'She was once the mighty Queen of Persia, the wife of a king who was defiant and unwilling to submit to a power far greater than his; but power crumbles like sand in the hands of men who know nothing of its worth. Now the only crown she wears is the rope tied around her neck and her only necklace is a necklace of memories of her former life.'

The emperor rose, expressionless, from his towering throne; softly he padded, like a lion stalking prey, down the lofty set of stairs to the others. He marvelled at how quickly the Queen of Persia's face had changed. Her glorious beauty had withered away like a rose battered by harsh winds; her once striking oval face, which had glowed with colour and life, had become dull and emaciated, her skin reduced to a sickly pallor and her nails broken and bruised. The queen shook her head, breathing heavily. The rope was slowly choking her; every time she drew in a breath she convulsed with strangled, wheezing coughs. Larsa watched the king stare at her. His green eyes were bright, like lanterns. Larsa noticed that his right pupil was not circular, but almost slit-like. It was strange. The more she watched him, the more desperate she felt to learn something about him, but every physical action seemed to be disguised by another. There was nothing she could learn about him unless he intentionally revealed it.

'Madness is in us all,' he said, standing in front of the Queen of

Persia and examining her. Everyone remained silent, waiting for him to reveal what lurked deep in his mind. 'Her madness came to her the day she saw her husband beheaded, her sons murdered and her people burned alive; and I know the same shall come to you if you disobey my commands.'

'Hasn't she suffered enough?' Larsa asked. She looked at the Persian queen, feeling intense sympathy for what she had endured; in one sense at least, they were cruelly connected.

'No,' he replied calmly.

'What are you going to do to her?'

'The answer lies with you.' Jaquzan turned to his cousin; he obviously had something in mind. 'Give the princess your dagger.'

Nafridos took out his dagger and handed it to Larsa. Like the princess, he had no idea what his cousin was planning.

'Your humanity may be your greatest strength, but in our world humanity is a hindrance to survival – only the selfish are able to survive, while the selfless are trampled on.' He began to circle the Queen of Persia, his steps soft and silent as if preparing an incantation of some sort. Finally he stopped and, unexpectedly, put out his hand. With his index finger he gently lifted the victim's chin, exposing her throat to him. Like a dazed animal, the Queen of Persia yielded to his power, tilting her head back and succumbing to his will without struggle or question.

'Let us see if your humanity is a gift or a curse. Kill this woman, and in exchange for her life I shall offer your people salvation. I want you to show me your inhumanity, and in exchange I shall restore humanity to your world. I offer you the chance to save your people. In your hands lies the life of freedom that they have always known …'

'How do I know you'll keep your promise?'

'I am a god. I am never in need of a lie.'

Larsa stared at the dagger which had been given to her; it felt heavy and cold, so foreign to her. How could she murder another human being, even if it guaranteed freedom for her people? It was surely wrong – or was it?

'I can't – I won't – do it,' she said, shaking her head, unable to comprehend what was happening to her.

'One life for tens of thousands of others – the choice lies with you,' said Jaquzan again.

Larsa turned to look at the queen. All she could see were the faces of her people, staring back as though taunting her, willing her to go ahead and become the murderer they needed at this moment. Was Jaquzan right? Did the life of one person really matter, if many thousands of others could be saved? Maybe it was more merciful to kill her; after all, the queen was practically dead, imprisoned in a life of madness. The choice was clear; she knew what she had to do – the only way Larsa could save her homeland was by killing the former Queen of Persia. The first step was the hardest, but she knew she had to do it. The question was, did she really have any choice? Did this all come down to her free will, or was it selfishness, her need to survive, that was drawing her like a moth to a flame?

Larsa walked towards the queen; with every pace she took towards the poor creature in the centre of the room, she felt her humanity shrink inside her like a dying star. *Could this actually be happening to me? I'm about to become a murderer.*

'You have chosen wisely,' said Jaquzan, watching her walk towards him, her movements revealing her choice to kill, rather than to save a life.

'I haven't got a choice; you're forcing me to do this.'

'Am I? There is no one holding the dagger but you.'

'I know she'd do the same for her people if she was in my position.'

'Or maybe she wouldn't – maybe her choice would be to save you.'

Larsa's hands shook. She tried to stop them by bringing the weapon closer to her chest, as if to reassure herself about what she was doing. Whatever happened, she knew she had to remain calm; it was the only way she could give the queen a quick and painless death – she deserved that at the very least. Larsa knew if she hesitated while committing this act of cruelty, the blade might not reach its mark, causing both of them yet more agony and trauma.

'One life for a thousand others – just one life to save so many,' said Larsa quietly, looking at the Queen of Persia, her neck still tilted back like the dazed animal she had become. Larsa was thankful that her face was partially hidden beneath a linen smock; at least it would hide the agony from her. She stopped in front of the queen. At first Larsa felt as if the dagger was stuck to her chest. She could not move it away, her hands were clenched so tightly around its steel grip. Then, summoning all her courage, she slowly moved it away and pressed the cold metal against the queen's unflinching throat. Larsa knew she would never forgive herself for this act. By killing the queen, she was killing her own innocence and damning herself to a life of eternal guilt.

'I'm so sorry, but I have no choice. I have to do this, I have to save my people. I know you'd do the same,' she said softly, her hand shaking. It seemed to those gathered that there was no chance she could give her victim a clean kill. Larsa was ready to use the sharp knife, and she took a deep breath. Just as she was about to glide her hand across the queen's neck Jaquzan did something which made her realise just how cruel he truly was.

'Everybody deserves to see the face of their killer, even a woman locked in madness,' said Jaquzan as he stepped in, the better to watch his sadistic charade unfold. He pulled back the hood of the queen's linen smock. Now, the two women could see each other. Their eyes locked.

'Forgive me,' said Larsa, trembling uncontrollably. Strangely, the Queen of Persia gave a small nod, as if to indicate that she was at peace with the prospect of being killed by her. She gave Larsa a look at once resigned and determined, as if she was desperate to die and be put out of her misery. It made Larsa hesitate for a second, until she gathered her courage again.

'Now end her life, so you can set your people free,' said Jaquzan.

'Freedom can never be born of compulsion; my people deserve better than that, and so does she,' said Larsa. She threw the dagger onto the floor. It was the reaction Jaquzan had anticipated, and only now did Larsa realise it. Jaquzan had proven his point: her humanity was her greatest gift and her curse. It was a lesson she would never forget. The emperor watched her step back. As she did so, he picked up the dagger and without hesitation he slid the knife across the queen's neck, slitting her throat and ending her life in seconds. Larsa gave a heart-wrenching scream; the queen slumped sideways, her muscles in seizure, until eventually she was still. All the while, her eyes remained open and fixed on Larsa, as if wanting to commit to memory the face that possessed the last traces of humanity left in the world …

20

For some people, dreams have a way of uplifting their soul in difficult times, but for others they act only as a reminder of things that have been lost. If they are not careful, a dream which once fuelled hope and happiness can destroy them, poisoning their mind with bitterness and regret, until eventually it kills them. Everything that Marmicus had dreamt of was now gone: the prospect of becoming a father and being loved eternally by his loyal wife had been taken away. There was simply no pleasure left in the world to taste or to feel; all that was left was the knowledge that his life would never be filled with beauty again. The enemy's plan had worked; Jaquzan had pierced his heart with one merciless blow, and there was nothing in the world that could ever restore it.

Marmicus sat alone in his thick-walled chamber. He hadn't spoken to or seen anyone for days, and his face was pale and almost unrecognisable. Underneath his eyes were dark circles; his face was dirty and unshaven and his body noticeably thinner. The old Marmicus had disappeared; all that was left was a skeleton of his former self, a reflection of a desolate man in need of comfort. Every time he breathed, a choking sense of guilt wrapped itself around his throat, squeezing him until he could no longer bear it. Sometimes he would bursts into fits of rage. Marmicus had never felt so much hatred before, but his real torture came at night. Since learning about the princess's death, he had had the same dream every night: she was standing in the middle of a battlefield, calling out to him, desperately needing him to come and save her from the army behind her, but every time Marmicus ran to her, she appeared to be further away. Her pleas grew louder, her lungs gasping with hopeless breaths, but Marmicus never got to her in time. His nightmare would always end in the same way: with a vision of her body lying lifeless on the ground, her arm broken, her eyelids blue and swollen and her nose broken and bloodied. She had been beaten to death while Marmicus watched helplessly from a distance.

'How can I forget the first moment I saw you and your pendant, sweet Larsa?' Marmicus whispered, clutching the royal pendant of Ishtar as if cradling his memories in his hands. The eight-pointed star shimmered brilliantly in his hands like the soft ripples of light scattered by the Tigris river. Pressing his lips against it Marmicus gently kissed the pendant, cherishing its scent, this tender act speaking of his desire to protect it from harm.

The doors creaked open, and a slender woman entered, rather hesitantly. Sulaf was immediately struck by the Gallant Warrior's change in appearance. She had never seen Marmicus look like this. She didn't recognise him at first.

'Leave me – I am in no mood for company.'

He began to sharpen his sword, using a rough stone that shot fiery sparks into the air. The dark circles under his eyes became even more obvious as the bright flashes of light illuminated his face. 'Why are you still standing here? I told you to leave!'

'I've come for the sake of the people; they fear for your well-being and so do I.'

Marmicus burst into laughter, like a madman, though his eyes remained intense. He was a completely different person, someone by whom Sulaf actually felt unnerved.

'When have the people ever feared for my well-being? They're afraid for themselves and their wretched possessions, not for me or anyone else.'

'Why are you saying such things? Your people love you deeply! If you wished it, they'd carve your name in stone and worship you as a god.'

'Then they're fools.'

He continued to sharpen his weapon, ever more vigorously; it was the only way he could take out his frustration without risking harm to others.

'What's happened to you? Where's the man I once knew and loved?'

'He's dead. Now go and tell the people that. Let's see if they truly mourn for me or for themselves.'

'Why are you tormenting yourself like this? You had no control over what happened. The gods give and take life; we can only submit to their will and pray for their blessings.'

'Then I'll wage a war against the gods and set men free from their tyranny; at least that way we won't blame them for the bitterness of our destinies.'

'If we don't win this war, the hearts of men won't belong to the gods, they'll belong to Jaquzan.'

Sulaf walked away angrily. It was the first time she had seen Marmicus behave like this. Although it was understandable for him to grieve, she did not expect him to turn away from the honourable code by which he had always lived.

She turned at the door. 'What's happened to you? If you had any respect for yourself, you would put down that weapon. Tonight you have chosen not to honour it.'

Marmicus continued to sharpen his sword, as if she had not spoken.

'Are you willing to sacrifice everything because of the death of one woman you have loved and lost? What about the lives of thousands of others who love you? They will die in the same way if you stand by and do nothing, or do their lives have no value to you? Have they lost their worthiness to be protected?'

'I told you to leave me.'

'I won't go; not until the man I once knew returns to me,' Sulaf said. Rushing to him, she placed her hand on the sharpened blade, momentarily forcing him to pause. It was an act of bravery; Marmicus looked up, giving credit where it was due. 'Many people have loved and lost; remember that you can always live once more and love once again.'

'I don't care about love. Vengeance is all I want; without it I have nothing.'

'Then fight for your vengeance: murder, destroy everyone who has aggrieved you, and avenge the death of anyone you have loved! All we ask of you is to save this kingdom when war comes. Then, once you have taken your vengeance, return to me, for within me you shall always find the love you need.'

The funeral chariot bearing the body of the princess entered the

Garden of the Gods, and with it came an eruption of mourning. Crowds from all over the kingdom had gathered, all of them coming to pay their last respects to a princess who was dearly loved by her people. No one could have anticipated that such a tragedy would occur so soon, for it had only been a month since her father, King Alous, had died. Today the kingdom had been left with no ruler to lead the people in troubled times or comfort them when in need.

'By the grace of the gods, I think our plan has worked,' whispered King Nelaaz as he followed the royal procession to the magnificent Temple of Ishtar. His knees began to hurt; he was not used to walking. He much preferred being carried by his servants, but in these circumstances it seemed inappropriate.

'I knew it would, Your Majesty; gold always deceives the eyes.'

'Yes, but the question is, will it deceive Marmicus? What if he recognises that it's not her? What are we supposed to do then? Give him a pile of bones and apologise for our mistake?'

'We are favoured by the gods; they will make it work.'

'It had better work! I've not spent my entire kingdom's fortune on one servant girl for nothing. Who would ever have imagined that my servant's death would outshine my own? I think the gods have made a habit of cursing me these days.' The king had spared no expense in attempting to conceal the young woman's true identity: it was either that or reveal the dangerous truth, that the princess – so they all believed – had been barbarically raped and mutilated in the desert, and that his army had not been there to protect her.

'Look at how the people mourn her, Your Majesty; she was clearly loved by them all,' said the advisor in astonishment. He had never seen such an outpouring of grief and love in all his life; the only reaction King Nelaaz ever received from his people was abuse. He would not be surprised if King Nelaaz's death led to celebrations in the streets of Aram. Here, the sense of loss was palpable.

'Yes, yes, I can see that they loved her; there's no need to rub it in.'

The chariot halted in front of the colossal Temple of Ishtar, and a thick fog of aromatic musk poured out from the gigantic entrance like a cloud of grief sent from the heavens. People threw rose petals and lilies at the casket as final sentiments of affection, for this would be the last time they would see her body before it was buried. But there was one woman among the crowd who did not mourn or shed a tear for the princess; instead, Sulaf watched and secretly rejoiced, a faint smile showing beneath her veil. Now that Larsa was dead, there was nothing to stop her from claiming Marmicus's heart. She had always loved him. *Finally his heart has been set free*, Sulaf thought, as she coldly tossed some petals onto the slab of gold. *I shall make you love me and, once you do, I shall help you bury your memories of the princess beneath the earth, beside her wretched body.*

21

The Grand Priest of Ursar walked out of the Temple of Ishtar to be greeted by a crowd of thousands. He waved to them as if he were their newly appointed king; as if, now that the princess had died, he had become their divine ruler. He was the head of the Counsel, and so by default their ordained leader. Few loved him; even so, their allegiance to the Counsel remained firm – nothing could put him in disrepute. Marmicus watched him from the palace balcony; even from there he could see the Grand Priest's lust for power. If Marmicus was not careful, he would have more than a war on his hands.

'Bring forth the eight sacred rams!' yelled the Grand Priest of Ursar over the drums. The animals were brought, and each was positioned around the majestic funeral chariot; together they formed the shape of an eight-pointed star, representing the symbol of Ishtar.

'With every curse there comes a blessing. Oh, Ereshkigal, Lady of the Underworld, we offer you these eight sacred rams as a sacrifice in your name. Let their slaughter hasten a blessing on our kingdom so that our moons will be eclipsed no further. Let their blood quench your thirst for taking further life from our lands. With their beating hearts, we offer you our own, and with their blood, we ask you to free the princess's soul to the afterlife, where she belongs. Today the Garden of the Gods mourns the loss of a ruler, but tomorrow we shall celebrate the birth of a new ruler from among the Counsel. Let this be the blessing born of our collective loss.'

He placed a sharp butcher's knife upon the throat of a restive ram. It struggled against the ropes that bound its legs. The poor creature's eyes were wide open, almost popping out. Suddenly, the Grand Priest of Ursar plunged the knife into the animal's throat, causing it to let out a strangled bleat before its head sunk slowly to the ground. The act had officially sent the princess's soul into the afterlife. Marmicus fell to his knees in his private chamber; for him, the only blessing was that there was no one to watch him break down.

The young Priest of Xidrica looked at the chamber door for a moment. Hesitantly, he knocked, and waited for a while, hoping that Marmicus would let him in, but there was no answer. Taking the initiative, he decided to enter. No one had seen Marmicus for days; the whole kingdom had gathered to say their farewells to the princess at her funeral, and it seemed that the only person missing from the ceremony was Marmicus. The young priest knew Marmicus wanted to be left alone. All his servants had been sent away, food had always been sent back, and so too had kings who had come to pay their respects to the grieving widower. Somehow the young priest felt he would not be treated like that; they shared a special understanding that was like a brotherly bond.

'I came to see if you needed anything,' said the Priest of Xidrica. He stood by the door, waiting for a response.

'I need nothing,' said Marmicus, watching the procession from the balcony, his back to the priest.

'I know losing a wife is the hardest thing any husband can face, but I do have some understanding of your grief – when I lost my mother as a child nothing anyone said could console me. But time and memories will heal us eventually, as they did me.'

'I don't need time or memories, they bring me no comfort. I just need her.'

The young priest nodded, understanding what Marmicus meant; his wound was still too raw; right now he couldn't see the beauty found in memories, in fact all they did was torture rather than heal him.

'There's still time to join the procession; come with me, don't regret not saying goodbye properly. I know she would have wanted this.'

'I won't show my weakness in front of the people. I don't need their pity, or yours.'

'You're too harsh on yourself; a man's grief is what makes him human – it's nothing to be ashamed of.'

'My weakness causes the people to fear and kings to rejoice; I won't let anyone use my pain as their weapon, they've already taken too much from me,' Marmicus said, choking on his words. He turned to look down at the burial chariot; the sight of the Grand Priests pouring holy ram's blood over the princess's corpse was too much to bear; he closed his eyes, unable to look. A vision of her lying in the desert, bleeding to death, came into his mind; no doubt she was calling out his name, wishing he would save her, but he didn't. 'I never knew how much I loved her, that's the worst part. I always thought my body would find its grave before hers, but now I'm forced to watch hers being buried before mine.'

'The gods are testing you, my brother. Hardship doesn't come without its rewards.'

'Don't talk to me about the gods! Where were your gods when she was alone out there? If they existed they wouldn't have let this happen! Innocence deserves to be protected, but your gods left her to die. If they are real then their hands are painted with as much blood as mine. No. Take your gods; I don't need them or anyone here, all I need is to be left alone.'

The young priest knew he had outstayed his welcome; he made to leave, feeling only sympathy for Marmicus.

'Wait,' Marmicus said. 'I may not respect your gods, but I respect you; I know you're different to the rest of the Counsellors and for that I value you. I want you to be careful who you place your trust with. I wouldn't be surprised if you have more enemies than I do, so be vigilant – more so now than ever before. There's a serpent in this kingdom – there was no way for anyone but me to know that Larsa was leaving the kingdom. Once I find him, he'll wish that he had poisoned himself before he struck others with his venom.'

Marmicus turned back to watch the funeral ceremony, his eyes firmly fixed on the Grand Priest of Ursar, whose exquisite robes were more suited to celebration than mourning.

'What makes you think there's a traitor?'

'There can be no fire without a spark! Someone in this kingdom sent word to our enemy, revealing our plans, and now he's unleashed a fire so great that no ocean in the world can extinguish the destruction I'm about to bring.'

'Then I'll do everything in my power to help you.'

22

'Drink this, Your Highness, it'll do you well,' said an old maid who had brought her some warm camel's milk; naturally Larsa was cautious, but there was no way to know if it was safe to consume. The maid placed the chalice in her hands, waiting for her to drink.

'What's in it?' Larsa asked, not knowing what to make of her kindness.

'Don't be afraid; it's nothing more than a warm drink that'll make you feel better.'

Larsa was hesitant at first; she looked at the old woman with distrust, not knowing if her kindness was genuine or just another sadistic trap dreamt up by the emperor to punish her. Her stomach was rumbling, and she knew that if she didn't eat soon she would collapse again. Taking a leap of faith, Larsa pursed her lips and in one go forced herself to drink the milk. It took just a couple of seconds for her to realise that the maid was right – it was nothing more than a harmless drink that would give her strength.

'Would you like some more, Your Highness?'

'I'm no longer worthy of that title; I'm a slave now, bound by the will of another. I deserve nothing but pity from you.'

'Nobody deserves pity, not even a slave; but you do deserve another cupful of milk,' said the old woman. She picked up the jug, and poured more camel's milk into the decorated clay cup.

'Why are you being kind to me? I have nothing to offer you,' said Larsa. It didn't make sense; she was a prisoner yet she was still being addressed as royalty.

'I don't need anything, just a thank-you will do.'

'I'm sorry. Thank you,' she replied, feeling ashamed of herself. She had seen so much cruelty in such a short space of time that she had forgotten kindness could still exist in others; it made her realise just how much she had changed. 'I wish all Assyrians were like you.'

'That's kind of you, but I'm not Assyrian.'

'You're not?'

'No, I'm not. A long time ago I was free like you,' the maid replied quietly, and slowly pulled up her sleeve, wanting to show her something. Larsa saw a green mark on her frail wrist; it was a symbol she immediately recognised, and one which truly surprised her.

'That explains your kindness,' said Larsa, recognising the tattoo of Azral, a small but ancient kingdom in the east. The maid knew she shouldn't be revealing her past life to the princess, but she had heard about the Garden of the Gods; its beauty was spoken of even by her people. It was a place of homage, so rich and pure with blessings, that somehow she felt by befriending the princess she might be doing good for her own people, or what was left of them.

'I'm sorry for branding you with the likes of them. I thought you were Assyrian,' Larsa said. She reached for the woman's hand, wanting to comfort her. She was glad she had shared her story; it made her realise that they were both victims, and that she could be trusted.

'I used to think that all Assyrian people were cruel, but I've realised over time that many of them are as oppressed as we are. You see, my dear, not everyone is born brave; in the end, many of us are forced to do things we don't agree with only because we wish to protect our families from harm. It's only human for us to keep silent for their sake.'

'Keeping silent is cowardly.'

'Maybe it is, but choice is a luxury that only a few of us can afford,' said the frail woman, returning to the table. Larsa had realised that her words were sharp and inconsiderate – cruel even.

'Are there more of your people in this kingdom?' said Larsa, wanting to strike up conversation again.

'Only a few of us survived.'

'Why weren't more of your people spared or taken as slaves?'

'The emperor doesn't need any more slaves; he has plenty.'

'Then what does he want, more gold?'

'You're thinking of the emperor as an ordinary man when he's much more than that; gold doesn't tempt him.'

'If he's not a man, then what is he?'

'He's an idea, and ideas that cannot be controlled grow to be more dangerous than the men that conceived them.'

'There must be something he desires.'

'The only thing he desires right now is you.'

Larsa felt her body shudder the moment the maid said that; she knew it was true but she didn't want to admit it to herself.

A loud thud came from behind them, and the maid jumped with surprise. She truly hoped that nobody had heard their conversation.

'You mustn't tell anyone what I've told you – it will lead to certain death for me and my grandson,' said the maid. She hurried to collect the chalice which she had placed on the wooden table while they were talking.

'I swear I won't say a word. You can trust me, I promise,' replied the princess. For a brief moment Larsa had been made to feel safe by the company of another; she needed a friend to confide in, especially when she was so alone in the world. 'Wait, before you leave will you tell me your name? I want to pray for both our souls.'

'It's Jehan, Your Highness.'

'Then Jehan, if the gods should ever grant me freedom, I pray that I will celebrate it alongside you and your people,' said the princess softly. A faint smile of hope touched her lips; but it vanished as soon as her enemy walked into the chamber.

'Leave us,' commanded the Dark Warrior.

The sacred ritual conducted by the Grand Priests had finally come to an end, and now the Temple of Ishtar could welcome the greatest mourner of them all.

Marmicus stared at the corpse, completely unaware that his grief was for another. Even in death, Larsa appeared beautiful; her body was dressed in a white silk gown and upon her head was a golden headpiece in the shape of flowers and leaves. Surrounding her were white lilies and lavender, and upon her face was a golden mask, to make her appear as beautiful as she once was.

'Why have they covered her face?'

'We thought it would be better to hide her wounds from you; we know how much you loved her,' replied King Nelaaz. From the tip of his nose there hung a single bead of sweat. He fervently hoped that

Marmicus's inquisitive mind would be distracted by the abundance of gold which covered her – a foolish thought indeed, as gold was never something Marmicus craved or loved. He despised gold – to him it was the source of all wars. 'I know my words will wound you, but I think you'd rather hear the truth than be lied to, am I right?'

'Speak it.'

'My advisors told me that the enemy neither spared her body nor her beauty. They mutilated her face – I don't wish to go into the details – and my advisors said that she was left with only her mother's eyes. That's why they felt – *we* felt – she should be buried with this mask; better the people remember her for her beauty than her tragic death.' The king hoped he had said enough to stop Marmicus from removing the mask. 'You know, I've spent a large part of my wealth on her burial; I wanted to make it easy for her people to say farewell; I loved her, you see, like my own daughter, really I did.'

'Then you have nothing to fear. You have my allegiance and thanks.'

'Thank you, I cherish it so very much, oh Gallant One, really I do.'

'Now leave me alone. I want to mourn my wife just as any husband would wish.'

'Of course.'

As the king waddled out of the enormous ziggurat he gave a huge sigh of relief. For endless nights he had tossed and turned in his bed, dreaming how Marmicus would slay him once he found out the truth. Thankfully, this wasn't going to be the case. 'At last I can enjoy the sweet pleasure of my food without having to choke on my wretched guilt,' King Nelaaz mumbled.

But every lie uttered by the lips is like a seed planted in the ground; all it needs is time to grow and become out of control …

⁂

'You asked me once if there was anything I feared in this world, and I told you that I feared nothing, not even death itself. But I lied to you, Larsa. I've always been afraid of one thing, and that is living a life without you.'

Marmicus felt empty and hollow inside. This was the first time he had been able to let out his emotions, something he really needed to do. The more he kept things in, the more his anger ate away at him, turning him into a person even he hated. His world had shifted overnight, and his only solace was seeing that the princess looked peaceful; it gave him unexpected comfort to see that she appeared to be sleeping.

'I would happily die for one more day with you,' said Marmicus. 'Every breath I take has always been for your sake, and now I'm suffocating without you.'

Summoning all his strength, Marmicus got up. It took all his energy and willpower to stand on his feet, but he knew he had to leave the temple before the undertakers came to bury his wife. He wished he could go with them and be buried alongside her; the only thing keeping him alive now was the promise he had made to her, for now he would live only for her sake, at least until his duty was done. Marmicus reached for her hand, wanting to kiss her one last time. He softly pressed his lips against it, and smelt her skin.

'When war comes you'll have the vengeance of which only a goddess is worthy, and after that day we can be together again,' he whispered, knowing that this would be the last time he would ever see her body lying peacefully. As he pulled away, he noticed something unusual, a small detail only someone who knew the princess intimately would notice, and it caught him by surprise.

Upon the princess's hand was a small birthmark about the size of a black seed. Marmicus had never noticed it before. Certainly, he would remember something like that – or perhaps the stress of everything that had happened had clouded his memory. Either way, something inside him told him to look closer; it was as if he could hear Larsa's voice urging him to remove the golden mask that concealed her face. Passing his hands over the heavenly mask, Marmicus slowly leant forward. He decided to remove it, and his hands felt heavy as he placed his fingertips around its edges. *Could this be happening? Could she still be alive?* he thought. Just as he was about to lift the golden mask he remembered what King Nelaaz had said moments before: 'She was left with only her mother's eyes'.

If Marmicus lifted the mask, he knew he would see the grotesque sight of battle scars. It would destroy him. It was wiser for him to hold onto the beautiful memories than replace them with a vision which could never be washed away from his thoughts; he knew that Larsa would have wanted that.

'I'm sorry for your loss,' said the Grand Priest of Ursar, who stood by the pillar. His hands were defensively folded on his chest, though his voice sounded genuine enough. Around his neck he wore a large pendant of solid gold, affordable only for the richest of men.

'Keep your pity,' replied Marmicus sharply.

'I'm offering you sympathy, just as any friend would offer to another,' replied the Grand Priest. Marmicus ignored his words completely. No matter what he said, he could never convince him of any kind of friendship between them. 'You know we are not so different, you and I; your allegiance is to your sword and mine has always been to this kingdom's throne. I shan't deceive you. I wish to be king – as any man would. If you love your people as you claim you do, you would offer your sword and fight with me, not against me. We both want what is best for this kingdom, and at this moment in our history I am the best that can be offered to the people.'

'I will never offer you my allegiance, not even if you offer me a life filled with the happiness I once knew,' said Marmicus. His uncertainty about the princess's birthmark had disappeared from his mind.

'Then you're making a mistake, Marmicus. Fight with me and together we can offer this kingdom everything it needs.'

'If I'm making a mistake then it's one I can live with.'

Marmicus walked away; he did not want to lose control, at least not within the temple where his wife lay lifeless. The Grand Priest stepped in front of him; he needed to convince him of what he was offering, it was crucial to his plans.

'If you love your people, you will do what is right for them. No one in the Counsel has the stomach to do what needs to be done for this kingdom.'

'What has my love for my people got to do with one man's greed and his desire to be king?'

'It's got everything to do with it! If we build the greatest empire known to man, then we will have built the strongest weapon, to be feared by all men: no enemy would dare attack our walls. So, you see, your love for your people has everything to do with it, oh Gallant Warrior. Join me in my cause and together we can protect our people from wars they dare not fight. The choice is entirely yours.'

'I've made my choice. I'll never use my sword to serve the desires of one frail priest who longs to be crowned a king,' said the Gallant Warrior. He would not back down from the decision that he had made. This, the Grand Priest knew, would have negative repercussions for his plans. Winning the Gallant Warrior's allegiance was essential.

'Then you've made the wrong choice,' said the Grand Priest of Ursar. His cold look was enough to lash anyone to whom it was directed. 'I warn you not to make an enemy of me, Marmicus; it serves no one well.'

As Marmicus attempted to make his way out of the burial chamber the Grand Priest of Ursar abruptly grabbed his arm, causing him to pause in his tracks. It was a show of unexpected bravery from the frail priest, whose talents lay elsewhere.

'Remove your hand, old man, or I shall remove it for you.'

'This kingdom needs a ruler, Marmicus, you can't deny it any longer. The princess is dead. Now the people need a leader who is capable of ruling over them. Don't make a decision without carefully considering the risks; it's not a wise tactic for you or the people you claim to serve.'

'This kingdom will have its ruler, but it will never be you, old priest, I'll make certain of that,' said Marmicus coldly. 'Now remove your arm or be prepared to use it as a walking stick for the rest of your days.'

The Grand Priest of Ursar removed his hand. Resentment coursed through his veins as he did so; he had hoped to persuade Marmicus to join his cause willingly, but their loathing for one another had prevented it. The traditional route of diplomacy had failed to work its charms; now the great scholar would have to think of other methods to achieve his vision. Friendship is always better than war, but when all else fails, what option remains?

23

Nafridos entered the room; he looked at the princess lying on the bed, so helpless and susceptible. In his mind she was naked, with only her beauty to cover her.

'There are two things I've desired in my life. The first is a throne to call my own, and the second is a woman worthy of me; at least tonight I know that one of my desires will be fulfilled.'

Nafridos took his sword from his belt, and removed his tunic, revealing a toned, muscular chest. Battle scars ran along the length of it, reminding Larsa of claw marks made by dogs, except they were probably the last marks made by innocent men who had died trying to protect their families. Larsa didn't want to look into his eyes; somehow, she feared him more than Jaquzan. His intentions were clear: he wanted to rape her, just like every other woman who caught his attention.

'Tonight, I'm going to make you feel like a queen, and all the people will know when they hear you,' he said, approaching her.

Larsa leapt up and tried to run out of the chamber, but Nafridos grabbed her by the arm, stopping her. She was as a wild gazelle locked in his jaws. She was light and delicate; he knew he would enjoy every moment of this. He threw her onto the bed, pinning her with his weight.

'Let me go!' she screamed, thrashing her arms and legs, trying desperately to free herself.

'You put up a better fight than your slaves.'

'You can mock my servants, but you'll never take away their honour.'

'Then I'll have to settle for yours,' Nafridos sneered, as he ripped off her shawl.

Brazenly, he began to kiss her neck, tasting her skin; she tasted so good. Larsa screamed, her fingernails clawing at his flesh, but it did little to stop him. His muscles strained as he tried to force himself between her thighs, but Larsa kept moving, determined not to make it easy for him.

'Marmicus, where are you?'

'Hush, princess, I'm here for you – think of me now,' Nafridos whispered, as he grabbed her throat violently with his left hand, and kissed her cheek. Larsa felt the bones in her neck bend like straws; she gulped and choked at the same time.

'Please just let me go ...' Larsa murmured.

'You can't blame me for this, princess; blame yourself. Your beauty is too much for any man to resist. Now, try to enjoy this; it will go better for you.'

He swept his rough hand up her thigh while licking her neck, savouring the smoothness of her skin.

'Kill me, but don't kill my honour. It's all I have left.'

'No whore has the privilege of honour.'

Larsa fell still. She had given up her struggle; he would have his way now. She could feel him beginning to push inside her.

'My lord!' a guard knocked on the door, shouting urgently.

'Not now! I'm busy.'

'The emperor desires your presence, my lord.'

Nafridos snorted like an angry bull. The princess had been saved by unfortunate timing. Delaying meeting the emperor was an unwise move – for some it could even be fatal. He lifted himself off her, freeing her body from his heavy weight.

'Be thankful to your god; it seems he has finally answered your pleas. We'll continue this later and next time there'll be no interruptions. I'll make certain of it.'

Nafridos stormed out of the chamber. The moment he left, Larsa burst into sobs, her body shaking from the hatred that boiled up inside her. Some of it was directed at Marmicus. He had failed to protect her as he had promised her he would. She had finally become a martyr to suffering; every inch a victim. There was only one thing Larsa craved, and that was the sweet intoxication of death. The barbarity of the world had left her wishing to die; taking her own life was the only prospect of freedom she had left …

24

Despite the royal burial procession ending hours earlier, the people of the kingdom had chosen not to return to their homes; instead they had congregated outside the great temple, looking for the one man who could restore their faith. Their fiery torches lit up the night sky like floating lanterns; their heat warmed them all as they huddled in the cold midnight air.

'He's just come out of the temple – look, over there!' cried one boy who had climbed a tall palm tree in hope of seeing the Gallant Warrior. As Marmicus left the temple, thousands of people flooded towards him like a human tsunami, all seeking to take refuge in his strength.

'Gallant Warrior, bless my infant, please,' said one mother as she shoved her newborn into his hands. Her maternal instinct had taken hold of her manners; rumour had it that a kiss from his lips would forever protect the soul that had been honoured by it. Everyone watched as he held the baby uncertainly; it brought home to him the fact that he would never become a father.

'Take your infant and return to your home. He should be sleeping in his bed, not wandering around the streets with you.'

'But you haven't kissed him!'

'A kiss won't save him from what's coming,' he replied bluntly, giving the baby back to his mother. He was emotionally exhausted; he did not need anything else to tire him. 'Now, return to your homes, all of you. Let me be; let me be!'

The change in Marmicus's appearance was shocking and so was his unexpected reaction; nobody had ever seen him brush the people aside and behave like this. Of course, none of them could hope to understand the burden under which he laboured. Normally he was strong; tonight, however, he looked like a defeated man, incapable of carrying on.

'He's lost faith in us; that's why he wants us to leave.'

'You won't abandon us, will you, Gallant Warrior?' said a little boy pulling at his robe. Marmicus ignored him and walked on. The crowd began to behave erratically, some shouting at him, while others sided with him.

'Before you judge him harshly, let us remember that the Gallant Warrior is in mourning. Every soul has a right to bear his grief upon his back, including him! He's no different to us – let him do the same as we would!' declared Sulaf from among the crowd. She had anticipated that something like this would happen, and like any loyal friend she wished to protect him from their misguided and malicious comments. *Oh, Marmicus, human emotions are not fitting for gods like you. They are as lethal as flying arrows unleashed against the body …*

'The woman is right; let the Gallant Warrior mourn his loss just as any man would wish to mourn his wife.'

'Well, let's hear it from him. Why doesn't he address us?'

'What's going to happen to us?'

The people waited uneasily. They needed him to instil in them some of his strength; with one breath he could embolden defeated hearts and send a fearless army into battle. However, Marmicus could think of nothing to say. His lips remained sealed, as by sap from an injured tree.

'Why isn't he speaking?' asked one young man with distaste. The sight of human weakness was never admirable.

'Speak to us, oh Gallant One, tell us that our children and homes will be safe. Tell us that you'll protect us – we need to hear it from you,' said one fearful woman who grovelled before his feet. Even that failed to provoke any kind of reaction from him. Marmicus simply stood there, neither trying to help her up nor to put her at ease. Tonight he had lost more than his strength; he had lost his desire to help others. *Meaningless words stir meaningless reactions*, he thought, unable to take any more of their pathetic behaviour. He began to push through the crowd, ignoring everyone around him; their hands tugged at him as they tried to pull him back, desperate to stop him from leaving them.

'Marmicus, remember that your tragedy is our tragedy. We mourn the princess just as you do!' cried Sulaf. He could not turn away from them now, not when they needed him most; the people needed hope, as a dying flame needs one final breath of air. The Gallant Warrior stopped. As he turned around, everyone stood back; they could feel his anger.

'Don't speak to me of tragedy! What do any of you know about it? Tonight you mourn the princess, but tomorrow you'll forget her name and go on with your lives. You'll see your children grow and hear their voices change; their laughter will fulfil you and carry you in bitter times. All the while I'll be cursed with visions of yesterday, while your eyes will be given the gifts of tomorrow. Your children will play and your wives will sing, all while the woman I love will lie cold beneath the ground you walk on. That is the tragedy.'

'You're entitled to grieve, Marmicus. All we ask of you is not to grieve at our expense.'

'You're mistaken, Sulaf. I'm not grieving; I've passed the point of grieving. I feel only one thing now, and that is mortal rage. I feel it burning inside me and if any of you were wise you'd leave me alone, because I shall soon erupt with vengeance. So go home, make love to your wives and sing to your children, for you have nothing to fear. Freedom will come to you the day war begins; the heads of our enemy will fall like rain from the sky. There will be no tyrants left among men, nor swords untouched by their blood. I will kill every man who has injured me, their annihilation will be my gift to you. All I ask from you in return is that you honour the princess's memory – for with her heart lies the allegiance of our swords.'

The crowd began to roar, but Marmicus felt nothing as they applauded and called out his name. Every word he had spoken was born of his hatred. Never had he wanted to kill a man so much as he did now …

25

Hiding behind the statue of Ishtar, concealed in the dark shadows, was the Serpent, who eagerly awaited the arrival of a messenger from the Assyrians. His sinful eyes flickered, soulless and unremorseful. More importantly, they revealed no sign of who he really was. If it had not been for the faint light from the surrounding torches, he would have been granted the power of complete invisibility, but that was not what he needed. He had patiently been waiting for the messenger to bring further instructions from his master.

As the Serpent stood there, he thought of Marmicus. Nothing needed to be done to destroy him; he was doing a good job of that all by himself – it was thrilling to watch. Even so, the Serpent found enjoyment in imagining how he would torture him once he had obtained the throne to the Garden of the Gods: the many ways he could kill him; thinking of it had become a ritual. He wanted Marmicus to endure a long and excruciating death; the Serpent wanted him to be alive when his hands and feet were hacked off using the same Sword of Allegiance he carried so confidently. They would be offered to the gods as a token of thanks for the Serpent's appointment as the divine king of the Garden of the Gods; as for his head, it would be placed on a long spear, which would be carried around the four corners of the kingdom. These dark thoughts comforted the Serpent every time he stared into Marmicus's eyes, and made him look forward to tomorrow. *The Gallant Warrior's punishment will come in good time and I will savour every moment of it.*

At last the Assyrian messenger had entered the ziggurat; it pleased the Serpent that someone else knew of his treachery.

'Here I am ...' whispered the Serpent quietly from the shadows. Only the reflection of his eyes could be seen; they glowed brightly like a cat's eyes, guiding the messenger towards him.

The Assyrian messenger walked to him. No one else was in the temple. He had hoped to catch a glimpse of the traitor who had done more damage than he could ever imagine, but the Serpent was well camouflaged in a shroud of darkness that was as dark as his soul.

'What are the commands of my master?'

'Only this ...' said the messenger, as he pretended to pray to the stone statue of Ishtar. 'Let the Gallant Warrior find out nothing of the princess's whereabouts or that she is alive. As long as she's believed to be dead, he'll remain vulnerable to attack. By your actions, divide the people and the Counsel: make them fight one another so that their minds are not focused on war. Above all, don't let the Gallant Warrior recover his strength; do everything in your power to make him fall to his knees, we want him weak when war comes. This is all my master has desired, and all that he has asked of you.'

'In return for all my efforts, will he fulfil his promise?'

'Our master is a god; if he has promised you the sun then he will shape it with his hands and grant it to you.'

'I don't long for the sun, I want my rightful throne, and I want to watch the Gallant Warrior suffer!'

'You'll have your throne once you have fulfilled the emperor's commands, and as for the Gallant Warrior's death, you will sit beside the emperor and watch him being slaughtered like an animal sacrificed in his name.'

'Good,' said the Serpent with a reptilian smile. 'In that case he has my loyalty. I will follow my master's commands and unleash a war so great from within these walls that no soul will be spared ...'

With these words the Serpent felt a rush of joy take hold of him; the realisation that he would soon be one of the most powerful men on earth made him feel that all the hardship he had faced to get where he was had been worth it. And as for the slaughter of the Gallant Warrior, it was the jewel in the crown he had been promised.

26

'Your Highness, you need to be careful how you address the emperor. If you show him any disrespect, he'll be unforgiving,' said Jehan. She gently plaited the princess's long hair as if she were her own daughter; with every twist she entwined within it flowers and golden beads.

'I'll treat the emperor the way oppressors deserve to be treated.'

The maid pulled the princess's hair back as she reacted; the Assyrian emperor was more than callous, he was sadistic; it made her stomach churn just to think of how he could hurt the princess, in ways she barely understood.

'Look, my dearest, I've seen all the queens who have entered this prison chamber. One of them looked disrespectfully at the emperor and she was killed for it. I can't imagine what would become of you if you should do something more grave. I'm just asking you not to provoke him. Think of me as a mother advising her daughter; you'll only regret the act, if not now then later, when they make you suffer the consequences.'

'What kind of world are we living in when it becomes an offence to look into a man's eyes?'

'You're living in Jaquzan's world now, and you're forgetting that, in his kingdom, he is a god – and if you look into the eyes of a god you will be burned by his power.'

'I understand your concern for me, really I do, but I'm not like the other queens who have passed through these walls. My backbone is made of stone now and nothing can reduce me to rubble; not after what I've seen and gone through. I've got nothing left to lose.'

'Hush ... you mustn't speak so loudly; it's not safe here. Courage offers only the gift of death here,' responded the maid. She looked over her shoulder, hoping that nobody had heard their brief exchange. Though there was no one else within the chamber, there were guardsmen standing by the door, making sure that the princess could not leave. 'I was like you when I first came here; I felt so much anger towards the world that I didn't care if I died. In fact, I had always imagined that I'd be buried beside my husband with the soil of my homeland as my resting cover, but that was taken away from me. I didn't want to carry on, but over time I accepted my new life, and had to move on; and so must you.' The frail old maid, with her motherly aura and her reminiscences, warmed the cold interior of the chamber. 'You're so young and brave, there's so much left for you yet; don't act in rage unless you're prepared to die. Believe me when I tell you, the human soul can endure more than it can imagine.'

'Thank you for being kind to me, and honest, but I can't force myself to be like you; I won't accept my slavery. I won't live a life chained to falsehood; my beliefs are all I have now, and I'd rather die for my freedom than have it taken away from me like a ring stolen from my finger. The battle starts here, tonight, but tomorrow the war shall end in my kingdom. I may not be there with my people, but I'm going to fight alongside them from here.' The faces of her dead servants flashed through her mind. Whatever happened, she could not let others die in the same barbaric way; she would rather die fighting for her freedom than accept her slavery.

'Then you'll need my help, and I'll do everything I can to help you,' smiled the maid. She dipped her finger into a chalice of rose water, then gently dabbed the water against the princess's lips and cheeks. The natural colour of the petals stained a woman's lips, drawing the eyes of onlookers towards their lusciousness.

'It's time ...' said a tall guard, ready to collect the princess and take her to her fate. 'The emperor awaits you ...'

27

Unable to sleep due to his wretched guilt, King Nelaaz of Aram tossed and turned like a buffoon, itching with lice. Each time he closed his eyes he heard the Gallant Warrior's words repeat in his mind. They were eating away at his conscience, causing his already unhealthy heart to become strained with fretful worry.

'By the gods, what am I going to do? I can't sleep! I can't eat! There must be a way out of this misery!' declared the chubby little king. He had tried thinking of naked women pampering him with food to relieve his unsettled mind; this had always worked in the past – but not tonight.

'I owe everything to the Gallant One. He's been my loyal friend when everyone else has mocked me as a clown king. There must be a way I can undo my wrong!' he moaned to himself. If he was not careful, his stomach would begin to harbour new ulcers from the added stress. His belly heaved up and down as he panicked, trying to think of an idea. The more he thought of possible solutions, the more he persuaded himself that he only had one choice.

'I must tell Marmicus the truth – it's the only way. I have to tell him that the woman he mourned wasn't the princess. By the gods,

I pray he's forgiving, otherwise I shall be roasting on a skewer by sunrise!' King Nelaaz was prepared to do anything in his power to ease his guilt, even if it meant biting off more than his chubby little mouth could chew ...

28

Dressed in silk and drowning in beauty, the princess sat silently waiting for the Assyrian emperor; she had been taken to another magnificent throne room which stood as testimony to the emperor's wealth and love of luxury. Rich textures and colours filled the colossal throne room, drawing gasps of envy from other kings who had paid homage to him; the high walls were intricately carved and painted with images of Jaquzan as an almighty god. On one wall was painted an enormous tableau of the emperor cradling the sun and the moon within his palms. His hands were so tightly gripped around them that he appeared to be squeezing them of light, implying that Jaquzan was the master of the universe and giver of all seasons. But the eyes were easily distracted from these arrogant depictions. The presence of two enormous winged bulls made of solid granite, standing either side of the emperor's colossal throne, created the focal point of the chamber. The Assyrian emperor had indeed built himself a palace worthy of a god, and Larsa despised him for it.

Larsa felt her eyes begin to blur and her throat tingle with irritation; the emperor's evil presence seemed to drain the air of its purity.

'The emperor is coming,' said one guard. He hastily knelt down, then prostrated himself, the line of guardsmen following him; their faces were level with the mosaic floor like a pack of submissive dogs waiting for their master's arrival. It was an act of pure obedience. Larsa could not hear his footsteps, but she did not doubt her nose. Jaquzan's body was always showered in powerful musk that marked his arrival in the divine chamber, acting as a warning sign to all those who served him. *It seems that the emperor's perfume is as intolerable as his aura*, Larsa reflected with distaste as she knelt, ready to bow before her master ...

29

Rising from the floor after bowing obediently before the mighty Emperor of Assyria, Larsa watched Jaquzan take to his throne. His cold, hard eyes were like the sea at night; they revealed nothing apart from fragments of obscure light that reflected off them.

'You have done well, oh glorious princess, for it is never easy for a lioness to be obedient to any master,' said the emperor coldly. His face was proportionally perfect except for his pupils, which were slightly different sizes.

'I bow before you only because I'm forced to, not because I wish to.'

'You deceive yourself. Every soul is blessed with choice, and you have chosen to bow and live, whereas others before you chose to disobey and die. That is the difference between a slave and a martyr; the slave is the one who surrenders his free will, knowing that he will live in shame, but the martyr is the one who dies to protect his free will, knowing that he will die with honour. You have chosen the life of a slave and you have chosen to submit to the power of your god.'

'I've chosen to bear the life of a slave only because I wish to save my people from the same plight that I've endured through this journey: sacrifice is what humble rulers do and what arrogant kings know nothing of. It's the choice I've made, and my people will know about my sacrifice in time.'

'If you believe that I'll offer your people mercy simply because you've shown me an act of obedience, then your beauty outweighs your intelligence. Princess, I don't *desire* obedience, I *expect* it from all my creatures, and you are no exception. Your people will die either way, and as for your Garden of the Gods, it will be flattened by the storm that I command. This is the will of your god and the order of things.' The emperor was watching the princess from the canopy of his throne; for some reason, Larsa held his attention, unlike other queens before her.

'Your poison will never run through my waters and it will never taint my soil,' replied Larsa with conviction. 'As long as Marmicus is alive, he'll fight to protect my land and preserve the sanctity of my kingdom. There's never been an enemy that Marmicus could not destroy. I assure you, your army will be annihilated by his sword.' Her head was tilted towards the ceiling like any royal soul; she would not be belittled by the emperor's overwhelming power or the intensity of his presence.

'What we have built with our hands reveals what we have achieved in our lives, and I have built an empire worthy of gods, not of men. Your Gallant Warrior is no match for my army; he is a mere thorn in a lion's paw. His efforts will not change what is already destined, and the fall of your kingdom is destined, princess.'

'No man is immortal, and your grip on the earth will be undone eventually; time will make certain of this. No amount of stone shaped by your hands can undo your mortality. The only immortals are the great warriors who are remembered by the people long after they die; tyrants like you are easily forgotten.'

Suddenly, the emperor's vacant face twitched with irritation. His dark eyebrows drew together and his lips tightened like two powerful ships colliding. The reaction was uncontrolled and inhuman, almost alien. For the first time, Jaquzan had allowed himself a recognisable expression of anger, which even Larsa feared.

'You make a habit of being unwise, and wherever there is foolishness there will always follow regret,' said Jaquzan.

'If my words have offended you, then give me your punishment; let's see if mankind truly fears a mortal god.'

'Your punishment will come, oh glorious princess, but it will not come to you in the form of death. No, your punishment shall be far greater than your heart can ever endure,' said the emperor. He rose from his empyrean throne and stepped towards her; his dark shadow swept against the enormous walls of the throne room, shrouding it almost completely in darkness.

'I'm already living my punishment,' said Larsa. 'Nothing you do can worsen it. Death will only ease what my heart has already endured!' She was certain of her words. At this point slavery was her greatest enemy, and death was her cherished ally, but the Assyrian emperor knew of a punishment far crueller then she could ever contemplate. It would be a punishment that would fulfil a godly purpose for him, something that would leave the scribes of history forever revisiting it.

'You underestimate the power of your god; death is a luxury, it is a most merciful act, and I am rarely merciful to those who have transgressed beyond my bounds,' he said as he walked around.

'Then declare your sentence and be done with it. Whatever it is, I will not fear it and I will not fear you!'

She remained unaffected by the power that terrified others; nothing that the Assyrian emperor could say or do could frighten her in the least. Her body and mind were prepared for the greatest torture possible. When you have been broken once, you can never be broken again; you become unbreakable ...

'You're an intriguing creature. Queens from afar have bowed before me in abundance, all of them longing to seduce me, so that they may live for another day longer, but I have spared none of them. Their lives had no value for me, and their beauty served me no purpose. However, your living has value, far more than you can comprehend or imagine, princess; your body is a symbol of sanctity admired by all men. Your blood is holy and your womb is powerful. You are fit to be touched by a god and to carry his crown within your womb.'

'Touched by a god?' whispered Larsa.

'Yes, you will be touched by a god; it shall be your blessing and your curse, for I have chosen you to be the mother of my kingdom and my legacy.' Jaquzan stared deeply into the princess's eyes as he paced slowly around her. His bone structure was emphasised by the tight skin that moved over his bones with every word he uttered. 'You were born for a purpose, one that is entwined with mine: with your womb you'll provide me with an heir of pure blood and bring forth an infant worthy of my name. Our infant will be mothered by a deity and fathered by a god; he shall be the new ruler of men and the next punishment of mankind. So you see, oh glorious princess, this shall be your greatest purpose and your greatest punishment in life.'

The emperor's plan had been revealed. Every detail had been thought of, but the plan was as salt in Larsa's wounds.

'My womb will never belong to you; I'd rather kill myself than succumb to your touch,' Larsa declared. Her confidence had quickly turned to fear.

'Then I must make certain that you bring forth my infant before you depart from this world,' smirked the Assyrian emperor. He gently placed his hand upon the princess's stomach, visualising what was soon to come ...

30

My lies have gone on for far too long. I must put a stop to them! King Nelaaz banged on the doors, hoping to wake Marmicus from his midnight rest. He was ready to confess everything he had done to his loyal friend. Unable to contain himself, King Nelaaz swung the doors open; his impatience had filled him with ample courage to do what was right for once.

'Forgive me, Gallant Warrior, but I must reveal something to you …'

'Let it wait until the morning, maybe then the curse of the night will not follow me into the daylight,' said Marmicus. He was standing alone on the balcony, simply staring out into the distance, waiting for the dawn. A faint foretaste of the sun was slowly spreading across the valley, the pale first light contrasting with the darkness which covered the rest of the sky. He had been unable to sleep.

'But it's of great importance you should hear it now.'

'Will your words bring the princess back to life?' asked Marmicus. He turned towards King Nelaaz, knowing full well that the answer would be no.

'I'm afraid that nothing I say can bring her back to life or change what's already come to pass.'

'Then let your words wait until the morning; let me mourn in the night and let me fight in the day, only then will I have the strength to endure my tomorrows,' said Marmicus, looking at him.

'If that's what you want, then I'll honour it,' said King Nelaaz. 'I just wish I had known how much you loved her. I would have done everything in my power to safeguard her.'

'Every husband loves his wife.'

'No, not every husband, my dear friend. I have four wives, and if any of them died I'd celebrate, not mourn.'

Marmicus smiled; it was the first time he had done so since the princess's passing. The feeling sparked a sense of life back into him, but it quickly disappeared.

'You have no reason to feel guilty. Let the guilt rest with me. You've honoured the princess with your burial gifts; that is more than enough.'

'I only wish my gifts were made for celebration, not for mourning. You see, your grief has touched me so very deeply, Marmicus. I've always had women surround me, but I've never won their true love or affection. I suppose what I'm trying to say is that I would trade my gold for just one day of love.' King Nelaaz had never known what it meant to really be wanted by another. He had bought hearts with gold, but women were never in love with him – they were only in love with his wealth and power. He envied Marmicus, because he had stolen hearts without having to offer anything in return, except his loyalty and honour. As he walked towards the open door, he realised that no amount of guilt or words would change a thing: the princess was dead, and nothing in this world could bring her back. Somehow the flabby king would have to live with himself, knowing full well that her headless body was buried somewhere in the desert, and not beneath the shrine made specially for her.

'Is there anything that I can do for you before I journey back to my kingdom?'

'There's only one thing I want from you.'

'Whatever it is, you will have it.'

'I want you to attend the Counsel tomorrow. I have something important to tell them. After that, you're free to head back to your kingdom and I'll ask nothing more of you,' said Marmicus, revealing nothing else about his intentions.

'What are you planning to say to them?' asked King Nelaaz, palpitating.

'It will be revealed tomorrow and no sooner. For now, all you need to know is that it shall align the allegiance of men.'

31

'Of all the kings of Babylon, why has the Gallant Warrior chosen to call upon you to join us, oh King of Aram? Doesn't he know that buffoons have no place among great men?' The Grand Priest of Ursar loathed King Nelaaz with the utmost passion; sophistication was something he desired in every friendship he forged, and King Nelaaz possessed none whatsoever. Today, the chubby king wore bright orange robes that exaggerated the roundness of his belly, making him look ridiculous.

Marmicus had summoned the whole Counsel, but for what reason was a mystery; the priests sat within the lush palace gardens making light conversation as they drank red wine and nibbled on sweet fruit; the swaying palm trees and flowering bushes easily distracted them from the looming threat of war.

'It is at the Gallant Warrior's request that I join you, and whether you like it or not I'll uphold his command.'

'By the gods, what's the world come to? Has the day come when our kingdom relies on the advice of a sweaty clown king like you?' heckled the Grand Priest of Ursar, enjoying the roll of laughter behind him. His words had obviously amused the scholars, who enjoyed themselves while they relaxed in the gardens. 'They say sorcery is still a poor man's trade; perhaps someone has cast a spell on him. I can't think of any other reason.'

'There's no sorcery in our friendship, there's only mutual respect; besides, I may be chubby and sweaty but at least I am always loyal to the Gallant Warrior's cause.'

'Be careful with your allegations, clown king, there is no man here who would ever question my loyalty to this kingdom. Isn't that right?' asked the Grand Priest of Ursar, bullying his fellows into agreement. His words were delivered with sophistication, unlike King Nelaaz, who stuttered and splattered as he spoke.

'Your loyalty has never been doubted by any of us!' said one Counsellor, hoping to gain favour.

'You see? No man here would dare question my authority or allegiance to this kingdom. Your remarks are as foolish as your pathetic robes.'

'These priests are inclined to say that they trust a dog even if it's bitten them on the arm. You've trained them to say whatever you command, not what they truly think,' responded King Nelaaz, struggling to keep his posture straight. He was trying his best to appear polished and poised, just as any king would, but it was a game at which he was miserably failing.

'Please, gentlemen, calm yourselves. We are all allies here; let our soldiers draw their daggers and let us promote the peace,' interrupted the young Priest of Xidrica, trying to be the voice of reason. 'I think it's best if we sit in silence; that way no man can be offended by another.'

'Your peaceful words deceive no one here; every day is a battle worthy of a cause and at this moment the battle is between men and fools, so take your own advice and silence yourself,' replied the

Grand Priest of Ursar, determined to divide the Counsel into friends and foes. He had always disliked the young priest; he never trusted anything he said, and every time the man spoke he felt an immediate desire to quiet him.

'We may be at a time of war but let's not mistake our friends for our enemies: King Nelaaz of Aram is a friend to this kingdom and to this Counsel; he shouldn't have to defend himself from an attack by you.'

It was the first time the young priest had challenged the Grand Priest of Ursar's command; he knew he would be opposed by everyone else, but even so, he would not watch the little king being bullied by a line of priests.

'Thank you for your support, noble priest,' said the king. 'It's very kind of you to stand up for me, but there is really no need for you to defend me. I've always fought my own battles and I've always won them.'

'It's not a matter of defending you: it's simply a matter of principle.'

'You grow unwise, young priest,' said the Grand Priest. 'A battle against me is a battle you can't win. It seems you've forgotten who I am, or do you need to be reminded?' There was no trace of humour left in his voice.

'I haven't forgotten who you are; in fact, you remind us every day. But it does seem that you've forgotten why we've gathered here. It's for the brotherhood of peace, not for the declaration of war, or do you purposely want to divide us?'

'Do not try me, boy, you'll regret the day that you provoked me!' declared the Grand Priest of Ursar. His fist tightened around the golden cane he always carried. There was nothing wrong with his ability to walk; rather, it was used to show off his grandeur, wealth and power.

'If I've offended any man here, then I sincerely apologise; it wasn't my intention to offend any of you. I simply want to preserve the peace of our kingdom, something we won't be able to do if we squabble among ourselves.'

He could feel them staring at him, they were all glaring disapprovingly. None of them had ever liked the young priest; in fact, his modesty and politeness were seen as more of a threat to them than a quality to be admired. The young Priest of Xidrica knew it was better to keep silent from now on; they would never ally themselves with him even if it was the right thing to do.

'No traitor deserves forgiveness,' said Marmicus, his words bold and loud. The birds in the palm trees scattered; it seemed that even nature itself had recognised his anger. 'The only man who has wronged this kingdom has been you.' He was looking at the Grand Priest. 'Your lies and your deceit have left this kingdom bleeding, but it won't bleed for much longer. Tonight the kingdom's mourning will be over and the punishment of traitors shall begin.'

He walked towards the Counsel, drawing all their attention. 'There is a serpent among us; he is sitting with us now and he is rejoicing at this kingdom's downfall,' declared the Gallant Warrior. His eyes were like a hawk's, fixed on the old priest.

'Are you certain of this?' said the young Priest of Xidrica above the shocked whispers. It was fair to say that he did not like the Grand Priest of Ursar very much, but he would never have expected him to be a traitor; it was an act of total defiance, punishable as treason.

'I am as certain about it as I am that the sun will rise each day, and I shall have my vengeance before sunset!'

'You have no power to judge me; only the gods can do so.'

'Then call upon them now! Let them defend you, because tonight you will be judged by the weight of my sword.'

'Marmicus, I urge you to be rational; think of what you're saying,' said the young Priest of Xidrica.

'If you trust this man, then you too are a collaborator and a traitor to this kingdom,' responded Marmicus coldly. Nothing anyone said could change his mind, even if it came from a friend. He had come for a purpose and he would not leave without achieving it.

'What are you intending to do with him?' asked one priest, while everyone else shifted nervously in their seats. Most of them had chosen to keep silent; they knew they were at the mercy of his sword, and right now there was no leverage to bargain with.

'What every traitor deserves.'

'Me, a traitor to this kingdom? It's an absolute lie!' yelled the Grand Priest of Ursar with anger. 'I will not be treated in this manner!'

'The only lies spoken here have been drawn from your lips, but not for much longer. From every curse there comes forth a blessing, and yours has been the chance to claim this kingdom's throne. With our king dead and the princess buried, this kingdom has no divine ruler, no loyal heir to the throne, no progeny to pass on its sanctity and no power to oppose you. You wanted Larsa dead, and you sent word to Jaquzan, telling him everything he needed to know about her journey. Only this Counsel knew about it, and you were the one who proved where your allegiance truly lies.'

'I am no traitor! The only treachery here is your wretched accusations. Will nobody speak up?' declared the Grand Priest, rising to his feet. He had expected an outraged reaction from his comrades, but the Counsel remained silent.

'Silence, old fool!' roared the Gallant Warrior, unsheathing his mighty Sword of Allegiance. The air rang with a metallic hum: Marmicus had raised the heavy weapon to the priest's neck in one deft and unforgiving movement; he could kill him at any second.

'Nothing you say can change what you are; you are a traitor and you are a serpent. You are an enemy of our kingdom and a liar among men, and now you'll pay for the wrongs you have committed against us all.'

'Marmicus, be rational!' said the young Priest of Xidrica. 'You've fought for justice all these years, but what you're doing at this moment is unjust. If you kill this man, you'll be killing everything you've stood for all these years. Be sensible; put down your weapon and let's discuss this as civilised men.' His face became pale as he intervened; he had hoped that his words would somehow extinguish his friend's fiery temper, but nothing the young priest could say or do would stop him from doing what he desperately needed to do, and that was to exact revenge.

'I know exactly what I'm doing.'

'No you don't, you're acting on impulse. As your friend, I urge you to restrain yourself. Violence is not the way to settle this battle; give this man a fair trial. Right now, you're angry and you wish to blame him because it would ease the burden you're carrying.'

'Listen to his wise words: don't do this, you'll only regret it,' said another priest, summoning the courage to speak up.

'The only regret I will have is allowing this man to live when I've had the chance to kill him,' Marmicus whispered as he peered into the eyes of the frail priest without pity.

'Wait! He's not the traitor – I am,' cried King Nelaaz, jumping up, wanting to stop the madness before it got out of hand. If only he had known that by saving one man's life, he was actually putting an end to another ...

32

Hopelessness is the one enemy that can threaten the survival of a soul: for the desire to survive is bled from the veins, and optimism is slowly dissolved until nothing remains. Tonight Larsa's hopelessness suffocated her like a pillow over her face. She lay on the stone floor, curled up in a ball and crying loudly; Jehan sat beside her trying her best to comfort her. With every breath Larsa remembered Jaquzan's face; it frightened her to close her eyes and be left alone with him in her imagination. If she were not careful she would lose her mind, just like the Queen of Persia.

'Take a deep breath; it's not right that you treat yourself like this. You have to be strong,' said Jehan. She brushed the princess's fringe from her eyes, and began to dab her fevered forehead with a wet cloth. Nothing the maid said could reassure her; the emperor's punishment ran through her mind. Jaquzan was right, he had given her the worst sentence imaginable, and it had broken her in two.

'I can't fight him any more; I'm so tired, I want to die,' sobbed Larsa, covering her face with her hands. Her lungs hurt and her head throbbed.

'Don't say such a thing! There's still hope yet, you must believe it.'

'Hope can't change my fate, nothing can now.'

Larsa grabbed the maid's hand, squeezing it tightly as she forced out her words. There was only one thing she needed from her; it would save her from all of this, offering her the salvation she needed.

'You've been very kind to me, and I hate to ask anything else from you, but I need you to bring me something.'

'I'll try my best. What do you need?'

'I need you to bring me the petals of the handiguk.'

'But they're poisonous, Your Highness, they'll kill you in an instant,' said the maid, removing her hand; she did not want to contemplate Larsa's suicide. Larsa understood the gravity of what she was asking her, but her plan made sense: she needed Jehan to hear her out.

'I'm not afraid of death, I'm afraid of living and what would become of me.'

'There must be another way I can help you – I cannot bring you poison,' said Jehan. She had seen so much death over the years, she did not want to be party to one.

'We both know there really isn't any other way. Your emperor wants me to bring forth an infant worthy of him; if I don't kill myself my womb will carry his child. I can't let that happen, you must understand that.'

'I know the emperor's your greatest enemy, Your Highness, but imagine if you were to give him an infant and raise him yourself – the child might become good like you and bring hope to those who so desperately need it.'

'There's more to it than that; we both need to die,' wept Larsa. She pressed her hand against her stomach. 'Only death can save us now.'

'Who are you talking about, Your Highness? Who else needs to die?'

'My baby,' replied Larsa, turning her face away.

'Are you with child, Your Highness?' asked the maid. Larsa's hands were clasped around her belly. She could feel her infant growing inside her, becoming stronger and more alive each day.

'Yes,' whispered Larsa. 'Before I left my homeland I thought I might be, but I wasn't sure, and I didn't want to tell Marmicus in case I wasn't. But now I'm certain of it: I can feel my womb growing; my baby is growing inside me and sharing my pain. That's why I can't let your emperor touch me. If he does, the baby I'm carrying inside me will be forever thought of as his, and that's a lie I can't allow the scribes of history to write. But if I don't submit to him, then he'll kill both of us.'

'Does anyone else know?'

'No.'

'There must be another way I can help you. Ask anything else of me, except this,' urged the maid. She had never imagined helping someone to take their life, let alone that of an unborn child; it was against everything she believed in.

'I have no other choice. No mother wants to kill her own child, but you have to understand, there's no poison deadlier than the infant that grows inside me right now; if he's born here within this kingdom and raised by your emperor, then he'll become the shadow of my enemy and the tyrant of all mankind. No child on earth deserves to be born with such a curse as his crown – even my own.' Larsa shook her head; she had lost the faint light of hope that could once be seen in the sparkle of her eyes. She had been thinking about it for some time, and she knew it was the right decision, since motherhood had blessed and cursed her at the same time. 'I'm begging you to bring me the petals; the poison must run through my veins and prevent the seed that grows inside me from blossoming. It's the only way to protect the future of mankind. We both need to die, or my baby will belong to him.'

'I can't help you kill yourself. I'm sorry,' whispered the maid, taking Larsa's hand. She could feel the princess's hand immediately tighten in response to her words. They were not what Larsa had wished to hear.

'Why won't you bring me the poison? It's all I ask of you. There's no need for you to watch me take it, or stay with me until the end.'

'I'll tell you why, and maybe then you'll understand,' replied the maid. It took a lot of courage to say what she was about to say. 'I had a daughter once, who was brave and stubborn like you. In fact, when I look at you I am reminded of her. Just like yours, her fate was awful. When the Assyrians came, they rounded up all the women in our village. Anyone who was beautiful and young was picked out from the crowd, while older women like me were forced to watch as they were raped. I saw them rape my daughter, as so many mothers did that night. Watching my daughter being stripped of her dignity and beaten by men who laughed at her when she tried to fight them off was the hardest thing I've ever had to endure. She may have been spared death, but on that day she died inside. I didn't see her smile again – not until she gave birth to my grandson, Paross, nine months later. I cannot say which monster was the father, because she was raped by more than one. When she thought no good could ever come from what had happened to her, she was surprised to find that it did. After the greatest of hardship came her ease; she loved the baby so much. He healed her from within and gave her hope when before she had none. He was only two when his mother fell ill and died, but I try to remind him every day that his mother loved him. So, you see, my child, when the world seems so cruel and everything has turned to dust, all you need is one tiny drop of rain to make a seed of hope grow. So long as you're alive, and you still believe in the goodness of others, even if there's only one person left in the entire world they become that seed, and your tears become the rain that will nourish it. I'm always hopeful that life can change, Your Highness. After all, there's nothing in this world that remains the same: night always turns into day, and oppression can always turn into freedom. The moment we give up is the moment we accept the world for what it has become.'

'I'm sorry to hear about your daughter. Thank you for telling me. When one feels hopeless, it's easy to forget that others can be hopeful.' Larsa hugged her tightly. She felt as though she was hugging her own mother; it felt beautiful and comforting. Larsa had grown up without her mother, but she had imagined her to be wise and kind, much like the maid. Larsa got up and walked towards the open balcony, wiping the tears from her eyes as if to make her appearance more beautiful for the setting sun. Her bare feet felt cold from the tiled floor. 'Even so, I don't know what I'm supposed to do to change anything.'

'There's only one solution for you, Your Highness; you must let the Gallant Warrior know that he will be a father. I suggest you write to him tonight and let him know about the infant growing inside you. I'll give your letter to my grandson, who will take it to your kingdom. Once Paross arrives in the Garden of the Gods, he'll secretly deliver the papyrus to your Gallant Warrior; maybe it will force Marmicus to come to you. There must be a reason why he hasn't come.'

'I don't want to burden you with my troubles.'

'There's no trouble.'

'There's one problem. The guards protecting my palace won't let your grandson enter, and if my letter lands in the wrong hands it'll be dangerous for both of us.'

'Then it's up to you to think of someone who can enter the palace gates without any trouble. Is there anyone who knows the Gallant Warrior intimately, someone who you can trust to bear such sacred news?'

'I think so. There's a woman Marmicus knows very well and speaks highly of; they've known each other since childhood, I'm sure we can trust her.' Larsa had met Sulaf only once; she had seemed like an intelligent woman and Larsa trusted Marmicus's judgement of character. He would never speak highly of someone unless they deserved his approval.

'What's her name?'

'Sulaf, daughter of Nazzar,' replied Larsa softly, remembering her face.

'Then we'll send your letter to Sulaf and she'll deliver it to your beloved warrior. All our hopes rest on her now.'

33

'How have you betrayed us?' asked Marmicus. The confession had taken him aback. Marmicus was right – there was a traitor – but he had not expected it to be King Nelaaz of Aram; in fact, no one had. The short little king quivered like a child afraid of what his punishment might be. King Nelaaz had always had his friendship; now he would find out what it felt like to be an enemy.

'I've … I've …' gulped the king, staring at the Sword of Allegiance. He wished he had not said anything now, but of course it was too late to go back on his words. He had openly made the confession, and unfortunately for him there was no one standing beside him to whom he could shift the blame.

'Answer me, or move aside so I can finish what I've started.'

'I would, if only I knew how to tell you …' he mumbled. He stepped back, trying to keep some distance between himself and the blade. The more he looked at it, the harder it became for him to whisper a word.

'The gravest mistake you could make right now is remaining silent when I've commanded you to speak, so either tell me what you've done or regret the day you chose to remain silent.'

'Believe me, if I could go back, I would. My wretched advisors made me do it; they're to be blamed, not me, I just followed them. Really I did,' gulped King Nelaaz. He wanted to make sure that Marmicus understood the full picture first. He could see the anger on Marmicus's face – his jaw clenched, his eyes narrowed. Whatever friendship they once shared had been thrown out of the window.

'What have you done?'

'Well, the woman you buried … how do I put it … well, she wasn't really the princess …' said King Nelaaz reluctantly.

The news was bewildering, stupefying; it made no sense at all. Everyone had seen Larsa's body lying on the royal burial chariot, her lifeless body dressed in the robes of the afterlife; each priest had conducted the sacred rituals of death over her and none had suspected that it might not be the princess. Could they all have been so blind?

'He's lying! It was the princess; we saw her with our own eyes. He's trying to conceal something else he's done,' declared a priest, his nose twitching with suspicion as he thought of what it could be.

'I've got no reason to deceive any of you. I'm telling you it wasn't her – I swear on my people's lives.'

'You would swear on any life as long as it wasn't your own,' yelled another angry priest.

Marmicus felt confused. What if the king was telling the truth? What if it hadn't been Larsa lying lifeless before him? He remembered noticing the unfamiliar birthmark on her hand. Could this really be happening to him? It made no sense; he had mourned his wife and now he was asked to believe that his grief was a sham of some kind. He needed answers, and he needed them quickly.

'If I believe you, then where's Larsa now? Is she in hiding? Doesn't she want me to find her?' asked Marmicus, his heart pounding. He felt alive again. The prospect of seeing her face, kissing her soft lips and embracing her made him burst with energy and happiness. Since Larsa had died, he had been battered by emotions that would have destroyed a lesser person.

'No, she isn't in hiding, I wish she was,' King Nelaaz said, not knowing how to break the news to him. He could not bear to look into the Gallant Warrior's eyes; for a brief moment they had gleamed with restored hope. He looked down at the floor in shame, suddenly noticing his swollen feet – all this standing up in the hot sun had made them swell like goat sacks filled with water.

'Then where is she? What have you done with her?'

'I haven't done anything. There wasn't much we could do, you see ...' replied King Nelaaz, wheezing. He felt a sharp pain in his chest, as if he were about to have a heart attack.

'Just a moment ago you said she was alive,' said Marmicus, lowering his weapon.

'I didn't say that exactly. Let me explain. After your messenger came to my kingdom, I commanded my soldiers to look for her – I hadn't heard from the princess either. My soldiers went to the desert only to find the Royal Caravan attacked, as you know, but what you don't know is that the princess wasn't alive when they found her, and she wasn't intact. I mean to say – how do I put it? – her beauty was scattered on the desert floor. My soldiers buried her the moment they found her; they couldn't bear to bring you her headless body, so they lied, and I only found out about what they had done when it was too late.'

'See? I was never the traitor here. It was him all along,' interrupted the Grand Priest of Ursar. He pulled himself up to his full height once more. Thanks to Nelaaz's confession, he was no longer in the line of attack.

'Do you mean to tell this Counsel,' said the Priest of Xidrica, 'that you secretly knew that the body we prayed over belonged to someone else? And, even so, you went ahead with these lies, this manipulation, to save yourself?'

'I can explain ...' replied King Nelaaz. The flare of the sun burned his pale skin, making him appear even more ridiculous in his orange attire.

'Then go ahead – explain, you insolent buffoon! Who was the woman you brought with you?' demanded the Grand Priest of Ursar.

Marmicus said nothing. He just stood still. King Nelaaz stared at him, having expected a reaction which had failed to come.

'She wasn't important; she was just a temple maid we found. No one shall miss her.'

'So your advisors killed an innocent woman to carry out this lie, and you did nothing to stop it?' asked the young priest, shaking his head in disbelief.

'I ... I ... I just followed their advice ...'

The king's words had sealed his fate; he had dug his own grave with that one sentence.

At last, an expression of madness came over Marmicus's face. He clenched his fists so tightly around his weapon that his fingernails turned white like teeth; the power of his grip was enough to force the metal blade to bend. A fit of rage had taken hold of the Gallant Warrior. Marmicus suddenly lifted his weapon above his head and swung it round like a deranged forester about to chop down a tree. He had unleashed a move normally reserved for the heat of battle. King Nelaaz shut his eyes. The weapon came towards him, and gasps from all sides burst through the silence.

'Give me a reason why I shouldn't kill you right now,' said Marmicus, stopping the blade at the king's throat. It took an extraordinary degree of finesse for him to stop the blade at that precise moment; only an exceptional swordsman could have done so.

'Because I'm your friend?' he whispered, opening his eyes. He could feel the cold metal press against his flabby neck.

'You're not any more. Now give me another reason not to kill you,' said Marmicus.

'What insolence is this? Our traitor stands openly before us, yet you choose to reason with him? The foolish king must be punished. What say you all?' said the Grand Priest of Ursar.

'Punish the traitor!'

'Kill him!' ordered the line of priests, raising their fists above their heads. The whole Counsel joined in, apart from the young Priest of Xidrica, who watched them act like wild animals, scenting blood. King Nelaaz looked terrified. He could see the desire in their eyes to have his body strung up and roasted; it was as if they were watching a theatrical spectacle. Marmicus noticed King Nelaaz quiver, and in the same moment, as though from afar, he saw his own behaviour. What had he turned into? He remembered what Sulaf had said; how he was no longer worthy to carry his Sword of Allegiance; how he had turned into a totally different person, someone to whom Larsa would give neither love nor approval.

'Mark my words, our serpent will be punished, but we won't follow the path of our enemies. We won't butcher kings or mutilate queens on our soil because, the moment we do, we become no different from them. So let our punishment reflect who we are and what we're fighting for. The King of Aram will remain alive, but he'll live in disgrace. This shall be his sentence and if there is any man who dares question my authority then they'll answer to my sword.' It took a great effort of will to say this, but even though Marmicus had spared King Nelaaz's life, the look on his face was far from merciful. He had spared his enemy only because he knew that Larsa would want him to do so. Quite clearly, King Nelaaz had offended the wrong man and now he desperately wished to ask for forgiveness.

'Thank you, I know I can't bring back what's wrongfully been taken away from you, but let me redeem myself. What if I give you a thousand gold amulets? Better yet, take my wives and daughters as a replacement for your loss. Let me suffer as you have suffered – that way we'll be equal, and can be friends again.'

'We'll never be equal. I've spared you out of pity for what you are: and that's a fool. Your people deserve better than to be led by an imbecile. I will make sure that your people know what you've done, and the moment they do, you'll wish you could hide forever. Everyone will remember you as the cowardly King of Aram who betrayed his people and the Garden of the Gods so he could save himself from harm; every man will mock you and every child will laugh at you when you walk through the streets. Even after your bones have dried and your skin has turned to dust, you will still be called the king of fools. It'll be your legacy, and it will never be washed away.'

34

Wealth without friendship is meaningless. It is like having a golden chalice, yet never being able to take a sip from it because you have no water or wine. Without genuine affection and smiles from friends, the heart can too easily become heavy with loneliness, and no palace, no matter how beautiful or extravagant, can fill the void of empty silence. This was how King Nelaaz of Aram felt. He had every worldly possession, but emotionally and spiritually he had nothing. No matter how much gold or wealth he spent on kings and beautiful women, indulging them all in his lavish parties and bestowing gifts upon them, no one truly cared for him or honoured him for who he was. He was a means to an end: guests would flatter him for their own purposes, and in this sense he was as cursed as any man without a fortune.

King Nelaaz understood that most of his friendships had been bought, but tonight, for some reason, he missed the only genuine friendship he had ever enjoyed, which had been with the Gallant Warrior. He had stood side by side with him, encouraging him to be all that he could be, believing in him – only to go behind his back and betray him. *The Gallant Warrior was right. I am a clown king and a mockery to my people*, he thought bitterly as he twiddled his plump fingers, lying on his bed, ashamed. He could not wait to leave the Garden of the Gods, but he knew that the moment he walked into his own kingdom, he would be taunted and abused by his people; once they heard about what he had done they would no doubt agitate for another rebellion.

King Nelaaz despised himself. He curled up into a ball, pulling the cotton sheets over his head, trying to hide from the world. In reality, his flamboyant clothes, the layers of robes, were nothing more than a façade used to distract others from his sensitivity. If he did not mend his ways, he would be forever known as the Clown King of Aram. For once the foolish king pondered hard on what he could do, this time using no advisors to help; he knew he had to obtain Marmicus's forgiveness.

Who could have imagined that a fool would become a genius?

35

'What's the matter? Haven't my hips satisfied my master? Shall I try something else?' asked the concubine. She lay naked beside the Dark Warrior, stroking his face. His body was hot and sweaty; she had done everything a woman could do to make a man relax and to satisfy his desires, but it seemed that neither kiss nor tender touch could relieve the tension in his muscles. Nafridos looked at her face for a moment. She was beautiful, but he felt annoyed and agitated by her presence. Something inside him had changed; he didn't want to be with her tonight – or with any of the remaining concubines in the palace. Nafridos hungered for one person, and until he had her, no other woman would do.

'The hips of a whore woman will never satisfy me,' he said, pushing her hand away from his face.

'Then let me try again; I'll be better this time, you'll see.'

'Lie down and be quiet,' he said, wanting to silence her. He hated women who talked too much. He wanted sex, not conversation. She followed his instruction, doing it with a cheeky smile and a giggle; but she stopped laughing the moment she saw him take a dagger from the table by the bed. Nafridos looked at the weapon. It had just been cleaned and sharpened; he smirked as he hovered it over her face.

'You're beautiful, but you're not as beautiful as she is,' Nafridos said as he kissed her on the cheek, then traced the dagger against it, making faint scratches like a pencil drawn over paper.

'What are you doing?'

'I told you to be quiet,' he said. He covered her mouth with his hand. 'Don't move.'

Nafridos would do anything to amuse himself, even killing the woman he had just made love to. He pressed the metal tip into her cheek, slicing into her skin as if he were cutting an apple. The concubine tried to scream, and flailed her arms, but Nafridos grabbed them and held her immobile.

'Stop, stop!' she cried, as he slid the knife deeper into her cheek, drawing a cuneiform word. Blood poured from her face onto the white pillow. Her beauty was all she had, and he was taking it from her.

'No, don't …' she pleaded.

'Don't move again, otherwise I'll kill you.'

He wiped off the blood against his hand, and returned to her, showing no sympathy for her agony.

Nafridos closed his eyes, and bit his lip hard. He imagined the princess lying on top of him, touching his body everywhere, screaming and quivering just like the whore was doing right now. He wanted to taste her, and feel her body move on his own; the thoughts gave him more satisfaction and pleasure than anything the whore could offer him.

'Beg me to stop, say it louder,' Nafridos whispered into her ear, as blood poured onto her neck and hair. He was using the dagger to etch a name into her cheek.

'I beg you, stop, stop!'

'Good,' Nafridos laughed as he opened his eyes and looked down at the name he had etched onto her face – 'Larsa'.

'You were right, you were better this time, but you'll never taste as good as she does. Now leave me,' he said pushing her off his bed. She quickly ran out, covering her face with both her hands as she tried to stop the bleeding. Nafridos smirked as he watched her run; even so, he felt frustrated and irritable. Bitter jealousy ran wildly through his veins. He wanted the princess; he needed her like the opium that poisoned the mind. His blood, his every sinew needed to either have her or draw blood. Nafridos had heard about his cousin's plans to have a child with the princess, and was uncharacteristically hurt. Nafridos felt something for the princess. No woman had ever made him feel like this; clearly, his obsession was beginning to spiral dangerously out of control. Jaquzan had always been the visionary, while Nafridos had always submitted to his rule; but now Nafridos had found a reason to wage his own war, and to stray towards disloyalty. *If I can't have the princess's heart, then I'll have what her heart desires the most.* His battlefield scars testified to his destructive malice. He had never lost a battle and he would make certain that he maintained this record. *Your glory shall never outweigh mine, oh Gallant Warrior. When the war comes I will make sure she remembers the way you died …*

36

Marmicus galloped across the fields where he had grown up. His wild horse pounded the earth with its hooves, and his body moved in sync with it. Together they were an unstoppable force; they chased freedom, determined to catch it as it appeared with the soft light of dawn. The peaking lantern of the sun grew stronger, appearing over the valley, growing powerful and more brilliant. Marmicus reached out his hand, wanting to touch the sun before it rose higher into the sky, away from his reach.

'Unleash your fury, Orisus, unleash it so freedom can come to us,' said Marmicus as he tightened his grip on the leather reins, and kicked his heels into his horse's sides. The stallion charged forward at full gallop, jumping over fallen trees, beating his hooves deeper into the wet ground; it was as if he understood his master's pain. There was no horse faster or more powerful than Orisus, everyone knew that, and everyone knew that whoever finally defeated Marmicus would not only inherit his Sword of Allegiance but would also claim Orisus.

'Orisus, you'll always be the envy of the winds,' he said, feeling the jealous winds thrashing his face. Together man and beast were united, free and untrammelled in that moment. The forest opened up, giving way to a lush green valley that was empty of any homes or nomadic tribes; all that stood were several large oak trees, and a derelict mud-brick house. The rains had destroyed much of the house; only the stone foundations had survived. Without them, it would have completely disappeared into its surroundings, only to be found by someone who purposely searched for it. Marmicus pulled the reins and came to a stop. For a moment he felt free – he had finally reached the place where all his dreams of glory had been born.

'We're here.' The horse threw his head back, and snorted loudly. His black coat shone in the misty light.

'This is the centre of the world, Orisus, and everyone's fighting for a piece of it,' he said as he jumped off the stallion and knelt down. All his dreams lay rooted here, borne by this very soil, grown with every sunrise and made stronger by the rain. Marmicus reached for its soil. Taking some in his hands, he looked at it and breathed it in, wanting to smell the scent of his homeland. As he did, he remembered the faces of everyone he had loved and lost: his mother and father, his wife and the family he had never had. Marmicus remembered his childhood; how his mother used to watch him from the front window of their mud-brick house, smiling and waving at him as he ran across the valley with Sulaf; but instead of seeing his mother's face, he saw Larsa's and saw her as the mother he had always wished she would be. 'If there's nothing worth living for, then there's everything worth dying for.' Marmicus clenched the soil tightly in his hand, squeezing it hard, his veins expanding, his fists burning, all his hatred squeezed into his fist; the wet soil moulded itself into the shape of his palm, as if it were testifying to everything he felt.

'You want a war, then I'll give you one. When it comes, this soil will turn into a river of blood, and you'll be the first to drown in it,

Jaquzan.'

37

The maid had brought Larsa everything she needed to reveal her profound secret. Gathering her thoughts, she gazed at the papyrus. Between her fingers she held a charcoal rod that had been entwined with a golden coil; using this, she would tell Marmicus of his impending fatherhood, and the blessing and curse of her motherhood. Larsa knew she did not have the luxury of time to contemplate the words to use. The guardsmen were always there, listening, watching; they stood beside her door like bloodhounds, carefully listening out for the soft tread of a feline's paw; any movement would alert them. Thankfully the Assyrian guards were distracted, giving Larsa the rare opportunity she needed to write down everything.

Two nights have passed, but a third shall not, she thought as she embraced the rare opportunity to write. Brushing the parched charcoal against the papyrus, Larsa finally began to write, her thoughts making their way onto the papyrus like a loving kiss blown from her lips. The sound of the charcoal rod stroking the delicate paper was enough to ruin her chances, but she would not draw back in fear. Larsa watched as the fine granules of coal began to splinter from the entwined rod as she drew the cuneiform symbols on the golden sheet.

To the one I adore and cherish with every breath that still lingers in the depths of my soul, oh sweet protector of heaven and earth, Gallant Marmicus,

Oh my love, I pray these words reach you safely, for it is this hope that leaves a candle burning brightly within my soul. Fate has overwhelmed me, sweet love, but the heavens are yet to collapse, for with this letter no wildness or grief can echo within my heart. Though our hearts are far apart, you are here with me in memory and in dream. Even among the tears that I have shed – plentiful in number and enough to fuel oceans far and wide – my grief is kissed with the remembrance of you. Oh, light of all that is good, tonight I bow before you, as do the heavens, the sun and the moon, for within my womb the jewel of your majesty grows. You are to be a father and I a mother. But among such glad tidings, oh my love, the fate of our unborn rests heavily on your shoulders, on your sword and the will of the gods.

For my enemy has decreed the darkest kind of punishment: that I will bear his crown within my womb and thus grant him an heir of royal blood. If I should refuse the pleasure of my enemy, then such infant that clings onto my womb in refuge will fall to the same fate as all those I have loved. And if I should accept, then woe upon my soul, for I have submitted to the devil's request.

Oh, Gallant Warrior, I fear above all other things for your safety and that of my people. My fate rests with the gods, I have come to accept that, but the fate of our people rests with you and you alone. Alas, do not fear for my burden, dear husband, think of your own and think of our people; they are all that matters. Although these three months have been unkind, I thank the gods more now than ever before, for even among the masked night of my enemy's kingdom and the wretchedness that my heart has come to know, I thank the gods for the gift embedded within my womb.

If we should ever meet once more, whether it is in heaven or on earth, know always that I love you, now and forevermore.

Allegiance lies in the heart of the sword …

Your love,

Larsa

38

The morning light shone over the valley, glorifying it with a white brilliance. From her mud-brick house, Sulaf had seen Marmicus ride off in the early hours of the morning. Somehow, she felt he would come here, and she was right.

'How did you know I was here?'

'When your stallion gallops as fast as the wind, every soul can feel the storm approaching,' replied Sulaf. She looked at him, sitting on the ground, doing nothing but thinking. 'I see Orisus is as untameable as ever. I never knew that animals could inherit the hearts of their masters.'

'Be careful; he's not a horse that likes to be touched,' said Marmicus, watching her.

'How do you know, if you never let anyone touch him?' replied Sulaf. She gazed at the wild animal, her brown eyes peering into his; she wanted to entrance him with her hypnotic stare, thinking that it would make him trust her, but it had the opposite effect. Orisus began to shake his head and stamp his hooves on the ground, tossing up clumps of grass. The more Sulaf stared, the more agitated the stallion became. Few people dared to come too close to him. The stallion was infamous; his reputation ironically mirrored the Gallant Warrior's own; but Sulaf was not like most people, she had learnt to be as daring as her childhood companion. The stallion watched her nearing him, flicking his long tail in protest as she approached.

'He'll hurt you if you go any closer.'

'No, he won't. Animals are no different to men; all they need is a little bit of affection to make them do anything you want,' said Sulaf. She reached out her arm, wanting to touch him. 'Every heart can be tamed if it willingly chooses to surrender,' she said, grabbing the reins.

'Don't!' shouted Marmicus. But he couldn't stop her in time. Orisus reared, jerking his head back, and the reins with it, and Sulaf slipped, falling to the ground. The fall was sudden and painful. She looked up, seeing a flash of hooves above her, her body at his mercy. Marmicus jumped up quickly, reaching to pull Orisus back before he trampled her. 'I told you to let him be; ill-tempered hearts can never be tamed,' said Marmicus, as he pulled the horse away and wrapped the reins around a tree. 'Are you hurt? Give me your hand; let me help you up.'

'I'm fine, just a little shocked,' Sulaf said. She slid her hand through his, clasping it tightly, and an energy passed through her, one of undeniable lust and desire. Touching him was worth the fall.

'You're lucky he didn't land on you. Even if he had, he's not the one to blame; you always cause trouble wherever you go,' Marmicus said. But he knew exactly why she had done it; it had been to prove her courage.

'I think you'll find it was Orisus who was the troublemaker here. What horse doesn't like to be touched? They are meant to be ridden.'

Marmicus shook his head. Sulaf's stubborn nature never failed to amaze him; she had not changed. Either way, he was glad she had come. He looked out over the valley, breathing in the fresh air and feeling calmed by its serenity. This place did wonders for his mind.

'I've seen so many kingdoms and palaces, but if I could choose to spend the rest of my life in any place in the world, I would choose to live here, away from the troubles of men, and the spoils of kings,' said Marmicus.

'There was a time when you hated this place,' said Sulaf.

'I didn't understand the world then; now I do,' said Marmicus, looking at her. For a moment he forgot she knew almost everything about him; now and then he would always be reminded. 'How's your son? Is he still practising his sword fighting?'

'He doesn't miss a day of training, and every part of his body is now bruised, thanks to you. I should never have introduced you to each other; you're all he can talk about, even when he sleeps.' Sulaf placed her hand on his arm, as if wanting to thank him for spending time with her son. Marmicus looked at her, saying nothing, but responding to her sensual touch. 'You would have been a good father. I hope you know that, Marmicus.'

Sulaf may have failed to hypnotise his horse, but Marmicus had certainly fallen for her magic. He looked at her, staring deeply into her eyes. Although he didn't say anything, he silently gave her permission to do what she had always wanted to do. He looked at her lips, as if hypnotised by them, and for the first time he wanted her to kiss him. Right now, at this moment, he had neither the wish nor the willpower to refuse her.

'How do you know?' whispered Marmicus, still looking at her lips.

Sulaf drew closer and tilted her head, recognising that he wanted her.

'Just a woman's intuition,' she whispered, as her lips touched his.

They brushed against each other softly, and then more passionately. Sulaf closed her eyes; she could feel his strong hands around her face, and feel his lips moving against hers. Their mouths opened and closed as they touched and tasted each other, savouring the moment. The colours of the world disappeared, leaving only a tingling sensation inside her that made her feel alive. *Is this really happening?* she thought, as she felt him breathe against her ear as he kissed it. Her heart pounded. Every second was bliss.

'I've always been yours,' Sulaf murmured as she wrapped her arms around his neck, hoping that their kiss would lead to much more. She knew she was exploiting his vulnerability but she didn't care; this was what she wanted …

⟨flourish⟩

Sulaf pulled at his shirt, wanting him to follow her onto the ground; there was no better place for her to cement her affections than here, where they grew up together. Marmicus looked at her, knowing exactly what she wanted from him. He followed her, lying on top of her as she stretched out on the grass. He knew he didn't love her, but selfishly he wanted to feel loved by her. Sulaf was powerfully seductive and confident; they were traits that few men could resist. She ran her hands across his chest, and up through his hair, biting her lips as she did so. Marmicus wanted to feel her body against his. He missed the closeness; the feeling was new and different and meant nothing emotionally to him, but at this moment it felt good. Sulaf moaned as he ran his hand up her thigh, and began to kiss her neck, enjoying the sounds she made when he did.

'Take me now; make love to me as I've dreamt you would,' Sulaf said, only to regret her words. Marmicus stopped kissing her and pushed himself back, breathing heavily. His rational mind had broken free of her hypnotic clutches.

'Desire can never replace love; if that's what you want, I can't give it to you,' whispered Marmicus as he drew his lips away from hers; and he looked at her, waiting for her answer.

'Then don't love me, just desire me,' Sulaf whispered, pulling him back and kissing him again, secretly hoping her words would satisfy him.

'I can't, not now,' said Marmicus. He slowly untangled Sulaf's arms from around his neck; a cold and humiliating gesture in the circumstances.

'I'm offering you my heart without any expectation of receiving yours.'

'I can't take your love and offer you nothing in return; you might not hate me now, but you would later.'

'No I wouldn't,' said Sulaf, trying to stop him from getting up. 'I'm offering you my body and heart freely – are you too perfect to accept it when every other man would? What's been taken can never be brought back to life. Marmicus, you love the princess, but she's dead and so too is her love for you. I'm giving you my body and heart instead – take them.' A rush of raw emotions left her reacting without restraint. Marmicus walked towards his stallion, saying nothing, not even acknowledging what she had said.

'Well? Won't you say anything?'

'It is not about perfection; it's about principle. I don't want to be the man who ends up hurting you.'

'Principled men can't exist in this world. If they do, they either lose their convictions along the way or are killed fighting for them.

It's in our nature to be human; to desire things we can't have or to love things by half-measure. You make yourself inhuman by what you expect from others and yourself. I don't need you to love me; all I need is for you to want me.'

'Maybe you're right, maybe truly principled men don't exist, but it's better to be a visionary or idealist than to be a man or woman who believes in nothing and settles for less. I've always been the former. I thought you knew that.'

Marmicus mounted his horse in one swift motion, gripping the leather reins tightly in his hands, wanting to leave her. 'You'll find someone worthy of you. One day he'll cherish you and love you, the way you deserve to be loved; but I can never be that man for you. I'm a warrior who's already sacrificed his heart in the name of someone else. And, as you said, what's been taken away can never be brought back to life. Your heart can never restore mine, and my heart can never offer you the love you wish for. All I can offer you is my friendship; it's up to you if you want to take it.'

The Gallant Warrior rode away, leaving Sulaf to pick up the pieces of her heart. Unrequited love had stabbed her in the chest, showing no remorse or consideration for her feelings. She felt cheap and used; bitter and jealous. Marmicus had glorified the princess to the point that nothing could tarnish her; she was absolutely perfect to him, and Sulaf was nothing but filth by comparison. Even though he was trying to protect her, what he had done to her then had hurt her more than he could possibly have imagined. *She was never perfect, Marmicus*, thought Sulaf. *I know you love me; I can feel it – you just need to realise it. I'll journey to the Black Mountain for you, and when I'm there, I'll make sure I greet the oracle with your heart in my hands* …

39

Past memories of love have a way of strengthening the soul whenever it is faced with times of calamity; Larsa pressed the letter against her lips as if she were clutching her last hope in her hands. She imagined Marmicus holding the papyrus just as she did, touching the soft paper against his fingertips, reading every single word that was written on it. She wondered how he would react to the news of her pregnancy. Would his eyes well up from happiness, or would it make him even more worried about her safety?

'Nothing can harm us as long as our hearts are bound together,' Larsa whispered. She kissed the letter, cherishing this brief, and well-earned, moment of happiness; that is, until she realised she was no longer alone. Larsa rushed from the balcony, her hands trembling. She looked around the room, trying to find a safe place to hide the papyrus. Everything seemed too exposed and open; if anyone found it she would risk losing the one thing that kept her fighting to survive.

'Too frightened to sleep, princess?' said Nafridos, looking at her. He was surprised to find the princess awake at this late hour. Larsa still clutched the papyrus, hiding it behind her back.

'What do you want?' asked Larsa. She stood still, secretly praying that he would not come any closer.

'What every man wants from a beautiful woman at night,' he said, resting his back against the door, looking her up and down.

'If you touch me before your emperor does, you'll die, so leave before he finds out; or else, come closer. Either way, I'll be happy to know that I'm the reason you die.'

Nafridos laughed, admiring the fact that she was calling his bluff; it was good to be on the receiving end of a woman's power. She was right, though – as long as Jaquzan wanted an heir from her she was protected, making her off-limits to any man, including him.

'Touch you, princess? I'm a grown man; we hunger for much more than that,' said Nafridos, walking to her. Larsa's hands sweated as she watched him approach. She thought what she said would have stopped him, but it had the opposite effect; it enticed him. Larsa tried her best to act normally, but she felt her body shake with every step he took. The papyrus was still in her hands; there was only one thing she could do. Larsa dropped it behind her back, praying and hoping that it would fall where he would not see it.

'What a man can't have, he desires more,' Nafridos said, stopping in front of her. He raised his hand. At first Larsa thought he wanted to hit her, but instead he stroked her cheek, looking at her with burning desire. 'Be careful who you choose to side with, princess; it's better to side with no one than to make an enemy of everyone. The emperor may be my cousin, but my loyalty only lasts up to a point. If I can't have you today, then I'll have you tomorrow.'

Larsa said nothing. All she could think about was the papyrus and how she could potentially lose everything. At last, Nafridos turned away; the tight knot in the pit of her stomach disappeared immediately, only for it to come back in a matter of moments. As Nafridos walked away, he saw a flicker of gold like that of a flame on the floor. Lying upon the stone floor was the epistle that contained of all her hope: the papyrus, a letter that had been written with love – words poured onto it with passion – and inspired by hope. The wind from the open balcony had carelessly blown it towards her enemy's feet …

40

The Dark Warrior had seen the papyrus. The folded sheet lay in front of his feet; nothing could conceal its existence now. *Help me please, goddess Ishtar; save my infant, please.* Nafridos reached for the papyrus, his fingers outstretched, ready to clasp the golden sheet. Remembering his words, Larsa realised she possessed something of a distraction. With no time to spare, she prepared to enter the battlefield, with her beauty as her only weapon.

Larsa remembered her father's words: *Power is a simple game of exploitation and tactic; find out your enemy's weakness before he finds out yours, Larsa. Be sure to understand it well. Once you've learnt your enemy's flaws, be aware of your strengths, and use every method to break him by exploiting them. Eventually the lion will kneel before you in surrender and you'll be his master.*

'You're right, I shouldn't make an enemy of you, not when you could be the most powerful man in Assyria,' said the princess. She walked to him and stopped in front of the papyrus. She stood on it. Nafridos looked up. Her white dress and dark hair blew in the wind. She looked like a goddess, but something had changed about her; her eyes were filled with a darkness that he had never seen in her before.

'Let me help you become what you're capable of being,' she said. 'All I ask is one thing in return.'

'What's that?' Nafridos whispered, drawn to her like a moth to a flame.

'I'm a slave who needs her freedom. Give it to me, and I'll thank you with more than words,' Larsa promised. She came to him like a glorious feline seeking affection; she seductively lifted his chin up with her fingertip, making sure he looked only at her face. Following the pull of her beauty, Nafridos rose. The plan was working; he was distracted from the papyrus, looking only at her. He desired her more than he could ever have imagined, which left him unable to think with clarity – precisely what she had intended.

'What about the Gallant Warrior?'

'My love for him has turned into hatred. How can I love someone who has chosen to leave me here alone?'

'Then you give me permission to kill him,' said Nafridos.

'Yes,' she whispered, looking into his eyes.

'How do I know you're not deceiving me, princess?' asked Nafridos.

'I have no reason to deceive you,' she whispered. 'But I do have every reason to support you. There's an ancient proverb in my kingdom which says, "allegiance lies in the heart of the sword". Grant me my freedom and I promise you that I'll offer you my heart, my body and the allegiance of my sword.' The princess was attempting to lure him with her lips, pronouncing every word and syllable. Larsa knew that words would make no difference to a man who communicated only with actions; she had to convince him by some other means, and she knew what method would do the trick. She grabbed his head, pulling him forward, and kissed him on the lips, wanting to blind him to her true intentions. Her purity meshed with his brutal aura as water mixes with oil. *Forgive me, Marmicus, it's the only way I can save our child*, she thought, as her lips locked with his. The vision of her butchered servants came to her mind, filling her with guilt and disgust. Nafridos opened his eyes, watching her for a moment as she kissed him. He wanted to know if she was enjoying it; it seemed that she was. She let go abruptly, leaving him crazy for more. Nafridos licked his lips like a dog satisfied after a meal, and wiped his mouth. He knew he would have to wait.

'Do you know what I'll do to you if I find out you're lying to me?' whispered Nafridos. His warm breath flowed against her skin as he kissed her neck and licked her ear; she felt her skin almost rupture with revulsion, but she hid her feelings well.

'What?' Larsa said, her voice still filled with false pleasure.

'I'll cut out your tongue so you won't be able to tell another lie. I'd like to think of it as a service to every man who has been deceived by a woman. Do you understand?'

'Yes,' Larsa whispered. She was under his control and at his mercy. But despite his vulgar words she showed no sign of turning back. Instead, she looked into his eyes and smiled. Larsa knew that if she hesitated for the briefest moment Nafridos would distrust her, with consequences beyond imagining.

'Good girl,' he said, stroking her face; then he walked away, still tasting the sweetness of her purity. Fortunately for Larsa, her ploy had worked. However, it had come at a price: her self-respect. She burst into tears, collapsing to the floor. *Forgive me, Marmicus …*

41

In a bid to revive his friendship with the Gallant Warrior, King Nelaaz of Aram had finally come up with a strategic plan that could potentially erase his past mistakes. He had thought long and hard about what he could do to regain Marmicus's allegiance and trust, and after many hours of twiddling his thumbs and sweating profusely, he had thought of a plan that was exceptionally tactful, considering the size of his intellect.

However, formulating a plan was very different to implementing one; to have influence you need to be influential, and to be influential you need someone with standing to support you in your enterprise. This was precisely why the king had called upon the Grand Priest of Ursar and the young Priest of Xidrica to help him in his bid to persuade Marmicus. The hard part was trying to convince them to follow him into his personal battle.

'Give me more air; I'm bathing in my wretched sweat,' the chubby king demanded. The servants waved the ostrich fans; over time their skinny arms had developed muscles the size of watermelons. King Nelaaz patted a cloth over his forehead and used the same material under his armpits. The Grand Priest of Ursa looked at him with revulsion.

'Why are you still here? You were ordered to leave this kingdom; I see you've disobeyed even those simple orders,' snorted the Grand Priest. He sat down, the Priest of Xidrica following suit. They had no idea why King Nelaaz had wished to see them both.

'I won't leave this kingdom, not until I've restored my friendship with the Gallant Warrior, and made amends for my mistake,' said King Nelaaz, shooing away his servants, wanting space to talk openly without unnecessary eyes and ears listening in.

'Do you take us for fools?' said the Grand Priest. 'You don't care about your treachery! The truth is, you need Marmicus to protect you from the savages who are waiting to kill you in your own kingdom; your concerns have nothing to do with making amends.' He stroked his white beard; the sight of the king perspiring in front of him left him feeling sick. He would have preferred the sweaty king to keep the servants next to him, fanning him, rather than have to watch him melt in the heat.

'Gentlemen, please let's cast aside our mutual loathing for one another. Carry on, King Nelaaz, explain to us why you've summoned us both. We don't have much time; preparations for war have started,' said the young Priest of Xidrica.

'Thank you, young priest. Look, I admit I need the Gallant Warrior's allegiance. Just as you said, if I return to my kingdom without his protection, I shall be roasted like a swine on a stake and tossed into a peasant's fire for supper. His friendship was the one thing that sheltered me from the damnable revolt of my people. But that doesn't mean to say that I can't offer your kingdom something in return. You see, I've got a proposition for you, one which could save us all.'

The Grand Priest of Ursar raised his eyebrow, intrigued. *Could it be that our clown king has played us for a fool all this time?*

'What is it?' asked the young priest.

'Let's be honest. Even with the Gallant Warrior leading your army, your kingdom is still greatly outnumbered. In exchange for redemption, I'll offer you my army to fight for your cause; I've got ten thousand men who will fight and die for you. All I ask in return is forgiveness and the Gallant Warrior's allegiance.'

'Your offer sounds reasonable,' said the Grand Priest of Ursar. 'But, my unfortunate friend, it seems you'll still have to get used to living in exile; even if I wanted to help you, I don't have the power to sway the Gallant Warrior. Marmicus listens to no one; he follows his wretched, moralistic heart, and the truth is, your treachery runs too deep for his wounds to heal. He would never accept your pledge. It's a pointless pursuit. Go back to your kingdom and enjoy your last days as king.' He was taken aback; he had not expected the fat king to have any intellect beneath all that flab. The Grand Priest of Ursar rose from the cushioned chair, expressionless, and walked away. He had spent enough time looking at the king, whose ear lobes resembled those of an elephant. But as he walked away from the canopy, he came to realise that King Nelaaz of Aram did possess a measure of tact after all; something he would not underestimate again.

'Wait!' King Nelaaz shrieked, longing to keep him for a while longer. 'You've misjudged me for too long, old priest. I realise you've no power over Marmicus, but that doesn't mean to say that no one here does.' King Nelaaz glared at the Priest of Xidrica, who sat silently. 'I think you'll find our good friend here has the power of persuasion.'

The Grand Priest of Ursar looked back. He was right, Marmicus did value the young Priest of Xidrica's advice more than anyone else's in the kingdom; he stood for something, which meant Marmicus respected him and was willing to listen to him. The young Priest of Xidrica stood up, realising that they were placing all their hopes in him. 'Even if I could persuade Marmicus to accept your proposition, we still have a problem – we don't have enough men to defeat the Assyrian army. Ten thousand men, combined with our own, are still too few. There'll still be a massacre on the battlefield.'

'How did I know you would say just that?' said King Nelaaz. He wrapped his arms around his belly and laughed. He had thought of everything. 'I've called upon the kings of Babylon to help us; I think you'll find they're willing to join forces if the Gallant Warrior could lead them.'

'Impossible,' whispered the Grand Priest of Ursar, but without conviction. The king had thought of every detail.

'Not at all. The kings of Babylon are coming; all we need to do is convince Marmicus, and I leave that up to our friend here.'

King Nelaaz of Aram had proved himself to be a genius in disguise, and for that reason he was worthy of respect, even from his enemies.

42

Threatening ideas must either be controlled by the hands or stamped out by the feet; the foolish king must be silenced before his ideas grow out of control, the Serpent thought. He glared at his finely engraved ring, which showed him to be a man of great calibre, and wondered at how quickly things had changed. He knew he had to act quickly before everything he worked for was ruined. He had not paid much attention to the king; in fact, he had never suspected him of becoming any kind of threat. Everyone knew his only genius lay in eating and tasting food, but it seemed he had been outsmarting everyone all along. King Nelaaz was right. There was only one man who could unite all of the kings of Babylon, and it was Marmicus. If the armies of Babylon came together, they would be strong enough to defeat the Assyrians. He could not let that happen, not when he was so close to winning his throne. He had to act quickly.

The Serpent rushed through the temple; the sight of godly statues filled him with revulsion and made him feel nauseous. He looked forward to the day when he could openly declare his hatred for them all, but in the meantime he had to hide his thoughts beneath the virtuous fabric of his gown.

The young Priest of Xidrica possessed the power to influence Marmicus. The question was whether he would use it. Even though the Serpent despised Marmicus, he did possess an uncanny respect for him. *He is a rare breed*, he thought as he traced his finger along the scar that flowed from his elbow all the way down to his hand. And like every rare breed, he would soon become extinct …

43

The Serpent stretched out his left hand and peered at the green mark etched into his palm; he ran his index finger over the cuneiform symbol, remembering the intense fire and the sharp needle that had pierced his hand. Nothing could make him forget the day he lost his childhood. He remembered crying loudly, feeling agonising pain as the woman brushed granules of black charcoal into the wound, smiling at him as she did so. He remembered the intense burning, as if his hands had been placed in a fire. At the time, the Serpent did not know what the woman had written, but now he did. He read the word 'slave', and thought about the way the world had treated him.

From the moment the Serpent was born, he was cursed with an impure soul; for he was the son of a whore, born through sin. Every man in the village knew his mother well, and every wife hated her; as for their children, he became their punchbag, to be beaten and ridiculed whenever they saw him. He learnt to hide behind trees, and run as fast as he could, so that he could avoid the scrapes and bruises that came with being the son of a whore.

The truth was, he hated his mother for all the pain she had

unknowingly put him through; yet, no matter how hard he had tried to forget her, he could not rid himself of memories of the warmth of her love. Without a father or loving husband, all they had was each other against the world.

He had tried his best to make his mother happy, wanting so desperately to ease her hardship, so that she could live a better life. At the tender age of five, he tirelessly ploughed the land, and collected wood for fires, earning goat's milk and bread as his reward. He remembered watching children play on the fields, some laughing and pointing at him as they saw him struggle to pick up heavy tools. He could barely stand on his feet due to his sheer exhaustion, but he carried on, doing it all for his mother. Deep down he hoped that it would be enough to make her happy and change her ways; yet no amount of help he offered stopped her from her doing what she knew best.

At night, while he was sleeping, she brought men to their home. Their voices often woke him; whenever he was awake, she would tell him to close his eyes and tightly cover his ears. Not knowing why, he followed her commands. No amount of pressure could block out the noises they made. Sometimes he would hear his mother laugh loudly or giggle. He wanted desperately to see what made her cheery, but he didn't possess the courage to open his eyes. Other nights, he would hear crying, and in the morning he would find marks around her neck and bruises on her face. On those days, she would plead with the gods to end her life; it was at these times he would tremble, and hate himself for not being able to protect her.

But there were nights he cherished, when life seemed perfect, when she snuggled up with him on the straw bed, with the light of the stars and moon flooding through the windows. His mother would tell him stories about her homeland, and how his father was the king of the Garden of the Gods.

'Why did you leave, Mama?' he asked, playing with her hands.

'Sometimes the wind draws us in a different direction than we hoped …' she whispered. She kissed his cheek and smelt his neck. He was absolutely perfect to her.

'What does the Garden of the Gods look like? Is it beautiful?'

'Yes, it's heaven on earth. You'll see it one day. I'll take you there when we have enough food for the journey.'

'But what does it look like?'

'It looks like a big garden, filled with flowers and palm trees everywhere. And in the middle, running through it, is a long wide river that sparkles when the sun hits it, and glows brightly when the moon appears. I used to take long swims there with your uncles when I was your age, and we'd pick fruit from the trees whenever we were hungry. At night you can smell the sweet scent of orange blossom; it blows with the wind, and makes you so calm. It's a beautiful place, for a beautiful prince like you. And when you go back, you'll see all the people waving at you, happy to know that you've come back to be their king. My precious little boy …' She hugged him tightly and watched him slowly fall asleep. In that brief moment both of them escaped their day-to-day reality and entered a new world but, as with all dreams, brutal disappointment can easily follow.

One night, life had unexpectedly changed. His loving mother had not returned home as she usually did. For two nights he sat, cold, hungry and alone, waiting on his straw bed, which he had once called his throne, watching the door, hoping that she would walk in, even if it were with another man. But she did not. A third night passed, and the hot bread he had made for her on the first night had grown hard like dried clay. He knew then he had to do something; he began to search desperately in the village, asking everyone if they had seen her. Some people were helpful, but most were not; many women smiled, realising that she had disappeared; others shunned him as if he had a contagious disease. Eventually, the little boy's energy drained away, and the small light of hope that shone brightly inside him disappeared.

His struggle to find his beloved mother took its toll on him. Eventually he collapsed, waking up only to discover that he was trapped in another nightmare. While he slept he had been sold to a wealthy but cruel man, and the boy who thought he was a prince was now a slave. It was that night that both his palms had been tattooed with the word 'slave', using a sharp, hot needle. The poison spread through his veins, leaving him in excruciating pain for endless days; his hands, which had never stolen food to survive or harmed others, were no longer his to command. However, the absence of his mother's kiss on his cheek was more unbearable than all his master's blows.

Soon his love for his mother drained away until it could never be restored. He secretly feared that she had abandoned him and returned to the Garden of the Gods without him. Beaten each night for what he was, a lonely slave born of a whore, the little boy would cry, knowing only that life was wretched and cruel. Eventually his eyes became bloodshot and his mind became bruised with sheer disappointment. He could no longer see the world clearly or revive in his heart the warmth it had once felt. The only comfort life afforded him was the knowledge that somewhere in the distance, beneath the lofty mountains and hidden among the plains of the desert, was a throne that sat waiting for the return of its king.

44

M armicus rode into the palace. He had hoped to clear his mind of all his troubles, but he had made things worse for himself, now that he had kissed Sulaf, and shunned her as he had. He knew she would never forgive him for what he had said; but in the long run it was for her own well-being, and he hoped she would realise that.

'Where did you go, my lord?' said a servant, taking hold of the reins of his horse. He led Orisus forward, steering him to the stables.

'What concern is it of anyone's where I've been?' Marmicus asked. He removed the Sword of Allegiance from his belt and gave it to the servant to hold for a moment as he dismounted from his horse. The weather had changed: the wind had become cold, and thick clouds spread over the kingdom.

'Forgive me, my lord. I've been asked to find out.'

'Who asked you?' said Marmicus, taking back his weapon as he landed on his feet.

'The Grand Priest of Ursar demanded to know where you've been; they were his orders, my lord.'

Marmicus stared at him, clearly annoyed.

'If every man followed orders without question, there would be more war than peace; remember that before you submit to another order, even if it's my own,' he said, storming into the palace.

Marmicus still believed that the Grand Priest of Ursar was a traitor; he had a hunger for power that would lead many a reasonable man into the realms of treachery. Marmicus had a feeling that he was also spying on him; he just hoped that no one had followed him to the valley. If they had, they would have seen him kiss Sulaf and betray the princess's memory. Now that he had returned to the palace, he felt a great guilt; he felt as if he had cheated on Larsa. Marmicus slumped down onto the wooden chair in his chamber. His back felt sore from his journey. He stared at the wall, not knowing exactly what he should do.

'Whenever honourable men disappear, they're sorely missed,' the young Priest of Xidrica smiled. He walked towards the Gallant Warrior, embracing him with brotherly affection. 'You look better than you did a few days ago. I'm happy to see that.'

'I still don't feel it,' Marmicus said as he let go, and poured some barley beer into a cup. He needed a strong drink to make him feel better.

'Well, that's to be expected,' the Priest of Xidrica said solemnly. He felt burdened by what he had to tell the Gallant Warrior. He had gone through enough already, but the Counsel had forced him to act; if he did not, he would be in the line of fire. The priest asked if they could go to the garden where no one could hear them talk, and directed Marmicus out of the chamber. It was an odd request: the weather was not fitting for a stroll, the wind was harsh, and it was beginning to pour with rain. Something was obviously on his mind. Marmicus obliged, and they walked around the palace gardens, silent at first. Eventually the priest stopped, and turned to him.

'May I ask you a question? It's not why I've come to you, but I am curious to know the answer.'

'You can ask me whatever you wish; there are no boundaries between brothers,' said Marmicus, trying to put him at ease.

'I am a man of faith, who knows very little about war and death, but somehow I imagine that if I saw a man die, it would strengthen my faith in the gods – not the opposite. You've seen death more than anyone else in this kingdom, but you don't seem to believe in the gods. What makes you doubt their existence?'

'Is it my lack of faith that's troubling you?'

'Nothing in your character troubles me, Marmicus. I'm just curious to know the answer …'

'I can't believe in the gods, not when I know innocent people die, and oppressors live. If there's a god out there, I'm still waiting to see his justice. Until then I'll rely on myself for it.'

'Well, you may not believe in the gods, my dear friend, but you do possess a godly spirit I admire and respect,' said the priest. He placed his hand on Marmicus's shoulder, squeezing it tightly. 'Now I must tell you something which requires courage to forgive, and strength to accept.'

'What is it?'

'As you know, we're on the brink of war, and in times of war, your greatest enemies can become friends. The King of Aram has made an offer of allegiance to you. He wants your forgiveness and in return he'll offer this kingdom his army to fight in our cause. The Counsel has accepted the proposition, but it means nothing without your forgiveness.'

'If they think I can forgive him, then they're asking the impossible. I'll never forgive him, not after what he's done to me.'

The Priest of Xidrica understood how difficult the request was; it was natural that Marmicus would refuse – he was only human. The

Gallant Warrior would have to swallow his pride and publicly pardon someone who had grossly and hideously deceived him.

'I know it's not a simple request, and I don't blame you for rejecting it, but I've been compelled to ask you by the Counsel. They're waiting for an answer.'

'Then the Counsel has proven itself willing to accept bribes from men who offer no real allegiance,' replied Marmicus. He walked to the stone table. Placing his hands flat against it, his hatred boiled inside him. The more he served the kingdom the more he began to loathe the Counsel and its politics. Counsellors thought only of themselves, and had sent the one man who did good to exploit him. 'Go back and tell them that I don't want his allegiance or his men. Nothing he can offer can make me forgive him, not after what he's done.'

'Are you certain of your choice? I know you hate him, Marmicus, but he's offering this kingdom a way out. If you accept, ten thousand men will join our army, and fight alongside us. Without them, we are left alone to defend ourselves.'

The young priest was right. Marmicus was lost, on the horns of a life or death dilemma he had never expected. He had always tried to be just in everything he did; now he realised that the compassion of his heart had limits. In the end, he was like any other man, afflicted by a human desire to avenge and hate.

The priest looked steadily at the Gallant Warrior, waiting for an answer. The fate of the kingdom depended on his ability to forgive. The question was, could he find the strength to do that?

'If I don't accept his pledge I become the oppressor of my own people. If I do, I become the oppressor of my soul,' he whispered, turning to the young priest, searching for an answer. 'What would you do, if you were in my position?'

'I can't tell you what you should do, Marmicus; the load you carry upon your shoulders can only be felt by you. No advice I offer will make the load lighter, or ease the journey you'll have to take. But I will say this. Forgiveness is no different to any battle: it takes strength and sacrifice, and in the end there's no guarantee that peace will follow.'

Hearing these words, Marmicus tried his best to rationalise his actions. Today he was fighting the hardest battle he had ever encountered in his lifetime; it was a struggle from within, his enemy was himself and the battle was for his pride.

'What's your decision? Are you prepared to pardon the King of Aram for betraying you and this kingdom?' asked the priest. He looked at Marmicus, with no idea what the answer would be.

'Forgiveness is but a word. If that's what the king desires to hear then so be it. He shall have my forgiveness, and in return I shall have his army. I mourn my honour so that others do not mourn their fathers or brothers on the battlefield,' Marmicus whispered.

'Freedom means nothing without sacrifice. Your sacrifice makes you the wise leader you are; for this you've earned the people's admiration and my sincere respect,' said the young priest. He moved closer to the warrior, who stood in silence. Although his words were soft, they echoed powerfully with meaning.

45

Tapping his plump fingers against the arm of his chair, King Nelaaz of Aram fidgeted. He sat slouched, with his belly rolled forward, and his nose twitching from the bristles of his ginger moustache. He felt like a prisoner waiting for his fate to be revealed. The Grand Priest of Ursar watched the king scratch his belly; the sound of his nails digging into his skin made him feel queasy.

'Do you find pleasure in irritating all those around you, or is it just me?' asked the Grand Priest of Ursar. Too anxious to care about the remark, King Nelaaz of Aram began to bite his already short fingernails to the point that he made them bleed.

'Do you think the young priest has persuaded him to accept my pledge?' King Nelaaz whispered. His voice cracked with nervousness. The more he thought about it, the less optimistic he became.

'Only time shall tell, and in that time we'll know the direction of our fate,' said the Grand Priest of Ursar.

46

Larsa needed all her strength today. Her day of reckoning had arrived: the slaves had come into her chamber to purify her body so that she was worthy of being touched by the Assyrian emperor. They had purposely waited for her body to heal from all its bruises – Jaquzan was not one to touch something that was unworthy of him. Every morning she was examined by slaves. Now the hourglass offered no more grains to spare; the time had come for her to kneel in surrender to the master who commanded it. Powerless to stop her imminent rape, Larsa cried and trembled. Repeating the poem written by her father, she hoped that it would instil in her the same courage.

> *'I am not afraid,*
> *I will speak louder,*
> *I will be braver,*
> *I will be all that I can be,*
> *If I believe then I become,*
> *I am free, even if shackled as a slave,*
> *I am pure, even if painted by the hatred of others,*

I am my own,
I will not hide in shadows, or disguise myself in another's
presence,
I am the love of my people.
What is destined can never be undone, but what is
unwritten belongs solely to me ...'

Larsa thought about Marmicus; she remembered his love, how pure it was and how lucky she had been to experience it. She thought about the way he had made love to her on their last night, how he had cradled her, wiped her tears and stroked her cheek. Never in her whole life had she ever imagined that she would betray him like this. *Forgive me*, she thought, unable to understand what she had done to deserve this. The more she thought about her ill fortune, the more her heart sank. She read the poem again, this time louder and more passionately. The slaves watched her as they began their preparations, the princess choking with every helpless breath. They sympathised with her, but they did nothing to comfort her. They led her to a pool filled with camel's milk, in which she was to be forced to bathe. Larsa looked into it. All she wanted to do was drown in it, and the only thing stopping her from taking her life was the little life growing inside her.

Larsa felt her knees shake as she dipped into the pool. The slaves held her by the arms, trying to give her the strength to walk. She closed her eyes and dipped her head into the milk, thinking of everything she had endured up to this moment.Finally, they helped her out, and led her to another pool, filled with rose water. There they washed her body and moisturised her skin with lavender oil until it glowed brightly. Her long brown hair was combed; her lips were reddened with the pigment of saffron and orange lily pollen, and her eyes were darkened with kohl. They placed a white silk robe over her body to symbolise her rebirth, and clipped a heavy necklace made of pure gold around her neck.

'Tonight you are a goddess,' said the slave woman. She placed a crown upon the princess's head, signifying her readiness for the emperor.

'Wait. I need to see Jehan, I won't go without speaking to her, not even if you try to drag me,' said the princess.

'Why do you wish to see her?'

'I need her reassurance. I can't disappoint your emperor, not when he's spared my body and my life. Let her come to me, so I can be at my best when he sees me,' replied Larsa. It was the only answer she could think of that made any sense. She wiped her tears and stared deeply into the woman's eyes without blinking: unknowingly, the princess had mastered the act of deception; it was necessary for her survival.

'Wait here, I'll bring her to you.'

Larsa watched the slave women turn away. They walked out the grand doors of the chamber, one by one, like a line of soulless sheep. Larsa rushed towards the wooden divan. Her hands slid across and under the fabric, trying desperately to find the golden papyrus. Larsa grabbed it, feeling instant relief, and held it tightly in her hand, hiding it as best she could. The papyrus was the only way to protect the sanctity of her unborn child's name. *Marmicus must know of his infant! It is the only way to prevent the carvings of history from spreading deceitful lies for all eternity …*

'You called upon me, Your Highness?'

Jehan had been followed into the chamber by a guard. They knew they could not talk freely without drawing attention to their plan. Larsa embraced the maid tightly as if she were saying farewell to her own mother.

'Living a life without friendship is like becoming a prisoner of your own flesh,' she whispered, hugging her tightly as she rested her head against her shoulder. 'Please give my love to your grandson. I've been thinking of him all this while ...'

Larsa discreetly slipped the papyrus into the maid's hand, desperately hoping that nobody had seen her.

'I'll send him your love, Your Highness, you can be certain of that.'

Jehan took hold of the papyrus, slipping it into the folds of her shawl; whatever the risk, she would fulfil her promise and entrust the papyrus to her grandson. It was a pledge that she would not forsake, despite the obvious danger that threatened both of them.

'Hurry up, the emperor's waiting,' said the Assyrian guard.

'Be strong, Your Highness, your freedom will be neither aspiration nor myth: it will be real', the old woman whispered into her ear, hoping to comfort her. She could feel the princess's body trembling in her arms. The guard's patience had run out; if the princess was late he would be the one in serious trouble with the emperor. He tugged at her arm, trying to pull her away. Larsa held onto the maid, squeezing her hand tightly, not wanting to let go; their arms straightened until eventually Larsa was forced to let go.

'Don't forget, I need you!' she shouted.

'Be quiet, whore,' the guard said, pulling her away.

Larsa wept all the way to the emperor's chamber.

Rape would not be the only calamity to befall her that night. Unknown to the princess, one of the slave women had been secretly watching. She had seen Larsa slip the papyrus into the maid's hands, and like any slave who longed for freedom, she hoped that her knowledge would be enough to win it.

47

The sinful deed was done. The Assyrian emperor rose from the princess's unclothed body and drifted away without thoughts or feelings about the wrong he had committed against her. Larsa remained still, her thighs – her whole body – aching. Disgrace and shame left her in an unearthly trance, as if her soul now mimicked Jaquzan's inhuman aura; perhaps the closeness of his body against hers had left some unseen imprint upon her, like a fingerprint on a pure and untainted surface.

Larsa's hands and feet had been bound. They now bled. She had been defiant, lunging and biting, hoping somehow she could save her integrity. Eventually, their bodies had connected like a rosebud to a stem; Jaquzan's movements were rhythmic, his touch was passionate and his kiss was poison to her flesh. He stared unashamedly into her eyes throughout the ordeal, his pupils enlarging the moment he insinuated himself between her thighs. Larsa closed her eyes, thinking only of revenge: she knew if she did not, she would die from her heartache. Sounds of pleasure came from Jaquzan's lips the moment he was inside her. Larsa cried, knowing that she had lost the battle to save her sanctity and that of her infant. His sounds reminded Larsa that he was indeed like any man. As soon as Jaquzan had finished, his cold exterior returned like plates of armour being strapped onto his chest. Larsa curled up in a ball. She felt dirty and impure.

'You've been blessed tonight, princess – what woman can say she's been pleasured by a god?' said Jaquzan. His slaves came to him; they wiped his toned body, cleansing it with aromatic water and perfume. The rich musk sickened Larsa; it was the scent that she now associated with him.

You are no god but you'll meet him soon enough, and when you do, he'll be unmerciful to you just as you've been unmerciful to others, Larsa thought with hatred.

Once the slaves had finished with him, they quickly freed the princess's hands and attended to her wounds, patting her wrists and ankles using a damp cloth. Larsa's skin burned from the sharp tang of the lemon water, which irritated her open wounds.

'Leave us,' said the Assyrian emperor. He wrapped a swathe of long black material around his waist, and walked towards the princess, who lay on the bed curled up in a ball. Larsa thought he wanted to rape her a second time, and she closed her eyes. Surprisingly, Jaquzan sat on the bed, staring at her, doing nothing at first. 'Now that we are united by the spirit of another, you will honour me and love me as your god, and in return I shall reward you with a hanging garden to remind you of the mountains your kingdoms once had before I flattened them. It shall be my gift to you, and your gift to me shall be the infant born of your womb, and blessed with my name.'

Larsa looked at him, knowing that what he presented as a romantic gesture was just another means to taunt her. Should he offer her the world, she would always choose to live with the stars.

'A man who claims victory before winning his war is like a blind man who claims he can see in the darkness,' said Larsa, looking at him. Her eye make-up had smudged, and her skin was yellow from fatigue.

Jaquzan took a deep breath. He understood she was angry, but that was no excuse for impolite behaviour.

'I'll tell you a secret, princess, one that will burn your heart with agony,' said Jaquzan. He pressed his lips against her ear, and Larsa moved her face away, but Jaquzan quickly grabbed it in a shocking fit of rage, his fingers pressing into her cheeks. Larsa felt a shooting pain at the back of her neck and across her head. Jaquzan squeezed her skin, pressing her chin into her neck. Larsa looked at him as he covered her mouth with his hands, but Jaquzan's facial expression remained unaltered; he was emotionally disconnected from what he was doing, showing anger only through his actions.

'You have chosen a life of hardship, when you could have enjoyed a life of ease. Because of this, you will remain alive only until the day your womb brings forth my infant. I want you to hear your son cry for the first time, just as he hears your cry for the last time. So, love me or hate me, you will obey me ...'

48

'If the gods offered me the entire world I would still trade it in for your love,' Sulaf whispered to herself. Her eyes followed her son Zechariah, who was playing with his dog, oblivious to war's final approach and to his mother's suffering. Rejection was beginning to tear her heart, shredding it into small pieces; she hated herself for allowing a man to have so much power and control over her. She had promised herself never to let that happen again. When Sulaf was married, she had fallen victim to her husband's fists and his need for control: she may have possessed a mind and heart of her own, but her body had become his to direct, manipulate and abuse. She had promised she would never let that happen again, but it was a broken promise: her heart and mind belonged solely to Marmicus. They had become his to love, or hate, need or reject; and all she could do was wait on the sidelines, hoping that somehow he would see the good and beauty within her. But she knew he would never change his mind, not when he loved the princess so much.

She sat on the grass, recalling the cursed day when she found out that Marmicus had fallen in love with another woman. It was a memory embedded in her mind like a thread woven into the fabric of her anatomy; nothing could loosen it without damaging the rest of her body. Sulaf needed a way out. All she could think about was Marmicus and how he had humiliated her that morning, when all her dreams were about to come true. Something had to be done.

Sulaf remembered a story which she had heard as a child about a woman who lived in the cursed Black Mountain outside the kingdom. She had no idea if the story was true, but rumour had it that a powerful oracle lived there, who was able to grant requests so long as a sacrifice was made to her. The long journey to the oracle was most often made by those aggrieved souls on the verge of insanity and now, for the first time, Sulaf actually sympathised with them. Somehow she felt that the oracle possessed the answers she needed, and possibly the cure for the disease that had taken hold of her mind and body.

The day she had found out about Marmicus and the princess, she had gone to the marketplace to buy some beads to make a beautiful necklace for herself – the last one she made had been ripped from her neck by her brute of a husband, who had beaten her for serving him food he did not like. Sulaf was standing by the stall when she heard two old women gossiping. She ignored them at first; it was only when she heard the mention of Marmicus's name that she began to pay attention. She heard them say that the king had given his blessing for his daughter to marry the Gallant Warrior. Sulaf listened to every word. She was surprised that he had not mentioned anything to her. The more the women spoke, the deeper her heart sank. Sulaf pretended that she was busy searching for azure beads; she scattered them across the wooden table, searching for the most beautiful ones. She hoped the rumour was not true, for her own sake. Although Sulaf was married, she still felt connected to Marmicus, as if they were two petals from the same flower. She thought about him every night, even when her husband lay on top of her, pleasing himself but doing nothing to satisfy her needs. She only endured his touch by imagining that it was Marmicus.

The rumours continued for weeks. Sulaf heard various stories, but the underlying story remained the same, that Marmicus had fallen in love with the princess. Wherever Sulaf went, the rumours followed her, as if chasing her through the streets, but Sulaf kept dismissing them. Then, one day, a messenger came to her door and delivered to her a clay tablet. Marmicus had invited Sulaf to meet the princess at the palace. It was like a knife in her heart. Sulaf did not wish to go, but she forced herself to, taking comfort from the fact that any escape from her husband's violent temper was welcome. The moment she entered the palace, her world collapsed, burying her. Marmicus and the princess's happiness and love for one another were a reminder of how deeply unhappy and lonely she felt herself, sparking resentment and jealousy within her: feelings that over the months following grew out of control. Marmicus invited Sulaf to the palace many times, wanting her to be close to his wife, but she never went back again. Eventually they lost touch with one another; the stem had been cut.

Sulaf needed to rid Marmicus's mind of the princess, and ultimately to take her place. This was her only hope. Sulaf began to tangle locks of her hair around her fingertips and think cruel thoughts about the princess. Even though she believed her to be dead, she hated her with a passion: like fire and water, nothing could have made them friends or allies.

'Don't turn in your grave, princess, I'm merely undoing what you did to me,' Sulaf said, standing up. Her hair blew in the wind as she looked out, seeing the bulk of the large dark mountain in the background. Somewhere, in the distance, was a woman who could set Marmicus's heart free, untangle it and hand it over to Sulaf to keep forever.

49

'With age comes wisdom, but in your case I see you've traded it in for treachery,' said Nafridos. He crouched down, glaring menacingly at the old woman who lay on the hot dusty ground. She had been left out in the sun for two days like leather being dried. Her frail hands and feet were bruised, having been handled roughly by brute soldiers. Each limb was tied to a wooden post. Nafridos held a green apple in his hand. Skilfully he twirled his knife, peeling the skin in front of the elderly woman whose torture he had ordered. He cut a piece of the green apple, and dangled it over her nose and her lips, trying to tempt her to talk. She moaned. Her lips were chapped, the flaky skin clumped and hardened by the sun.

'Are you hungry?' he asked, as he bit into the apple, crunching it loudly with his teeth. Juice burst from his lips. 'You can have it. Just tell me what you know.'

Jehan refused to answer his question. She moaned again, turning her head from side to side in painful protest.

'You're an old woman. This isn't the time for you to be brave. You should carry on living out the few miserable years left to you in peace. Now, tell me, what did the princess give you?'

'Courage to dream ... once again ...' Jehan whispered faintly, struggling to speak. She looked into the sky, feeling the white light of the sun against her face; and she imagined heaven, how pure it was, and free from suffering.

'You mean, courage to die,' Nafridos mocked. He rose from the burning ground and walked around her, flicking sand onto her face with his sandals. Jehan closed her eyes and remained silent. She had no idea what they were going to do to her; it was the not knowing that frightened her.

'Where's the informant who saw everything?' Nafridos asked a soldier.

'She's not here, my lord.'

'Go and get her.'

'Yes, my lord,' replied the Assyrian soldier, departing swiftly to carry out his orders.

'Why do you want to die for the princess? She's not one of you. She's never been like you.'

'I'll die ... for ... my freedom,' said the maid, using all her strength to speak. Her throat had become so dry that it felt like a hot stone had been wedged there; she could no longer see the Dark Warrior's face; she could only hear his words.

'You'll never have your freedom, not while I'm alive.'

For no apparent reason, Jehan smiled. Her torturer looked at her, not knowing why she should react like that.

'You're wrong ... I've already ... set myself free ... with my voice ... and my words ...' she whispered, looking up at him. Jehan felt reborn, finding inner peace at last after all these years of suffering.

'If you're free, then why can't you stop me from doing this?' said Nafridos as he crushed her hand with his foot, using his whole weight. Jehan screamed. Her body shook violently, but she was held in place by the wooden posts. Nafridos heard the bones inside her frail hand crack as he stamped on it.

'This is only the beginning; by the end you'll be begging me to kill you. So why waste my time? I'll ask you one last time: what did the princess give you? If you tell me now, I will set you free to live out your miserable existence.'

'My lord, here's the informant,' interrupted the soldier, pushing her in front of him. Nafridos looked at her. Like all men, he hated traitors, even if they had provided him with valuable information.

'What happened? What did you see?' asked the Dark Warrior. She was youthful and striking, with smooth brown skin and short plaited hair, but her treachery made her appear grotesque to Nafridos.

'I never saw much, just that the princess gave her a letter. She took it and hid it beneath her gown,' the woman said, taking long deep breaths. Nobody wanted to stand in front of the Dark Warrior; in some ways he was more frightening than the Assyrian emperor because he lacked logic and reasoning.

'Who did she give it to?'

'No one; she took it home with her, my lord.'

'How do you know that?'

'I followed her, my lord. She doesn't live far from here.'

'Is that everything you know?'

'No. The princess asked about her grandson; I think she wanted him to take the letter somewhere.'

'He's … innocent …' moaned Jehan, using all the energy she had left. She opened her eyes crazily as if some spirit possessed her.

'No one's innocent in this world; the day we're born is the day we're destined to do evil,' said Nafridos. He looked at the informant with disgust; for some reason he felt that a woman betraying another woman was far worse than a man betraying a man, but right now he needed her to lead them to the boy. 'You'll take us to her grandson. If you try to mislead us you'll join them both in the afterlife.'

'I won't fail you,' she said, kneeling and kissing his feet. She was just grateful that they had not killed her. Of course, there was no guarantee they would not do so at a later stage; she knew that the only way to escape their brutal hands was to lead them to the boy. And, like any traitor, she had no second thoughts about the well-being of others, even if the person being hunted was but an innocent child.

50

'What's the matter with your robes now? I see no fleas upon them,' the Grand Priest of Ursar puffed with irritation. He did not know what was worse – waiting for their fate to be revealed or having to spend another second with the nauseating King of Aram. *Give me patience before I lose my calm with this idiotic buffoon ...*

'The gods have cursed me with a blasted sweat. I wouldn't wish this wretched curse on my worst enemy, including you,' King Nelaaz howled. Even his scalp seemed to sweat. He scratched his head and looked at his fingertips, picking out the white bits that stuck beneath his nails. The Grand Priest placed a handkerchief over his mouth and shut his eyes; he could not bear to watch the ghastly sight of the king picking at his flaking scalp; it made his stomach heave. Fortunately for the Grand Priest of Ursar, he would not have to endure it for much longer. Both of them had noticed the young Priest of Xidrica walking towards them – hopefully, bringing with him some favourable news. Whatever the news, their destiny had at last been sealed.

'Where have you been? If you had taken any longer, the war would have been fought and lost by now,' said the Grand Priest of Ursar, watching him walk back slowly as if he were some kind of passing shadow. They could only guess at the outcome; it did not help that the young priest wore a blank and empty expression, with a hint of disappointment. The truth was, he felt used, like a sacrificial goat, in pursuit of their interests, and because of this he felt ashamed of what he had become.

'Well, what did the Gallant Warrior say?' asked King Nelaaz, shooing away his servants.

'Everything and nothing,' said the Priest of Xidrica dejectedly. His eyes fell to the mosaic floor as if they were lost in memories.

'What does that mean?' said the king.

'Be quick, your patience serves no one but you,' said the Grand Priest, demanding an answer with no hidden meanings.

'Yes, put us out of our blasted misery, we've been waiting in the sun for hours; if it weren't for my sweat cooling me down I'd have roasted like a pheasant,' said King Nelaaz as he staggered, with difficulty, to his feet.

'Your misery is nothing compared to what Marmicus endures because of you – remember that,' snapped the Priest of Xidrica. All they seemed to think about was themselves, nothing more.

'Well, what did the Gallant Warrior say?'

'He said forgiveness is but a word, and he grants it to you for the sake of the people. So there's no reason for your betrayal to torment you any longer, King of Aram. You finally have what you desired: the gods have spared you from shame, but as a friend to Marmicus I feel it's only right to tell you that it has come at a great cost to him. Not only has he had to sacrifice his ideals, he's had to bury his dignity along with them.'

'Forgiveness is all I wished for,' said King Nelaaz. Even though he felt a release of tension in his neck, he remained stricken with a guilty conscience. He had thought that his pledge would remove his feelings of guilt; truthfully, it did nothing but reinforce his deceitful nature.

'And you, oh great scholar, you're free to call upon the kings of Babylon and do whatever you wish with the Counsel. Whatever command you choose to make, the Gallant Warrior will follow and uphold it. Power means nothing without purpose. I just hope that the purpose is one that serves the interests of us all, not only you.'

'It will,' replied the Grand Priest of Ursar, acknowledging that he had been given real power.

'If only you knew the gravity of your actions,' said the young priest, ready to walk away.

'Why are you so against the idea of uniting Babylon? It's a wise idea, isn't it?' asked King Nelaaz. He was beginning to distrust his own idea; the young priest's hesitation was enough to induce reluctance in anyone.

'A good idea? You've plunged this kingdom into a war that's now far deadlier than it initially was. If the armies of Babylon unite but don't win, there'll be nothing left of the city of Babylon but the dust fallen from its demolished walls. Jaquzan wants just this kingdom; this land possesses the spirit of the gods, and that's why he wants to destroy it. He never had his heart set on Babylon, but now it's his for the taking. Everything that is Babylonian will become Assyrian. We'll watch our future become our history, and our present become our past. I've followed your orders to the letter, but I'll take no more part in destroying Babylon. I've already done my fair share to destroy it.' The young priest was astounded by his own stupidity. He looked at the king, waiting for a response, but none came. King Nelaaz had learnt that sometimes the best answer was silence, and so the chubby king remained silent.

51

Paross heard men's voices outside his house; he ran through the small courtyard that led to the front door and placed his ear against the wooden door, hoping that he would recognise the voices, but he didn't. His grandmother had told him not to open the door to anyone, not even the neighbour's children. Paross ran back through the courtyard and up the spiral staircase; the only safe way to know who was outside was to see them from the roof. He opened the door and shooed the chickens away. They always ran to him whenever they saw him, since he was the one who fed them in the mornings. Finally, he looked over the wall. To his horror, he saw Assyrian soldiers everywhere. They had gathered around his house with their horses.

'Burn it to the ground,' said Nafridos, seeing the boy's face appear.

Paross heard a loud thud downstairs, and looked over the wall. The soldiers were throwing burning missiles through the open windows of his house. Then he heard what sounded like a rush of air above his head and looked up to see something falling from the sky. Instantly he ran, kicking the chickens out of his way and wrenching the door open as he tried to escape whatever was heading towards him. Arrows thudded into the roof, narrowly missing him and killing the two chickens nearest to him. Not knowing what to do, Paross stumbled down the stairs, his hands reaching out as he tried to make his way through the dense smoke. He could barely see through it. He ran into the bedroom and crawled beneath his bed. Whenever he was scared he would hide there and wait for his grandmother to pick him up after he had fallen asleep. Paross shouted for help as parts of the roof crumbled and fell around him. His lungs felt tight, as he inhaled thick smoke and dust. If the soldiers didn't kill him, then the fire certainly would. Paross closed his eyes and waited for his grandmother to reappear, like she always did. Then by some miracle he heard her voice; she was calling out his name. He opened his eyes, not knowing if it was really her outside – or his imagination. Another loud thud came, and this time a whole section of the roof crashed down into the next room; his home was ready to collapse. Paross let out a loud scream; he kicked his heels into the ground, feeling completely helpless. He didn't want to die here, all alone, but he was too afraid to leave his bed.

'Paross, Paross!' yelled a voice from outside.

It was his grandmother's voice again; this time he knew it was real, and she was outside waiting for him. He took a deep breath and crawled out from beneath his bed. With his small hands he covered his head and ran towards the faint light that came from the windows. Just as he was about to leave, he remembered something. There was little time left; he had to get out before the house collapsed on him. He threw his pillow aside and grabbed the papyrus, remembering everything his grandmother had told him. *Find a merchant who will take you to the Garden of the Gods, and deliver the letter to a woman who bears the name Sulaf. She'll know exactly who to give it to. Whatever happens, don't return to this kingdom. I'll be waiting for you in spirit in the Garden of the Gods.*

Summoning all his courage, the little boy placed the papyrus in his pocket, and ran towards the front door, ready to face the men who were waiting outside.

∽

A thick cloud of rippling smoke rushed into the air, and searing flames soared higher into the night sky – sharp, dancing daggers that probed the heavens. Paross looked at his grandmother. The Assyrians had brought her along with them; her eyes were swollen and bruised, as were her arms and legs. She had been cruelly beaten. Paross held her hand tightly, and together they watched their home burn to the ground; everything that had value for them was slowly turning to charcoal, and by morning would be reduced to ash.

'Grandma, wake up. I'm scared; please wake up.'

'Don't be afraid, I'm here,' Jehan said, trying to open her eyes.

Deep down, she knew she could not protect him from the savages that surrounded them; all she could do was lie to him and tell him that everything was going to be fine. Jehan reached out and touched his face. She looked at him, remembering her daughter's face. He looked so much like her: so innocently beautiful and too good for the world they lived in. Paross had large brown eyes and a snub nose, common in any child his age, but he was smaller than most eight year olds. He hated being small; he wanted to feel like a man, especially since he looked after his grandmother. She had always said that when he reached the age of twelve he would shoot up and become tall like his father. It made Paross look forward to his twelfth birthday.

'Rope her and throw her into the fire. Let her scream for her freedom just like she promised us she would,' said the Dark Warrior, the red flames painting his face the colour of blood. Paross yelled and clung to her, hoping somehow that he could protect her body from them.

'It's time to let go,' said Jehan, hugging him. 'Be brave like your mother.'

'Don't leave me, I won't let you die,' said Paross, kissing her. Even though he did not want to admit it, even to himself, he was saying goodbye.

'Be brave for me,' she said again.

Paross screamed as the Assyrian soldiers moved in and grabbed her; he tried to fight them off, but he couldn't. They pulled him away and made him watch as they strung his grandmother's wrists and ankles together with a thick rope as if she were an animal. The only person who could possibly stop this madness was the man who had ordered them to throw her into the fire. Paross looked at the Dark Warrior; he sat on his horse, smiling as he watched. Paross ran to him; a courageous act for such a small boy.

'Make them stop! Please make them stop!'

Paross kissed his feet and clung to them; he looked up, hoping that the man would offer his grandmother mercy. Nafridos remained silent for a moment, then his lips curled.

'Only a boy of courage would dare kiss the feet of a man who's murdered men ten times his size; you have my respect for that. What's your name, boy?'

'Paross.'

'Then wipe away your tears, Paross, and give me your hand,' said Nafridos as he dismounted from his horse. He took the little boy's hands, opening them out, and looked at them for a moment. They were small compared to his brutish fists. His men had all noticed the connection he had made with the little boy; it was unique for Nafridos, and rather extraordinary. They walked together towards the fire; a surge of bright sparks flew into the air.

'Do you love your grandmother?'

'Yes, she's all I have.'

'So you would do anything to save her?'

'Yes, anything!' cried the little boy, looking up at the man who offered him some hope.

'Then she will be spared, but only if you can prove your courage to me like you did before.'

'I will,' cried the little boy. Tears rolled down his cheeks. He quickly wiped them away and looked up. Nafridos turned, and ordered his soldiers to untie the rope around Jehan's feet; it was his way of persuading the little boy to trust him.

'Have you ever played with fire?'

'No,' said the boy.

'There's a game I used to play when I was your age. All you have to do is stretch open your hands like this, and stand in front of the fire for as long as I can hold my breath. If you can keep them there for longer than I can hold my breath, then you've proved your bravery, and your grandmother will remain alive.'

'But my hands will burn,' said Paross, looking at the flames; he could feel the intense heat from where he stood.

'Saving a life takes strength; you can either be brave like a warrior, and take the pain like a man, or you can turn away like a coward and watch your grandmother die. It's up to you.'

Paross looked at his grandmother, uncertain what to make of the Dark Warrior's game. The heat was ferocious; it left his skin sore. He could barely endure its wrath from where he stood, so how would he be able to stand so close to it, and for an indefinite time? Ultimately, he knew he could not live with himself if he did not try to save his grandmother's life and, like any brave soul, he took his first steps towards the fire, wishing that the gods would bestow upon him the courage he needed.

⁙

The midnight winds grew stronger, causing the fire to grow into gigantic fireballs; the closer Paross got to the raging fire, the more bitter his saliva became. It was as if he were chewing and swallowing a lemon pip. Unbeknown to him, his lungs were filling with toxic gases that ran into his bloodstream. Paross felt light-headed and dizzy; every breath he inhaled drew in more poisonous fumes.

'Show me your courage, and in return, I'll show your grandmother my mercy,' yelled the Dark Warrior from a distance. He watched the little boy descend towards the inferno, the outline of his small body flickering in the intensity of the flames.

Finally, the child reached the place where he had been told to stand. Paross stretched out his hands towards the mountain of flames; they were ready to roast like skewers of meat. Raising his arm into the air, Nafridos signalled for his heartless game to commence and took in what appeared to be a deep breath.

'Don't hold your breath for too long, Commander; he'll be a pile of ash by the time you finish,' the soldiers laughed. They all knew from experience that the Dark Warrior was breathing through his nose.

Paross began praying to the gods to bless him with the endurance and strength he needed to win the game. He coughed loudly as the smoke blew in the wind, blackening his face and burning his nostrils. Paross closed his eyes, his hands trembling in agony. He could feel the skin melting; he desperately fought against his instincts, wanting to keep them in place. He knew if he pulled his hands back, his grandmother would die, and he would be unable to live with the guilt. The only way to make it through this battle of endurance was to let the pain out. Paross screamed and stamped his feet. He could not take the agony; every second that passed was more torture. Blisters began to form on his hands. The agony was unbearable. His mind and body told him to pull his hands away, and each time he was about to, he remembered his grandmother lying, half-conscious, on the ground. He could not let her die, not when he had the power to save her. The Assyrian soldiers watched, some feeling nothing, others feeling emotions they thought had died long ago. Either way, the boy was truly brave, and for that he had won their respect.

'He truly loves her,' said one Assyrian soldier to another.

Paross fought on; his fingers swelled up as his blood boiled beneath the surface of his skin. He opened his eyes to see excruciating blisters the size of cardamom seeds on his palms. They were bursting, and it felt as though his skin was being smothered with lava then lashed off with a whip made from thorns. Eventually, the pain was too much for Paross to endure. He abruptly pulled his hands away from the fire, and fell to the ground, weeping; he had failed to save his grandmother from her killers.

'I thought you were a courageous man; now I see you're nothing more than a pathetic boy. Throw her into the fire!' Nafridos roared. His top lip lifted in a snarl, revealing his gums and teeth. Any kindness that had briefly appeared on his face had completely vanished, as if it had never been present.

'No!' Paross yelled.

'Throw him too – let his innocence light up the darkness!' said the Dark Warrior as he remounted his stallion and galloped away, leaving the soldiers to fulfil their orders without him.

'Stay with me!' Paross cried, reaching for his grandmother. His eyes widened in horror as he watched two Assyrian soldiers lift her and carry her in the direction of the fire. They swung her from side to side, and in one single action, they released their grip, throwing her into the mountain of fire. Paross screamed as he saw his grandmother being flung into the fire as if she were nothing more than a piece of firewood. Her eyelids remained closed; she was now, mercifully, in a state of unconsciousness. Paross ran to the fire, hoping he could pull her out, but he was powerless; she lay asleep on the burning wood, until eventually she disappeared in the smoke.

'Let me kill the boy! I want to be the one who throws him into the fire,' said an Assyrian soldier to the rest of his companions. He grabbed Paross, who had refused to move from the bonfire. Paross did nothing. He was in shock, completely unable to comprehend what had just happened. Fortunately for Paross, not all of the soldiers had lost their humanity.

'Listen to me now,' said the soldier. 'I'm going to let you go, but you've got to run away as fast as you can, because if you don't they're going to catch you and they'll kill you. Do you understand?' Paross was staring straight ahead, blank and heedless, and the soldier tapped his face as though to wake him.

Paross nodded, looking at him.

'Then go! Run, boy, run as fast as you can, and don't look back.'

Paross did exactly what he was told. He ran for his life and he did not look back for a second. At one point he thought he could hear his grandmother calling out to him, but he kept running. Adrenaline rushed through his veins, numbing the pain in his swollen and blistered hands and instilling power into his tiny legs. Behind him, the orange fire that was so brilliantly alight slowly faded, until eventually there was only darkness. Paross kept running until the dawn arrived, and all the while he remembered his grandmother, and everything she had told him before she had died, and how he had to be brave like his mother. He took the papyrus from his pocket and held it in his hands. His journey to reach the Garden of the Gods would become a great battle of endurance, and he would do it all for his grandmother, who had given him the love of the mother who had died when he was too young to remember her.

52

'From my womb I give you life. From my heart I give you love. From my soul I give you all I that I have,' Larsa softly sang. It was a lullaby that her mother used to sing to her when she was a child. Her mother's gentle voice soothed her to sleep like the fine strings of a Babylonian harp played into the late hours of the night. Larsa intended to do the same for her infant – if freedom should ever return to bless her. With each new morning she could feel her body physically changing: day by day, her womb was rounding. Larsa placed her hands upon her belly, and slid them down, feeling its shape. Her belly even felt heavier. The subtle change was only noticeable to her: even so, it filled her with joy to know that her infant was growing stronger, and every time her womb grew a little bigger, she felt reassured that her baby was healthy. Larsa had also noticed her emotions changing; most nights she felt suicidal, but since her baby had grown stronger, she had begun to feel inexplicable bursts of happiness. She closed her eyes, and imagined watching Marmicus hold his son or daughter in his arms; she envisioned him smiling as his baby's tiny hands wrapped around his finger.

'You've got a beautiful voice.'

Larsa opened her eyes. A long face with a crooked nose poked through the door. Larsa recognised him as one of the Assyrian soldiers who had attacked her Royal Caravan in the desert; it was the same guard who waited by her door each night.

'Won't you sing me a little song of my own? I'm in need of some entertainment,' said the guard as he entered the room. He placed his sword on the table, his crooked nose twitching.

'You're not allowed in here,' Larsa said, standing.

'You're right, but who's watching? Go on, sing for me,' he said, walking to her. He had always been tempted to enter her room, and had controlled himself until now, but with her beautiful voice he could resist no longer.

'Get out of here before I scream,' Larsa said, rushing to the door. He ran after her, determined to stop her leaving the prison chamber. Larsa kicked him back, but he quickly grabbed her, and threw her against the table. Larsa felt a sharp pain in her stomach: she immediately thought of her baby. He had cornered her against the table. 'Go on, sing me a song.'

'I wouldn't do that if I were you,' said Larsa, and her hands stretched behind her back then reappeared.

'Why not?'

'Because I have your sword,' she smiled.

53

The powerless princess had been transformed into an opponent of unexpected potency. Larsa realised she had one chance to take vengeance. The guard looked behind at the door, and thought about running. Larsa shook her head, and pushed the tip of the sword into his throat: if she pushed it any deeper, it would certainly wound him.

'Don't be foolish. I may be a woman but I possess the hatred of any man.'

She glared at the guard with sheer disgust for what he was, a vile creature who bullied her into entertaining him. The tables had been turned.

'My father was right; temptation is the first spark of sin. Perhaps if you hadn't been so tempted to touch me, I wouldn't have your life in my hands.'

'I wasn't going to touch you. I just wanted a song, nothing else.'

Larsa began to laugh, so hard so that her cheeks went red; she had so much anger built up inside her that the only way she could express it was through laughter; it felt as though any other way would destroy her.

'Look, if you let me go, I'll help you,' said the guard, lifting his hands up, fearing that she had lost her mind. 'The palace is filled with guards – you can't escape. The truth is, you're never going to leave this place, unless as a corpse. But if you let me go, I'll help you.'

'Do you really think death frightens me? I've stared into death's eyes, and I've seen more humanity lying within them than in the eyes of men. Death is a friend to me: it is the ripeness of the apple when everything else has withered. Now, take me to your emperor,' said Larsa. She tightened her grip on the heavy weapon and stared, unblinking, into the guard's eyes.

'What if I don't?'

'Then love death just as I've learnt to love it; for it shall be *your* corpse that's taken out to be buried in the morning,' replied the princess.

At last, she would have the opportunity to kill her greatest enemy and save her kingdom from the barbarity of his wretched war!

54

The most dangerous of spirits is the one unafraid of death and willing to sacrifice life to achieve its ends. This is what had happened to Larsa; she had befriended death as though it were her companion in life. Larsa followed the guard out of the prison quarters into unknown territory: she had been caged there for so long that she felt like a bird that had forgotten how to fly. It felt strange and unnatural to be walking where her consciousness commanded her; the prison chamber had in a sense become her home. Larsa looked up. The Assyrian palace was gigantic; it was similar in size to the Temple of Ishtar, which had been created for thousands to worship, unlike this palace, which served the pleasure of only one man. The stone corridor they followed seemed to carry on forever, and she was impatient; she needed to face Jaquzan. It meant more to her than anything else; motherhood, for the moment, could wait. Jaquzan had taken so much from her: his death would restore to her the life and dignity she had once possessed.

'I told you, you won't get far,' said her captive.

Soldiers ran towards them, encircling her and her prisoner. Larsa looked at them, remaining calm despite being completely surrounded.

They made a human wall, encircling her as a ring encircles a finger. She was trapped, but unafraid of the arrows pointing at her chest. The Assyrian emperor had thought her perfect enough to bear his crown, and she knew she could not be harmed: her womb had given her prestige and power above all others; she must exploit it to her advantage.

'Lightning is never far from thunder; whoever strikes me with their sword shall be struck by the emperor in anger. My soul belongs to him alone. If you kill me, then you dare to insult his authority and power,' declared Larsa.

'Ignore her words. She wants to kill our emperor. Kill her now!' yelled the captured guard.

'Choose wisely. If you kill me, you kill yourself.'

Realising her power, two soldiers stepped aside from the human wall, creating a small passage for the princess to pass through. She smiled, nudging her captive forward: she still needed him to lead her to the emperor's chamber. No one knew with certainty that her actions were the folly they appeared to be: but they would soon find out ...

Sulaf made her way towards the Gallant Warrior's chamber, her tall slender body walking past lofty white pillars and the endless number of guards who stood beneath them protecting the palace walls. They all watched her, but she ignored them as if they were stone statues collecting dust. Finally, the door she had been searching for appeared. She breathed in, then came a rush of self-belief.

'Open it, quickly,' she instructed, without thanking the guard who stood by it.

He nodded and pushed it open for her, watching her pass through.

⚜

'In every kingdom you'll find a palace and in every palace you'll find a struggle for power. Isn't that so?' she said loudly.

'Kingdoms may change in name, but human nature remains the same across all shores,' replied Marmicus. He turned, surprised to see Sulaf, who had not informed him of her visit.

'Then we've agreed on something at last.' Sulaf gave a false smile, then paused. 'I'm glad you're here. I wanted to speak to you about what happened.'

'There's no need to talk about what happened,' Marmicus replied. 'It's in the past. Today is all that matters, not what has happened in the past.'

She did not want to hear his polite dismissal; it would only make her feel worse. And she knew she could not face another rejection; it would be like a knife in her heart.

'Well, it's good to see you,' he said. 'The smile of a loyal friend is always a blessing in cruel times.'

'Friendship is never free from expectation, you understand that more than me. We both know that a person who offers loyalty to another is always in need of something in return.'

'If that's true, what do you want from me?'

'What I want from you has no significance for the fate of our kingdom. The question is, what do the kings of Babylon want from you? I hear they've gathered in our kingdom, no doubt sipping wine at the expense of our people.'

'Who told you that?' asked Marmicus, curious. He suspected everyone of treachery now.

'You forget that the people have eyes and ears too, Marmicus. When a king enters a kingdom it's only a blind man who can't see his endless train of horses and slaves walking behind him,' said Sulaf, staring at him. He looked healthier than when she had last seen him; it was as if he had come to accept his loss. It pleased her to see this; it meant that his heart was ready to heal, and to accept another. 'So why have the kings of Babylon come here? Are they offering their allegiance to us?'

'Kings never offer allegiance; they offer what is in their interests only. They toss their armies into battle like pebbles thrown into the river, for more land and power. That's why they're here, so they can bargain over what's left of our enemy's kingdom.'

Marmicus clenched his jaw. The cold breath of war was never far from him; wherever he went it followed him.

'Then it's up to you to safeguard the people's interests when you're in their presence. Remember, you are the voice of the voiceless and the hope of the hopeless. If you speak for the people, you can ensure balance in the affairs of selfish men. Be the leader you were born to be,' said Sulaf. She walked to him, hesitantly at first. Her desire for him drove her to the depths of madness, but she would always force herself to journey back to sanity. The boy who had once loved her was still trapped in there somewhere; she just needed to find him, and release him from his imprisonment.

'I'm only one man, Sulaf. I can't change the world if it's unwilling to change,' he said, looking into her eyes. Sulaf knew he needed her, and for the first time she wanted to reassure him without any agenda of her own.

'You're not one man, Marmicus. In you lies the admiration of thousands. If you wished the day to turn into night, the people would raise their shields to the sky to cover the sunlight for you: can't you see that kings are powerless when they stand beside you? You wear the crown of the people's love upon your head, when they don't.' Sulaf pressed her palm to his cheek with a hunger that was urgent and irrepressible. She needed him to believe her. If he did not, there was no hope left of them winning this war. 'Believe me when I say this: one day, all of mankind shall know your name, and the gods will envy you because of it. This war has been destined for you, and nothing on earth can move you from the path you were born to tread. Embrace it so that your destiny can pay homage to you.'

'I don't need the gods to envy me or destiny to bow before my feet; I just need a sword to claim my vengeance.'

She could see his anger in his eyes for what had been wrongfully taken from him.

'Then let your vengeance be the gift you offer to your people in this war.' Sulaf stepped back; she had done her duty as a friend, now she needed to free herself from the one man that had unknowingly ensnared her.

'You asked me what I wanted from you. Do you want to know the answer?' Sulaf asked, walking towards the door. She wanted to leave; it was not like her to give in to her emotions, but she no longer had the energy to fight in silence.

'Yes.'

'I want to be free from you, so that I can live again. I know you can't offer me the love I need – I understand this bitter truth – but if I stay here, I'll die.'

'What are you saying?'

Marmicus looked at her, not knowing what she meant; her

feelings of rejection had obviously crushed her more than he had imagined. Marmicus sincerely wished that he could give her what she wanted – but he could not.

'My father was right,' she said. 'Even love can turn to poison, and it seems that I've been drinking from its deadly chalice all these years. That's why I've got to go. It's time I saved myself because, if I don't, who will?'

She pushed the door open, and looked back, not knowing if this was the last time she would see him.

'Where are you going, Sulaf?'

'A place where I can find my freedom. Don't worry, I'm a strong woman. I have fought many battles. Just because I don't carry a sword it doesn't mean I haven't won them.'

Sulaf closed the door behind her, ready to make her journey to the Black Mountain in search of the oracle. Even though she wore no shackles around her wrists, she had been enslaved by unrequited love. Sulaf knew that if she did nothing to save herself, she would eventually die from the weight of her broken heart.

55

Larsa knew she was close to the emperor's chamber; she could see it
in the guard's face; he was more fearful of entering it than the tip
of the sword that was held against his neck. The long corridor opened
up into a huge space; the ceiling soared and the walls immediately
widened. Larsa felt dizzy and lost in this empty space; she knew from
that moment that she had finally entered the emperor's abode. It
occurred to her that whatever danger she encountered now, so too
did her unborn infant, and together they entered the lion's den with
only a sword to protect them from harm. Larsa looked around her.
On one side of the chamber was a gigantic wall with a large carving
that had been intricately painted. It told the sacred story of creation,
but from Jaquzan's perspective. Larsa looked at it. She saw the sacred
twin rivers, the Euphrates and the Tigris, which joined together;
sailing upon the river was a royal boat belonging to none other than
the Assyrian emperor, and across the river was a huge fishing net,
bulging with the catch. Larsa squinted. Looking more carefully, she
noticed that the net was filled, not with fish, but with the heads of
kings and queens. Larsa looked at them with disgust, wondering if
a likeness of her own head would be carved into the wall should

she fail to kill Jaquzan. She carried on walking, reaching a second carved story that spoke of the Fertile Crescent; like the first painting, the second revealed a distorted tale of creation, with the mountains appearing in the form of Assyrian winged bulls, and the land being ploughed by the emperor himself. He rode a chariot pulled by lions and in his hand was a bow, from which flew hundreds of arrows, as if to imply that he had sent the blessing of rain to nourish the dry land, turning it fertile once again. Larsa looked away, unable to stomach the sight of one man's self-glorification. Suddenly, she heard a strange noise, as though from the throat of some unearthly creature. Perhaps she was imagining things? She ignored it and instructed the guard to walk on.

The walls and floor seemed to stretch away to nothingness on all sides so that it became impossible to focus. It was as if there was some kind of magic present. There was a subtle movement of some kind in the background. The guard was completely oblivious to it, and Larsa thought it best to say nothing. On one wall was a set of swords aligned row on row like pieces of art. Strangely, Larsa had noticed that the hilts were not engraved with Jaquzan's name.

'Whose are they?' she asked, peering at the array of weapons that stretched across the wall.

'They're the emperor's trophies. Every time he triumphs in battle he takes the sword of the fallen king and puts it here. Each one represents their fight, each one their annihilation. I've never seen them before, but everyone knows about them.'

As the princess peered at the swords, she could almost feel the blades slice her skin. Larsa secretly feared that the Gallant Warrior's Sword of Allegiance would end up here and, if it did, she would use it to kill herself.

'It's an unholy cenotaph,' Larsa whispered, looking at the endless rows of weaponry. Her reflection was mirrored in them. They were all magnificent in their own way, some possessing golden pommels and quillions, while others were made from the strongest iron.

'You could say that.'

A piercing roar shook the room; the guard heard it this time. He turned around to see what lurked behind him, and as he did so he felt a slight prick on his neck where the tip of the weapon had scraped his skin. He stared. All this time he had been worrying about the blade pointed at his neck, when there was far greater danger lurking behind him.

Larsa could not believe her eyes. She had heard stories of such creatures, but she had never seen one in the flesh. Two lions sat on either side of the emperor's large divan, their honey-coloured eyes fixed on these intruders who had entered their realm, bringing with them the smell of fresh meat and awakening their hunting instinct. Larsa lowered her sword in respect. This was not the time to be bold – the wild lions were free to do as they chose; no rope held them back. But they simply stared with curiosity at the two feeble creatures before them. The guard covered the scrape along his neck with his hand, hoping to stem the bleeding, but the scent of blood was enough to bring from the lions a low, throaty growl.

'What do we do?' he whispered.

'Stand still, don't move.' Larsa lowered her eyes to the floor in an effort to compose herself. Her father had spoken of these creatures; and now she needed to remember every single word he had said, if she was to survive.

'Be wise, my dear child, and never look into the eyes of the mighty lion; you'll only regret it,' King Alous had said, handing his daughter a small wooden carving of a lion. He had made it especially for her; the wood had been taken from the finest willow tree in the neighbouring kingdom, from where he had recently returned.

'Why mustn't I look into them, Father?' Larsa had asked as she sat on his lap. The sun's glorious rays had streaked her hair with golden tones. She loved the stories her father told her; they were so exciting and filled to the brim with adventure.

'Because if you look into a lion's eyes you'll reveal everything about yourself to him. You see, a lion's very clever, Larsa, and more than that, he's cunning. Before a lion attacks he tests his prey; he stares into his victim's eyes, wanting to know more about who is standing before him. If they don't move, and stand firm in their place, the lion then will give a ferocious roar, designed to intimidate. But if his prey continues to show no fear and stands still, he will turn away with respect for such a creature. So, never turn your back on a lion. It would be an insult to a beast that prides itself on honour and glory.'

Larsa's eyes froze and her mouth opened. She was fascinated by his story; she had never seen a lion. Of course, later her father regretted telling her that story; she suffered nightmares, imagining that lions were chasing her within the castle.

Who could have imagined that her nightmares would become reality?

Time has a way of pausing when the soul finds itself in mortal danger; all that can be felt are one's human senses, while the world moves on, oblivious. Even though Larsa was unafraid of death, she had never imagined standing between two fully grown lions. Both beasts sat up and sniffed the air; they grunted as the subtle smell of blood and flesh roused them from their sluggishness. The larger lion stood, and moved closer, head lowered as though stalking, its muscles rippling beneath sand-coloured fur, coiled like a spring. Larsa understood why her father had told her to respect these creatures; she could see the power and strength in their bodies in the way they moved. Their golden manes were like a ring of fire burning fiercely around their faces.

'Enough of this – give me that sword,' said the guard, snatching the weapon from her. The abrupt action triggered a violent reaction in the larger lion, which roared and swung its enormous head, revealing black lips and sharp canines. This was his territory and – like any predator – he would dictate what happened within it.

'Don't move – it will anger them.'

'You can stay here for all I care, I'm leaving,' said the guard, turning to go. It was a mistake. He had aroused the lion's hunting instinct. Its honey-coloured eyes followed him and it gave another savage roar, but the guard broke into a run. Larsa noticed the muscles on the back legs of the animal were rippling and twitching; he was in hunting mode. Larsa's first instinct was to shout a warning, but it would only turn the predator's attention to her. In an act of selfishness, she chose to remain silent. The lion leapt into the air, charging towards the guard as though hunting an antelope on the open plain, his muscular legs pushing him forward at astonishing speed. The guard turned back and as he did so, he saw the lion twist slightly in mid-air, and his claws extend from his massive paws, ripping into his shoulder. The guard gave a screech as he felt the razor-sharp claws ripping through the muscles of his shoulder and chest.

'Get him off me! Quickly, get him off!' the guard screamed, trying to fight but pinned to the floor by the lion's immense weight. Blood gushed from the man's face as the lion's sharp teeth tore through his skin and bit into his feeble neck. In seconds his windpipe would be crushed or his neck broken. The second lion lunged, intent on scavenging. Bloodcurdling screams echoed across the chamber. Larsa could only imagine the agonies the guard suffered as the second lion dug his claws into his leg and bit into his calf.

'Give me the sword! The sword!' pleaded the guard, his voice almost lost in a muted gurgle.

Larsa moved in to kick it to him, but the moment she reacted the lions turned towards her. Their blood-stained muzzles crinkled as they each gave a savage roar – a warning not to interfere. Larsa staggered back; she closed her eyes, trying to block out the grotesque sight. The lions were clawing at the guard, tearing his limbs and shaking him like a rag doll. Eventually the gargling noises stopped, only to be replaced by the sound of bones splintering. The lions chewed on his limbs, tearing away the flesh until the brown muscles were exposed, and finally the white bones of the soldier's rib cage.

'It's never wise for a lioness to be in the company of two lions; she may unleash war between them.'

The Assyrian emperor had entered his chamber, and was surprised to see that the princess was still alive. He was glad all the same, for now she was at the mercy of a greater predator than the lions …

56

The kings of Babylon had assembled in their hour of great uncertainty; collectively, the fate of their kingdoms was under threat by the coming of the Assyrian army. If the Garden of the Gods fell, then all the provinces of Babylonia would certainly follow suit. The only possible solution was to join forces so they could increase their chances of survival. However, these were men who had fought each other for years; their first instinct was to distrust one another. The only reason they had accepted the invitation was because they had been summoned by the Gallant Warrior, who had helped them individually, advising them and offering his Sword of Allegiance whenever the cause was worthy. It was clear that only he had the power to unite them, but Marmicus remained silent. He watched them sitting together, dressed in their formal attire, representing their kingdoms and their gods, their extravagant headpieces bearing the symbols of their land, and their long black beards braided with gold and silver. The Grand Priest of Ursar led the discussions in the palace gardens. It was obvious he was enjoying the moment: it was affirmation of the power he had always wanted.

'Let's not delude ourselves, great kings of Babylon; the time has come for war. If we do not join forces now, all that will be left of your kingdoms will be the relics of your gods. I call upon you to join us. Let our swords and arrows be unleashed together so that the mighty gates of Babylon can shine in the light they scatter. Let today be a day of proclamation, where we resolve to fight not alone, but together, as brethren, our victory shared between us and the stories of our triumph told for a thousand years. Only the gods can judge us, for we are men of stature. The events of today have been predestined by the gods; so let the people do what is expected of them and fight for their leaders in the hour we call upon them. Their deaths will guarantee your lives. If we win this war, Assyria will fall, and the lands that come with it shall be split equally between you all. The spoils of this war are great indeed.'

Marmicus watched the Grand Priest enjoy the attention. He had intended to stay for the whole discussion, but he could not stomach the Grand Priest's arrogance.

Marmicus got up abruptly. 'Forgive me, I must attend to the preparations for war,' he said, storming off.

The kings of Babylon looked after him in surprise. They said nothing, but his departure left them hesitant. They needed him to lead their armies. Without him, the venture was suicide, and they all knew it.

'Your vision is a great one,' said King Salazar. 'No king here can deny that it is in all our interests to unite and work together. But there's a flaw in your plan.' The king was staring at his finely engraved ring as if totally absorbed by the large blue stone inlaid within it. 'Even if all the kings of Babylon agree to your proposal, how can we be certain that Marmicus will care about our thrones or the splitting of power? All he wants is vengeance. Without his commitment to the outcome you have so eloquently described, the doors of Babylon shall remain locked.'

The point raised by King Salazar was valuable and intelligent: while others thought of power and land, he thought of strategy and commitment.

'You make a valid point,' replied the Grand Priest of Ursar. He walked towards the stone statue of Ishtar that overshadowed every man sitting within the palace gardens. She watched them all with her magnetic, cat-like eyes. 'It's true that all Marmicus cares about is his vengeance, but that is precisely what we require of him. Never before have I seen one man carry such hatred for the world that his skin burns with rage. Although the princess's death was unfortunate, it has guaranteed our victory, for it has unleashed a fire within Marmicus that can only be extinguished by the beheading of our enemy.'

'So do we have your allegiance?' asked King Nelaaz of those assembled. He was responsible for contriving the master plan. His short legs swung in mid-air below his lofty chair. All those present looked at each other, waiting for someone to either approve or disapprove.

'You have my army and my allegiance,' said King Hasabi. He rose from the chair, took his royal ring from his finger and placed it in the centre of the stone table. The act was powerfully symbolic.

'I offer mine too,' declared another king, who copied his gesture.

The kings of Babylon rose, and one by one they placed their royal rings in the centre of the long stone table and returned to their seats. As they began to settle down, the Grand Priest of Ursar felt exhilarated. *Tonight the gardens of the palace are filled with the aroma of my victory*, he thought, admiring the beauty of the kingdom that was falling further under his command with each passing night.

57

The Assyrian emperor walked into his quarters. With every step closer to the princess, he appreciated more how steadfast she really was. She possessed an inner strength that could not be toppled or destroyed, no matter how many attacks were made upon it. Unlike other kings and queens, Larsa would not surrender to his power; instead she fought him, refusing to yield to his supremacy. She had empowered herself, when her predecessors had not.

'I've come for my freedom,' said Larsa. She reached for the sword and dragged it across the floor, ignoring the lions behind her. Incandescent sparks flew from the tip of the blade as it slid across the rough stone slabs; she wiped the guard's blood from her brow, and took her position, ready for combat.

'You speak as though you're a warrior.'

'I've become one.'

'Then killing a god shouldn't be difficult for you, should it?'

The Assyrian emperor walked to his collection of prized weapons. Jaquzan closed his eyes and ran his fingers over the hilts as he walked by them, searching for the right sword; the one that called out to him. He could feel the last traces of their energy running through his veins, as if they were pulling at the very core of his being. Finally, Jaquzan stopped in front of one. He opened his eyes, and as he did so his frosty expression altered. It was an unexpected choice.

Jaquzan wrapped his palm around the grip, and lifted it off the carved wooden cradle on which it rested. The reflection of the princess's face appeared in the long blade as though she had been painted onto it. He had chosen a sword like none other: it was beautiful, its metallic shine was like a stream of light, its weight was in perfect balance, and along its length were the words 'Shield of God'.

'Do you know who this sword belonged to?'

'Let me guess. It's another king you callously murdered in cold blood.'

'On the contrary – it's never been held by a mortal. It was made for a god, and now you'll understand why it carries such a name.'

Both lifted their weapons into the air, ignoring the roars of the lions in the background, and moved in a slow circle, their eyes locked on one another, every fibre of their beings prepared for mortal combat.

Larsa swirled the deadly sword above her head, her dark hair and bloodied dress twisting with her movements. Marmicus had taught her everything she needed to know about defence and swordsmanship; his training had made her a formidable opponent. Suddenly, Larsa heaved the sword, striking her blade against Jaquzan's with power and deadly accuracy, but the moment her blade touched his, she was doomed to defeat, for the Assyrian emperor had indeed chosen a weapon suited to a god. With this single touch, Larsa's sword shattered as if it were made of glass, and small metal pieces flew across the room like arrowheads; the hilt was all that remained in her hands. Larsa fell to the floor, her back soaked in the guard's blood and her hand numb from the force of the blow.

'You make a habit of error, princess; a slave can never conquer a god, just as the moon can never conquer the sun. This is the rule of law. Accept it, for you can never change it,' said Jaquzan, holding the sword to her neck.

'I would rather live in darkness for all eternity than accept the light cast from your tyranny,' said Larsa. No sword of god or mortal would silence her.

'I've offered you my light but you've shown me ingratitude time and time again. Now watch as your world falls into darkness.'

Jaquzan whistled softly. The larger lion rose to his feet and walked stealthily towards his master, the embodiment of strength and pride. The emperor had taught them the obedience of dogs. He stopped in front of the emperor, waiting for his master's instructions. Jaquzan pulled the princess closer. 'I know your instincts are urging you to hate me, just as his instincts are urging him to kill you, but a powerful soul is always in control of his instincts. Let me show you.'

He took the princess's hand, placing it directly underneath the lion's wide nose; Larsa flinched as she felt the warm vapour from his nostrils on her skin. The creature remained still, observing her distrustfully with his honey-coloured eyes. Her hand was in front of him; he could smell her skin, but still he remained motionless.

'Open your hand, let your mind become the master of your instincts.'

Larsa opened her hand, revealing to the animal the cut that ran across her palm. Every instinct implored her to pull her hand away, but she did not; despite herself, she wanted to prove her courage to the Assyrian emperor. The lion turned his head and sniffed at her skin; saliva dripped onto her hand. Jaquzan watched the princess tremble, and was impressed. Larsa had seen the same creature shred to pieces a fully grown man, and he could easily do the same to her, yet she remained unmoving, containing her fear. Jaquzan took hold of her hand again, raising it higher this time until her fingertips touched the lion's majestic mane. His coat was rougher than it looked. The mane ran around his head all the way down to his belly.

Larsa's breath quickened as she touched his head. This time, she tried to pull her hand away, but Jaquzan held it in place. With a gentle rhythmic motion, he drew her hand across the lion's mane, down towards the wide bridge of its nose. Clots of blood caught beneath her fingernails as her hand slid across the royal beast's face.

'You will never be more alive than you are now,' said Jaquzan, watching her. He began to walk back, leaving the princess alone with the lion. In a split second the creature reverted to instinct: he lifted his head and roared, revealing blood-stained teeth.

'Can you see how he's fighting his instincts? You are his gazelle, and if he so wished he could kill you in a moment.'

With no emotion, Jaquzan held out his hand. Larsa saw it from the corner of her eye and walked backwards very slowly; she knew she should not turn her back on the beast. Jaquzan stared into the lion's eyes and raised his hand; a silent command to remain where he was, and not to attack. The lion lowered his head and obediently returned to the carcass, knowing that this was a battle he could not win.

'If I was his gazelle, why didn't you let him kill me?' asked Larsa.

'Because some things are meant to be saved,' said Jaquzan, touching her cheek softly. He looked at her, feeling some distant relic of humanity stir within him. It was a strange sensation, and one that he knew, if left uncontrolled, would lead him to weakness.

Larsa turned her cheek away. Even though Jaquzan had spared her, she was disgusted by the act; she preferred it when he showed no emotion.

'So be it, princess. I see you desire death more than life – now I shall offer it to you.'

Suddenly, Jaquzan grabbed the princess's throat with great force. Larsa squirmed as he locked both hands around her neck, suffocating her.

58

'Please …' said Larsa, her voice coming in choking gasps. 'Release … me!'

She smacked her hand against his arm, trying to stop him from suffocating her, but Jaquzan continued to hold her. He lifted her up until her legs dangled in the air. Larsa fought for breath. Her mouth was wide open and she tried to suck in air, but it was no use. Jaquzan's hands were wrapped around her throat like an iron cord strung around her neck.

'Give me a reason to spare you,' said Jaquzan as he watched her consciousness slowly ebb away. Her rose-coloured lips turned blue. Her lungs were caving in inside her; it felt as if they were being beaten flat with a wooden mallet.

'Don't spare me. Spare … your … baby,' rasped Larsa. The veins in her eyes exploded. This was her last chance to live: it was now or never. Jaquzan released her, throwing her to the floor. She collapsed on her back, her lungs bursting with the oxygen that came flooding through her open mouth. She had bitten her tongue and she coughed so intensely that the blood flowed out between her lips.

'Love me as your god and I'll reward you with continued life,'

Jaquzan whispered as he knelt beside the princess. He moved her dark hair away from her face, and raised her chin so that she could look into his eyes. 'But if you should come to deny me again, then I shall rip out this infant that clings to your womb, and I will feed it to my cherished lions, for I fear this child may be as disobedient as its glorious mother.'

He rose from the floor and left her lying in overwhelming pain. Her eyes filled with tears, not because of the pain, but for the crime she had committed against Marmicus. *Oh, my love, forgive me for this act of betrayal; it was the only way to save our infant.*

59

'Here it is,' said the guide, hesitantly. He had taken Sulaf as far as his courage would allow him, and it was now up to her to make the rest of the journey alone. They both looked at the imposing mountain that lay in the distance. Sulaf noticed that all around the mountain there was vegetation, yet nothing seemed to grow on the mountain itself: perhaps the plants had either died in the harsh winter or were too afraid to blossom there.

'Can't you take me any closer?' asked Sulaf, squinting; the afternoon sun was still strong.

'My journey ends here.'

'Just take me a little closer. I'll give you this ring as extra payment; here, you can have it,' she said, struggling to take the gold ring from her finger. It was worth more than the journey itself. She looked at it, wishing she had something less sentimental to trade, but it was the only thing she possessed that could tempt him to accept her proposition. Her mother had given it to her before she died, and Sulaf had never taken it off since. Under it there was a white band where her skin had been shielded from the sun.

'Nothing you have can make me take a single step closer to that mountain. This is where my journey ends – at this spot.' He pointed downwards. Beside his left foot was a large stone which had been painted with a white cross.

Sulaf huffed, irritated by his stubbornness. He understood her frustration; everyone he brought out here reacted in the same way.

'You don't understand. I've come to see the oracle – she's the reason I'm here, and she lives up in that mountain.'

'Everyone who comes here is looking for her, and I always tell them the same thing: it's better to go back to where you came from than climb that mountain and find her. This place offers no blessings. If you plant a seed of hope here, it'll be eaten by the soil. And even if by some miracle it does manage to survive this place, it won't offer you fruit; it'll offer you poison. That mountain and that oracle are cursed. You should leave before you become part of the curse.'

'I won't turn back, not when I've come this far.'

'Why do women never listen?' the guide mumbled to himself. 'Everyone who comes here regrets the day they did, but they never listen to me. Never.' He returned to his camel, and unpacked the sack which carried Sulaf's belongings. He placed it on the ground at Sulaf's feet. 'Now I must go before the light fades. I'm offering you one last chance to come back with me.'

'I'll take my chances here.'

'Very well,' he said, disappointed by her decision. 'Then you should climb that mountain before the darkness falls. May the gods protect you – you'll need their guidance more than anyone.'

60

I *hope you were wrong about this place*, Sulaf thought, following the path up the mountain. Night had fallen; the moon sporadically appeared from behind the thick clouds, its misty light pouring down. The air was cold and damp. The guide's words resonated in her mind. She clutched the blazing torch above her head, raising it higher to guide herself through the rough wilderness of jagged stones and dead trees. She was not afraid of walking alone in the darkness – in fact, she was used to it – but this place was unlike anything she had encountered before. There was an unnatural silence; no birds sang, no trees rustled. It was as if nature itself was afraid to occupy this place. It occurred to Sulaf that if anything bad should happen to her, no one would know where to find her. She had hinted to Marmicus that she was embarking on a journey, but she had not told him precisely where she was going, or who she was intending to meet.

Sulaf sat down for a moment. The ground felt wet, but she needed a rest. Her feet were sore, so she took off her sandals and put them aside. Small blisters had appeared on her toes. She examined them, drawing the light closer, and warming her feet as she did so. Her shadow seemed to be her only companion in this forsaken place.

Sulaf looked around. There was nothing but dead trees and stone ruins – or so she believed.

But her presence had not gone unnoticed. She was being watched. The sound of twigs cracking behind her startled Sulaf, but she thought it was probably a small animal of some kind. The sound stopped, only to be replaced by something stranger; a barely-audible tapping. Sulaf had no idea what it was, until she felt a blunt pain on her back. Someone had thrown something at her – a pebble perhaps.

'Who's there? Keep away!' Sulaf exclaimed, straining her eyes to look among the trees. No one answered her. The trees began to move, though the wind had not grown any stronger. Sulaf heard a whistling sound, and the sound of human voices, coming from all sides, and she grabbed her bag, quickly untying it and pulling out a knife. She waved it around, hoping that it would frighten off whatever it was that was lurking beyond the light of the torch. It worked: the voices hushed and the branches stopped moving. Whatever it was had gone. Sulaf sat back down and put on her sandals. She thought everything had returned to normal, until she felt another thud on her back – another pebble. In a rush of panic Sulaf grabbed her bag and ran, trying to follow the path between jagged rocks and dead trees. The fiery torch flickered as she sprinted. A large root poked out of the wet ground; missing her footing, Sulaf stumbled, gasping as she twisted her ankle. A pain shot up her leg. Sulaf dropped the fiery torch, which rolled several paces until the wet soil extinguished the flames. Her only source of light had disappeared before her very eyes. Now she was completely alone in the darkness …

61

I t was virtually impossible to continue her journey without light. Sulaf could hardly see the back of her hand, let alone the stone path from which she had wandered. With no other option, Sulaf decided to stay where she was. She lay down on the uneven ground. It was damp, and her cotton shawl absorbed the moisture, making it extremely uncomfortable. She tried to sleep, but she kept thinking about everything the guide had said. He was clearly frightened by the mountain; she wondered what kind of stories he had heard. The more Sulaf thought about it, the more alarmed she became. She shook her head, trying to push out every scary thought. All she wanted was to fall asleep, but it was too cold. It was obvious that she was ill-prepared; if she had known that the guide would abandon her here, she would have thought twice about coming. Sulaf wished she had taken the sheepskin blanket, but it was too heavy so she had left it.

It was so cold. The chill winds climbed up the mountain, becoming stronger as the night passed. Her muscles tensed up; they felt hard, like blocks of ice, and she was shivering uncontrollably. Sulaf placed her goatskin bag beneath her head, using it as a pillow. 'Even love can turn to poison,' she murmured to herself. The words of her dead father echoed in her mind, for reasons she could not understand. Each word he spoke was like a knot in her throat being untangled and tugged at by her reason. Her only source of comfort was the knowledge that Marmicus would fall in love with her, thanks to the oracle's powers. Just as she drifted into the realm of sleep, a faint noise came from behind her – the sound of leaves being crushed underfoot. Sulaf wanted to turn around; she knew she should, but in the dark she lacked the courage. Instead she shut her eyes, closing them so tightly that it was painful. She hoped that, by ignoring the noise, it would disappear.

Sulaf remained still, every muscle in her body clenched like a rope being twisted to breaking point. She heard another movement, this time louder. And closer. Sulaf felt helpless. She could see nothing: even if she plucked up the courage to turn her head, she would not be able to see what was behind her. Her instincts were telling her to remain still; perhaps the presence would not see her and would disappear. Then she felt a warm tingling sensation that seemed to brush against her neck. It was someone's – or something's – breath.

Sulaf slowly turned her head, her heart pounding so violently that she felt a cramp in her chest. It was the last thing she had expected to see: standing next to her was a child no older than eight, watching her intently. Her skin was white, almost glowing, as if illuminated by the purest light. The child smiled as she got up, and held out her hand. Oddly, her bare feet appeared clean, as if the soil could not stain her skin. Whoever she was, she did not belong in the wilderness.

'Come,' the young girl whispered as she held out her hand. 'The oracle awaits your presence.'

The child guided Sulaf up through the Black Mountain, passing large stones that resembled the figures of men, women and children. The final steps, the little girl told her, were to be walked alone. Sulaf crossed a small stream, walking slowly towards a wooden shack that stood alone in the wilderness. A dim light coming from the windows guided her towards it. Finally she reached it. She pressed her hands against the wooden door and it creaked open. She had been surrounded by darkness for so long that the rush of colour from the light instantly burned her eyes. She entered the shack, and the wooden door shut behind her with a loud thud.

'Is anyone here?'

There was no answer. A tight feeling gripped her; she felt claustrophobic and scared. It was the kind of feeling a child has when they enter a new place alone. Sulaf looked up at the ceiling. There were small straw dolls hanging from hooks let into the timber roof beams. They were tied by the necks with horse hair and an all-seeing eye had been painted on their heads, and words stitched into their bodies. They twisted eerily in slow spirals. Sulaf looked at them closely. They were each a different shape and size; it looked as though they were in pain, from the way they hung by their necks, each one glaring at her with its painted eye. Sulaf crouched down, trying her best to avoid hitting them. They covered the entire ceiling, and crouching seemed to make no difference at all; they were everywhere, clawing at her head and catching her hair as she walked below them.

'What is this place?' Sulaf whispered. She pushed aside some of the dolls, trying to make a path for herself, and it was then she realised that what appeared to be horse hair tied around their necks was altogether finer. *Human hair?* Sulaf looked at another doll – one which caught her attention. Unlike the rest, its hair was blonde, and unlike the rest, upon its chest were the words 'jealous soul'. It was staring into Sulaf's eyes, as though it was a reflection of her inner self.

'You must learn to control your curiosity, Sulaf; it has always led you into trouble,' croaked a voice. Sulaf turned around, her spirit almost escaping from her body as she looked at the hideous creature hiding in the shadows. Lying on the floor was what Sulaf assumed to be the oracle; no amount of darkness could conceal her ghastliness. Her back was hunched, like the crescent moon. Sulaf tried to control her reaction; she tried to keep her eyes on the oracle's face but they naturally slipped to the rest of her body. Her legs were most frightening of all: they were long and deformed, appearing as the twisted roots of an oak tree, flowing free from her body in either direction.

'How do you know my name?'

'I know much more than that, my child ...'

62

The oracle neared Sulaf, dragging her body across the floor like an animal that had lost the use of its hind legs. Her sharp nails scraped against the ground, making a dreadful splintering sound. Sulaf tried her best not to be frightened by her ghastly appearance, but it was hopeless; she could not conceal her fear. The oracle's eyes were a clouded white, with neither pupil nor iris. Sulaf thought she must be blind, but oddly, the oracle appeared to be glaring at her, as if she could see her clearly. The oracle dragged her body further into the light, her hideousness becoming more apparent. Her lips drooled with thick saliva and the muscles of her eyes seemed to be in spasm. She had no trace of beauty; instead, there was only ghastliness to shy away from. Her fingers were deformed. They were long and thin, curling round, like her feet, the joints bulging out like the stumps of withered limbs.

'Will you help me to my seat, dear child?' the oracle croaked. Her breath poisoned the stale air. Sulaf clutched the old woman's hands; she felt the oracle's long, dirty nails dig into her skin as she did so.

'Who told you I was coming?'

'Why, it was you! Or have you forgotten all that was said between us?'

'You're mistaken. This is the first time I've ever met you,' Sulaf said, lifting the old crone from the floor and helping her to sit on a wooden log that had been carved into a seat.

'That may be, but I've met you many times before this moment – in spirit.' The oracle whispered the words, almost in a hiss. She directed Sulaf to sit beside her on the floor.

'I've no memory of our encounters.'

'No memory?' the oracle shrieked excitedly. The muscles of her eyes flickered madly; her spit burst out of her mouth. 'Do you remember your infancy?'

Her question seemed bizarre. *Perhaps she is mad …*

'No, of course I don't. Few do.'

'Then how do you know you've lived through it, if you can't remember all of it? Memories mean nothing; we only remember what we choose to, and never the whole journey of our lives.'

'That doesn't explain how you know my name, or that I was coming.'

'I heard your voice in my dreams, just like all the others who call out to me,' the oracle whispered as she traced her dirty nail over Sulaf's cheek. 'You see, my dearest, when a mortal sleeps, he does not die, nor does he live; instead, his spirit wanders across the earth, looking for something that will guide it to its destiny. Some spirits wander into peaceful sanctuaries, thinking of places they've seen or lost; they find comfort in these petty things. But other souls, like yours, wander further, into places that call out to their desires. I call them the wanderers of the night, for they are lost, and the only power that can bring them back home is the fulfilment of their desires. So you see, my child, I know everything about you. I summoned you to come to me so that I may free you.'

As Sulaf listened intently, she understood what the oracle

had meant: she had become so consumed by Marmicus that she depended on him entirely, needing his love simply to survive. Every day she yearned for him, both awake and asleep. *As long as the princess remains alive in his memories, she will drag his heart to the bottom of the sea and he shall never come to know the pleasures that lie upon the shore.*

The oracle watched her attentively. Unbeknown to Sulaf, she possessed a rare and powerful gift; the oracle could hear Sulaf's thoughts as if she were speaking aloud. She had been born with this gift, and curse; it was the strongest weapon she possessed, for it allowed her to sift through past memories until she found a person's greatest weakness. Sulaf turned towards the oracle, her heart awakening with new hope. She would seek her powers to grant her the man she adored.

'Then you know why I've come here.'

'I do, but you must say it out loud so that you give me permission to convince the forces of our universe.'

'I will,' said Sulaf. 'I want you to free the heart of the man who clings to the love of another woman. Kill her from his memory, so he doesn't think about her or feel for her any more. Let her die in his mind, just as she has died in spirit, and in body.' Her voice trembled in desperation.

'Is that all you wish for?'

'No. Give me his heart, and make him become mine. I want him to fall in love with me and desire me, just as he loved her. Give me his heart, and I'll reward you with all the gold I have.'

The words have finally been uttered, the oracle thought. *Her soul shall soon belong to me …*

'Come, dear child, lay your head to rest upon my lap. I've always longed to be a mother and tonight I am proud to be one,' hissed the oracle. Her smile became all the more frightening for her display of affection. Sulaf began to lower her head. As she did so, she heard a voice crying; it sounded like the girl who had taken her up the mountain. She was calling out to her, warning her to leave this place now. But Sulaf was focused on getting what she wanted, and she would not leave without the oracle's blessing. The crying ceased as soon as she laid her head upon the oracle's withered lap. The foul stench of her body pricked her nostrils, but Sulaf would tolerate it as long as the oracle granted her what she desired. She would even come to love her as a mother if she offered Marmicus's heart and placed it in her hands.

'Listen carefully, precious child. The man you love is like no other soul that breathes. His soul is chaste and his heart is pure. He's true to his heart, just as he's true to his Sword of Allegiance.' The oracle gently ran her bony fingers through Sulaf's hair. The dirt from her nails trickled into her hair. 'The love this noble warrior possesses is rare. It cannot be destroyed or tainted with black magic, for wherever there is true love, my dear, magic has no power or place. As long as the Gallant Warrior thinks his princess to be dead, he shall love and cherish her memory as if she were alive. But the Gallant Warrior carries a guilt which should be laid to rest, for the woman you hate is in fact still living. The princess is alive and she will return to him soon – if you stand back and do nothing.' The oracle's thin whisper was barely audible, and she poisoned Sulaf's ear with her foul breath.

How could the princess be alive if I've tossed petals at her burial chariot? The oracle's lying; she's deceiving me …

'Wretched girl, I'm no liar!' screeched the oracle, in a rage. Sulaf jumped back. The oracle's murky white eyes filled with blackness, and her long, knotted hair rose up as if caught by a gust of wind. Sulaf wished she could take back her thought. The straw dolls swung erratically, twisting and shuddering as if they were in pain. Their painted eyes were fixed on her, as if trying to warn her not to anger the oracle.

'Forgive me for thinking that; I'm just desperate for his love,' Sulaf cried. Begging for forgiveness, she kissed the oracle's deformed hand. The moment she did so, the oracle's eyes reverted to their colourless shade. The dolls were still turning.

'A mother always forgives the wrongs of her child,' said the oracle as she lifted Sulaf's chin with her long fingers. 'Tonight you have become one of my own ...'

63

I n the blink of an eye the oracle's anger drained away as though it had never been. It unsettled Sulaf, who tried her best to hide her inner thoughts, but the oracle seemed to possess a sixth sense that could catch her by surprise.

How could the princess be alive when I saw her lying lifeless? Sulaf wondered.

'Is it so hard to believe in miracles, my child?'

The oracle dragged her deformed body across the floor until she reached a low wooden table in the far corner of the shack. Her long arms pulled the weight of her body, causing her twisted legs to fold over with each movement.

Miracles are words used by those who believe in the gods, not for those who practise the dark art of demons.

'You're surprised by my choice of words?' the oracle mused, turning her head. The bones of her neck cracked like twigs being broken.

'I'm just a little confused. I never imagined you to believe in the gods or their miracles.'

'What an absurd remark; every sorcerer believes in the gods, and those who don't are foolish creatures indeed.'

'Then why do you practise the art of black magic?'

'My dear child, I said I believe in gods – but I didn't say that I side with them. There's an unseen war going on between gods and their angels, one that shall continue to be fought until the fire of our sun dies out,' said the oracle. The muscles in her face were twitching. She rested her hands on the wooden table, upon which was a large basin, filled to the brim with water. 'Come close to me; the time has come for us to call upon the angels of the fire for guidance.'

Sulaf stood up, keeping her intrigue to herself. She had already offended the oracle, and she did not wish to repeat the same mistake.

'Give me your hand, my child.'

Sulaf presented her hand, uncertain why exactly she wanted it. As soon as she held out her hand, the oracle snatched it and reached for the sharp knife lying on the table.

'What are you doing? Let go of my hand!' screamed Sulaf. The oracle's brittle body was deceptively strong, and her grip sure.

'Don't be afraid, child. I'm doing what you've asked of me,' screeched the oracle. Her tongue hung from her thin lips in her excitement.

'You are hurting me!'

'Love hurts, my child. If you want it you must be ready for the pain.'

The oracle slid the sharp dagger across Sulaf's forefinger, cutting into her skin. Her blood poured out into the basin, turning the clear water a cloudy shade of red. The knife was rusty; Sulaf had felt the iron granules enter her skin like grains of salt.

'Look into your reflection, my child, and tell me what you see.'

Sulaf peered into the water. Instead of seeing her reflection, she saw a dark shadow ripple across the surface of the water. It only appeared for a second or two, but it was long enough for her to notice that it was not her, but some unearthly creature.

'Who was that?'

'The master of all angels, the one who's come to accept your blood and sacrifice,' said the oracle. She poised herself over the bowl, holding back Sulaf's hair, then reached for something that lay at the bottom of the basin.

'What sacrifice are you talking about? I haven't offered you anything; I thought I'd be paying in gold.'

'Fallen angels have no need for gold; gold is made by mankind to serve men alone. With your blood you've offered me something else entirely, something that is more rare, infinitely more precious. He wanted your soul and you freely gave it to him. The moment you looked into his eyes, you pledged your soul to him. There's no going back now; you're one of us.'

The oracle pulled an object from the large basin. She grinned with excitement, revealing her yellow-stained teeth. Sulaf quickly covered her mouth as the foul stench of rotting flesh filled the room, and she moved into the light, wanting to see what excited the oracle so much.

'A man's heart is a precious thing; it's always so sensitive to a woman's touch, and can be so easily torn apart by her hands,' said the oracle. She laid the human heart on the table and reached for the rusty knife, then changed her mind, instead reaching for the axe. She hacked through it as though through infested fruit fallen from a tree. Brown blood squirted everywhere, and there was the sound of gentle dripping against the slate floor. Sulaf covered her face with her hands. The oracle showed no sympathy, while Sulaf thought about the person who had died and offered their heart – willingly or unwillingly. Then, in a seemingly haphazard manner, the oracle began to run her bony fingers across the heart's blue veins, looking for symbols to foretell the future. Sulaf tried not to contemplate whose heart it had been, or whether they had been killed for it.

'What future do you see?'

The oracle did not reply immediately. She elongated her neck, turning her head from side to side like a mad creature.

'When the full moon glows with the colour of blood, the war for the Garden of the Gods shall commence. The armies of Babylon will gather together like clouds uniting in a storm. On that day, the winds shall be driven by the screams of men who will die in their thousands fighting for the taste of freedom.'

Her voice had changed from a screech to a lower, unrecognisable, masculine voice, as if she had been possessed by the heart she had sliced apart. 'Before that happens, there will come to you a child with great innocence in his heart and a powerful message carried within his palms. Make no mistake: this boy is your enemy. In his hands he holds a dagger capable of killing any hope of love offered to you by the Gallant Warrior. Kill the boy or kill his message. Whatever you decide, be sure that Marmicus knows nothing about the golden papyrus, for it is as much your enemy as the princess herself ...'

64

S ulaf looked back at the Black Mountain with unease. She had journeyed to the oracle for one purpose alone: to obtain a potion that would somehow cure Marmicus's heart from the disease of love that ravaged it. But her journey had been fruitless. The oracle could provide no such cure, for she had said that, wherever there is true love, magic has no power or place.

However, she would not return to the Garden of the Gods completely empty-handed. The oracle had warned Sulaf to beware of a young boy who possessed a golden papyrus. If revealed to the Gallant Warrior, it would destroy any seed of love that could grow between them. *It's a secret that shall of course remain hidden,* Sulaf thought, as she made her way back to the Garden of the Gods.

65

'Wake up, boy, you're not here to daydream, you're here to lead my camel,' the merchant yelled angrily. He sat comfortably on his camel, gurgling water and spitting it out like a llama. The merchant was a man of moody disposition, and poor Paross was bearing the brunt of it. The little boy had been pulling on the leather reins for two days without any token of appreciation from the merchant; he was allowed to journey with him on the condition that he made himself useful. Paross felt his head thump: he could barely lift it, it felt so heavy. The afternoon sun was at its strongest, sucking all the moisture from his body and leaving him dehydrated. Paross looked up at the merchant, who sat comfortably on his camel, holding a straw umbrella over his head, spinning it around as he sang, without a care in the world. The boy watched him untie the goatskin water bottle, and drink from it again, splashing it all over his face.

'Are you thirsty, boy?' asked the merchant.

'Yes, my lord.'

'Good, that means my kindness hasn't gone to waste.' The merchant laughed as he poured water over his head, with a dash for his shoulders and a sprinkling for underneath his armpits too.

The boy looked at his hands. They were blistered, the skin peeling off, and yellow pus oozing. Flies flew about him, and he knew he would not last long if he did not wash them.

'My lord, can you spare a little water for me?' asked Paross. His voice trembled.

The merchant glared at the feeble boy. He had already been kind enough to let him journey with him, and now the boy was showing selfishness.

'You want me to spare a little water for you? What do you think I am, a priest? I'm a merchant, we don't spare anything; we only sell. If I spared you a droplet of water, then all my slaves would want a droplet too, and I'd be left with nothing.' He pointed his finger at him angrily. 'Nothing in life is free, not even for a child. If you want my water, you have to offer me something; if you don't, you can die of thirst for all I care.'

Paross had nothing to trade apart from the clothes on his back and the innocence in his heart, and these were worthless to the merchant, who wanted gold or silver. The only possession Paross carried was the golden papyrus, and the loving words of affection that came with it from his dead grandmother. Knowing this, Paross remained silent; he looked at the merchant with helpless eyes, feeling no anger, but pity.

'Don't stare at me, boy, it's rude. Didn't your mother teach you any manners?' yelled the merchant. He took off his turban, scratched his bald head, then put it back on. Paross closed his eyes for a while. His legs carried on, one agonising step at a time, the rough granules of sand irritating his tiny feet. Every time he closed his eyes he saw his grandmother being thrown into the fire; the image inhabited his mind like a rippling mirage. Unable to endure the visions in his memory, he opened his eyes and looked at the blisters on his hands. They had dried up and were beginning to peel away, but the leather reins kept rubbing against them, making them bleed.

Paross bent down. Grabbing some sand, he rubbed it into his hands, hoping it would dry up the yellow pus. Maybe that would stop the flies from entering his wounds. It worked for a while, but soon his hands began to throb. The sand irritated his open blisters. Paross knew his life was worth nothing. He took out the papyrus from his pocket and looked at it. He wished he could read; then he would understand what had been written on it. He remembered his grandmother's words. He knew he would not find peace until he had delivered the letter to the woman known as Sulaf.

'What's that in your hand?' asked the fat merchant. The yellow object had attracted his attention like the flickering of gold.

'It's nothing.'

Realising that the child was reluctant to answer his question, the merchant became even more intrigued by the object; self-interest was the quality that seemed to bind all wealthy men. 'If it's nothing, give it to me. In return, I'll give you that droplet of water you wanted.'

The merchant smiled falsely and reached out, his flabby arm flailing in the wind as he tried to take hold of the papyrus.

'No, it's not mine to offer you,' blurted out Paross, shoving his hand away.

'Give it here, boy, before I give you a thousand lashes!' the merchant commanded. The lines around his eyes crinkled as his temper rose. Paross stood his ground. He would not trade it in, even if the merchant gave him a jug of cool spring water. His grandmother's last wishes meant everything to him.

'Impertinent boys should be taught how to respect their elders. I blame your parents for your rudeness; they've brought you up to be spoiled!' exclaimed the merchant, frothing at the mouth in his temper. The boy had insulted his kindness by denying his trade and snubbing him! In a rush of anger, he grabbed his whip and raised it above his head.

'You'll regret this day, boy!' he said. He swung his whip, using all his might, the sudden action energising him. Paross bravely stood his ground, clenching his fists. The whip came thrashing down, lashing the boy's back and leaving lacerations that oozed blood. Long red marks appeared beneath his cotton robes; every time the merchant struck him they ripped anew.

'Now give it here, or I'll whip you until the sunlight fades!'

'I can't – it's not mine to give you,' cried the boy. The slaves watched as the boy stood still, enduring every blow like an animal unable to defend itself. Among them was the Shadow, who stared darkly at the merchant, his eyes filled with a smouldering hatred.

'You stubborn child, I'll beat you to death. Now give it here!'

The merchant struck him again as he would a stubborn mule. He no longer cared about the papyrus; he just wanted to break the boy's will. He would not stop until the boy kissed his feet and begged for his forgiveness – it was up to him to encourage slaves and children to understand their place in society. He kept raining blows upon the helpless child. 'You wretched slave, you'll learn to obey. I swear by the gods you shall be buried here.'

Unable to stand any more, Paross collapsed onto the ground.

'Now …' the merchant mused with a childish sense of accomplishment as he jumped off his camel and reached for the papyrus that lay beside Paross. 'What do we have here?'

66

'Give it back to me,' Paross cried. He tossed and turned in agony as he lay on the ground, the sand sticking to his back. It felt as though a thousand wasps had stung him all at once.

'It's mine now – you traded it in for a droplet of water, remember?' said the merchant, who hastily opened the papyrus. He tingled with excitement: the boy was obviously carrying something of importance; no one in their right mind would be prepared to die for a worthless piece of paper. *It must be worth something; if not, it will come in handy for my fire tonight …*

The merchant read every symbol; the sweat from his forehead formed rivulets on the golden sheet. His eyes widened with every passing second. He learnt of the princess's infant, and how she planned to pass it off as the Assyrian emperor's own.

'Where did you get this?'

Paross remained silent; he knew if he spoke it would only make matters worse. The merchant became agitated. Whatever happened, he would not lose out on an opportunity to trade the letter for gold, but first he needed to know if the letter was real. His palms prickled with impatience. Time was of the essence! If anyone else learnt about the secret, it would lose its value.

'I've always disliked children, they're costly and stubborn. But if you tell me what I need to know, I'll treat you like my son. Now who gave you this letter?'

Paross deliberately remained silent; the slaves looked on, not understanding why he would choose to be beaten. The boy was either too loyal for his own good, or stupid.

'Very well. Since you don't want to talk like a human, you'll be treated like an animal. You're going to scream so loud that you will sound like a mule,' the merchant puffed.

He released his grip on the whip, wrapping the leather around his fist so he could control it better, then swung it with all his power. He struck downwards, this time aiming at the little boy's neck. He knew it would hurt him more. The slaves watched from behind as the merchant expressed his anger; they shook their heads, wishing that the boy would speak up, for his own sake.

'No more, no more!' Paross screamed. His lips trembled as his defiance finally caved in. The boy had finally been broken. In a whisper, Paross revealed how he had come to obtain the golden papyrus from his grandmother; she had told him that it belonged to the princess, that it had become her epistle of hope. His instructions were simple; he had to deliver it to a woman bearing the name Sulaf, and from there she would deliver it to its rightful owner.

The secret had now been revealed, and the princess had no idea that it had fallen into the wrong hands ...

67

Lying beneath the glory of the heavens, the merchant slept comfortably, drawing in deep breaths and blowing out large snores. His heart was content, for beneath his head lay the token of all pleasures, the golden papyrus. Tomorrow his caravan would change course and head back to the kingdom of Assyria to present the emperor with a secret that would certainly lead to the execution of the princess. *The emperor shall be pleased with me, and I shall live abundantly because of it,* the merchant dreamt, lying on a thick pillow stuffed with goose feathers. For him, resting in the desert was not much different to resting under a canopy in a palace. The merchant had everything. He lay on a thick mattress stuffed with sheep's wool, and covered his fat body with layers of material, while his slaves tossed and turned on flat beds of straw used to feed the camels and mules.

But there had been a time when the merchant had nothing to live on; he had lost all his wealth in one imprudent bet. He was given a choice: he could either die a rich man, refusing to give up what he possessed, or he could live the life of a poor man, with nothing. He had chosen the latter. Unexpectedly, he had found that life as a rich man was as worthless as a slave's and as miserable as a mule's, and from that moment forward he made a pledge to himself that he would never shun a man or harm an animal.

As the nights trickled on and his robes became dirty and fell apart, the merchant still found a strange sense of contentment in his life, something that he had never experienced before. He found himself being happy with the simple things life offered; he ate oats for supper and drank only water. Every day he watched the sun rise and set, hearing the birds jubilantly sing, when before he had scarcely realised they were there. With no wine to poison his thoughts or cloud his judgement, the merchant would smile and admire the natural jewels of the earth that lay before him. It was an unexpected gift; paradise had come to him when he had lost everything, until one day his life unexpectedly changed again.

The merchant was crossing the desert, hoping to find an oasis where he could live peacefully with nothing else but his camel and goats. He wandered for days. On his journey through the desert he saw a caravan that had halted. For whatever reason, the caravan had lost its way and had eventually run out of water. The penniless merchant had only noticed it because of the vultures circling above it. He kicked his heels into the sides of his camel and galloped until he finally reached the caravan, and by pure good fortune he had come to the caravan's rescue just in time. Lying on the sand were an old man and his dead slaves; the old man was dressed in exquisite gowns, like those the merchant had enjoyed in his past life. The merchant knelt down, and lifted the master of the caravan's head, wanting to revive him, but time was not on his side.

'I envy you,' said the master of the caravan, uttering his last words.

'Why? I have nothing,' replied the merchant, and put his ear close to the dying man.

The young merchant sprinkled cool water upon the dying man's lips, hoping to revive him. The taste of it was unlike anything else the old man had ever tasted. In his arms, the frail man slowly died and at that moment the penniless merchant, who had lost everything, was restored to wealth. Soon his robes shimmered again, and his belly grew. He had inherited everything material that the dying man had left, but over time he came to lose all that he had acquired in spirit. His heart hardened and his eyes lost the jubilant sparkle brought about by a simple life. Suddenly the sun did not seem so bright any more, or glorious; the stars appeared dull and common; and, as for the pledge that he had made to himself, it was but words lost with the breath of the wind. The compassion of his heart turned to stone, and his greed was fuelled by a desire for more, until one day he came to regret it. For the merchant was hated by many men, particularly by his slaves, who had suffered under his brutal tyranny and leather whip. He had beaten and tortured them until he had broken them; the marks on their bodies testified to this. But, wherever oppression exists, rebellion against a dictator is bound to follow ...

68

The stillness of the night was ruffled by a shadow, which crept secretly through the desert, nearing the merchant's resting form. He was sleeping peacefully, wrapped up in silk, unaware that a black figure was standing over his body, scowling at him. The Shadow's eyes were shaped like a hyena's; every time the clouds drifted away from the moon they faintly sparkled then disappeared again. He had seen how his master had treated the child, smiling cruelly as he whipped him. The boy had shown so much courage, when the men around him had shown none – not even he. For this, the Shadow felt ashamed, sickened by what he had become. How could a child who had barely lived possess so much courage and bravery? At that moment the Shadow had vowed that he would do all that was in his power to help Paross.

With his large hands the Shadow clasped a straw basket used to store hot bread; tonight, however, there was no scent of sweet dough in the air. The fire had died out, only blackened logs remaining. The Shadow had come for another purpose. He quietly lifted the straw lid, tilting the basket sideways, and began to rattle it as if he were sprinkling winter seeds over the merchant's body. Small yellow creatures began to fall out of the straw basket, making a scuttling noise. The sand crunched beneath the Shadow's feet as he hurried backwards, trying not to tread on the creatures. *Justice never forgets the evildoer*, he thought, lifting his arms into the lofty sky as if asking his god to send thunder down upon the merchant's sleeping body. He had been the victim of the merchant's torments for so long, had been ridiculed for the darkness of his skin and struck for his belief in a One-God. Each night, when the Shadow knelt before his god in humble prayer, the merchant would whip his back and the soles of his feet; for years he had clenched his fists, enduring the pain much as Paross had, but tonight he could no longer remain silent; something inside him had snapped.

Suddenly, the merchant felt a tickling sensation on his arm; he grunted as he scratched his skin, hoping to rid himself of whatever insect had landed on him. The ticklish feeling disappeared for a moment, but immediately returned. This time he felt it everywhere. Only half-awake, he rolled over, trying to change position, wanting to go back to sleep, until he felt a sharp pain, as if someone had prodded him with a needle. He woke up fully and opened his eyes to a nightmare. The merchant screamed: he was covered in desert scorpions. They were everywhere, scuttling across his bedding and among the folds of his robes, their segmented tails curved over their backs. Every time the merchant moved they stung him, injecting their venom into his bloodstream.

'Now you'll shriek like a mule and we'll all be here to watch,' the Shadow said, emerging from the darkness like the angel of death itself. Nothing could save the merchant now; the paralysis had begun and he was drowning from within. A trickling numbness spread throughout his body, with hot lumpy patches emerging all over his skin from the stings of the scorpions.

'Help me, you wretched fools!' cried the merchant, trying to wake his slaves, realising his predicament. He needed them to help him. 'Wake up quickly! Wake up, he's trying to kill me!'

The slaves were already awake. Not one of them moved an inch. They watched as their master struggled to breathe. Each time he moved it became far worse for him; the scorpions were darting their venomous tails into his back, leaving his joints to stiffen and his blood vessels to burst. His muscles were going into paralysis, his lungs filling with fluid. The slaves watched their master bristle in agony; instead of feeling pity for him, they felt a wave of relief. Many of his slaves had died at his hands; and finally their deaths were being avenged.

Lifting the merchant's head, the Shadow slid his fingers beneath the silk fabric and reached for the golden papyrus which lay underneath.

'Get away from it, it's mine,' the merchant groaned. Saliva ran out of his mouth. His eyes were so bloodshot he could hardly see.

'It was never yours to start with,' said the Shadow. He put his head next to the merchant's ear, making sure that he could hear his every word before he entered the afterlife. 'A poor man may have nothing, but he always has justice on his side.'

The Shadow stood up. He had at last been reunited with justice after so long. He walked towards the feeble boy, who slept on the ground, and gently woke him up. Paross rubbed his eyes. He thought it was already morning, but it was still the middle of the night.

'Take this, I know it belongs to you,' the Shadow whispered. He leant in and handed him the papyrus. Paross looked at him, completely unaware of what had happened or how he had come to be in possession of the papyrus. He turned around and saw the merchant lying dead, flat on his back.

'May the gods bless you,' said Paross. He took the papyrus from the Shadow's hand, holding it to his chest.

'No …' the Shadow smiled as he looked towards the heavens and pointed upwards. 'May the One-God bless you.'

'Be sure to savour the warmth of the sun on your skin, because by nightfall your bodies shall be buried beneath the damp soil!' said Nafridos. He marched past a long line of men who stood in a single row, each dressed in thick armour. They wore iron helmets, and their bulging muscles were covered in heavy metal plates to shield them from the impact of their enemies' blades. They had all been rounded up for the same purpose; to fight the Dark Warrior on the training field so that he could strengthen his swordsmanship for the battlefield.

'Remember my face well; it shall be the last thing you see on this earth. If any of you desire vengeance in the afterlife, then wait for me beside the pits of hellfire.'

The Dark Warrior searched for the strongest opponent who could match his fighting prowess. His eyes flickered across the long line and came to rest on one man. He was in luck. Standing at the far end of the line was a black slave whose biceps were thick like the brute muscles of a stallion. *His death is worthy of glory …*

'You shall be the first to die,' Nafridos said, pointing his blade towards the tall man. It had been a long time since he had enjoyed a challenge, and today he would make the most of it.

The Nubian prisoner stepped forward, his shadow covering the two men who stood either side of him.

'I'll take pleasure in killing any Assyrian where I may find them. I'll crush you with my hands and leave you begging for air,' said the Nubian.

He twisted his head from side to side, clicking the bones in his neck, than spat into his hands, the better to grip his sword. 'Your men robbed my wife of her dignity, and killed my child; now I'll take your life just as you took theirs.'

'Did your wife squeal like a pig when they ravaged her or cry like a whore who enjoyed it?' Nafridos laughed, goading him. He began to undo the black swathe which he wore around his burly chest, revealing his sculpted muscles. Unlike his challengers, he wore no armour or helmet to protect his body from harm. A slave stepped forward, holding the Dark Warrior's armour. He lifted it to place it upon his master's shoulders, but Nafridos pushed him away.

'I can see your desire to kill me in your eyes, so I'll make it easy for you, giant. Choose whatever weapon you want from my collection, and wear your armour, and I'll fight you with only a sword in my hands. What do you say?'

There was a long silence from his opponent, laden with distrust; the Nubian slave knew that he already possessed the advantage due to his sheer size, so why would he need anything else to improve his chances of killing his opponent?

'My lord, are you sure you don't want your armour?'

'If I need a shield on the battlefield I'll use your body as one. Now choose your weapon, giant; I want to bury your body before sunset.'

The Nubian nodded, agreeing to the conditions of combat, then walked past the weapons, considering each one carefully. On the ground were a long line of swords, axes and spears used to hunt lions and butcher soldiers. Eventually he paused at one weapon designed to bludgeon any opponent to death. He was imagining how he could use each one to kill his opponent, trying to anticipate his moves. He looked at a mace made from solid iron, with razor-sharp spikes running round the ball. Connected to it was a long metal chain with a thick handle for the warrior to clasp as he swung it.

'I've made my choice. I choose this. When it hits your face it shall crush your bones from the inside and leave you bleeding until death greets you.'

'Only a giant would choose this weapon to defend his honour,' Nafridos laughed. He directed his guards to lift up the mammoth mace and hand it to the Nubian. 'Your words excite me. Every man I've met upon the battlefield knows for certain that he shall die. When I kill you I shall watch your hope die with you.'

Nafridos knelt on the ground to carry out his sacred pre-battle ritual. He took out the sharp dagger he used to slice tongues, then slid the blade against his hand, cutting into the skin. His shoulder muscles clenched for a moment than relaxed, as if being massaged by the sadistic feeling that rushed through his veins. The giant watched, slightly unsettled by the strange ritual. Nafridos grabbed his sword from his slave, and wiped his blood across the hilt and down its length. Taking sand from the dusty ground, he sprinkled it across the thick metal grip, creating a grit paste which dried instantly as his blood coagulated. Now he had the best grip possible to kill any enemy that approached him.

'In death we find solace from life; today I'll offer it to you freely,' said Nafridos …

69

Silence filled the training courtyard. The giant faced his opponent, ready to fight to the death and obtain the justice he deserved and craved. The remaining prisoners looked on, feeling relief; they were grateful that they could live another day. Of course, it was only a matter of time before their luck ran out. Their hopes rested on the Nubian giant, who was athletic and strong. If he could not kill the Dark Warrior, what chance did they have?

The Nubian prisoner closed his eyes, remembering the faces of his wife and child; the last time he had held his daughter was when he had buried her in a shallow grave. She had appeared to be sleeping peacefully in his arms, just as she had done at night. He remembered untangling her hands from his, and placing her in the wet ditch, knowing that he would never see her again.

'Let the battle between giants commence.'

The Nubian prisoner hoisted the mace above his head. His muscles flexed as he twirled the chain in a vicious circle, creating a destructive force capable of killing anything that stood in its path. The iron ball was flung towards Nafridos; he bent his knees, reacting quickly as the sharp metal spikes flew past him, narrowly missing his face.

'Is that all you've got, giant? I expected better.'

'I've just begun,' said the Nubian, and flung the iron weapon again, this time using all the strength of his upper body, his massive shoulder flexing to the rhythm of his swing. Nafridos rolled across the ground, dodging the spiked ball. Dust flew up as he twisted his body quickly; every movement was imprinted on the sand like footsteps. Nafridos laughed. He was enjoying this battle; most of his opponents failed to put up a good fight. He watched the iron ball swing all the way back again. The Nubian clearly had an advantage; the iron chain was long, and the circle it described created a fearsome barrier, so that there was no way for Nafridos to get to his opponent without being hit by the flailing weapon.

'You disappoint me, giant; I expected more from you. I'm sure your wife fought a better battle.'

The Nubian roared with rage, spit bursting from his lips. He grabbed the thick handle with both hands, gripping it tightly, and again hurled the mace.

'Enough,' said the Dark Warrior, who was starting to get bored. 'Your footsteps shall be the last walked by giants. The time has come to die.'

The Dark Warrior stood up. The long metal chain spun towards him but Nafridos simply stared at it without moving an inch. The iron ball curled, ready to smash into him, but Nafridos remained still. He watched it spin. As it was about to make contact, Nafridos jumped into the air, twisting his body like a lion in mid-flight. He stretched out his sword, and the long iron chain caught around it. The tactic was truly genius. The giant desperately tried to draw his weapon back, but it had already wrapped itself around the Dark Warrior's weapon. Sparks flew; the two weapons were being pulled in opposite directions. Using the full weight of his body, Nafridos leant back and dug his heels into the ground; he was ready for the kill. The next instant, he let go of his weapon, releasing it like a bow shot from an arrow; only a god was capable of judging the moment so that the sword would find its mark. The Nubian looked up, expecting the weapon to land behind him, but the sword arced into the air, spinning in a silvered blur, and embedded itself in the Nubian's neck.

'Every man I kill shall die on their knees,' whispered the Dark Warrior.

Nafridos walked towards the giant, whose head was flung backwards as if he was searching for his loved ones in the sky. Nafridos looked deeply into his opponent's eyes, watching them slowly roll back into their sockets. It was the sign Nafridos was waiting for; the look of hope dying just as he had promised it would.

'Ask a healthy man what he wishes for in life, and he'll always reply "more gold", but if you ask a dying man what he wishes for, he'll always say "one more day".' Nafridos tilted his head back as if mirroring the Nubian's skyward stare, a cruel smile of satisfaction on his face. He wrapped his hands round the grip of his sword, still staring into his opponent's eyes, and abruptly ripped it out of his neck. The giant's body was flung sideways, his mouth open wide as he landed at his murderer's feet. It was yet another number to be added to the Dark Warrior's belt of death. 'Farewell, giant. I shall wait for you by the pits of hellfire; maybe then you will redeem yourself and win your glory.'

70

Now that the merchant's brutal whip was buried with his body beneath the desert sands, the wretchedness of the desert was transformed into a sanctuary of security for the little boy who had endured so much agony in his short years of life. Paross knew he owed a great deal to the slave who had not only returned the golden papyrus to him, but given him his freedom.

'I never thanked you for saving my life; one day when I've grown tall like you, I'll repay you with gold,' said Paross, sitting on the back of a groaning camel. He looked at the golden papyrus, wishing it was a plate of gold, but even if it was, he knew it was not his to offer. His body rocked from side to side every time the camel took a step, leaving even footprints in the sand. He clutched the sheepskin saddle, trying hard not to fall off; it was the first time he had ridden a camel.

'I don't need gold as my reward.' The Shadow looked up at the boy with fondness as he led his camel in the direction of the Garden of the Gods.

'You don't? Everyone wants gold or silver.'

'Only a fool needs gold; he thinks it'll make him happy, but it can't settle his stomach when he's hungry, or cover him when he's cold. It's the only thing he sees in the darkness. But a wise man dreams of greater things, like justice, because justice settles the heart when gold offers only envy.'

'You're right. I want justice for my grandmother,' replied Paross, who looked down, remembering what had happened to her. 'What's your name?'

'I wasn't given a name at birth; only free men are given names.'

'Then what did your master call you?'

'He called me Shadow because my skin is black like the night. I've known no other name – apart from worse ones,' said the man.

'But you're free now, so surely your soul deserves a name it can be proud of?' Paross smiled, hoping to comfort the man who had saved his life.

The Shadow smiled back fondly at him. He had shown so much bravery throughout his beatings; there surged through him a paternal feeling of protectiveness.

'Then to you I shall be known as Abram, the guardian of my people,' he replied, holding on to the long rope which led the camel through the stillness of the desert. The hot sands were turning cool with the arrival of dusk. The orange light of the sun was mixed with a deep blue, painting the sky in a myriad of colours.

'I like that name. Is that the name of your god?'

'No, it's the name of a man who my people loved and followed for guidance. He was a man like you and I, with a body made of flesh and bones, but a soul pure as daybreak.'

'So he's like a human god then?'

'No, my people don't believe in human gods or in their powers. We believe in an unseen god, who rewards and punishes. When someone needs guidance, He draws him close to Him and helps him, and when someone does evil, He either forgives or punishes him,' Abram whispered. He looked towards the heavens, as if offering repentance for his mistakes; he found peace there. 'Today I've taken a man's life; my god may strike me down with fever because of it, but I feel it was the only way to stop him from killing you. If there's a punishment from my god for what I've done, then I'll accept it proudly.'

Paross listened to him speak, captivated by Abram's belief in a One-God; he had never come across a man who prayed to an unseen creator who was neither made of stone nor covered in gold. It was all new to him, and did not seem to make much sense in relation to his own way of life.

'My grandmother used to say that when a star flickers in the sky, a god is reborn. Now I think my grandmother was wrong – how can a god be reborn if they're supposed to be everlasting? And what happens to them when there's daylight? Where do the gods go when the light falls upon us in the day?'

'A wise man first questions his beliefs before he pledges his loyalty to an idea. Now that you've started to question your beliefs, you have a lifetime to think of the answers – be assured, they are there.'

From the first moment Abram had seen Paross, he knew he possessed wisdom beyond his years. There was something about him. He continued to pull the camel's reins, his bare feet sinking through the bed of sand, which rippled endlessly into the distance.

'Do you have any children, Abram?'

'No, I can't have children.'

'Why not? Don't you like women? Aren't they beautiful to you?'

Abram laughed, surprised by his words; they were the very opposite of what he was thinking.

'A slave isn't allowed to give life; it's a rule forced upon us by our masters. When I was your age, my master took away my right to have any children; it means I can never be a father, even if I've been freed.'

Paross did not understand exactly what Abram meant – he knew little about intimacy or the way the human body worked – but still he felt sorry for Abram. The man appeared uncertain of his newfound freedom, as if he did not know exactly what he should do with it.

Abram halted, as did the rest of the slaves who trailed behind the long, winding caravan. The camel groaned loudly as the rope tugged back.

'What's the matter, Abram?'

Paross felt unnerved. He turned, looking back at the other slaves who were now free from the merchant's tyranny. They too had stopped and were looking into the distance, mesmerised by something that sparkled high up in the sky. Paross looked into the sky, following the direction of their gaze, but could see nothing apart from the deepening colours of the sunset. Everything seemed normal.

'What are you looking at?' Paross asked, his curiosity getting the better of his manners.

'Look up into the sky – you'll see it too.'

'I don't see anything.' The young boy frowned, feeling rather stupid. Everyone else saw it, so why couldn't he? All he could see were an array of endless stars shimmering like pearls on a necklace. There was one star that shone more brightly than the rest but, other than that, the horizon was normal.

'Don't search with your eyes – search with your heart. It will guide you,' said Abram.

Paross closed his eyes then slowly reopened them; as he did, his blindness was healed. He saw that the brightest star was in fact the hearth of the Temple of Ishtar, the magnificent burning torch which sought to guide the dwellers of the desert towards the Garden of the Gods. It was a spectacular sight, and one that drew the soul towards it. His grandmother's words flooded back into the boy's mind, and his heart filled up with indescribable happiness that showed in the endless tears which rolled down his cheeks. Although his grandmother had not made the journey with him, Paross felt she was near him, protecting him all the while.

'We're here at last.'

71

Larsa stared at her hands as if seeing them for the first time in her life. Across her palms and along the middle of her forehead were a series of tattoos – unwanted but drawn with great artistry. It was her punishment from Jaquzan; now anyone who looked at her would know that her soul belonged to him. A long metal needle, heated in the flames and dipped into a mixture containing copper metal granules, had been used to colour her skin, changing it into a dark brown like the dye of the henna leaf. Using her fingernails, Larsa peeled off a scab that had formed on her hand, desperately hoping that somehow she could save her skin before it was forever tarnished by the ink. Her flesh had already changed colour; the brown had turned into a dark green.

'If I could have stopped my cousin from spoiling your beauty, I would have. Now, when I look at you I'm reminded of him,' said Nafridos, admiring the curves of her body. He had met few women who could seduce him without having to do anything; he rested his broad shoulders against a pillar and watched her.

'Even if your emperor stoned me to death I still wouldn't call for your help; my lips call for Marmicus only.'

'Here, take my sword,' said Nafridos quickly. Larsa was puzzled by his words; they appeared out of context.

'If you offer it to me, then you willingly hand over your life.'

'On the contrary, I think it'll be more dignified for you to take your own life instead of watching it drain away because of a man who's forgotten your existence,' said the Dark Warrior, pulling out his sword.

'What do you know of dignity? You strip it from men like meat torn from a bone.'

Nafridos laughed loudly, glad to see that the princess still retained her fighting spirit, despite everything that she had endured. Of course, Larsa had meant what she said. He walked towards the chair where she sat. She looked broken and miserable. Nafridos crouched down and glared at her, wanting to look at her tattoo. It had been drawn across the centre line of her forehead, like a fine engraving etched across a ring. Larsa turned her face away, humiliated at having Jaquzan's name inscribed on her skin. The defiant and courageous look she once possessed had for the very first time changed to one of utter shame.

'Do you still think that the Gallant Warrior will save you from all of this? Even I'm not too proud to recognise when a battle's been lost.'

'I don't *think* it – I'm certain of it.'

'What makes you so certain?' asked Nafridos.

He stared at her lips, wanting to kiss them, like the last time they were together. Their fullness called out to him, making him unable to concentrate on anything else. But Larsa was the forbidden fruit that could not be touched or tasted unless by permission of the Assyrian emperor. Every time she breathed in, he felt a pressure on his chest like the push of a sweeping tide. A surge of lust urged him to touch her and be done with the desire that engulfed him.

'What makes us certain that the sun will rise tomorrow or the next day? We know it because the sun has always promised it shall, and delivered on its word. It's the same with Marmicus: our love is like a lantern that guides us to one another in the darkest night when the stars themselves are lost.'

Even though Larsa had proven that she believed in their love, it made her appear pathetically naive. Nothing, it seemed, could destroy her irrational hope of survival.

'Then where has he been all this time?' asked Nafridos, biting his lip. 'If there's any lantern, it'll come from the fire that burns his body. What you witnessed in the desert when I captured your Royal Caravan is nothing compared to what I'll unleash when I'm on the battlefield.' He clamped his teeth together then stood up, wanting to leave her. She knew nothing of his abilities; somehow, this amused him and frustrated him at the same time. He had a deep streak of competitiveness which made him lust for her attention. It was the same egotistic desire that propelled him to kill so savagely.

'You'll be glad to know that my cousin wants you to join us on the battlefield; he says he wants his infant to watch his mother's homeland being flattened by the feet of his soldiers. When your kingdom loses this war, you'll beg me to offer you my sword. Just you wait and see ...'

72

'Blessed is our almighty God, for His heaven has fallen onto our earth,' said Abram in sheer awe. He walked through the fertile land holding Paross's hand, and the rest of the free slaves walked behind them, enjoying their new freedom to wander without fear of being beaten. The Garden of the Gods was like an oasis in the desert; whoever had named it had indeed done it justice, for there was no other kingdom quite like it on earth. This was the first time they had been here, and already they felt as if they had come home.

Paross looked around, unable to contain his excitement. They had decided to walk throughout the night and, just as tradition dictates, they had finally reached the kingdom at the break of dawn. Paross let go of Abram's hand and began to run across the oasis kingdom, feeling the cool wind blow against his skin as he dashed in and out of palm trees, orange blossom and pomegranate trees. There were streams running under the shiny evergreen foliage, birds and little animals everywhere. The lush green grass felt like an exquisite rug which cushioned his feet as he ran on it. Spreading his arms out like a bird wanting to fly, Paross spun through the valley of palm trees. His reflection rippled across the crystal-clear Euphrates river, which nourished the fertile land. Some pelicans had gathered, resting in the shallows in a large flock, but they rose the moment Paross came near.

'Are we dreaming? Can this place be real?'

Paross boyishly ran back towards Abram, who stood under a fig tree, hoping to find some ripened fruit which had fallen onto the rich soil. He did not need to look far; they were everywhere. One by one Abram collected the ripe figs, placing them in the same straw basket which he had used to collect scorpions to kill his master, and feeling no regret at all for the lethal act. With his blistered hands Paross began to help his friend collect the figs. Thick sugary syrup coated their hands and lips as they ate the fresh fruit without fear. Eventually the straw basket was full of ripe figs, and they sat down for a while under the shaded palm trees. The scent of wild jasmine flowers flew with the winds that kissed this perfect landscape. Wherever Abram and Paross looked, beauty caught their eyes, calming their souls after all the suffering they had endured.

'Where are all the people?'

'They live over there. I've heard it's called the City of Flowers,' said Abram. He pointed into the distance; they were still some miles away from it. Paross repeated the name to himself; the city sounded glorious. The Assyrian kingdom may have been impressive, but the Garden of the Gods had a natural simplicity that beautified it. It was coloured by flowers and palm trees, while everything in Assyria was built by man and spoke of darkness and destruction. Abram and Paross walked together along the stone path, the other free slaves following behind. Paross looked again at the Temple of Ishtar, standing against the clear blue sky. Birds were circling it as if paying homage to its brilliance, their wings decorating the sky like scattered petals falling from a white cherry tree.

'Now that your friends are free, where will they go?' Paross asked.

He held Abram's hand tightly, knowing full well that their journey together would not last much longer.

'They'll remain here for a few days, then they'll follow the sun back towards their homelands. Many of them have families there,' said Abram. He looked over his shoulder at his comrades, who joyously entered the kingdom, this time as free souls, not slaves.

'What about you? Where will you go, Abram?'

'I'll come with you until you're free of your duty,' replied Abram. He did not wish to leave the boy.

'But you're free! You can go wherever you want!'

'A free man has nothing in this world if he does not have a friend by his side.'

Paross looked up at the man who had not only saved him from brutality but had offered his friendship, like the loving father he had never known.

'My journey will end as soon as I find the woman my grandmother told me about.'

'Then we'll find her together …'

73

King Nelaaz of Aram had been regarded as an insult to the line of kings, yet somehow he had managed to cling to his throne despite the constant revolts that occurred in his homeland. But a man's reputation can change as easily as the direction of the wind; after all his years of ridicule, the sweaty king had at last proven himself to be anything but stupid. For King Nelaaz had potentially saved the lives of thousands without having to bribe or lie to anyone, and for this he was loved by his people. But the world can be a cruel place; for, unknown to King Nelaaz, death was hovering over him. The Serpent slithered into his bedchamber, his nose and mouth covered with a cotton handkerchief.

The Serpent waited for several moments, simply staring at the king as he held a pillow with both hands. Whatever happened he could not afford to make a mistake. If he did, he would risk revealing his identity. *I must be prepared for all eventualities …*

He breathed in and out again. It was the first time that the Serpent had felt a rush of nerves before killing someone: it was a new experience for him. He smiled to himself. Of all the people he had murdered, he would never have imagined feeling nervous about killing the chubby little King of Aram; he was someone who could barely frighten a child. Then again, the Serpent had underestimated him before: anything was possible; after all, luck had always proven to be on his side. The Serpent sensed the right time had come. Like a ghost, he held the pillow, hovering it over the king's face. Suddenly he brought it down, using the whole weight of his body to suffocate him. King Nelaaz woke up immediately, his vision blackened by the pillow which pressed tightly against his face, scarcely able to breathe.

'Guards! Guards!' the king yelped. His cries came from his lips as faint whispers. The Serpent pressed the pillow harder, watching the king's legs jerk manically, and feeling his nose squash into his face. He knew he had to be careful; he could not afford to leave his victim with a broken nose; this would only alert suspicion. The king's chin squashed into his neck; his lungs were bursting.

'Those who smile foolishly in life, die with an unwelcome frown,' said the Serpent. He watched as the king's toes curled in pain, and the sheets slipped off his bed. His body shuddered; strangely, it took the Serpent back to a childhood incident long forgotten. When he was eight his beloved cat had been bitten by a snake. As the venom had spread through her body, the animal's suffering became more obvious. At first, he had thought she was recovering, because her muscles were twitching erratically as if she were waking up, but eventually she died in his arms. Unlike for his cherished cat, the Serpent felt no sympathy for King Nelaaz as he suffocated. Finally King Nelaaz's eyes rolled back into their sockets, his scrabbling feet relaxed on the bed, and his body fell still. The Serpent lifted the pillow from his round face, then reached for the cotton handkerchief that lay on the divan. Leaning over the king, he dabbed away any traces of sweat on his face. In the last few seconds of his life, King Nelaaz had recognised the voice of his murderer: it was the voice of a man so revered that he could hardly believe it.

'Farewell, dear friend, your laughter shall be missed,' the Serpent smiled. He reached for the linen sheets, which had slipped onto the floor, picking them up and placing them over King Nelaaz's still body. Whoever was unfortunate enough to find him would think that he had died naturally in his sleep. The Serpent gently closed the king's eyes and walked out of the chamber. Tonight he had drawn nearer to his goal of the throne promised to him; but something else had taken over his thoughts, a secret which he could not wait to reveal to the Gallant Warrior …

74

'My lord Marmicus, you're needed urgently,' said the messenger who barged into the chamber.

'Whatever it is, it can wait,' Marmicus replied, brushing aside his words and returning to his generals, and the map spread out before them. This was a critical time for the Gallant Warrior; the commanders of the Babylonian armies had arrived, bringing with them their forces. They now gathered to discuss potential strategies of war. There was no time to waste. They all knew that they were greatly outnumbered, and if they were going to defeat the Assyrians they needed to work together as one force. Without an effective strategy, it would be suicide for each commander and his men.

'My lord, I'm not permitted to leave this chamber without you. These are my orders.'

'Get him out of here! He's not allowed to be here when we're discussing strategy,' yelled one of the generals, who was used to dishing out orders. Marmicus understood his concerns. In the affairs of war no man could be trusted unless he stood to lose as much as he gained.

'Who's ordered you to remain here?' asked the Gallant Warrior.

'The Priest of Xidrica, my lord. He told me to either bring you to him or wait with you here, until you finish.'

Marmicus knew he should leave. If the message had come from the Priest of Xidrica, it must be something of great importance.

'The only reason I'm coming with you is because I don't trust you to stay here. Now take me to him.'

The Gallant Warrior followed the messenger out of the chamber, uncertain of where exactly he was being taken. As soon as he entered the sunlit corridor, he noticed a thick wave of smoke drifting through it. The powerful incense smelt the same as the one used at the princess's funeral, and instant memories of that awful day came back to him.

The messenger halted abruptly outside one chamber. The large wooden doors were bolted open to allow Marmicus to enter. As he walked in, he saw dark, shadowy people standing round a bed. Despite the thick cloud of smoke, and his blurred vision, he immediately recognised them to be Grand Priests, from their long headdresses and gowns. They were conducting a sacred ritual, but the ring of scholarly men was missing a very important leader.

'Why isn't the Grand Priest of Ursar here?'

'We've searched everywhere for him; he's nowhere to be found,' replied the Priest of Xidrica, who placed his hand on the Gallant Warrior's shoulder, greeting him in mourning.

75

The Gallant Warrior glared at the lifeless corpse of what once had been a cheerful king who enjoyed life's pleasures to the fullest. Whether you loved him or hated him, King Nelaaz's presence could certainly never be ignored. His cheeks were always rosy and vibrant with colour – some jokingly referred to them as ripened apples of summertime – and his laughter was always loud, like his flamboyant character. But now the cheerful king was dead, lying flat on his back with his eyes closed as if he were still sleeping. The glow of life had disappeared; his flabby chin had sunk into his neck, with his skin turning blue as his muscles hardened. Marmicus looked at his body, not expecting to feel any emotion for a man who had betrayed him. Ever since Larsa had died, he had felt nothing but anger; however, King Nelaaz's death reawakened some emotions within him.

'It's always a blessing for a king to die in his sleep and not at his enemy's hands,' the Priest of Xidrica whispered dejectedly. He had abandoned the line of priests who were reading sacred prayers over his body. Even though Marmicus had said nothing, the young priest could tell that he had been affected by the king's death, irrespective of the bitter feud between them.

'Death makes no distinction: whether you're a poor man or a king, death will always find its way into our lives and men will always try to escape it.'

'Death may make no distinction when it selects its victims, but men always do,' Marmicus said quickly. He looked at the body, searching for something.

'Leave us,' instructed Marmicus to the surrounding priests.

'The ritual isn't complete yet; we must prepare his body for the afterlife,' said a priest.

'If you don't leave us, you can join him.' Marmicus had lost his patience with them all; he expected everyone to do as he commanded without question. The Grand Priests abandoned their posts, breaking the circle of death; they could see that he did not trust them.

'You need to be careful, Marmicus; making enemies isn't a wise tactic, irrespective of how strong an opponent you may be,' said the Priest of Xidrica. He had thought about keeping silent, but he felt it necessary to speak up. It was never right to bully anyone.

'Who told you that the king had died in his sleep?'

The priest was baffled by the question. It was obvious that he had died in his sleep.

'No one told me; we all assumed it. He was found like this.'

Marmicus looked more closely at the body, wanting to inspect every detail. He lifted King Nelaaz's chin; his skin was cold and dry. His muscles were beginning to stiffen, making it hard for Marmicus to lift his chin. Marmicus saw purplish blotchy patches running across his flesh, and looked at them closely, then pulled away the covers that concealed the rest of his body. The blotches looked like leopard spots. It was not unusual for someone who had been dead some hours.

'A poor man who has nothing is far more blessed than a wealthy king who has a surfeit of enemies and a mountain of riches,' Marmicus whispered. He traced his fingertips down the length of the king's neck, looking for something unusual, but he felt no trace of strangulation. There were no tears or scrapes to the flesh; no sign of a struggle.

'What are you doing?' the Priest of Xidrica asked.

Marmicus said nothing.

'Not everyone who has died has died unjustly. Death isn't always committed by men, Marmicus; the gods have this power too.' The priest clasped the Gallant Warrior's hand between his own, sensing desperation in his behaviour; it was obvious he wanted to find some kind of answer for the unexpected death. 'Do you dream of her?'

Marmicus looked up, taken aback by the question, and how well the young priest had got to know him; it seemed the priest could see his inner thoughts when he had managed to conceal them even from himself.

'Every night.'

Marmicus peered at the floor, his mind flashing with the visions he saw in his dreams. They were images that haunted him at night and tormented him during the day. Just as he was about to speak of his recurring dream, he saw something that caught his eye. There, lying by the foot of the bed, was a white cotton handkerchief which he recognised as belonging to the Grand Priest of Ursar!

Marmicus knelt down and reached out for the handkerchief.

76

'There are people coming, Mama!' called Zechariah. He rushed into the large mud-brick house, wanting to tell his mother the news. He had seen them approach from a distance when he was playing in the gardens behind the house. At first, Zechariah had thought they were just passing by, but then they walked along the stone path that led towards the house.

'Who is it?' asked Sulaf, glad to have company. Despite resting for several days, her journey to the Black Mountain had mentally exhausted her. Since she had returned, she could not eat or drink, or even bring herself to leave the house. Sulaf sat on a chair, stringing together lapis lazuli beads to make a necklace for herself. It was nearly finished; the bright blue beads would look glorious against her sun-stained complexion.

'I don't know who they are. I've never seen them before. They look like slaves; their clothes are all torn, Mama.'

Sulaf stopped what she was doing, somewhat unsettled by her son's remark. The beads of her necklace fell, spinning, across the table and onto the floor.

'Come inside quickly, I don't want anyone to see you. Do you understand?'

'Yes, Mama,' said Zechariah. The tone of his mother's voice had changed. He rushed into his room and hid behind the wooden door as he always did whenever there was danger. Sulaf had taught him to hide there; it meant he could easily escape the house if anything happened. With no one else to protect the boy, Sulaf had always thought about these things; it was ingrained in her. Her paranoia came from the beatings her husband had inflicted on her over the years – they remained with her even after his death. Sulaf hated him for hurting her, but she hated herself more for not standing up to him when he did. Her experiences had made her strong and independent, but at the same time they had instilled bitterness within her, which had been directed at the princess.

The hardest times for Sulaf had been when she lay with her husband. Every night and each waking morning she would look into his eyes, knowing that the man she loved was looking into someone else's. She endured her husband's touch only because she imagined he was Marmicus.

All the while, Marmicus was in the arms of another woman who never knew him the way she did. Larsa had the pleasure of seeing his face while Sulaf would lie with her tormentor and cry herself to sleep.

With war looming, the need to take precautions naturally resurfaced. Sulaf grabbed her shawl, draping the soft material over her head and across her shoulders, wanting to conceal her beauty from those who were coming. She could not think of a reason for anyone to journey out here; it was so far from the city. Someone was either lost, or had come with the intention of robbing her. Sulaf grabbed her dagger as a precaution, concealing it in the folds of her shawl. She had no intention of using it, but it made her feel safe as she walked out of her house. Sulaf looked behind her, making sure her son was well hidden. Walking towards her were a small boy and a man. It was a relief to know that there was a child; it surely meant that there was less chance of danger. Sulaf looked at the boy. He was no older than her son, possibly younger, but he wore the same wild smile as any enthusiastic child. It never occurred to her that the oracle's prophecy was about to come true; in fact, she had entirely forgotten about it, believing that the woman was mad.

'It's her; she's the woman my grandmother spoke of; I know it,' said Paross to Abram. He saw Sulaf standing a short distance ahead. Although Paross had yet to speak to her, something inside him made him certain that she was the person he had been searching for. After all the miles they had walked, they had found her. The child had overcome every obstacle trying to reach her, and at last his journey was nearing an end. Paross ran to her, leaving Abram to trail behind him. He watched as the little boy sprinted to Sulaf. At his age, Paross could have no idea about women and their jealousies; if he had, he would have known that the greatest poison that can run in their veins is envy, and that Sulaf had plenty of it.

77

Sulaf looked at the boy's hands. They were tiny, like her son's. Unlike his, this boy's hands were covered with brown blisters, some the size of shekels. Under his fingernails was a line of dirt the same colour as wet mud. Sulaf immediately knew that Paross was not from the Garden of the Gods, because of his unclean appearance. No child who lived within the vicinity of the Garden of the Gods appeared so filthy; even peasant men took the time to swim within the cool Euphrates river to cleanse themselves.

'Are you Sulaf?' asked the boy.

'Yes, I am.'

'I've crossed the desert searching for you; you've been the one thought that's travelled with me,' said Paross.

'Why have you been searching for me?'

Paross looked up, feeling embarrassed, as would any child in front of a stranger.

'So you can grant my grandmother peace in her grave.' He was fighting to hold back his tears; they gathered at the corner of his eyes, until his long eyelashes forced them to roll down his dirty cheeks. He quickly wiped them away, using his tattered sleeve, and sniffed.

Paross didn't want Sulaf to feel sorry for him, but he could see pity in her eyes.

Paross had asked many people within the kingdom where Sulaf lived. Finally someone had told him where to find her. He had run eagerly, with Abram following behind. Every step closer to her house had made the burden he carried a little lighter.

'My grandmother wanted you to have this letter before she died. She said that once you have read it you'll know who to give it to. I've travelled a great distance to find you, so I can give it to you.'

The little boy dug deep into his pocket and took out something wrapped in cloth. Paross had ripped the material from his own clothes in his desire to protect the papyrus.

Sulaf watched him remove the cloth. As soon as he did, she remembered the oracle's words. She stepped back, feeling frightened by the child who warmly extended his hand to her. It was as if the oracle's breath had touched her skin, making her jolt. She remembered what the oracle had said: *There will come to you a child with great innocence in his heart and a powerful message carried within his palms. Make no mistake: this boy is your enemy. In his hands he holds a dagger capable of killing any hope of love offered to you by the Gallant Warrior. Kill the boy or kill his message. Whatever you decide, be sure that Marmicus knows nothing about the golden papyrus, for it is as much your enemy as the princess herself …*

Sulaf could not believe it. The oracle had been right. Everything was happening just as she had described; she could clearly see the papyrus in his hands. Her eyes were drawn to it but she was frightened, unsure what the message would say. Paross looked at the papyrus for the last time, knowing that one final act was all that was needed; he hoped his grandmother would find peace at last.

'I tried my best to look after it for you. I'm sorry if it's a little dirty,' said Paross, looking at the papyrus. It was torn around the edges and had little brown blotches of blood on its surface.

'There's no need to be sorry. The main thing is that you've brought it to me,' said Sulaf, with a false smile. She reached out her hand, waiting for the boy to hand it over. 'Have you read it?'

'No, I can't read.'

'What about your friend? Did he read it for you?'

'No, he can't read either; he used to be a slave,' said Paross, giving more information than was necessary. He turned to see where Abram was; he had chosen to remain some distance away, wishing to give the boy some space to carry out his final duty.

Sulaf believed the boy, and was sure that no one had read it: when children lied, they always showed it. The anticipation was killing her; all she wanted to do was snatch the papyrus from the little boy, and read every single word. But the boy had grown attached to it and did not want to give it to her immediately. Instead he began to rant about his dying grandmother and how she had been thrown into the fire because of the papyrus. Sulaf knelt down, wanting to move things along more quickly.

'I promise you, your grandmother will find her peace as soon as you give it to me. I'll protect her letter just as you did. Now, let me ease your burden by taking it off your little shoulders.'

Suspecting nothing, Paross kissed the papyrus as if saying farewell to his grandmother for the last time. It was one of the last objects she had touched when she was alive; he could almost smell her beautiful fragrance upon it. He then softly placed it in Sulaf's hands, and looked into her eyes. As soon as he let it go, Paross saw Sulaf's expression change, from kindness and affection to malice – the same malice as those who had killed his grandmother …

78

Spoken or unspoken, each Assyrian soldier had an understanding that his life meant nothing to his emperor. He amounted to dirt beneath the emperor's sandals, to be trodden on and used without any gratitude for his sacrifices. Not even a nod of appreciation would be offered by Jaquzan. The time had come, yet again, for their lives to be sacrificed. Thousands of men marched together, heading towards the Garden of the Gods, ready to destroy it. They understood that they were waging a war against a sacred kingdom that believed in the sanctity of peace. It was one that brought no threat to them, but the Assyrian soldiers were all subject to the commands of their emperor. So large was the Assyrian army that the warriors marching in their thousands were as ants moving in a swarm across the landscape. No opponent had been capable of stopping them; this war would be no different. If anything, the Assyrian army looked stronger than ever before. Jaquzan had summoned all his troops, sparing no man from his duty. It was a precaution he had taken after the Serpent had sent him news by messenger, warning him that the kings of Babylon had joined forces, uniting in their allegiance to the Gallant Warrior. But even if the kings of Babylon came together, Jaquzan knew that no enemy could penetrate his army; the Babylonians would be as a mere droplet of water in a sea of men.

Jaquzan gazed over his unending army, his eyes outlined in thick black kohl made from lead granules. Larsa looked at him. His sculpted face showed neither pride nor arrogance. He was simply staring at them, unmoved by their presence or influenced by the proof of his supremacy. She sat beside him, dressed in the most exquisite white gown, totally unsuitable for war; her hands were decorated with henna paintings and her hair perfumed with the fragrance worn only by the Assyrian emperor. She was like a rose among thorns, fragile and out of place in the army of soldiers who carried heavy shields and swords. Her shapely lips were stained a bright red with ochre oil, and her eyelids shaded with pollen. Larsa clutched her womb as the emperor's slaves carried them both on processional chairs, which bumped over the wasteland. The orange fabrics sheltering them both from the burning rays of the sun that blew on the wind. Larsa sensed that the Assyrian soldiers were looking at her, and she knew what they were thinking: everyone believed that she was carrying the emperor's unborn infant in her belly, and they feared her because of it – but only she knew the truth.

Larsa looked away. Her golden headdress made metallic sounds with every step the servants took. Long golden leaves draped across her forehead, running around her head. She was grateful that it partially concealed the tattoo that had been etched into her skin. In the middle of the elaborate headdress was the symbol of Ishtar. She had been forced to wear the very symbol that belonged to her own kingdom; Jaquzan wanted her people to recognise her, so that when they were slaughtered they would know that it was under the watchful eyes of their ruler.

Larsa began to recognise where she was in the desert; she could see the green mountains in the far distance, revealing themselves as if inviting the enemy to come towards them. A tiny flickering light could be seen in the blue sky; only those familiar with the kingdom would know that it was the enormous hearth of the Temple of Ishtar, the sacred place where Larsa used to pray and where the body of her beloved father lay buried. Now she was powerless to stop its destruction. With every breath she took, Larsa whispered a prayer to the great goddess Ishtar, hoping that she would hear her pleas and protect her kingdom from what lay ahead. She thought about Marmicus, facing the Assyrian army on the battlefield while she sat beside the emperor as though in thrall to his supremacy and power. Deep down, Larsa knew that Marmicus would never believe that she had willingly betrayed him, but the thought of it still frightened her. *What if the papyrus hasn't reached him? What will become of our love when the world is torn apart?*

79

After putting her son to bed, Sulaf left the mud-brick house and walked towards an old willow tree that had stood there for as long as she could remember. She had chosen this spot to read the papyrus; for some reason it called to her, reminding her of all the childhood memories she shared with Marmicus. Sulaf felt the need to be close to him now.

She looked at the old tree. Its branches flowed with green leaves that draped beautifully down, almost touching the grass; Sulaf remembered the thrill of climbing it. Whenever she and Marmicus had wanted to escape the world, they would race each other towards it and climb its branches; whoever reached the top first would be the winner. Their shared competitive streak was what had made them best friends. Sulaf remembered the feeling when they reached the top: they would stare out over the valley, feeling like kings who commanded their own future, saying nothing – the scenery had enough to say for both of them. It was a wonderful feeling. At other times, they would tell each other stories, and sometimes, when Sulaf felt angry, she would throw small pebbles at those who passed by. Sulaf was always the one to throw them, but Marmicus would always take the blame; it was his way of protecting her, not wanting her be punished by her father. She loved him for what was, itself, an act of love. Sulaf could still hear their laughter, even now as she stood alone beneath the tree on this dark night. The child she once was remained alive inside her.

A crisp wind rushed through the valley, chasing away its warmth, but Sulaf decided to stay. She made a small fire, watching its golden flames dance in front of her. Sulaf sat down, crossing her legs and resting her back against the old tree. She finally opened the papyrus and began to read the letter, her face turning pale as she did so.

'It can't be,' she said. Her eyes flickered across the page. She read it again, and again, until every word had become engraved on her mind. Sulaf now understood what the oracle had meant by her prophecy: the secret in question was not that Larsa was alive, but that she was carrying Marmicus's infant in her womb. Sulaf shook her head. Part of her wanted to run to Marmicus and tell him the news; but no matter how many times she tried to convince herself she should go to him, her jealousy convinced her not to. *You dreamt of happiness, but all you got was heartache …*

Sulaf stared at the papyrus, unaware of how much hope had been invested in it, not only by the princess, but by the woman who had sacrificed her life so that it would reach Sulaf, and by the little boy who had been entrusted with its safekeeping. Perhaps, if Sulaf had fully understood this, she would have thought twice about throwing it into the fire. But envy has a way of hardening the heart. The answer was clear, just as the oracle had prophesied: if Marmicus knew about the papyrus and that the princess was alive, he would never fall in love with Sulaf. Sulaf had no choice but to destroy it. Yet there was still something inside her that stopped her from doing it. Even though she despised Larsa, the words inscribed in the letter revealed love, a feeling she herself wanted to experience with every heartbeat. Sulaf looked at the fire again. It was flickering, slowly dying as if it did not want to be part of her selfish betrayal.

'I want you to know that, even though I envy you, I don't hate you for loving him. I understand why you love him because I love him too,' said Sulaf. She spoke loudly, as if she was speaking to Larsa, wanting to explain herself. 'The world offered you everything: beauty, power and admiration. You had all of this from the moment you were born; but from the moment I was born I had only one thing to cherish, and it was him. I loved Marmicus from the moment I could say his name. But you stole him from me, and I watched you do it, saying nothing and letting him go to you. Now I've got the chance to revive our love. If I give Marmicus this letter, there'll be nothing left to revive between us except heartache. I cannot let that happen to me again. I died the day he fell in love with you, and I won't die for a second time, not when I have the power to save myself.'

Sulaf lifted up the papyrus, and gently kissed it as if saying farewell to a beloved friend. As she dropped it, the crisp wind sent it drifting it towards the flames like a leaf fallen from the willow tree. Sulaf watched it land on the fire. The edges were the first to burn, and soon the golden sheet carrying the princess's hope had completely disappeared.

80

With the approach of the Assyrian army, thick grey clouds began to descend over the Garden of the Gods from nowhere; it was as if the gods themselves had sent their army of chariots to protect the kingdom from harm.

'Cleanse my kingdom of the blood of barbarians, and with the honour of heroes instil it with a new life,' prayed Larsa. She looked up into the skies: a thunderstorm was swelling, ready to drown her kingdom in rain and strike it with lightning. There was a risk that the Euphrates would burst its banks; it had happened a decade ago and it had never been forgotten. It was a bad omen for the Assyrian army, and equally bad for her own people; fighting through a deluge would be a challenge for both armies.

In a way, Larsa wished she could go back to her prison chamber, preferring a life of slavery and exile to watching her kingdom being threatened by war. It made more sense for one person to sacrifice their happiness and freedom than to sacrifice thousands of lives for a possibility of freedom that was far from guaranteed. Larsa knew that it was a cowardly thought; something Marmicus would disapprove of if he had heard her say it.

The shadows of soldiers covered the desert dunes, turning them dark like the skies above. Larsa looked at the mighty hearth of the temple that burned in the distance. The raging fire appeared brighter than ever before because of the dark clouds that robbed the skies of light. Larsa also noticed something else on the horizon; something she had never seen before. Orange flickers of light could be seen across the length of her kingdom's walls. Larsa instantly knew what they were: they were beacons of war. Marmicus had seen the enemy coming, and it was his way of warning the people. The gigantic beacons were lined up on the stone walls, running in an enormous crisscross around the kingdom's walls, proclaiming war. From where Larsa was they appeared faint, although the message they carried was clear – defiant and heartrending at the same time …

81

The weather had changed so drastically. Sulaf looked into the sky and saw clouds coming ominously together, merging, becoming larger, until they were so dense and thick she could almost touch them. Sulaf looked back at the fire. *If Marmicus finds out about the papyrus, I'll say no boy ever came to me,* she said to herself. The fire had died, taking with it all traces of the papyrus, as if it had never existed; but Sulaf started to feel paranoid, and kept looking at the burnt charcoal, imagining that the papyrus was still lying there on the ground. She feared more than anything that someone would find it and give it to Marmicus. Sulaf wished she had chosen a different place to burn the letter. Whenever she walked past the willow tree she had always enjoyed fond memories of their childhood; now this place had become tainted with what she had done. Sulaf felt ashamed, but she knew she had made the right choice. *Marmicus has enough to worry about*, she thought, trying to make herself feel better.

She looked at the willow tree again. Its heavy branches were shaking in the powerful winds that heralded a thunderstorm; it was no longer safe for her to sit there. She hurried towards her home, her hair blowing in all directions in the wind. Just as she reached the mud-brick house, she noticed something in the distance; something small but with great meaning. Across the horizon were small flickering lights, as though stars had fallen to the ground. She looked more closely, trying to work out where they came from and what they meant. Sulaf ran quickly into the house, wanting to wake up her son, who was sleeping peacefully, unaware that the world had changed. Her heart thumped in panic. She had no idea how long the beacons of war had been burning; she had been inside her house for most of the day. It made no difference now; there was only one place they could go, and that was the Temple of Ishtar, like all the other women and children.

82

Peace had shattered like a glass dropped by the hands of chaos. Time was no longer on the side of the people; the Assyrian forces had crossed the border and were marching closer, their drums beating ever more loudly; it was the dreaded music of war, and everyone recognised it. Hundreds of people had gathered outside the Temple of Ishtar. Paross looked back at the queue, which had grown in only a matter of minutes. It went on and on, twisting around the walls of the temple like a giant snake that was trying to suffocate the building. He felt the weight of their bodies press against him; thankfully, Abram was there, and he tried his best to shield the boy from the constant pushing of the crowd. Paross watched as husbands and fathers knelt down and kissed their wives and children, some making false promises, telling them that everything was going to be alright and that they would return to them safely in the morning. Others remained silent, choosing not to lie to them or themselves.

Paross watched them closely, until a group of boys ran past him, laughing loudly as they played among the crowd. Their behaviour seemed different to everyone else's; they were either completely unaware of the army's approach or bored of waiting in the queue with their parents.

'Why are all the men saying goodbye? Aren't they going inside with them?' asked Paross.

'Don't be frightened; just stay close to me and focus on yourself,' said Abram. He held Paross's hand as they waited by the large doors of the temple. They were just another two people in the hundreds of others who fought for a place inside the temple. Paross wanted to sit down, as his knees hurt, but he had seen an old man do the same thing and almost get trampled. It was not a good idea.

'Only the boy can enter; you must join the army or look elsewhere,' ordered a soldier who checked the front of the queue, making sure the right people entered. Abram turned to Paross and his heart sank for him. He felt the boy's hand squeeze tightly around his. Paross had come all this way, expecting to find happiness, and for a few hours he had, but now he would be forced to fight another battle all alone.

'It's time to say goodbye, little scholar,' Abram whispered. He knelt, and looked into the boy's eyes, wanting to reassure him that everything was going to be alright. 'I can't come with you.'

'No, I won't leave you, we will go inside together,' said Paross, clutching his hand and trying to drag him into the temple. The soldier leapt forward, blocking his path, not letting him enter with Abram: 'There's no space for cowardly men …'

'Don't worry about me Paross, I'll go somewhere else,' said Abram, trying to reassure him.

'Then I'll come with you.'

'No, Paross, you can't come with me.'

'Hurry up, you're holding back the queue!' yelled an angry woman who was waiting to enter.

'If you're not going in, then get out of the way,' yelled another. He waved to the soldier, trying to grab his attention so that he would remove them.

The crowds were beginning to turn hostile; people were desperate to get inside. But Paross did not care what they thought. They could wait for a lifetime – he would not leave his friend.

'There's no time, Paross; you must go inside. Please. It's the safest place for you. I must fight.'

'Don't fight, please, I don't want you to die.'

'I must, little scholar, it's my duty. All my life I've been a slave. I was born one, and if I don't fight in this war as a free man, I'll die as one. I don't want to leave you, but I have to do this for myself. Remember when I told you how my masters used to whip me and beat me every night? When they did, I never stood up for myself. Now I have the chance to stand up.' He wanted to make Paross understand. Abram had never cried in all his life, but his eyes welled up with the emotions of a free man. It saddened him to abandon the child, who had never looked at him differently because of the colour of his skin or his status in the world.

'My prophet says, a wise man can never celebrate his freedom when his brothers in the world are imprisoned. You'll understand this when you grow older. Now, please, Paross, you must go inside.'

Paross turned, trying to force himself to walk away from his friend, but he could not; his feet felt glued to the ground. Instead he hugged Abram tightly as he had his grandmother, not wanting to let go. His cheek rested against Abram's shoulder. In that moment Paross felt the loneliness sweep back into his heart; for a brief moment it been washed away by happiness. 'I don't want to be alone.'

'You'll never be alone, Paross, not when you remember the One-God – He's always with you, even now.'

'But I can't see him as I can see you.'

'He can see you and hear you, little scholar. He'll protect you better than I can. If you ask sincerely for His help, He will reach out to you even if you're at the far end of the world.'

'Will he bring you back to me?'

'I can't promise that, but the One-God says that no burden is ever too heavy to be carried. He'll make your heart strong like a ship, so that you can carry any load and sail through any storm,' replied Abram. He untangled the boy's hands, not wanting to give the child false hope of his return. The enemy army was vast, and the likelihood of his survival was small; but, even so, he would rather fight.

The soldier's patience had evaporated; there was no time for bittersweet goodbyes, especially ones that obstructed the gates of the temple. Something had to be done. The soldier grabbed Paross by the arm and marched him away. His clasp was painful, unlike Abram's – he had held Paross as if he were his own son. Paross cried out for Abram, hoping that his friend would save him as he had done in the desert, but this time he would not. His eyes were fixed on him; he stood out, a single figure of courage in a crowd of people fighting for their survival.

'Forgive me, my child, forgive me for letting you down,' said Abram.

He watched the little boy disappear into the temple. Eventually, his cries faded, along with the cries of others, until they could not be heard above the clamour of the crowd.

Paross could no longer see his friend. He had disappeared, abandoning him just as his grandmother had done, and once again he was alone in the world, with no family or friend by his side.

83

Dawn had finally arrived, giving birth to war and a guiltless new morning. The soft light of the sun hid behind a phalanx of stormy clouds as the morning light fought its perennial enemy, darkness. The armies of Babylon stood shoulder to shoulder with their brethren-in-battle from the Garden of the Gods. Their metal shields clattered against one another and a sand-laden wind blew hard against them, stinging their faces. Together they stood in silence, watching the sun burn the clouds with its flaring light. None of them had ever seen a dawn quite like it before: the sun was unveiling its glory before an audience of thousands, freeing itself from the horizon and crowning itself king of the sky. In the stiff silence of nothingness, the soldiers thought of their loved ones, remembering the affectionate gazes of their wives and the laughter of their children. Under their heavy plates of armour some wore locks of their wives' hair, while others carried flowers given to them by their children before they departed for war. Unlike his men, Marmicus stood watching the sunrise, feeling only one emotion: rage. Rage was all that he carried in his soul. It burned inside him, keeping his body warm in the stormy dawn. Marmicus looked out and could hear Larsa's voice against his ear in the wind, as if she was sitting behind him on Orisus, wanting to remind him of the love they once shared. *Your love is my throne, Marmicus. I would never need anything else in the world to make me feel like a queen, apart from you ...* With those words echoing in his mind, Marmicus felt his blood boil. The final hour had come.

'All I ever needed was you, Larsa.'

Every soldier turned his attention to Marmicus as he lifted his helmet, placing it over his head, ready for battle to commence. No man on earth could mistake the Gallant Warrior for anyone else on the battleground; his bronze helmet was one of a kind, brilliantly sculpted into the face of a fearless lion with only his eyes and wide jaw visible behind the mask of war.

'This shall be our last battle together, Orisus. Today we fight for love. Today we die for Larsa,' said Marmicus. From the stallion's nostrils came vaporous plumes, as his warm breath challenged the icy winds. Orisus was a temperamental creature; his hooves kicked up the dirt as he waited for the signal to gallop into battle with his master. Marmicus reached forward and ran his hand down the animal's long neck, seeking to calm him; Orisus would need to save his energy for the long hours of combat. Marmicus grabbed the leather reins, wrapping them tightly around his left hand, his fists clenching until his knuckles turned pale.

The time had come for the ancient ritual of battle to commence. Marmicus dug his heels into his stallion's sides; Orisus began to trot across the open terrain, gathering speed until his hooves left the ground in a full gallop. The commanders of the Babylonian army watched from a distance as the warrior who united an army of thousands reached the centre of the battlefield and came to a stop, waiting for Jaquzan. Only the whispers of the wind could be heard. Marmicus looked out over his enemy. Thousands of Assyrians glared back at him. To them he was a faint figure in the distance, but to him they were as a thick blanket that covered the ground.

Suddenly, came movement. The Assyrian army was stirring en masse, but they were not marching closer; they were parting, making way for the godly presence of their emperor, Jaquzan. Soldiers in their thousands dropped their sword arms by their sides, wall after wall, each man bowing low in respect for the power commanded by one. Jaquzan stood on a chariot drawn by the two lions he had raised from birth. Their honey-coloured eyes searched through the crowds of men, their instinct to hunt and kill an easy prey. For now the lions would have to wait; battle had not yet commenced. Riding on a horse behind the chariot was the Dark Warrior, his armour blackened by the smoking fires of the cities he had burnt to the ground. Today Nafridos had sharpened his sword with special care. His main intention was not to kill an entire community of men as he usually did, but to slit the throat of just one. His lips curled upwards with eager anticipation as he envisaged the Gallant Warrior standing in the middle of the battleground waiting for them.

'Let me kill the Gallant Warrior now! I'll rip his flesh from beneath his armour and feed it to your lions,' said Nafridos to his cousin.

'I want a war, not a battle. Today Babylon will be buried beneath the heads of its people, and their gods will mourn it.'

The Gallant Warrior watched the chariot draw nearer until it finally halted; the roars of the lions did not instil fear within him. Instead he glared at Jaquzan, looking squarely into his eyes where others were terrified to peer at his shadow. His desire to kill him had burnt a hole in his heart. Marmicus knew he could kill Jaquzan at any given moment; the only reason he did not was because it would bring shame to his kingdom – the ancient ritual between leaders had to be observed. The Gallant Warrior abruptly unsheathed his Sword of Allegiance. The large weapon glowed, its silvery metallic light unsettling the lions so that they lunged against their chains, wanting to attack.

'You have no cause to be here. Take your army and leave this kingdom at once. Babylonia stands free, and she will remain free for all eternity. But if you want a war, then your lions will not go unfed; I'll make sure they taste the blood of tyrants.'

'My army will crush yours before you have the chance to scurry back to where you came from. Every man here will die, and all of Babylonia will bleed until her womb has nothing left to give. There is no mercy for men of courage.' replied Jaquzan.

'Then we've agreed on war. By nightfall freedom shall belong to the people, and vengeance shall belong to me.'

'Be careful what you desire, Gallant Warrior. I'll make sure that you see your men die first, before your head joins them,' said the Assyrian emperor. He turned his chariot towards his marquee, from where Larsa watched, wretched and helpless.

'Let the battle of the gods commence.'

84

The Gallant Warrior galloped towards his army, wanting to reach his men, his stature among men magnificently proclaimed by the brilliance of his Sword of Allegiance and the light that glinted off his bronze armour. The Assyrian chariots were assembling behind him, straightening into a single row as they tried to create an attacking wall against the Babylonian army. Their horses snorted loudly, jerking their heads and stamping their hooves in the dirt.

Marmicus knew he had to lift the morale of his soldiers. Wars were won by breaking the enemy's will, and he knew there was a danger that his men would become victims of hopelessness. If they had any chance of winning this war, they had to believe that they could. Marmicus removed his glorious helmet from his head, in order to speak to his soldiers as a man, not as a warrior. This was the time to awaken their spirits with the hope they needed.

'There was a time,' roared Marmicus as he rode across the front ranks, 'when I thought that every war was fought for land and wealth; but I was wrong, loyal warriors of Babylonia, because today this army shall fight for something other than a king's greed. Today we fight for what's right. We fight for our freedom and for the freedom of our homelands.' Thousands of soldiers stared back at him, wishing to be reassured of victory, though knowing that they were greatly outnumbered. 'I have learnt that death is not the heart pausing, or our breath ceasing; it is hope fading and dreams shattering. For, without our hopes and dreams, we are already dead. Today your sword shall be the guardian of life; let no enemy take it away from you. Your convictions shall be your armour; remember them when you stare into your enemy's eyes. Freedom is born from the seed of sacrifice, so I say this to you now, brothers of Babylon: fight well and embrace your swords, for the sake of all those you love. If death should relieve you from your duty, then remember this: one day of freedom is worth more than a thousand years of slavery. It is better to die as a free man than to live as a slave. So embrace your swords, guardians of Babylon, and do not release them until freedom is yours once more. Know that I shall fight alongside you until the light of the sun burns out; if I should die then at least I will have fought bravely alongside my brothers in battle. For empires rise and empires fall, but the names of their warriors will live on forever. Let victory be ours!'

The army of thousands roared. The Gallant Warrior had lifted their spirits, steeled their hearts and settled their nerves. They were ready.

'Allegiance lies in the heart of our swords!' they roared in unison. Their eyes locked like falcons on the lines of men that stood in the distance. Their hearts had become fearless, for today they were defenders of freedom. The moment had come. The drums sounded. The horns blew. The battle for the Garden of the Gods had begun ...

85

The Assyrian chariots began to charge in their hundreds, dust whipping into the air, as their wooden wheels ran across the uneven battlefield.

'Hold the lines. Raise your shields. Be the gods of courage,' roared Marmicus. The Babylonians stood their ground; they would not move unless the command was given. Marmicus watched as the Assyrian chariots bolted towards his lines; the charioteers lashed their horses, and hundreds of arrows rained down, landing on the ground, missing the Babylonian front lines. Marmicus knew it was only a matter of time: every stride brought them closer, and his army would soon fall within their firing range. Another wave of arrows darkened the sky, and the first screams of war were heard.

'Close your positions. Wheel left! Stand behind the wind! Stand behind the wind!' yelled Marmicus. The Babylonian soldiers began to move; they lifted their shields higher, holding them above their heads, blocking out the onslaught of arrows that continued to rain from the sky.

'Hold your ground; be the mountain that cannot be moved!' ordered Marmicus, galloping past the front lines. Seeing the

Babylonian manoeuvres, the Assyrian chariots began to alter their line of advance to align themselves with the enemy. They raised their bows again, pulling back their bowstrings; they fired again, and hundreds of arrows shot into the air, then hailed down, but this time the winds curled them away, blowing them off-target. The tactic was brilliant: the Gallant Warrior had turned the stormy weather into an ally, using it to his advantage. The charioteers tried to swerve again; they needed the wind behind them. They lashed their horses harder, urging them to gallop faster, at a different angle. This was exactly what Marmicus wanted: they had fallen into his trap. He knew that the Assyrian chariots could only be driven in straight lines, and that if the horses galloped at such speeds without slowing before they turned, the chariots would overturn. Marmicus watched, holding his breath. The Assyrians galloped and the chariots continued to turn; this was the pivotal moment of his plan. Every frenzied lash on the horses' backs brought them closer and the Assyrian chariots curled across the battlefield like the rings of a giant whirlpool. Suddenly, their wheels began to buckle one by one and come loose, ripping off the wooden axles, and the shrieks of the charioteers rang out as their bodies were flung into the air, many of them trodden beneath the hooves of their own horses. It was a humiliating start for the Assyrians.

'Your arrows, men. Now!' ordered Marmicus. This was the time to exploit the Assyrians' weakness. The order was passed instantly down the lines, and the archers moved to the front, the shield men moving behind them. They fired, and their arrows pelted into the gloomy sky, seeming to cut through the clouds as they came down in a long, shallow arc upon the Assyrian ranks. Marmicus watched, feeling some relief as more Assyrians fell; but new weapons of war had emerged, ones that they had never seen before.

'Bring forward the catapults! We will crush them one by one,' declared the Dark Warrior. His teeth clamped together as he watched his front line break and flee, trying to escape the arrows. Hundreds of slaves began to push enormous catapults over the ground, their muscles protected by leather armour, unlike that of the Assyrian soldiers. They had all been brought to war for one reason – to push these towers across the battlefield. The arms of the catapults were constructed from massive timber beams that seemed to reach to the sky, towering over the battlefield. They were weighed down by boulders that dripped with black Baba Gurgur oil. The oil would be set alight by the slaves; once ignited, rocks would be launched in volleys and hurled across the sky with an unstoppable and terrifying force, obliterating swathes of men across the battlefield, setting soldiers alight and crushing them where they stood.

Giant, fiery rocks emerged through the thick clouds, as suns falling to the earth, and the screams of burning soldiers filled the air.

There was chaos.

Marmicus felt the ground move with every volley; he dug his heels into his horse's flanks, racing towards the centre of the battlefield. He raised his Sword of Allegiance, trying to grab his soldiers' attention. Fiery missiles fell around him like volcanic hail. Orisus reared, lifting Marmicus's body high so that he could be seen by every one of his men.

'Change formation! Make space in the middle – attack like the crescent moon eclipsing the sun!'

The Babylonian soldiers began to change their formation again. This time they turned the front lines into the shape of the crescent moon. It was another clever tactic: the heavy catapults were cumbersome to move, and boulders began to fall in the space created. Marmicus continued to gallop through the lines, roaring out his orders to everyone who had not heard him. They had to act as one unit if they wanted to survive. A large boulder blasted across, and Marmicus jerked the reins to stop Orisus from galloping into its path. The horse pulled his head up and back, to within inches of his rider, and Marmicus took the opportunity to murmur encouragement in his ear. The boulder crashed into the ground, sliding across the mud and killing instantly those unfortunate enough to be in its path.

'Aim your arrows at the slaves! Fire!' yelled Marmicus. He felt guilt and pity for the slaves, who were not his enemy, but if they had any sense they would run away, and leave warring to the soldiers. The Babylonian archers locked their eyes onto them; they knew the slaves were practically defenceless, but this was war, and empathy had no place in war. They fired, and hundreds of arrows spun across, striking the slaves' legs and necks; their leather armour made little difference. Marmicus watched as most of them began to run; it was an instinctive reaction, and he felt only relief.

'Break the lines! Pursue them to their deaths!' roared the Dark Warrior, realising that the time had come to charge. Following his command, thousands of Assyrian foot soldiers ran towards the Babylonian army. Every man now fought for his life against the onslaught of the enemy; spears flew and swords were thrust into soft flesh. Men trod on corpses, while others lay in agony, slowly dying beneath the soldiers' feet.

Marmicus fought through the oncoming swords and arrows; sand and earth scattered and dust rose. Enemies fought each other, staring into death's eyes, each hoping that the man in front would lose his life, and not he. Marmicus swung his sword, killing everyone who attacked him, blood splattered on his face and armour. Another boulder blasted across his path; Marmicus swung to the side, dodging it.

All the while, Marmicus had no idea that he was being followed. The Dark Warrior was manoeuvring himself towards him, determined to reach his opposite on the battlefield; Marmicus embodied everything he wanted to destroy. His pupils grew larger as his eyes focused on the moving object he desired to kill; Nafridos was slaughtering a tide of men to reach one man. Leaning out of his saddle, Nafridos swung his weapon through the men, hacking into limbs; a metallic taste seeped into his mouth as their blood splattered across his face. Arrows were fired from both directions; Nafridos raised his shield, holding it above his head with one hand while he swung his sword, hacking into bones as though chopping reeds. His skill with a sword lay in the movement of his wrist, but there were too many soldiers between him and his target. Nafridos needed another kind of weapon. He looked at the ground and smiled as he ripped a long spear from one Assyrian soldier, who had not yet died.

'I need this,' said Nafridos as he held up the spear. His eyes squinted as he focused on the Gallant Warrior, and in that moment his world became still. All he could see was Marmicus, and the spear in his own hand. Nafridos waited for the right moment. With great deliberation, he leant back in his saddle and threw the spear, thrusting it powerfully across the battlefield. Nafridos watched it soar above the heads of soldiers, flighting towards its target. An arrogant smile spread across his face as Marmicus remained oblivious to its approach – or so it seemed. Just as Marmicus struck his sword against another, he caught the reflection of a spearhead hurtling down towards him. He instantly raised his shield, covering his head, and the long spear sliced through his shield, penetrating it and scraping his shoulder. He turned his head to see who his enemy was; something inside him warned him to remember it well – Marmicus had never seen such skill before. The Dark Warrior was staring back at him, his eyes unmoving and his body coated in blood. There was pleasure on his face, which spoke of excitement at Marmicus's death. In that brief encounter both warriors knew they were made to destroy one another. The question was, who would leave the battlefield alive?

For now the battle between the two warriors would have to wait, for more pressing matters had emerged. The Dark Warrior heard his name being called, and looked over his shoulder to see the position of his soldiers on the battlefield. As he did, he saw something moving in the distance. It was a trap! A tactic which no previous enemy had ever tried. Another army, vast in number, was approaching from behind, loosing their arrows and trapping the Assyrian army in between two enemies. Marmicus had wanted the Assyrians to charge from the beginning; that was why he had not advanced – he needed to keep his front line intact. All this time Nafridos had believed that they were fighting the whole of the Babylonian army, when in fact his enemy had been divided into two sections; it was a decisive and brilliant move for the Garden of the Gods and Babylon; now the Assyrians would be locked between them, with arrows hurled at them from both positions. The Dark Warrior galloped towards the emperor's marquee. Nafridos knew what had to be done, but he did not have the stomach or power to do it. *We will lose this war if we do not retreat now!*

86

Larsa had been forced to sit beside the Assyrian emperor in an extravagant marquee hidden away from the battlefield. Despite being some distance away, Larsa could still hear the horror of war, knowing full well that she sat beside the one man who could stop it all. Unknown to her, missiles were being launched into the gloomy skies, the burning rocks landing on her soil, rolling and flattening anything that stood in their path. All that Larsa felt was the flutter of the tent, not knowing what awesome weapon had been unleashed against her people.

Jaquzan walked out of the marquee. His exquisite cape was held by his slaves, who made sure that the divine fabric would not touch the unconquered soil.

'Bring the princess outside; I want my heir to see the glory of war through his mother's eyes.'

Jaquzan believed that the horrific battle scenes would make Larsa's womb become stronger, so that his son would be trained to love war almost before his life had begun, and to embrace the life of a conqueror. The guards moved in to take the princess. Knowing her, Jaquzan expected Larsa to refuse them, and put up a fight as she always did – but Larsa gave in without protest. She stood up and walked out, following her master from the tent towards the living portrait of war. Larsa wanted to see war for herself. All this time she had spoken of freedom as if she knew everything about it, but in reality she knew nothing. The men who were being slaughtered outside were paying the price for her freedom. Larsa knew that if she did not have the courage to look into the eyes of war, then she would never be worthy to enjoy the subsequent freedom. She placed her hand on her womb and walked out of the marquee, feeling the beauty of life growing inside her, just as the world around her was being stripped of life. The need to protect her unborn infant grew stronger; it was the last remaining granule of happiness she had left in the world. Her belly had become larger, her womb shaped by the glory of motherhood. Anyone who looked at her could see she was carrying a child.

'Today the mighty rivers of Babylon shall run with the blood of gallant warriors, and by nightfall they'll become an extinct breed,' Jaquzan whispered. He stared calmly into the sea of soldiers, who hacked away at one another in the distance. Larsa stood beside him, saying nothing. She simply watched as her glorious homeland fell towards destruction. Never had she imagined looking out onto her kingdom and hearing the piercing shrieks of men replace the songs of wild birds. Thousands of soldiers were dying on her soil; their blood draining away into the land. All the dense palm trees which had once grown wild around the edges of her kingdom had been chopped down, making way for war. The long green grass had been scorched, creating a flat piece of wasteland for the battle. Larsa quietly wept, reacting to the first signs of war, and for the first time she found relief in her tears.

'You can cut a rose from its stem,' she said. 'But it will always grow back from its roots. The same goes for courageous men – they will always rise up, and you will always cut your hand trying to tear them down.' She stood beside Jaquzan, breathing heavily, the scent of blood heavy in the air. Jaquzan turned towards her, placing his hand affectionately on her belly as any father would. It seemed that even in the chaos of war Jaquzan embraced his fatherhood.

'Then you'll be the one to bathe our infant's hands, because they shall bleed from tearing out those roots.'

Suddenly, Nafridos appeared in the distance, galloping as fast as he could towards the emperor's marquee. Something was obviously wrong – he cherished combat; there was no reason for him to rush back if the war had not yet been won.

'We've been deceived!' Nafridos roared as he stopped in front of them. His skin was covered in blood. He had lived up to his reputation as the Dark Warrior: just as he had told the princess, every part of him was soaked with blood.

'We've been trapped! The Babylonians are attacking us from behind and—'

'Then fight from the front – their army is like a grain of sand compared to mine. They will die either way,' replied Jaquzan.

'You're missing the point, cousin – my men will be unable to fight like that, our soldiers will be attacked from both sides. They'll be trapped in the middle. We'll lose this war if we don't retreat, cousin. We must fall back now.'

Nafridos knew his men well; they were accustomed to using the same military tactics they had used in every other kingdom they had crushed, and there had never been a need to change them, until now.

'Order the retreat!' Jaquzan blasted angrily. The Dark Warrior darted back towards the battlefield: for now, the Gallant Warrior had saved the Garden of the Gods, but the emperor would make sure that the silence would not last for long. His army remained vast; he still had a strong chance of winning.

Marmicus, my love, there's hope yet because of you, Larsa thought. She knew then that Marmicus was still alive, and that her kingdom still had hope.

'Wherever there are tyrants, there will always be freedom fighters to oppose them,' she said.

'Then tomorrow I'll rip them out from the roots so that they can never rise up again,' Jaquzan replied bitterly, turning back into the marquee.

87

Time meant nothing now. It was drifting aimlessly like the stormy clouds in the sky, without any kind of purpose. Paross rocked back and forth, waiting for war to end and peace to arrive with the new morning light. Silence gave people room to think; everyone's minds were united in the same place, each of them thinking about the battleground where their loved ones were fighting for survival. Paross thought of Abram, and glanced at the empty space beside him where he could have sat. What had become of him? Was he dead? If he was, was his body being trodden on by soldiers, or had it been thrown onto a stack of bodies, ready to burn in a mass grave? He missed Abram's wisdom, and the way he spoke lovingly about the One-God as if he were a friend of his who had travelled alongside him throughout the harsh years of his enslavement.

Now Paross was alone, lost in the midst of people who didn't know his name or anything about the agonising journey he had undertaken to get here. His was just another face in the thousands who sat waiting for something to happen. Paross looked around. Women and children surrounded him. If they were not crying, then they were staring angrily at the soldiers who had refused to let their husbands and sons enter the temple for refuge. Paross could not blame the soldiers for what they had done. Deep down he knew that if Abram had been allowed in, he would still have given up his space to someone else, offering his place in the temple to another who needed it more. It made no difference now. The guards had locked the temple doors; no one could enter or leave. Everyone sat in silence, not knowing if the enemy would break down the doors or if the temple would be set on fire by the Assyrian army.

When the war began, Paross watched as mothers hugged their children tightly, showering them with kisses, perhaps for the last time, and wiping away their tears. It was during these moments that Paross felt the loneliest. He watched as toddlers buried their faces in their mothers' necks for reassurance. Others lay on the floor, crying for their husbands, their backs cushioned by sheepskin blankets they had carried into the temple, one of the few possessions they had taken with them. Paross stared at the goatskin sacks lying around the temple. He could not help but think how miserable an existence it was when the life of a person could be summed up by the few possessions they clung to. He knew his own life told the same story. In the darkest hour, when the screams of war were at their highest pitch, Paross thought about his grandmother; the way she used to hug him at night whenever he was frightened, the way she used lick her fingertips to wipe the dirt off his face. It was a sensation he had hated, but now he missed it deeply. Then the Dark Warrior's face entered his mind. Nothing could make him forget the look of his face: it was embedded in Paross's mind like a splinter embedded beneath the skin. Paross knew that if Abram had faced him on the battleground only his One-God could save him …

88

A man who is always victorious in his endeavours finds the taste of defeat far harder to stomach than those who are familiar with its bitter flavour. This was exactly how Jaquzan felt: tonight the taste of defeat was more intolerable then he could ever have imagined. He had never lost a war before, and now his pride bore the brunt of his humiliation. Seven loyal advisors prostrated themselves before his feet, each one pressing their foreheads so hard against the ground that red pressure spots appeared on their skin. They were hoping that the Assyrian emperor would show them mercy, but they all secretly knew why they had been summoned. Defeat was not an option; they all knew this.

'Forgive us. None of us could have anticipated his strategy. Tomorrow our soldiers will be stronger and more prepared,' said one advisor.

'I do not speak the language of forgiveness,' replied the Assyrian emperor. He clenched his hand into a fist, his fingernails digging deep into his skin. Jaquzan was not a man to show emotion, but today he found it hard to conceal his rage.

'You've made a mockery of my name and my empire; now I shall make a mockery of you all.' He turned to his guards. 'Round up the rest; I want them to watch these fools struggle for their lives just as my army struggled to be victorious today. Coat them with blood and feed them to my lions.'

The Dark Warrior stood at the sidelines watching intelligent men he had worked with in past wars being led away, to be killed like goats. The smell of bloody battle that lingered on his skin had been washed away and replaced with the fresh scent of lemon and oranges; it was the soap of war, cleansing all cuts and scrapes and removing from his skin the filth of his enemies.

'Are you sure you want them dead? If you kill these men our kingdom will have no advisors left!' said Nafridos.

'They've outlived their usefulness. The best advisor is one's own conscience, for there the tongue can never deceive the mind.'

'We still have a good chance of being victorious. Let the soldiers rest. By morning we'll have a new strategy, and a new victory. Now we know how large our opponent is, we won't be deceived again.'

'The Gallant Warrior is only one small problem,' said Jaquzan.

'What's the other?'

'My soldiers can longer be trusted to win this war. They've always feared me, but today they've been reminded that it's possible to defeat a god. We both know they don't fight out of loyalty, or love for me, but out of fear of what will become of them if they refuse.' Jaquzan ground his teeth as he considered his options. 'Victory does not come without loyalty to a cause. I need a warrior who has shown me loyalty; that's where you come into play. We'll settle this war using the ancient art of combat, one warrior against another. Whoever wins the battle will claim victory as theirs before the eyes of thousands.'

'Is this your way of instructing me to take up the challenge, cousin?' Nafridos smirked.

'It's my way of offering you the glory you've always desired. I give you permission to destroy the man you were born to destroy, and in return I'll burn this kingdom to the ground so that all memory of my defeat dies with it. There'll be nothing left of this Garden apart from the blackened statues of its gods.'

Nafridos understood that his cousin had not given him this opportunity out of generosity: he needed him and it made the opportunity even more alluring. This was exactly what the Dark Warrior had been waiting for all his life! Every battle he had experienced led up to this final moment. He had agreed to set aside his own share of the glory for the sake of the ultimate prize – victory. Every droplet of sweat that poured from his brow, every drop of blood, was precisely so that he could gain the skills necessary to annihilate the one opponent who matched his capabilities in combat.

'What if Marmicus doesn't accept the proposition? What then?'

'He'll accept it; we can be certain of that.'

'Why should he? Only a fool would accept it.'

'A man in love is always a fool. If Marmicus chooses not to fight, then he shall have to watch his beloved princess being slaughtered on the battlefield before his very eyes. That's why he'll accept the proposition – his heart will compel him to. I hold his heart in the palm of my hand, and it shall be crushed until its beat falls silent.'

'What about your child? If you kill her, you kill him too.'

'You overestimate my compassion. I'll be the one to draw the sword myself. This war shall be remembered as the battle for Larsa – one love dying for another.'

Nafridos looked at the emperor, realising that his cousin was a genius and his plan flawless. Marmicus would undoubtedly accept the challenge: he would do everything in his power to save the one he loved from harm, especially when he had thought she was dead.

'Before we kill him, there's work to be done and arrangements to be made,' said Jaquzan. No detail would be ignored.

'Arrangements to be made?' muttered Nafridos.

'Precisely.'

All that was left was one more stroke of wickedness. An act that could only be committed within the walls of the kingdom and by the most treacherous of men: a Grand Priest ...

89

At last the Serpent planned to come out of the murky shadows of deceit into the light of truth. The time had come for him to commit the final act of betrayal, sacrificing the Gallant Warrior's body in the name of the Assyrian emperor, a man he served without question or guilt. His final set of orders had been explicitly laid out, instructing him as to what to do. In exchange for his loyalty he had been promised a throne; but the Serpent sought a different prize altogether, one that had no equivalent in wealth or material goods. He wanted to reveal his true identity to the person that mattered the most. Revealing the truth was all that he needed; it would heal him as cool water heals a burn. He wanted Marmicus to know why he had betrayed the kingdom; telling him this would reveal a secret which had followed – and haunted – him since childhood.

'Tonight, you above all others shall know what it feels like to be bitten by a snake ...' the Serpent smiled as he slithered towards the palace gates in search of the Gallant Warrior's chamber.

90

Marmicus had returned to the palace after the battle, where his physician the Asu was waiting for him. The shoulder wound was deeper than the Asu had expected. He gently removed the Gallant Warrior's heavy armour and instructed Marmicus to raise his arm, trying his best to stop the bleeding. Squeezing the cloth free of blood, the Asu cleansed the large flesh wound, dipping the cloth into a bowl containing fresh salt water and yarrow. Even though the wound was not fatal, there was still a prospect of it becoming infected.

'I've met many warriors, but I've never met a man capable of throwing a spear like that. His aim was perfect. If it hadn't been for the wind, it would have been on target. Whoever he was, I saw his desire to kill me.'

'Then we must thank the gods for the strong winds they sent us,' said the Asu.

His enemy's face came back into Marmicus's mind; Marmicus remembered how he had looked at him with disdain, trying to intimidate him. He was confident in his abilities, and rightly so. Somehow, Marmicus knew they would meet again on the battlefield; if they did, he would be better prepared next time.

The Asu took a long iron rod, which had been heating in the coals of the fire for some time, and hovered it over the Gallant Warrior's shoulder. Marmicus could feel its heat against his body.

'I must seal the wound to stop the bleeding. If I don't do that, it will become infected. The battlefield is always filled with diseases.'

'Do it.'

'Brace yourself – this will hurt.'

'Do it. I am ready.'

Marmicus clenched his arm, trying to prepare himself for the pain that would follow. The Asu held the hot iron rod against the open wound, searing the skin with its ferocious heat. Marmicus bit his lip, tried to stop himself from yelling out. The pain was indescribable. Marmicus could smell his skin burning; it was the same smell that came after battle, when bodies were piled together and set alight.

Finally, the Asu lifted the hot instrument away and quickly dipped his hands into another bowl, filled with cloves, calendula oil and lavender. The mixture was intended to numb and disinfect the area, although it offered little relief from the pain. The Asu then carefully bandaged the wound.

'Can I come in? I want to congratulate the Gallant Warrior on his victory,' called the Priest of Xidrica. He entered the chamber holding a clay jug filled to the brim with barley beer.

'I recommend he rests.'

'No, he can come in.'

'Then I'll leave you to talk,' replied the Asu. He dried his hands using a cotton cloth then walked out of the chamber to attend to the rest of the day's injured.

'You shouldn't be too eager to celebrate victory: this kingdom may have won the battle, but we still haven't won the war. Tomorrow we face a new dawn filled with new challenges,' chided Marmicus, trying to get up. The Priest of Xidrica could tell he was in a lot of pain. He had difficulty in standing up; whoever had struck him must have been extremely skilled.

Marmicus walked towards his armour, which was covered in dried blood. Across the metal were scrapes from swords and spears. Marmicus placed his hand on the cold metal, remembering the faces of the men he had killed, though this time he felt nothing for them. He grabbed a clean cloth, squeezing the water from it, and began to wash away the traces of blood that lingered on the metal.

'Today our kingdom's walls will tremble with the cries of widows searching for their husbands,' he whispered.

'You obviously haven't left the palace; the people are already celebrating our victory in the streets. Besides, wives who have lost their husbands still have their children and their homes. That's enough to be thankful for.'

The Gallant Warrior said nothing. The truth was that he did not like the fact that the people were celebrating a battle that was half-won. Anything could happen – he had learnt that from life's bitter lessons.

'Has no one found the Grand Priest of Ursar?'

'That is partly why I've come to see you. There's something important I must tell you, and it concerns him …'

'What is it?'

'It can wait for a moment – you've already gone through enough trials to last a lifetime. Let's have a drink, at least to celebrate our small moment of victory.'

'I can't celebrate a victory when my soldiers are being buried and tyrants are still being feared.'

'Then let us pledge our allegiance to justice, and to the memory of the princess. She deserves to be honoured, no matter how small the victory may be.'

The Priest of Xidrica placed the clay jug on the table and began to pour the barley beer into two chalices. The truth was he needed a drink, but he did not want to drink alone. He offered the chalice to Marmicus, along with a reassuring smile, and lifted his own cup into the air in praise of his friend's remarkable success on the battlefield. With no reason to question his loyalty, Marmicus took the chalice, placing his lips to it, then drank the barley beer until there was nothing left. The young priest watched as the Gallant Warrior gulped it down, the alcohol immediately relieving the intense pain in his shoulder.

'You truly have a remarkable gift for war. Today the gods watched one man defeat an empire of thousands.'

'If knowing how to kill men is a trait envied by gods,' said Marmicus, 'then I've been cursed, not blessed by it … How did you get that scar on your hand?' He had never noticed it before today, as the young priest usually chose to cover it with his long sleeves.

'My master gave it to me when I was a child,' said the young Priest of Xidrica. He turned to the chair and sat down, looking at Marmicus as if waiting for something to happen. 'Whenever I look at it, I'm reminded of what's been taken away from me, and what I've struggled to take back all these years. If you look carefully, you'll see it looks like a snake writhing along my hand. Doesn't it?'

91

M armicus stared at the scar which stretched along the young
priest's hand. He was right; it did resemble a snake.

'I was a slave as a child, and I'm still a slave, even as a man.'

'If serving the gods makes you a slave, why don't you free yourself
from their rule and become the free man you desire to be?' asked
Marmicus. He could not understand why anyone would wish to live
a life that was not of their own choosing.

'You should ask yourself the same question, Gallant Warrior.
Aren't you the slave of the people, constantly fighting for them,
instead of yourself?'

'If fighting for justice makes me a slave to the people then I'm
content with that,' responded Marmicus. An odd tingling sensation
ran along the back of his tongue. 'What was in that drink? It doesn't
sit well with me.'

'It wouldn't sit well with anyone.'

The young priest gave him a long, penetrating look that was
uncharacteristic of him.

'What was it?'

'Do you really want to know?'

'Yes.'

'It's the same poison I gave to your beloved king.'

At first Marmicus thought it was a poor joke. The Priest of Xidrica knew how much he honoured Larsa's father.

'You offend our king with those words; he still deserves our respect, even after death.'

'If I wanted to offend you and your beloved king, I'd tell you everything that I've done to betray you both.'

The young priest had finally shed his cloak of false humility and revealed his treacherous self. He relaxed on his chair, watching his victim begin to show the first signs of being poisoned. Marmicus turned to grab his Sword of Allegiance, but the sudden movement made his nauseous feeling worse. His head began to spin, then throb.

'I see the poison's working. I have to say it's worked more quickly than I expected,' smiled the Serpent. He noticed Marmicus trying to focus on him, but his eyelids had grown heavy. The young priest chuckled. Now the Gallant Warrior was powerless to do anything: the poison was penetrating him, turning a strong man into a helpless weakling. Marmicus felt the tingling sensation in his mouth spread. It had moved to his hands and feet, and even his tongue felt heavy.

The Serpent watched, enjoying every little flicker of pain on Marmicus's face. He had been waiting anxiously for this, dreaming of it every single day like a child who eagerly awaits the arrival of a special gift. He threw his chalice onto the floor, and it rolled towards Marmicus's feet. It was time to reveal all.

'Your king was right. I remember him saying that a man will always carry two things in his hands: friendship in one, and a knife in the other. You should have taken his advice; you made a grave mistake placing too much trust in a person when you hadn't tested them.'

Marmicus sunk slowly onto his knees, then collapsed sideways onto the ground. He remained conscious, but his body began to tremble, and saliva poured from his mouth as if it were water coming from a well. Everything around him became distorted and cloudy.

'Why ... did you ... do this?' asked Marmicus, slurring his words. It was hard for him to speak, as the poison had numbed his tongue. He could feel it roll back into his mouth; if it did, it would block his breathing passage, and he would certainly suffocate.

'Never blame the enemy without first understanding his motives,' the Serpent said. Stepping over to Marmicus, he grabbed his jaw, lifting his head, wanting him to hear every single word. Marmicus could not fight back; he was at the priest's mercy.

'If I told you that your king had a son, would you believe me? Well, you should. After the Queen died, your king became lonely at night; he would call upon my mother to keep his bed warm. She did, until one day she fell pregnant. Who could have imagined that a whore would give birth to a bastard prince? When she told him, he banished her from the kingdom, he wanted to hide what he had created with his own body. My mother was forced to live in exile, and I was forced to grow up watching her sell her body to men just so that she could feed and clothe me. One night, my mother disappeared; I looked for her everywhere, but she had vanished like the cool winds from the desert. I was forced to fend for myself, a boy of eight, who knew nothing about the ways of the world. Eventually, I gave up, and was sold into slavery. I'll never forget the day when I pleaded with my masters to let me go, I told them that I was a prince from the Garden of the Gods; they laughed at me and beat me until I learnt to keep silent, but I never forgot who I was or where I came from. I endured the pain, biting my tongue, and enduring their punches just so that I could survive to see my father. No one imagines that their curse could become their blessing, but that was precisely what happened to me; I was sold to a Grand Priest who gave me my freedom on the condition that I loved the gods like he did. I was free in body, but my mind had become slave to a false love of temples and stone. I pretended to love them, believing in their wretched power just so that I could join the Counsel of Grand Priests and meet my father – who led them. I had pinned my every hope on that day.'

Marmicus began to lose consciousness at this point, but the Serpent would not let him slip away. He grabbed his shoulders, and shook him frenziedly, but it was no use, he had passed out.

'Stay awake!' the priest commanded. He got up angrily, and began to kick his chest, his heels digging into lungs and stomach. Marmicus stirred, he coughed spitting blood because he had bitten his tongue; the pain would keep him awake for a few more minutes.

'Welcome back,' said the priest as he knelt down, and grabbed Marmicus's jaw again. 'Now where was I? Ah, I remember now … after years of waiting and planning, I was summoned by your king; I saw him several times, but one night he invited me alone to his chamber. I took the chance I needed, and poured poison into his wine, watching him take sips until he collapsed. I called the guards and told them that I had found the king lying on the floor; I watched them lift him up, knowing full well that even though he was lying motionlessly, he could still hear and see everything around him. He was trapped in his own body: now he knew what it felt like to be a prisoner. I visited him every night with the rest of the Grand Priests, they were praying for him to gain strength but, unlike them, I prayed for him to suffer - I wanted him to hate his life just as he had made me hate mine. I would have been happy watching him lying there forever, but the Grand Priest of Ursar became suspicious of me when I asked to see him alone. It looked as though I wanted to confess something to the king. He began to watch me closely, but although he said nothing, I could see the suspicion in his eyes. Finally, I had the chance to see the king alone without anyone knowing, so I came to his chamber, and it was then that I noticed something – something I'd never noticed before. I saw myself in him: his eyes were the same as mine, so too were his nose and lips; and then it occurred to me why the Grand Priest of Ursar had been suspicious of me. It wasn't because I wanted to see the king alone; it was because of how similar we looked. The Grand Priest of Ursar had noticed it too, that I had my father's face, and when he noticed it, he must have remembered the king's secret after all these years. I knew then that the king had confided in him, telling him what he had done.'

The priest stared at his hands as if recalling the moment he realised this. The memory was crystal clear, like the Tigris river.

'On that night, I remember looking into my father's eyes, seeing myself within them. I told him what I'd done, how I had poisoned him, and how I'd planned to do it for years. I saw his face react, as if he knew already, and as if he were deeply sorry for every moment of suffering I'd endured because of him. But it was too late to be remorseful. Unseen scars can never heal when they afflict the heart and, just like you, I wanted vengeance, not only for myself, but for my mother, who had suffered alone, in silence. It wasn't enough that he was trapped in a body he could no longer control. So I strangled him. I remember looking at him, seeing his fear, and feeling absolutely nothing as I wrapped my hands around his neck. I kissed his forehead, just as any loving son would, and left, without a flicker of guilt for what I'd done. I may have killed him that night, but I killed my past too – there was nothing left to bind me to anyone, except for my half-sister. I was the one who told the Assyrians. She was another thorn in my flesh, but I didn't hate her for it, because she was innocent – unlike our father. So, you see, I killed your heart with my own hands and, if I could, I would do it all over again.'

For the first time, Marmicus had lost a battle on which his life depended. The venom had taken over his bloodstream, poisoning every inch of his body until he fell unconscious, his body tired from a world that had betrayed him in more ways than one. If only the Gallant Warrior had known that the princess was alive and that he had been blessed with fatherhood, maybe then he would have chosen to fight for his life ...

92

The Serpent's work was complete. The young priest looked at Marmicus lying still on the floor. He smiled and grabbed the Sword of Allegiance which lay beside him. He held it in his hands, marvelling at it for a few minutes; it was truly magnificent.

'Who could ever have imagined that the mighty Sword of Allegiance would be covered with the blood of its keeper?' said the young priest, raising it. The weapon would be proof of his treachery, showing the Assyrian emperor that he had done everything that had been asked of him. Once he showed him this, he would be in possession of a throne and a kingdom worthy of him. But life is never simple, for where evil conspires, so too does justice. The doors of the chamber were flung open, and guards rushed in, taking up position in every corner of the chamber, making sure that there was no place for the young priest to escape. They were led by one man – a person who had been misjudged, especially by Marmicus, who he had come to save.

The Grand Priest of Ursar rushed to Marmicus, the edges of his robes soaking up the blood that seeped from his injured body.

'Quickly! Call the Asu; tell him Marmicus has been wounded!'

yelled the Grand Priest. Deep down, he knew it would make no difference. Marmicus was lifeless, his eyelids closed and his chest unmoving.

'I owe you a great debt of gratitude,' said the Priest of Xidrica. 'It's because of you that Marmicus placed his trust in me. You should have told him of your suspicions from the beginning. You could have saved his life! Now nothing can heal him, for death has already collected his soul.'

'Silence the traitor!' yelled the Grand Priest. He lifted Marmicus's head, placing it on his lap, trying to somehow help him. The colour of his skin had leached away to the paleness of death. *If only I had said something … anything …*

The guards grabbed the young Priest of Xidrica, their fury taking hold of them as they manhandled him.

'What shall we do with the traitor, my lord?' They all hoped that he would give them permission to make an example of him, but the Grand Priest remained silent for a few moments. For the first time, he thought about what Marmicus would have done in his place.

'Set him free.'

'He deserves death. He's a traitor to our kingdom!' said Sibius, unable to comprehend such an order. The Gallant Warrior was not only a friend to him; he was a hero, worthy of vengeance.

'I said, set him free! He may be a traitor, but he sat within the Counsel, and our laws dictate that no man from the Counsel can be killed by his brethren. I know Marmicus would have willed this,' the Grand Priest replied evenly. Then an idea came to him. 'But that doesn't mean someone else can't kill him for us. Make sure he returns to our enemy – let Jaquzan do what he wills with the traitor.'

None of the guards could believe what they were about to do. Even if the law of the kingdom dictated such a thing, it should have been overridden in these circumstances. However, they were powerless to stop it. Respecting their orders, the guards dragged the young priest away. It was indeed true that the Gallant Warrior would have set him free and returned him to the enemy.

'Make space – the Asu's here!'

The guard pushed through the crowd that had formed, trying make a path for the Asu. Everyone looked anxiously at Marmicus's body, hoping that by some miracle he would wake up.

'I said move back! Move back!' yelled the guard again, this time pushing people out of the way.

The Asu rushed to help Marmicus. His frail hands trembled as he tried to heal the one man who everyone depended on for life. He hovered his ear over the Gallant Warrior's mouth, desperately listening for any signs of breathing, but the commotion around him made it difficult to hear. He could feel no warm breath against his skin. The Asu turned and pressed his hand heavily on Marmicus's chest, trying to feel a heartbeat through the palm of his hand.

'His soul is still alive – I can feel his heart beating.'

'What about the blood from his body? Where's it coming from?'

'It's not from a new wound; it's coming from his shoulder.'

'My lord, we have a new problem.' A messenger rushed in holding a clay tablet which had been sent by the enemy.

'What is it now?'

'We've received word from the Assyrian emperor! He wants to end this war using one-to-one combat.'

'That would save the lives of many soldiers,' said Sibius, grabbing the clay tablet from him.

'Go quickly and find the best warrior, one who can give this kingdom the greatest chance of victory,' declared the Grand Priest.

'I wish it was that simple, but it is not. The princess is alive, my lord! The Assyrian emperor says he is keeping her prisoner, and if the Gallant Warrior does not fight to save her life tomorrow, then she'll be killed in front of her own people.'

The news was astonishing. How could the princess be alive? It made no sense! They were all stunned, but they had no time to question whether it was true or not. The pressure was mounting. The Grand Priest of Ursar turned to the Asu, wishing for a miraculous answer. There was only one question in his mind: would Marmicus wake up, and if he did, would he be strong enough to fight in tomorrow's battle? He did not have to say anything for the Asu to understand what he was thinking.

'Only the power of the gods can heal him in time for tomorrow's battle,' said the Asu, shaking his head.

'Then we've lost the battle for Larsa.'

93

I f there ever was a time when the Gallant Warrior was needed by his people, it was now, in this lonely hour when hope and despair stood together, waiting for destiny to decide which one to choose. The news had spread like the plague; some people claimed that the Gallant Warrior was badly injured, though still alive, while others said that Marmicus had died at sunset. Whatever the truth, the people of the Garden of the Gods flocked en masse to the palace. In their hands they gripped flowers and incense, and placed them on the steps to the palace until there was no space left.

Rumours that the princess was alive also circulated around the kingdom, and with them came word that she was carrying an infant within her womb that had been fathered by Jaquzan.

Sulaf fought through the crowds, her heart beating so frantically that she could feel her pulse in her throat. She was fighting to get through, wanting desperately to see Marmicus.

'Please let me pass. I have to see him! I have to tell him something!' Sulaf cried over and over again, trying to squeeze through. The crowds kept pushing her back, as a strong wave pulls a small boat back to shore.

'It's no use – he's dead! Our saviour's dead!' one woman cried. She began to beat her hand against her chest as if she was mourning her own son; everyone knew that if the Gallant Warrior died, the kingdom would certainly die with him. Sulaf refused to believe her words – she would not let Marmicus leave this earth without him knowing that he would be a father. Everything Sulaf had done to harm him came back to her.

She could hear the oracle's voice again in her ears, the way she had hissed at her when she spoke about Marmicus and what should be done to free his heart. She felt the fire burn her fingertips again, just as it had when she dropped the golden papyrus into the flames; a missive of pure love, intended to carry the sweet fragrance of hope to the Gallant Warrior. No memory was unvisited in Sulaf's mind. Every time a memory came rushing back to her, she felt as though stoned by guilt, her skin bruising in shame. How could she have betrayed the man she loved so much?

Somehow she felt that his death was partly her fault. All this time Sulaf had rationalised her actions, believing herself to have committed them out of love for Marmicus, but in reality everything she had done was out of envy and hatred for Larsa. It was only now, in the final hours where hope and despair meshed together like a sunset in the evening sky, that Sulaf realised she had betrayed her friend. Then it dawned upon Sulaf: her father had been wrong all these years – true love could not turn to poison.

94

Fortunately for Sulaf, two guardsmen recognised her, and let her enter the palace without hesitation. When she asked them if he was still alive, they both ignored the question, choosing not to answer. Sulaf felt the knot in her stomach tighten when they said nothing. She saw them flinch as if they knew the answer, but they refused to say a word. The more Sulaf thought about Marmicus, the more she felt unable to cope with everything she had done to hurt him. Her hands sweated with anxiety. The guards walked at their own pace; they had agreed to take Sulaf to the Gallant Warrior. Sulaf wished they would walk faster: every second was valuable! Then it dawned on her that maybe Marmicus really had already died, and that time had no relevance at all. It was only a short journey to the chamber, but it felt like hours. Not knowing if he was dead or alive made the journey seem to last forever.

Finally the guards stopped outside the doors, pulling them open for her to enter. They stepped away, giving her the space she needed to talk to Marmicus. Sulaf walked through the doors. She could hear herself breathing heavily. No amount of air seemed to satisfy her lungs; she was choking on her guilt. Any hope of Marmicus being alive and well was crushed when she saw his body lying still on the divan.

'The time is drawing near. You must ready yourself for the greatest calamity,' said the Asu. He watched her walk towards Marmicus, her lips parting as if wanting to scream but having no strength to cry.

'Is there nothing that can be done to help him?'

'I've tried everything. Maybe the voice of a friend will have the power to reach him. Nothing else seems to,' said the Asu. He had given Marmicus the strongest herbs in the largest possible doses; they would have awoken a horse, but they could not wake the Gallant Warrior.

Sulaf looked tenderly at Marmicus's handsome face, the warmth of his smile lost behind the curtain of sickness. His eyebrows were clenched together as though he was in great pain. He was sweating profusely, his head turning from left to right, than back again, from the fever which his body had developed in trying to combat the poison. The only time Sulaf had ever seen him stricken with illness was when they had been children; even then it had seemed impossible that anything would harm him. Now Marmicus lay powerless, caught in the grip of a sickness that was slowly killing him.

'I wish to speak to him alone. There's something important I must tell him.'

'He may not be able to hear you,' said the Asu.

'Let me try for my sake, then. Don't deny me this final moment, please,' begged Sulaf. She would not give up now; she needed to tell him of his fatherhood, even if it was too late.

'As you wish.'

Sulaf watched the Asu leave the chamber, making sure they were left alone before she spoke. At first she did not know what to say; the more she tried to force out the words, the more she choked on them. The knot in her throat became even tighter, drawing the words back. Her suffering was nothing compared to that of the Gallant Warrior, who lay helplessly, as if in limbo, unsure of which realm he should enter. It seemed that his spirit had at last decided, as the rapid movements of his head began to slow down. He was no longer choosing to fight the fever; instead he appeared to have given up altogether.

'You once said that the smile of a friend is always a blessing in cruel times; I wish that were true. I wish I could smile at you, like the loyal friend you imagined me to be, but the truth is, I've been no better to you than your enemy,' said Sulaf. She took his hand, holding it against her cheek. The smell of his skin was everything she needed to make her happy: how could she live without it now?

'I know the gods are calling for you, Marmicus. I can hear them too, but you mustn't go to them – it's not your time to go. The princess is alive! She's waiting for you here on earth, and she carries a gift; a baby. You're going to be a father! I know that's what you've always wanted.' Sulaf kissed his hand, breaking down in tears. The same thought kept repeating in her mind: if only she had told him the joyous news when he was well, maybe then she would have seen his face react with the beauty of a smile.

'So, you see, you can't die now. This is the time to fight, to live – not for your people or for your duty, but for something more important than all of that; this is the time to live for your family. They need you now more than ever before. So fight with your heart, Marmicus, I beg you, fight like you have never fought before. Fight for them and live for them now. No war is worth fighting unless it's for love. Today, your battle is for love, so fight to protect it and live to embrace it!'

95

Larsa could feel her infant growing stronger inside her, warning her of his impending arrival into the savage world of men. She wished he did not have to leave his sanctuary, where it was safe and warm. His innocence was like a jewel among stones roughened by the passing of time and the learning of evil. Together, they had faced this burdensome journey, walking along a path filled with uneven stones and thorns that had only been lightened by a mother's love. Now the road was nearing its end. Larsa could feel her infant kicking at his walls, rolling around with life; he wanted to be set free. Every time he somersaulted inside her, Larsa felt a rush of excitement and unrestrained happiness. Even though she was only six months pregnant, she could feel that he wanted to be set free: his movements were stronger than ever; he was curious about the world, wanting to explore it. She imagined his tiny hands stretching open inside her, wanting to taste and touch using his own senses instead of his mother's. Larsa lovingly placed her hands upon her belly, remembering Marmicus's face as she did so. She wondered if her infant would look like him. Would he possess the same gentle eyes she had fallen in love with? She hoped so.

'You're strong, like your father, and brave like him too,' said Larsa. The softness of her voice soothed her infant, hushing him back to sleep; he had been kicking frantically all day. 'Be patient – you'll meet him soon. We both shall.'

96

Dawn had arrived, and with it came the final hour. The storm which had swept over the Garden of the Gods the previous night had grown stronger, and thousands of soldiers from either side lined the battleground. They watched as the Dark Warrior stood alone in the middle, waiting for the Gallant Warrior to come. Today these men would watch a war end by the bloody combat of two warriors, one who fought for love, the other inspired only by hatred.

They looked to the skies. Rain poured from dense black clouds, but no amount of force unleashed by nature could stop this battle. It had been destined, like the coming of the end of the world. The soldiers' metal armour, which acted as a means of protection, had now become a source of danger, as lightning struck the horizon, with thunder rumbling after it. Each time it did, the horizon turned bright white, then dark again. There was no greater battle on earth, nor one that carried so much glory. Nafridos glanced into the distance, looking at the faces of thousands of soldiers who stood like a crowd of powerless spectators. He was searching for Marmicus among the faces. But he could not find him.

'Babylon has a coward as its leader. Fight me and redeem your honour!' yelled the Dark Warrior. He dug his sword into the sand and spat on the ground in disgust; nothing could persuade him to abandon his conquest now, not even the end of the world. The rain began to pelt harder. It would be difficult to fight in these conditions, but it meant their battle would be even more glorious.

Nafridos turned towards his cousin, wanting to obtain his approval for what he was about to do. The Assyrian emperor remained still. Jaquzan sat upon a throne beneath a canopy, which sheltered him from the harsh rainfall, his lions guarding his feet. He enjoyed watching his cousin squirm with restlessness; it only meant that he was hungry for death – it was exactly what was needed for victory. Lifting his hand, Jaquzan gave the signal that offered Nafridos the blessing he so desperately awaited.

'Bring forward the whore of Babylon!'

The faint cries of a woman could be heard, and the Babylonian soldiers looked on, not knowing what was happening until they saw her: the so-called whore of Babylon was none other than Larsa, Princess of the Garden of the Gods. Two soldiers dragged her forward, her hands tied behind her back like any prisoner of war. They pulled her by her hair, ripping out chunks of it, and every time she fought back they spat at her. It was a humiliating spectacle. Some Babylonian soldiers jumped forward, unable to contain their anger, but their commanders looked at them, warning them not to react. This was not Babylon's battle; it was a battle between the Gallant Warrior and the Dark Warrior and it belonged to no one else. What was needed was a life for a life. This would spare a thousand others …

97

They dragged the princess to the centre of the battlefield and pushed her to the ground, leaving her beside the Dark Warrior, who stood waiting for Marmicus. Her long white dress soaked up the muddy water as the cold rain ran over her body, washing away the humiliating spit of her enemy. Larsa felt them push her, and she fell sideways into the wet soil, her hands tied behind her back. She lifted her head, trying to breathe, but the muddy water entered her mouth. If she did not die by the sword then she would drown in the floodwaters that swept over the land.

Larsa saw what looked like the entire world staring at her. Thousands of soldiers were watching her misery, doing nothing to stop it from happening. Not one soldier had the courage to step forward to protect her from the barbarity she endured; the knowledge that none did so was more agonising than any beating.

'Where's your humanity? Is there no one who will help me?' she screamed with hurt and desperation. Her voice was almost strangled by her anguish. 'Have you no compassion? Have you no shame?' There was no reply or movement; brave men had turned into cowards. Larsa rolled across the ground, her white dress turning filthy from the mud that stuck to her body. It tortured her to know that today her baby would die along with her. She felt his rapid heartbeat in her womb, sinking with hers to the bottom of a pit of filth and betrayal. Would she never get to see his face? Would she never get to kiss his cheek and hold him lovingly in her arms, just as every mother had the right to? How close he had come to living his own life … now it would be taken away from him.

The Dark Warrior hovered over her: if he could not kill the Gallant Warrior, then she would be the next best thing. Water ran across his sword, dripping onto her neck, and the sight of her lying at his feet made him feel more powerful than he had ever felt in his life.

'What hurts more, princess? Is it knowing that you shall die young, or realising that in this savage world of men, you don't have anybody when you need someone the most?' asked Nafridos. He knelt, lifting her chin from the muddy ground using only his blade. Even besmirched by mud and filth, her beauty shone like a star.

'Beg me to let you live, whore of Babylon, and I'll spare you. I'll give you your life back; all you have to do is beg me like the whore you are in front of all these men.'

'I beg you to kill me. Kill me now, while I'm dreaming of a better life …' said Larsa. Her breaths became shorter. Every muscle within her body was stiffening in the chill wind.

The Dark Warrior laughed. Her bravery never ceased to amaze him, the words poignantly poetic, summing up her futile existence. She had once had the world at her feet, now she carried only an unrealised dream in her hands.

'Very well, I shall.'

The Dark Warrior stood up. The time had come to put her out of her misery. Larsa closed her eyes, knowing that she was ready to die. As he placed the sword against her neck she dreamt of the two people she loved the most: Marmicus and her baby. She thought of Marmicus holding their infant in his arms, rocking him back and forth while they watched him sleep peacefully. This bittersweet thought filled her eyes with tears of sadness and joy, for she knew he would never see their child. The Dark Warrior watched as a smile slowly lit up her beautiful face, her eyes flickering as if she were dreaming, while tears rolled down her cheeks, washing the mud away.

Larsa clenched her hands tightly, as if holding onto her thoughts of love; they brought her the warmth she needed. The icy winds felt as though they were cutting to the bone through skin and flesh, reminding her how cruel the world was. The sharp tip of the Dark Warrior's weapon pressed into her throat, just below her windpipe, and soft tingling droplets of water fell onto her. This would be the last sensation she would feel in life. She took in one last deep breath while dreaming of a better life: none of the pain or the agony, none of the things she had endured, mattered any more. Her hurt and anguish would be buried here, in this place where her body would rest; after that, everything she feared would drift away.

'I'll give you a clean kill. Your bravery deserves that at least,' said the Dark Warrior. He curled his fingers around the hilt of his sword, his thumbs squeezing so hard that they turned white. Raising his sword above his shoulders, he prepared to bring it down with all his strength, severing her head with one clean blow.

'Dream, princess, dream of a better life where men like me are never born into existence,' said the Dark Warrior, with death ready to blow its tender kiss upon her soul ...

98

Every fire must die out eventually, no matter how fiercely its flames may have raged the night before; but love is unlike any fire, for true love is immortal – while mere conquest is not. Love can only die if it is not carefully tended; nothing else is capable of destroying it.

That day, true love had breathed life into the Gallant Warrior's lungs, awakening him from unconsciousness.

Marmicus galloped across the landscape, his horse unshaken by the bright bolts of lightning and the deep rumbling of thunder. It was as if all of nature's elements were standing against them, trying to stop him from reaching the battlefield in time to save Larsa's life. As he rode across the empty valley, Marmicus remembered what Sulaf had told him. He felt unable to comprehend what she had said, but he desperately wanted to believe that it was true.

Sulaf had stayed by his bedside all night, praying over him and cooling his head from the high fever. The moment Marmicus opened his eyes, she told him everything: that Larsa was alive and that he was blessed with fatherhood. The joyous news was quickly followed by a calamity, one which left Marmicus full of anger: he had been summoned to fight the Dark Warrior at first light. Should he fail to arrive on the battleground, then Larsa would be killed by the enemy. Marmicus immediately rose from his divan, grabbing his Sword of Allegiance and rushing to put on his armour, wanting to enter the battle. Nothing could stop him from fighting to save her life, other than the weakness of his own body. He nearly collapsed a second time; the poison had robbed him of his strength.

When Sulaf asked him if it was worth fighting, Marmicus said, 'I would rather die in battle knowing that I had tried to save her life, than know that I had done nothing at all.'

Sulaf watched him ride away, feeling that it would be the last time she would ever see him. If he fought today it would be with half his strength.

Orisus could feel his master's desperation. The stallion galloped tirelessly through the thrashing rain, his hooves pounding the sodden earth and whipping mud and water into the air. He galloped faster than all the temperamental winds and clouds that sailed above him through the stormy skies. But it was still not enough to make time an ally; every second lost was a second closer to the princess's death. The land began to rise. Orisus's hooves splashed through deep puddles, cutting through the wet turf that broke into pieces as he galloped over it. As soon as Marmicus reached the top of the hill, he saw the entire world gathered below him. The silhouettes of thousands of soldiers were visible on the open plain, armour gleaming, their flags flapping in the breeze as they silently waited. Marmicus saw movement on the battlefield; a man in black armour was standing over something. He could not make out who it was, the sheeting rain and dim grey light making it difficult to see through the haziness, and all he could see was what appeared to be a white object lying on the flooded ground at the soldier's feet.

Then Marmicus heard a familiar voice scream just one word,

not with fear but with defiance: 'Marmicus!' The woman who had restored him to life was calling out to him, and he spurred Orisus on, asking the stallion for one last effort.

'Larsa!' he cried, as rage ignited within him. He laid the reins across Orisus's shoulders each in turn, asking him for more. He crouched forward, trying to fight off the torrential rain and the wind slamming into his body, slowing him down.

'Release her!' roared the Gallant Warrior, as he galloped between the rearmost ranks of his own army. He unsheathed his Sword of Allegiance, raising it high in the air, trying to get the soldiers' attention so that they would know he had arrived. Tens of thousands of heads turned towards him as one and watched, transfixed, as one courageous man rode into battle, preparing to die for the woman he honoured and loved.

'Free her and fight me!'

Larsa opened her eyes, hearing a voice call out her name like a warm breeze flowing out from a raging storm.

'Marmicus …' Larsa whispered. As soon as she uttered his name the Dark Warrior knew he had arrived. Nafridos turned, and saw the man he was born to kill emerge at a gallop from the ranks and turn towards him, sending great columns of spray into the air. The black silhouette of his wild stallion and the white light from his sword seemed to disperse the mist and render the world, in one instant, a different place. Larsa's face began to stream with tears as she watched Marmicus ride towards her. Even if she died now, she was thankful that she had seen his face for one last time. The reminder of their unbreakable bond meant everything to her. She watched Marmicus, his armour gleaming like the rising sun lifting above a stormy battlement of clouds. She had made it through her darkest hour, and so too had her infant, but the danger was far from over, for there was one more obstacle left to overcome.

99

'I have seen this day in my dreams; now I know it shall be more glorious on earth,' said the Dark Warrior. He lifted his blade from Larsa's neck, sliding it along her chest, stopping it only at her heart.

'Let her go! If you want glory then fight me for it! Only I can offer it to you!' roared the Gallant Warrior. He jumped off his stallion, ready for combat.

It was the first time the two warriors had met face to face. Even though Nafridos had heard much about Marmicus, the Gallant Warrior knew nothing of Nafridos's cruel and lethal reputation. Marmicus remembered his face though – he was the one who had thrown the spear the previous day.

'No, Marmicus! No! Don't fight him!' cried Larsa. She did not want Marmicus to fight for her – how could she endure watching him being hurt or, worse, killed in front of her?

Marmicus had already made up his mind. The princess was the centre of his world and he would die to protect her.

'Hold your tongue, princess, or I'll cut it out.' The Dark Warrior jabbed his weapon against her cheek, almost slicing into her smooth skin. He had been waiting for this moment for far too long; he would not let it slip away because of her pathetic pleas.

'Let her go! She has no part in the destiny that binds us both.' Marmicus stared at Larsa, trying to reassure her that everything was going to be alright; she needed to trust in him now more than ever before. 'You'll have your battle. Take your glory as your prize; mine shall be her life,' continued Marmicus. 'These are my conditions. Either you accept them or you have declared war.'

The Dark Warrior turned to his cousin, like a dog wanting to gain his master's approval to fight, but Nafridos would have to wait before he received any kind of answer from the Assyrian emperor. The only movement on Jaquzan's face was the subtle twitching of his jaw muscles beneath his skin; even so, Marmicus could tell that beneath his expressionless appearance was a man who was deeply afraid of losing his power. The Assyrian emperor glared at the Gallant Warrior; he had almost destroyed everything the emperor had built, and the mere thought of him made him react in ways he had never before experienced. Jaquzan moved in his seat and his lions roared, twisting their heads from side to side. They clawed at the air, trying to reach the Gallant Warrior, but their iron chains held them back.

'I am the world and you are the dust crushed beneath my feet,' said the Assyrian emperor. He glanced at the Gallant Warrior's sword, admiring the sacred words of allegiance that ran across the metal blade. They would soon become meaningless words lost in the mists of time.

'I will make sure that nothing shall remain of you: not even the whisper of your name or the blade of your sword will exist. There will be nothing in this world that will speak of your story, not even the dust of your body, or the memory of your name.'

'You can have the world and everything that lies within it. Today

I fight for only one thing.' He turned to the Dark Warrior. 'Now let her go, and let us see where our destiny leads us.'

'Release her,' said the Assyrian emperor. He had given his consent to the terms of battle. He looked at his cousin, knowing that he only had one opportunity to kill the Gallant Warrior; whatever happened, Nafridos could not let it slip through his fingertips. He needed this battle as much as the emperor did. What would be done with his enemy's body after that would be up to him.

'If allegiance lies in the heart of the sword, then today the beating hearts of men shall surrender to me. The time has come for you to meet your equal upon the battlefield, oh Gallant Warrior … step forward, Dark Warrior. Kill him, and seize the destiny to which you were born.'

The Dark Warrior turned with excitement: this would be his greatest ever battle, and the princess would be the closest person to the fight. By nightfall, history would honour his name as the man who killed the Gallant Warrior from the beautiful Garden of the Gods. He grabbed the princess, pulling her up from the wet ground, slashing through the rope that bound her wrists. Larsa felt her heart sink the moment he cut it; somehow she wanted to remain prisoner. Only then could she guarantee that Marmicus's life would be safe.

'If there is a god in the heavens then he has sacrificed someone else for you,' said the Dark Warrior, as he turned to face his opponent.

100

The winds were singing on the edge of the Gallant Warrior's bronze helmet, making it difficult for him to hear. Marmicus needed to use every sense he had, so he lifted his glorious helmet from his head, revealing his face. The muffled echo of waves crashing against his ears immediately disappeared. He flung the helmet onto the wet ground, choosing to fight without it.

'Swear by your honour that you'll abide by the conditions of combat and that no harm shall be inflicted on her.'

'I have no honour to swear by,' replied the Dark Warrior. He followed his enemy's actions by removing his own helmet, as if peeling back the layers of his identity to reveal the inner sanctum of his barbarity. The grip of his sword had been moistened with his own blood and gritted with sand, as was his custom.

'Then let the scribes of history hold you to account, for you'll be buried without any,' replied Marmicus. He turned to Larsa; she stood in the rain, trembling, unable to absorb what was going on. Thoughts of despair kept running through her mind. How cruel could the world be? How could her army do nothing to help the man who had sacrificed so much for them? Marmicus understood that these few minutes of combat were going to torment her more than anyone else, and he remembered what he had told her the day he had returned home; how she was the heart of his sword, the very place where his allegiance lay. Now he would be fighting to save their love, using the same weapon.

Larsa cried out as soon as she saw Marmicus take the first step into battle. An Assyrian soldier held her back, stopping her from running towards him. Her hands reached out to him, desperately wishing to touch him one last time, but Marmicus had become a prisoner of this war as much as she had.

'If there is any cause worth dying for, then it is this. Allegiance lies in the heart of the sword!' roared the Gallant Warrior. His voice travelled across the battlefield and could be heard through the plunging winds. It was heard by the thousands who looked on, watching this epic battle unfold.

The two warriors began to circle each other, like lions stalking their prey. The Dark Warrior held his shield high, covering one side of his muscular body. Only his eyes could be seen above the circular disc that moved along with his stride. Along the metalwork of his shield was an array of iron spikes, so that anyone who brushed against it would find their flesh torn off. Marmicus knew that his opponent's strikes would be quick and clean, just like his own; he had had a glimpse of his fighting ability in yesterday's battle, and that had been enough to warn him what to expect. Using all his energy, Marmicus tried to focus on his moving target, but his vision was warped and hazy. Instead of seeing one opponent circle around him, he saw two figures, rotating and distorted as through a prism. He only had one chance to live, and he could not afford to make any rash judgements, not when so much was at stake.

Suddenly, the Dark Warrior threw himself into combat, moving his heavy shield aside and unsheathing his sword. Marmicus leapt back, his knees bending just in time as the sword curled across, sweeping past his head. Nafridos swung the heavy weapon again, this time striking at a different angle. His muscles pumped with hot blood and adrenaline. Marmicus threw up his shield, blocking the blow, his body jolting back as the sword met his shield, leaving a scratch across its full width. Nafridos laughed as he watched Marmicus struggle; he had just started to warm up. The Dark Warrior swung his sword again, rotating his wrists as he did. Each time he moved, he smirked. His aim was to make his enemy tire until he had no strength left, and it was working better than he had expected. Marmicus felt the strength being sucked out of him. His reactions were beginning to slow; it was the worst possible dilemma for any soldier on the battlefield. Blood dripped from his injured shoulder, and he felt the wound tear every time he raised his arm.

'There's only one entrance to the hall of death. Run to it and set yourself free,' said the Dark Warrior. He powerfully rotated his arm, slicing his weapon down. Marmicus threw up his sword, trying to stop the blow from slicing his neck. The deadly instruments clashed together with the force of a lightning strike. Marmicus felt his heart thunder against his chest. He was not frightened of death; it did not matter to him if he died at this very moment – all Marmicus needed before death was to know that he had set Larsa free.

Marmicus was doing everything he could to block the assaults, but they kept coming, crashing down with the pelting rain. Every time he blinked, he saw another blow coming, stronger than the last. It was getting harder for him to defend himself and control them. His enemy jumped into the air, hammering his sword down and punching it across. Marmicus raised his sword; their weapons clashed. This time the Dark Warrior did not pull back. Instead, he glared into the Gallant Warrior's eyes, wanting to strip him of all confidence that he could win. He needed him to know that he was going to die, and that the princess would watch it happen. Marmicus felt his body sink, his feet slipping into the mud. Nafridos was forcing his weapon down, using his full strength. With no choice, Marmicus rolled across the ground, unlocking the grip of his opponent's sword. It was a dangerous move. Nafridos followed him, hacking his weapon into the ground. Every time he missed him, large chunks of earth were thrown up. The lions launched themselves towards Marmicus, trying to swipe his head with their claws, but they were at the limits of their chains.

'You disappoint me, Gallant Warrior. I was expecting a challenge from you. I'm still waiting for it,' said Nafridos, wiping the mud from his brow. He was getting bored of the Gallant Warrior's defensive moves; the time had come to change his tactics.

'I'll give you three seconds to rise to your feet. I want history to remember the day you fell to your knees.'

Marmicus rose to his feet, feeling weak and disorientated. He could barely see, and could hardly stand straight. The poison had taken too much from him. The Dark Warrior began to circle him, but Marmicus could not concentrate; he could see three shadowy figures walking around him, and he had no idea which one was real. He squinted, trying to clear his vision, but it made no difference. The torrential rain grew stronger, seeming to surge over him. Suddenly, his enemy rammed the bulky edge of his shield into Marmicus's chest, battering his ribcage, the spikes tearing flesh from bone. A scream of agony came from Marmicus's lips. The air in his lungs had been expelled by the blow to his diaphragm, and he fought for breath. Marmicus fell to the ground, his body blackened by the mud. It was if he had come to accept his defeat; he had nothing left with which to fight. The last powerful thrust had broken him.

'Get up, Marmicus! Get up!' Larsa screamed, begging him to stand up. She reached out to him. Her fingertips were so near to him, and yet she felt as if she were standing a thousand miles away.

'Where's the mighty lion whose roar unsettles the hearts of men?' laughed the Dark Warrior, kicking dirty water on Marmicus's face. He had imagined their battle would last much longer; alas, it was almost over. 'Never trust a man who has no honour to live by. After I kill you, I'm going to kill your wife. But, first, I'll make her watch you die. Then, I'll take your sword and cut out your heart and give it to her. I think I can be sure that when she sees that she'll die from the heartache.'

The time had come for the Dark Warrior to make his kill. He walked backwards, laughing as he did so. The Assyrian soldiers knew how he would slaughter his enemy; the Dark Warrior had done it many times before. He would jump up high, holding his lethal blade above his head, before shooting it downwards into his enemy's throat and ripping it all the way down his chest. It was his signature kill, and a gruesome one. Larsa's eyes were streaming with tears, she did not want to watch the horror that was about to unfold in front of her. Her infant moved in her womb as if he too were screaming inside her.

'Marmicus, fight. Fight for us. Fight for your child!'

'If you are not prepared to fight for love, then you are never prepared to die for it,' said the Dark Warrior. He ran, then leapt into the air, holding his heavy weapon above his head. The surging winds swept over him, the rains ready to mix with the blood that would spill out from his victim's neck. As Nafridos swooped downwards, Marmicus looked at Larsa, as if absorbing her beauty for the last time. She was screaming at him, pleading with him to stand up. These were the final moments, the last time she would ever see him alive.

The blade shot down, ready to disembowel the man she loved with all her heart. But Marmicus rolled sideways, avoiding the oncoming blow by inches. Using all his energy, Marmicus stood up, flexing his muscles and roaring like the enraged lion he was. He threw his shield to the ground and wiped the mud away from his blade. The words of allegiance on his sword began to glimmer again, as if revived by honour and restored to youth.

'One day of freedom is worth more than a thousand years of slavery. Today mankind shall have its freedom, and today I shall have Larsa.'

He looked at the Dark Warrior, no longer seeing haziness or feeling any kind of weakness. His muscles were burning with fire and rage. The Gallant Warrior struck his mighty Sword of Allegiance against the Dark Warrior's weapon, his body twisting like a flame. Nafridos did everything in his power to defend himself, but with every blow his feet sank, and he fought to keep his grip on his sword. Marmicus had become the beast of the battlefield: all the anger rooted inside him now erupted. Larsa watched, feeling her hope revive. Marmicus had regained his strength, sprinting forward and bringing the fight to his enemy with the Sword of Allegiance. Meanwhile, the Dark Warrior's fighting had become scrappy; his feet were slipping in the mud due to the sheer number of blows that kept coming at him, pushing him back, disorientating him. His eyes remained focused on the swinging sword: each time it came at him, he raised his weapon, feeling its power sing through his body.

'Your time has come,' whispered the Gallant Warrior, as he struck his enemy's blade once more. The force was so intense that the Dark Warrior fell back, his head hitting the ground, and his weapon falling from his hands. Marmicus walked to him, ready to kill him.

'Death is no stranger to a man who has already killed. Your

death has come for you. Greet it with bravery just as you have forced innocent others to,' whispered Marmicus. He looked at Nafridos, who was crawling through the mud like a coward, trying to run away, his knees digging into the soil as he desperately tried to retrieve his sword, hoping to save himself from death. But the Gallant Warrior stood above him, digging the tip of his weapon into his neck, just as the Dark Warrior had done to Larsa. Marmicus showed no emotion or remorse.

'Wait, don't kill me. I ask for your forgiveness,' said Nafridos, begging for his life. He lay helplessly in the mud dignity, stripped of all dignity.

'Why should I offer you mercy when you've offered none to your victims?'

'I swear, everything I've done was forced upon me.'

'Don't listen to him, Marmicus. He's lying to you, don't show him mercy! Kill him now. Kill him!' the princess screamed. She knew the Dark Warrior; he would never beg to live. He was planning something.

'I'm not deceiving you. You've won this war and my respect,' said Nafridos. The soldiers could see what was happening, but nobody could clearly hear the exchange of words between them.

'If you kill me, you'll taint your sword with the blood of a man who longs to change his ways. Look at those men's faces – they see no sword in my hand, all they see is a man begging for his life.'

'He doesn't deserve to live. Kill him! Please listen to me, Marmicus. I know him better than you!' yelled the princess, begging him to do what she said.

'If I spare you, you must leave this kingdom at once, and take your army with you.'

'You have my word.'

Unable to kill a repentant man, the Gallant Warrior lifted his weapon from his neck.

'Know this – men you have fought and killed on the battlefield have shown more honour and courage than you. You may have lived your life by the sword, but today you've spat on it with your cowardice.' Marmicus returned his sword to its sheath.

He turned away, desperate to free the princess from her captives, and walked towards her.

'Marmicus!'

Suddenly he felt a sharp pain between his shoulder blades. He fell to his knees, blood pouring from a wound in his back.

Larsa had seen Nafridos heft his sword, throwing it across the battlefield like a spear. She had screamed Marmicus's name, trying to warn him, but it was too late – the weapon had already pierced his flesh.

101

The Dark Warrior knelt beside his enemy, smiling cruelly as he pushed the blade further into his back, twisting it round, wanting to make him suffer before death.

'If you have any humanity, you'll let me be with him when he dies,' said Larsa to the Assyrian soldier who was guarding her. He held her back, trying to stop her running to the man she loved, but as her words struck home, the soldier felt a rush of guilt for what he was doing. He freed her. Larsa ran to Marmicus, the wind pushing her back as if to shield her from further heartache.

'Can you feel their glare? They're watching you die – one life sacrificed for a thousand others,' said the Dark Warrior to his victim. Marmicus was gasping for breath. The world around him was disappearing. He could no longer see the thousands of faces that edged the horizon, watching him die. All Marmicus could feel was the immense pain of the blade twisting in his back, cutting his muscles and slicing his flesh.

'You should have listened to the princess; she understands what kind of creatures we are. We are men of war. Forgiveness is a gift we were not blessed with.' With a sudden, violent movement the Dark

Warrior pulled the blade from Marmicus's back. Blood seeped out of the wound. Marmicus fell sideways, rolling onto his back as he hit the ground. He knew he would either bleed to death or be decapitated. Whichever it was, he did not want Larsa to see. Nafridos reached for the Sword of Allegiance, lifting up his prize. It was a glorious instrument of death. The words of allegiance caught the light as he took hold of the weapon, clasping the hilt with both hands and raising it up into the sky for everyone to see that victory belonged to him. The time had come for one final act – the Gallant Warrior's beheading.

'All your life you have fought for justice. How ironic that at the moment of death the world should offer you none!' The Dark Warrior swung his weapon, ready to behead his greatest opponent.

'Stop!' Larsa screamed. 'Move away from him!'

The Dark Warrior turned to his cousin, seeking his signal. Nothing would give him more pleasure than to kill the princess while his victim was still alive. The Assyrian emperor gave a subtle nod, granting his blessing for Marmicus to die in her arms. Larsa rushed to him, gently lifting his head and cradling it on her lap, her eyes running with tears as blood seeped from his back, clouding the water around them.

'You should have killed him when I said. He doesn't deserve to live. You do.'

'I could never ... kill a man who's asked for my forgiveness ...' Marmicus whispered as he lay dying in her arms.

'Forgive me ... for failing you ...'

'Don't say that. You have not failed me. You never have and you never shall. Even in death – especially in death – you will have honour.' She stroked his face, all the while watching his eyelids slowly close, as though drifting into sleep.

'I shouldn't … have let you go that day …' he murmured as he pressed his hand to her cheek, absorbing her beauty for the last time. He remembered all the glorious nights he had lain with her, watching her sleep peacefully. He had smiled, knowing that she was his and that they would one day grow old together, but now his vision was fading as darkness began to sweep over him. Marmicus could no longer see her face; he could only hear her soft voice and feel the lasting tenderness of her touch, and her words.

'I buried my dreams the day you died, Larsa, and now they've come back to life with you.'

'Then live, so we can share our dreams together, as we said we would.'

'Our love … can never die, Larsa … not when it is true like ours. Even when we've submitted to death … a part of our love shall still live on in those we leave behind,' said Marmicus. He gently touched her belly, wanting to feel the movement of his child for the first time. He knew that he would never see his infant's face or hear his laughter across the green fields; even so, Marmicus loved him with every breath he possessed.

'I can't survive without you. I can't bear to even try. I'll come with you to the afterlife; we'll be together again, all three of us.'

'No, Larsa. No. Don't be afraid. Death is but a curse … if the soul has lived without purpose … My life has been for you. Now you must live for our child, just as we lived for each other … I know you'll be a wonderful mother … you already are …'

Her warmth had healed his wounds, but this time it was not enough to restore him to life. The enemy had prevailed. Marmicus had breathed his last. His hand slipped from her stomach, falling to the muddy ground. Heaven had lost its sacred guardian; the Gallant Warrior was dead.

Larsa began to wail in agony as she cradled his head in her arms, rocking back and forth in unendurable torture, not knowing what else to do. Her screams were so frightening that the lions began to roar with her.

'Stay with me. Don't abandon me here. Not now, not when freedom is so close,' Larsa sobbed as she kissed his face tenderly. She desperately wished he would brush his lips against hers as he always had, but they remained still. It was no use. The battle had been fought and lost; her beloved husband had died trying to defend her.

'Come back to me. Come back.'

'Move aside, princess, his body belongs to me now.' The Dark Warrior had returned to behead his victim; it was the last act needed to consolidate his victory in front of the armies of thousands.

'You shall not harm him; I won't let you! You've won this war, now let us mourn our defeat.' She attempted to shield his body from the Dark Warrior's lethal sword, which hung above them both.

'I said move aside, or let the world remember the tragedy of your love forever.' He directed his weapon towards her neck, his eyes lighting up with his desire to use it. Who could have imagined that he would kill the princess using the same weapon that had been sworn to protect her? Larsa turned towards the Assyrian emperor, who watched from his throne. Only he possessed the power to stop his cousin from mutilating Marmicus's body.

'I want the Gallant Warrior's head to be mounted on the last pillar still standing when everything else in this kingdom has been set on fire. The Garden of the Gods shall become the ashes of hell,' said Jaquzan flatly. He had enjoyed their display of affection, but now he longed to crush it with one last blow. Two Assyrian soldiers attempted to pull her away, but Larsa fought them, refusing to leave Marmicus's body alone on the battlefield.

'Where's your compassion? Is there no one here who will stop this? Is there no one with honour among you all?' Larsa screamed with burning despair. She looked around at the faces of the soldiers. Some turned to their commanders, waiting for a signal to help her, but none was given. 'If death returns, let him testify to the gods that only one man among a thousand others died with honour.' Larsa sank her head into the Gallant Warrior's neck, wanting the sword to sever hers as well; she could not live without Marmicus, and she would not even force herself to try.

'So you want to die?' asked the Dark Warrior. He lifted the Sword of Allegiance above both their heads, ready to swing it. The world watched in silence, unable to deny their overwhelming love for one another and the tragedy of their story, a tale which would forever be called the Battle of Larsa, painted with the blood from their bodies until the end of time.

'Death comes to us all, but only a few are worthy of dying for love. Today you are worthy,' said the Dark Warrior.

'We'll be together, soon. All three of us,' she wept, holding tightly to his lifeless chest, waiting for death to finally take her soul.

102

'We have to do something! We cannot let this happen. There is no honour in this.'

'Stay in your positions. The Gallant Warrior is dead and so too is our hope of freedom. The pledge we made must be kept if we wish to stay alive and keep our kingdom's walls standing,' responded the commander. He understood what that meant; every man here was a slave to his new masters, including him.

'Don't listen to him; the Gallant Warrior's not dead! He's still alive in our hearts. He can only die if we forget what he lived for. Remember what he said? That one day of freedom is worth more than thousand years of slavery. This is the time to fight, now, that a man of courage might be buried with the honour he deserves,' shouted a soldier in defiance. 'Who's with me? Who'll fight for the Gallant Warrior now when he needs us the most? Who'll embrace their swords and keep his spirit alive in the way in which he lived?'

'I'll fight for him! If I die for him, then death is a worthy friend of mine.'

Soldiers began to break the battle lines, steadily marching as one force. Each step took them nearer to the body of the man who had sacrificed everything for them. The Babylonian kings watched from above: their greatest nightmare had come to pass. Not only had the Gallant Warrior been defeated, but now their soldiers were disobeying orders to remain in their positions. It would be an act of disobedience for which they would pay with their lives.

'Who ordered them to move? They must stay in their positions!' a Babylonian king shrieked as he watched his men defy his orders.

'Even in death, the Gallant Warrior has the power to command spirits,' replied one of the generals.

Larsa held Marmicus's hand as she lay beside him; the last traces of his warmth deceived her into thinking that he was still alive. She imagined they were lying on lush green grass. Somehow the lie she told herself made death seem more bearable. She kissed his hand, smelling his skin, unaware that the Sword of Allegiance hovered above her neck, ready to kill her.

But nothing in life is ever written in stone, and her dreams of paradise would have to wait, as many voices called out to her, trying to wake her from her dream. A thousand soldiers lined the horizon, each one stretching out his hands to carry her away from the wreckage of war. The Babylonian rebellion was unexpected, but by walking forward the soldiers were unleashing war. The soldiers drew closer, all hungry for vengeance.

'Unleash hell! Let no man live to see tomorrow,' commanded the Assyrian emperor. Strangely, no movement came from his soldiers; it was as if he had said nothing at all.

'Archers, unleash your arrows! Flatten them as the earth is flattened by my feet.' Once again, there was no movement from the Assyrian lines; the soldiers remained where they were, their arrows still in their wooden quivers, unused. Although nothing had been said between the soldiers, there was silent agreement among them all.

'Do what your emperor commands! Move forward, and unsheathe your swords, or your bodies will be used as barricades,' declared the Dark Warrior.

Again the soldiers did not move. Instead, a loud chanting began to spread through the Assyrian army. The defiant soldiers began to roar the words of allegiance, their voices growing louder as their confidence grew. Today, at this moment, they were free. They were liberated to think for themselves and their minds submitted to the compass of their hearts. The mighty Assyrian emperor had lost control over his people, and he realised this as soon as Larsa rose to her feet, turning to him and looking deeply into his eyes with the new breath of freedom spreading through her lungs. The woman who had become the slave of an emperor had returned as the divine ruler of the Garden of the Gods.

'Fear is the weapon used by oppressors, but courage is the weapon held by the free,' said Larsa to her enemy. 'Your time has come.'

103

Upon the battlefield lay the bodies of the ruthless Assyrian emperor and his merciless cousin Nafridos, their heads raised on spikes, to rot in the same way as any wretched man who had met such an ill fate. Who could have imagined that the indestructible Assyrian ruler, who had created an empire from nothing, would finally meet his end in the same manner as all those he had sentenced to death? His curse, however, was a blessing for many other men: those who had been his slaves were now free men, able to live the rest of their lives safe from bullying and oppression.

As for the Serpent, he had been given what he had always dreamt of: a piece of land to call his own, and a throne where he would forever rest. But it was not one that would be envied by others, for the throne his body rested on lay with his body in a shallow grave, where the Assyrian emperor had buried him.

As for freedom, it is always born from the seed of sacrifice. The courageous lion among men lay dead, never knowing whether the woman he loved, and the child he wished for, would be able to live in the way he hoped and dreamt they would live.

'Who'll help me lift his body?' a Babylonian soldier asked as he placed the Sword of Allegiance in Marmicus's hands. Several warriors came forward to help lift his body off the ground. Together they walked through the ranks of soldiers, who knelt before him, placing their swords and shields on the ground as a sign of respect. The world had never witnessed such a thing: today, one man in death had united thousands in life. From this moment forward, the name of the Garden of the Gods would be changed to Larsa, reminding all others that true love had once lived here.

104

Paross looked into the empty blue sky, imagining what it must be like to sit with the One-God and look down upon the world from the glorious heavens. Would it be easy to find a loved one in an area covering so many kingdoms? Every day since the war had ended, Paross had come to the same spot, sitting on the large stone steps of the Temple of Ishtar, waiting for the arrival of one man. Now that Paross was free, he had become a victim of his own enslavement, choosing to believe in the false hope of a friend's return. But time has a way of eroding hope, no matter how strong it may have felt at first. Paross saw families come and go, children like himself waiting by the doors of the temple, some playing together while women stood gossiping, others trying to comfort their mothers when they fought back the tears as the disastrous news of their husbands' and sons' deaths was delivered to them. Even though the war had ended, the burning of bodies continued to light up the night sky.

The likelihood of Abram still being alive was slowly slipping away. Some passers-by sat with Paross, offering him bread and water to drink as they tried to console him. Others were blunt with their words, wanting to move him away from the gates of the temple, like unwanted vermin. One passer-by told him he was wasting his time, and that if Abram was alive he would surely have returned to him by now. The old man even went further, saying that a freed slave would find a worthless child-like him to be a burden, and that Abram had planned everything, leading him to the temple as a way of getting rid of him without guilt. Paross did not wish to admit it to himself, but the old man's words made sense. If it was untrue, then lying somewhere on the battlefield was the body of a man who had only experienced freedom for a few days.

Nonetheless, Paross waited by the temple, day in and day out. He could not forget Abram, no matter how many people advised him to. Something deep inside urged him to come back to this spot and wait for him there. During their short journey together, Abram had shown kindness to him as nobody else had ever done. When the entire world stood against him, he had become a friend, a father – and somehow, the homeland he needed. Paross cupped his head in his hands, the bright afternoon light stinging his eyes. It frustrated him to see the same passers-by staring at him, even if they offered him a sympathetic smile; he felt their judgement nonetheless.

'Please, One-God, answer my prayers. Let him be alive,' said the boy, trying to hold back his tears.

'Why are you crying on such a beautiful day?' asked a voice.

'Because I'm alone,' said Paross. 'My friend's dead, and I've got no one.'

'Nothing ever dies so long as you believe, little scholar …'

Paross immediately looked up. No one had ever called him that apart from Abram.

Paross leapt up, filled with emotion, bursting with tears of happiness and relief. The One-God had answered his prayers.

'Every dream has a window to reality: all you need is some faith to carry you there,' said Abram as he embraced the little boy. He thought of Paross as his son, as well as his friend.

105

Few men understand that war and peace are born of the same womb; they are brothers in battle, one fighting to preserve that which exists in the world, the other fighting to destroy it. What unites them is their mother and father for, in the world of men, light cannot be seen unless there is also darkness. The only gift of war is the prospect that peace shall follow it, giving birth to new hope and a new beginning. Larsa had learnt this in the most painful of ways, for death and heartache had been worn around her finger like a wedding ring. But after hardship there follows ease: the princess had given birth to a healthy baby boy, bringing her the comfort she needed to carry on living. As she cradled her newborn in her arms, she remembered Marmicus's final words:

'Death is only a curse if the soul has lived without purpose ...'

Although Marmicus was no longer with her in flesh, he had not abandoned her completely. Every day she saw part of him live on in her infant. His eyes and mouth had the likeness of his father, beautiful in every way.

'Are you ready, Your Highness?'

'Yes.' She handed over her infant, smiling at him as he slept peacefully, unaware of what lay ahead; how, in this brief moment, his mother's life would change forever. She walked out onto the palace balcony, her head bearing the glorious crown bestowed upon her by her ancestors, the crowds below her roaring as they greeted her with love. Thousands of people were waving their arms and cheering with excitement, for today was a new start for their kingdom. Their ruler had shed the title of princess, becoming instead their new queen.

- The End -

A NOTE ON THE AUTHOR

Seja Majeed is a British Iraqi with an Honours degree in Law from Brunel Law School and a Postgraduate Diploma in Legal Practice from the City Law School, London. She also has a diploma in Public Policy and Administration from the American University of Sharjah in the United Arab Emirates. She currently works for the Shell petroleum company, where she is a contract engineer working on the Majnoon Oil Field Project for Shell Iraq.

Seja's family left Iraq in 1980 due to the Iran–Iraq War, and Seja was born in 1986 in Algeria. One year later, her family moved to the United Kingdom, where they claimed asylum due to civil unrest escalating in Algeria.

In 1980 her uncle, Naeem Fadel Al-taki, was executed by hanging at the age of twenty-one. He was hanged because he had joined a university club that spoke up against Iraq's Ba'ath regime. In 1986, another uncle, Helmi Fadel Al-taki, was taken by the Ba'ath regime. He was placed in Abu Ghraib Prison in Baghdad, where he was frequently tortured. Seja's mother was pregnant with Seja at the time. He was last seen in 1991.

For many years, Seja's family searched for Helmi Fadel Al-taki, but it was only in 2003, after the collapse of the Ba'ath regime, that they realised it was most likely that he was buried in a mass grave, since he had not been released from prison. To this day, Seja's family have no idea what happened to him, or how he may have died. Seja says, 'From the moment I was born I knew about war and death, without anyone having to explain it to me. It became a part of my being, to know that people were hungry to kill and destroy everything around them. I was helpless to do anything but comfort my mother. I would hear her cry, knowing that so much injustice had been done to her family. She had lost everything, except her hope that maybe she would find her brother alive.'

In 2012, Seja was accepted on to the highly competitive graduate programme for Shell, the multinational petroleum company. She first worked in Scotland, on the North Sea oil fields, and was then transferred to work on the Iraqi Majnoon oil field. She now lives in Dubai and frequently travels to Iraq.

She is also a One Young World ambassador. One Young World is a premier global forum for young people of leadership calibre, endorsed by many political and social figures such as Nobel Peace Prize winner Desmond Tutu, humanitarian Bob Geldof and US senator John Kerry. Seja began writing her novel, *The Forgotten Tale of Larsa*, when she was just nineteen, while she was also studying law and working. It took Seja eight years to complete her novel; she has dedicated it to the memory of her uncles and the Iraqi people.

Printed in Great Britain
by Amazon.co.uk, Ltd.,
Marston Gate.